PRAISE FOR J.R. SEEGER'S ... RIES

Readers are encouraged to go to www.MissionPointPress.com to contact the author or to find information on how to buy this book in bulk at a discounted rate.

Published by Mission Point Press
2554 Chandler Rd.
Traverse City, MI 49696
(231) 421-9513
www.MissionPointPress.com

ISBN: 978-1-954786-06-6
Library of Congress Control Number: 2021902989

Printed in the United States of America

The Silicon Addiction

The Silicon
Addiction

J.R. Seeger

book 6 in the   MIKE4 series

The mystery does not get clearer by repeating the question,
Nor is it bought with going to amazing places.
— Jalaluddin Rumi Balkhi
From *The Essential Rumi, translations*
by Coleman Barks with John Moyne

A LITTLE FRIENDLY COMPETITION

August 2007, Camp Ederle, Italy

Master Sergeant John Carver, the senior range safety officer, or RSO, at the firing ranges for Camp Ederle, was waiting for his appointment with two Special Operations Force officers who needed their semi-annual range certification for both long guns and sidearms. Carver was a year out from a thirty-year career in the Army and retirement. He started in an armored cavalry unit during the Cold War, served as a platoon sergeant in an armored scout platoon during Desert Storm and a troop first sergeant in 2003 in Iraq.

He had seen plenty of combat.

He was convinced that "special operations" soldiers generally were not all that special, and often their operations were not all that important. Carver was not thrilled that he had to block off a half day at his range for some "special" troops. But orders were orders.

He watched as the two shooters arrived in an OD green Army pickup truck. The driver was an NCO who looked close to his own age. The passenger was a female. He couldn't make out her rank because she was wearing a Nomex flight suit. A pilot? Well, there were plenty of female pilots in the Army and he supposed SOF had their share. The NCO was in a worn set of Army BDUs in woodland camouflage. They could easily have dated from the 1990s. Still authorized for use in Europe and especially for field duty like a day at the range.

Once they exited the truck, they put on their berets. The NCO wore a green beret with a flash and insignia for the US Army Special Operations Command. Carver noticed the female wore a red beret with the same flash but with a rank insignia of a chief warrant officer. The two soldiers walked to the back of the truck and each pulled out a long gun case, a pistol case, and an OD green ammunition box.

Carver noticed the female had a very slight limp. War wound or just a recent accident? He couldn't be sure and he didn't really care. If they got on and off his range on time and safe, that was all that mattered to Carver. At least they came with their own firearms, their own ammunition and their own hearing protection. Carver nodded to himself: so far, so good.

Carver was waiting with a clipboard. After rendering a formal salute to the warrant officer, he got down to business. He checked their military ID cards to confirm they were who they said they were. CSM Jim Massoni. Check. CW3 Susan O'Connell. Check. Both affiliated with a unit he had not heard of in the past: Regional Logistics Support Unit. Well, the US Army Special Operations Command had plenty of admin units, this probably was one of them.

The red range flag was already flying so Carver took them to the range control building for the mandatory safety review. The CSM was polite though impatient during the briefing. Carver expected some sort of pushback on safety and was pleased that he didn't get any. However, the CSM did push the envelope when he asked Carver if they could move up and down the range as they fired their weapons. Carver looked at the CSM as if Massoni had asked if he had ever dined with aliens from another planet. "Sergeant Major, this is a qualification range, not a shoot house. You said you needed to complete a command mandated firearms qualification. I set up the range for you to qualify with pistols and rifles. I made sure you were not on the range with other units. You will stay on the firing line and follow my range safety protocol."

Carver noted with some amusement that the female warrant officer looked surprised at his response. He suspected the warrant wasn't used to anyone saying no to her CSM. Well, this was Carver's range and safety was his responsibility. If they wanted to use his range, they could damn well follow his rules.

The warrant said, "Master Sergeant Carver, we will do the needful and get off your range in under three hours."

Carver took another look at the warrant. Thirty something. Whip thin, so probably a runner. Short, auburn colored hair. She was wearing a sterile flight suit and a drop holster on her right hip. If she was a helicopter pilot, he would have expected to see a leather identification patch attached to the Velcro on the flightsuit. It should have had her name, rank and her pilot's wings. Instead, there was nothing at all attached to the pile portion of the Velcro. He said, "Thanks, Chief. The range is all yours. I will be up in the tower. Please listen for any safety instructions."

The warrant officer said, "Thanks." The sergeant major just growled.

As they walked to the firing line, Carver heard the warrant say to the sergeant major: "OK, we have a couple of hours. We don't have a conventional unit with us. As range regulations go, the RSO was easy on us. So, how about a little competition?"

The CSM grinned and said, "And what do I get when I win?"

"How about a pizza dinner and I deliver your coffee to you every morning for a week? What do I get when I win?"

"I plead with you not to tell anyone and I buy you two Italian dinners."

"Deal!"

Carver smiled. He decided to watch how this female did on the range. She was pretty cocky. Maybe, just maybe, she might also be a good shot.

He climbed into the range control tower. While he could control the targets from the tower, he usually just turned on the automated cycle and spent his time watching with binoculars for safety issues on the firing line and the range itself. The rifle range had targets that would randomly pop up for five seconds, at distances from 25 meters to 300 meters. Sitting in a concrete foxhole, a shooter had to first identify where the target was located and then hit the target with one round. The firing table for the qualification was 60 rounds. That meant the shooter would have to make one magazine change during the qualification.

Carver watched as the automatic cycle started. The warrant and the CSM began to engage targets as they varied from the closest position at 25 meters to the farthest. Carver was not surprised that the sergeant major was the more experienced of the two shooters and he knocked down all 60 targets with no difficulty. He watched as the warrant officer assumed her position in the foxhole. She was right-handed, but seemed to have an awkward stance. That limp he noticed early on pointed to an injury to her left leg, or her left hip, perhaps? She had a slow magazine change which he knew would mean she would miss at least one of the targets before it dropped out of sight. Still, the warrant recovered her composure and continued to hit targets. When the firing table was completed, she had missed two targets at ranges of 275 to 300 meters. Still, that wasn't too bad given the 300m target looked to the shooter to be the size of a thumbnail held at arm's length.

After cleaning up their brass under his watchful eye, he heard the CSM say, "I wonder if you might have your eyes checked, Sue. It seems you had some trouble on the farthest targets. Oh, and just remember, I like my coffee early in the morning."

The warrant nodded as she walked down to the pistol range. Carver noticed she didn't seem too worried about the competition. Would she be a better pistol shot than the sergeant major? It seemed unlikely. She said, "Sergeant Major, the competition is not over until it's over." Carver noticed Massoni just smirked.

The pistol range was set up as a fixed range of 10 meters. Each firing position had two targets that would randomly rotate and face the shooter for between one and three seconds. Sometimes a single target would open to the shooter, sometimes both targets would appear. The targets were known as e-type silhouettes, two feet wide and four feet tall. In the center of each target were three concentric rings labeled 8, 10 and X. Once again, Carver reviewed the firing table with the two SOF operators and showed them the target positions.

Pistol qualification required that 45 of the 60 rounds needed to be inside one of those three rings. Any hits on the targets outside the three rings would not be counted. Carver said that they would have 15 rounds in each magazine, so the qualification requirement would include three magazine changes to fire the full 60 rounds. Again, the CSM requested a modification to the firing table. He wanted to shoot two rounds at each target each time, a term known in the shooting community as a "double tap." Carver politely pointed out that while that was a very effective combat shooting technique, this was not a training session but an Army qualification session. Each target would be engaged with one round each time. That was the Army requirement and that was all there was to it.

Carver had been the senior RSO at Camp Ederle for two years. Pistol qualification for other units at the post was restricted to a small number of officers and senior NCOs. Since they were not expected to be experienced shooters, they would start the qualification rounds from what was called a "low ready" position with the pistol held in a double hand grip, pointed slightly down and toward the targets. This was as much for safety reasons as to make it easier on shooters who had little time to practice. As a small concession, Carver agreed to one modification to the normal range safety requirements. His two SOF shooters could start with their pistols holstered and return their pistols to the holster between shots. Once the target or targets rotated, the shooter once again had to draw the weapon, engage the target and then return the pistol to the holster.

On the pistol range, the two shooters were only five meters apart, so they could easily see each other's results as they proceeded through the firing table. Carver knew that if a shooter was distracted by another's results, it would guarantee a low score or even a failure to qualify. He didn't expect either of these two shooters to be distracted. He noticed that the CSM was wearing an ancient nylon pistol belt and nylon holster over his uniform. The female warrant had her pistol in a drop holster that placed the weapon at mid-thigh. He knew that there were many who said this style of holster made it easier during parachute jumping and more readily accessible in cramped quarters such as a vehicle or a helicopter. In his time in Iraq, the RSO had found that this drop holster was really little more than a style trait among the Special Forces troops. Conventional soldiers used either a standard holster like the CSM or, if they were assigned to an armor or scout unit, a nylon shoulder holster so that they could get in and out of a turret without difficulty.

Before they started, he heard the CSM said, "Don't you think that fancy rig will slow you down a bit? Remember, we are just shooting paper here not some bad guy in Afghanistan." If Carver had been advising the warrant, he would have said the same thing.

"Train as you fight, Sergeant Major. Some smart guy told me that years ago."

"Must have been a sergeant major. They are the smart guys."

At the pistol range, Carver was positioned behind the shooters in a small cabin protected by bulletproof glass. Again, the range was automated, but he could shut down the system if he saw a safety problem. His announcement on the loud speaker intruded in the back-and-forth between the two shooters. "The range is about to go hot. Put on your hearing protection, load your weapons and holster them."

The Sergeant Major was standing squared off to the targets in the standard Army posture known as the isosceles firing position; the warrant stood in a half-bladed position with her left leg slightly forward in a style known as a modified Weaver stance. Carver said to himself, "This definitely could be very interesting."

Both of the SOF operators were using Glock19 pistols, common enough in the SOF community. The pistol was smaller and lighter than the standard Army sidearm of the Beretta 92F. Easier to conceal and easier to operate. But, due to its size, the Glock was harder to shoot well. Carver knew a good shooter could excel with nearly any weapon. He had started his military career in armored cavalry wearing a 1911A1 .45 in a shoulder holster. He had reluctantly transitioned to the Beretta when the Army changed over. He won shooting competitions throughout the Army units in Germany and again as he moved to Camp Ederle two years ago to serve as the senior RSO at the post range complex. During the last two years, he had seen plenty of SOF operators training with some standard and some highly modified pistols. He didn't really care what they used so long as they used them safely and cleaned up after themselves.

Under his watchful eye, they loaded their first magazine into the Glock pistols, put their pistols into battery and holstered their weapons. They placed the three additional magazines in open magazine pouches on their opposite hip. Once they were ready, Carver repeated three times, "The range is now hot." A gong sounded and the targets proceeded to appear in multiple intervals.

Sixty rounds in less than five minutes might seem a reasonable pace for a qualification firing table. But when each scoring shot had to be placed somewhere inside a space the size of a dinner plate on the target, when the shooters didn't know if they would see one or two targets, and when each shot had to start with a holstered pistol, the time passed in the blink of an eye.

When the firing table was completed, Carver announced the range was clear. He instructed the two shooters to clear their weapons and leave them on a table behind them before he and his two shooters proceeded to the targets for him to grade the results. It was clear the warrant was the easy winner. The center of her targets, the X ring in shooting parlance, were completely missing. A space about the size of an old silver dollar was torn from each of the targets with the rest of the space clean. The sergeant major's targets had a mix of X ring and 10 ring punctures, but there were two rounds on one target that were right on the edge of the 8 ring, the outer scoring area. Carver looked at the sergeant major as he marked the two rounds as counted, but they both knew that another grader might have not counted them at all. He handed Massoni his graded range qualification card without comment.

Massoni said to Carver, "It looks to me like Chief O'Connell missed some. I mean, how can we be sure all 60 of her rounds went through those tiny little holes?"

Carver shook his head. "I watched her, Sergeant Major. She has an odd stance. Some sort of modified Weaver stance that we don't recommend, but every round went through the X rings." As he handed Sue her range qualification card, he said, "Good shooting, Chief."

"Thanks, Master Sergeant. I was on my school's pistol team before joining the Army."

Once again, Massoni did nothing but growl. He turned to Carver and offered a gruff aside, "Pistol team, my ass. She was one point away from shooting for the US Olympic team. Plus, she learned to shoot from her grandfather who is a legend in SF. I knew I was toast on the pistol range."

As they walked back to the pickup truck, Carver wondered what RLSU actually did for the Army. He suspected it probably wasn't normal Army logistics.

On their drive back to the RLSU building, Massoni said, "OK, so we call that a draw."

Sue was not about to irritate her sergeant major. She said, "A draw it is, Jim."

As they were pulling into the compound, he said, "How about this, we continue the competition as we make sure you stay on jump status. You need two parachute jumps to get back on track. How about we do a competition to see who can land closest to a marked spot on a drop zone here? Two jumps with the average closest distance to the mark the winner."

Sue knew better than to argue with Massoni. She said, "Sure, Sergeant Major. Sounds good. When do we do this?"

Massoni said, "I have a pair of jumps coming up tomorrow. I think I can get you on the manifest, assuming you have time."

"You know I have time, Sergeant Major. Jump certification is one of the things you already put on my schedule."

Massoni smiled and said, "And isn't that just perfect?"

NIGHT STALKER

CW3 Sue O'Connell, Special Operations Force warrior, walked through the remnants of the destroyed village. The mix of US Air Force fast movers and the Apache gunships left little but smoking rubble. Seen through night-vision goggles, the thermal signatures of animal and human remains glowed slightly more than the ongoing explosions of ordnance inside what had once been an al-Qaida logistics headquarters in Nangarhar province of Afghanistan. The goggles might create the impression of distance from the havoc, but Sue could smell the recent combat: smoke, cordite from small arms fire, and death.

Sue was leading a section of Special Forces operators along the middle of a muddy street. When the bombs hit the town, they had burst the local water tower and flooded the street. Afghanistan was mostly a desert so the water running down the street was nothing much more than a series of mud puddles that could be ignored. Her job was to find a set of computers that SOF analysts were convinced AQ used to manage the logistics effort. The shooters trailing Sue had the job of keeping her alive while she did her job. Sue used a small tech device created by SOF headquarters to locate the WiFi signature associated with the computer hub. She walked along the dirt street listening on headphones to the tone from the device. As she got closer to the hub, the techs promised the tone would increase in sound and in pitch.

Inside her headset, she heard the SF team leader cry out, "Chief, we're sinking!"

Sue looked back to see her mentor, Max Creeter, and his team-mates literally sinking into the mud. They were already up to their knees.

"Help us!"

Sue didn't know what had happened, but she needed to cover the 20 yards back to the team. If she could get to them in time, she could throw them the rope that she kept in her ruck. As she turned to run back, her left leg collapsed under her. Her prosthetic started to melt into the soil.

"Chief, don't leave us!"

Sue couldn't speak. As she fell, the weight from her rucksack turned her on her side and now her ruck was sinking into the mud. She could feel the ruck pulling her down. She knew she was going to drown in the mud.

Sue woke up from the dream. She was soaked with sweat and had sat upright in bed just as she had started to feel the mud filling her mouth. It had been months since she had endured a nightmare like this one. It always had some of the same characteristics. First, she was responsible for others who were in harm's way. Second, she would fail them because of her below-the-knee prosthetic on her left leg. Finally, she was about to die from whatever threat her brain had created.

Sue threw her legs over the side of the bed, turned on the light and looked around her bedroom. She went through her normal, post-nightmare routine. She said to herself, "I'm in Italy. That dream isn't real. I'm okay." She stood up on her good leg and reached over to grab the back of a chair. She hopped over the bathroom. She wondered if her time on the firearms range had triggered what she now called simply the Dream. As she looked at herself in the bathroom mirror, she said to her reflection, "No telling for sure, girl."

It might be 0325hrs, but there was no chance she could get back to sleep. She might as well shower, put on her prosthesis, change into her PT clothes and walk to the gym. A little PT was about the only thing that could wash away the night terrors. It was six years since 9/11 and almost four years since she lost her left leg in an ambush. Since then, Sue had seen more than her share of one-on-one combat and she had come to accept the fact that her nightmares would never go away. Years earlier, she had asked her mother, a retired CIA officer, when her own nightmares had stopped. She got a simple answer, "They haven't."

So, a shower and a workout and another day of hard work inside the US Special Operations Forces (SOF). That was Sue's world.

DID YOU LEARN YOUR LESSON?

Later that morning, Sue and Massoni drove out to the Camp Ederle airfield. They were jumping with a Special Forces detachment that needed qualification jumps after a year in Afghanistan. Massoni told Sue that he had already talked to the Drop Zone Safety Officer or DZSO, to mark a ring three meters in diameter on the DZ. The DZSO or his assistant would be the judges for this part of the competition. Massoni used his sincere senior NCO voice and said, "Now, Sue. This might be a competition, but safety first on this. If the winds don't work for us, they don't work for us. Check?"

Sue nodded. There were lots of airborne qualified personnel who loved to jump out of airplanes. And then there were qualified personnel who did the minimums so that they could remain in a specific unit. Sue was one of the latter. She figured parachute operations, even military free-fall operations, were simply a way to get to the battlefield: no more important than infiltration by ground, by helicopter or by rubber boat.

Before she passed selection and entered SOF, Sue went to jump school so that she could serve in a military intelligence unit inside the 18th Airborne Corps. Her unit was too small to have its own designated jumps, so she regularly had to jump with other units in the 18th Airborne Corps or even with the 82nd Airborne. She had heard stories from her grandfather of what it was like to jump with the 82nd. The stories were terrifying, but the reality for Sue was worse. The paratroopers were so ready to jump out the door when the green light came on that they could empty 64 paratroopers out of two jump doors on a C130 in less than 30 seconds.

After a year jumping as a "strap hanger" on another unit's jumps, where she had no control over her experience, Sue made another career decision. She would go to the 82nd Airborne jumpmaster school so she could be the one in control. The instructor cadre, black hats as they were known at the school because of their black baseball caps, were professional but not the least bit tolerant of a female warrant officer from 18th Airborne Corps. Sue took her lumps, but passed and was awarded the status of jumpmaster. After graduation, whenever she chose to do so, she could serve in her aircraft as one of the Army officers in command of the jump. It meant she was in charge from start to finish. That made it somewhat better. Somewhat.

Now, she was a below the knee — a BTK-amputee. Regardless of whether she started her career as one who loved to jump or hated to jump, Sue was now one who jumped so that she could stay in SOF. Airborne operations were one way she proved to herself that she remained an effective SOF operator, despite her BTK status. Sue was not the only BTK in SOF who was still on jump status, but she was the only female BTK SOF operator who was on jump status.

For Sue, parachute operations now fell into the everyday as a challenge category. Just getting into the aircraft pushed the limits of her ability to lift her left leg. Once inside, there was the risk her prosthetic could get caught in the roller conveyor system on the floor of any military cargo aircraft. She had to be certain that when she exited the aircraft, she pushed away on her good leg. Finally, she had to be sure to land so that she did a parachute landing fall on her right side.

Every time she completed a jump, she was that much closer to personal confidence that she was still a complete person with no physical limitations. Sue recognized now that she might never feel whole again, but that was about mental limitations. Still, every jump meant progress, and being under canopy at 1000 feet was wonderful all by itself even if it didn't last. Sue liked being under canopy and especially so with MC-1D steerable parachutes used by SOF.

As they drove up to the airfield, Sue said "I'm jumping with you,

Jim. But I insist on being jumpmaster. It's the only way I can be sure you aren't cheating on the spot for our jump."

Massoni laughed. "Do you really think I was going to let you take my job? The young captain in charge of this 10th Group operational detachment already tried that. He didn't have any luck and I am going to give you one guess on your chances."

"Perhaps zero, Jim."

"Precisely zero, Sue."

The pair of jumps went off without drama. The first from the tail-gate of a C130 Hercules and the second that afternoon from the door of a MH60 helicopter assigned to Southern European Task Force. The winds were perfect, the sky was blue and both Sue and Massoni landed inside the marked ring on the DZ. By the end of the day, the competition once again was a draw.

Massoni said, "I hope you have learned your lesson, Sue. You can't beat a sergeant major."

Sue couldn't suppress a laugh. "I didn't know that was the lesson," she said. "But I certainly learned it."

WOULDN'T THAT BE NICE?

T he competitions with Massoni marked the end for Sue of what had been a two-week "Permanent Change of Station" or PCS leave to settle into her new home base at Camp Ederle.

Her SOF unit, known as the Human Intelligence Collection Unit (HICU), had actually relocated in 2006 from Ft. Bragg to Camp Ederle in Italy. Due to a pair of assignments off base at the beginning of 2007, Sue had never fully in-processed at Camp Ederle or moved into her rooms at the Bachelor Officers' Quarters (BOQ). Now, she had finally been able to complete her PCS.

Her quarters were comparable to a small, one-bedroom condo in the US. Furnished in a style consistent with a high-end motel and wired with US outlets and cable TV, it offered little in the way of style or substance that would make a place home. Instead, it underscored the temporary nature of military life. It basically implied, "You are going to live here a few years and then a few years someplace else."

SOF personnel generally had a better structure to their career than conventional Army personnel. Once assigned to a SOF unit, the regular Army personnel system did not intrude. SOF personnel were expected to stay in a single unit for the rest of their career. They were expected to build their expertise over years of experience. It was one of the things that appealed to Sue when she initially applied to the SOF unit known as Surveillance and Reconnaissance or S&R. She was looking for a home and a family and found both in S&R.

Her traumatic amputation in Afghanistan ended that part of her career, but now HICU was her home and the men and women in

HICU were her family. Sue wondered whether she could live on this base in what she saw as suspended animation for another ten years. One possibility was to lease or even purchase a larger apartment on the Italian economy. It would take paperwork and a commitment to living with Italian as well as US government bureaucracy, but at least it wouldn't feel quite as sterile as these quarters.

As a first step in testing her tolerance for "living on the economy," Sue purchased a FIAT 500 Abarth from a local Italian car dealer. She obtained her US Armed Forces Europe driver's license and was off exploring the foothills of the Italian Alps. It wasn't her house in Virginia, which she continued to think of as home, but then again, it wasn't a bunk in some war zone, so she was satisfied. Until she decided to leave SOF/HICU or retire, Sue figured a nomad life was going to be her life. If that nomadic life allowed her to spend some time in Italy, it didn't seem all that bad. At that point, Sue decided that she was "settled."

Sue returned to work the next Monday and was quickly summoned into the office of the HICU commander, Colonel Jed Smith. Sue was expecting a new assignment to a war zone tour or, at the very least, a border state to one of the war zones. Her language skills in Dari and Russian argued for another trip to Afghanistan or, perhaps, Pakistan. Her work with Flash over the past two years on the nexus of Iranian operations and Russian criminal enterprises argued for a tour in one of the Persian Gulf States. And, given the fact that her last assignment had been in Cyprus which was hardly tough duty, she expected the worst. What Smith offered was a surprise.

Smith was never one for pleasantries. After receiving the response of "Enter" when she knocked, Smith waved her to a chair in front of his desk. Seated on the couch against the wall was Jim Massoni. As Sue looked around the room, all she saw were large-scale maps of the Eastern Mediterranean, the Persian Gulf, and Central Asia. No clue for the next assignment. Smith started, "I was pleased to see that you didn't cause a diplomatic incident in Croatia. I even got a note from the MILATT who said he would consider having you join his team." Smith looked up at Sue. He continued, "I thought you said he was a pain in the ass."

Massoni chimed in, "I think what she called him was a..."

Smith intercepted the comment, "I was trying to be diplomatic, Sergeant Major." As with every conversation Sue ever had with her commander, Smith did the transmitting and she did the receiving. He started right in. "O'Connell, I have a job for you. It isn't exactly the standard for HICU, but it is something the CG wants and we all know..."

Sue and Massoni spoke in unison, "What the Commanding General of SOF wants, the Commanding General gets."

Smith did not acknowledge their effort at amusing repartee. He just nodded. "The CG wants to have someone working the Eastern Med and the Gulf looking for new sources for the Special Operations Force counterterrorism missions. One of the ways that OGA captures new sources is through volunteers who walk into embassies. Not always great leads, but sometimes real gems. Through SOF Headquarters and the two JIOCs located in Balad and Bagram, we have real-time connectivity with the military attaché offices in the region. The CG asked me to have you serve as our circuit rider in the region. He said you did so well working with the MILATT in Nicosia and in Zagreb, he thought you would be the sort of warrior diplomat we needed making that happen."

Sue knew the Joint Intelligence Operations Centers managed by SOF ran 24/7, capturing intelligence feeds from every part of the Intelligence Community as well as monitoring reporting feeds from key departments in the government including State, Justice, and Treasury. She suspected the problem for the JIOC analysts was they didn't have anyone to task once they identified an intelligence lead. It looked like Sue was tapped to be that person who received the tasking. She said, "Boss, what are we talking about here? Do I meet these volunteers and then...?" She held up her hands expressing confusion.

"You talk to them, you sort out which ones are nuts, which ones should be debriefed and which ones either we or OGA put on the books. You are the focal point for this job. Beyond that, I don't know how it's going to work because we haven't done it before."

Sue nodded though she still wasn't sure what the new job would look like.

Smith continued, "OK, so get out of here and get wired into the JIOCs in Balad and Bagram. Get your kit ready for travel, get over to the post hospital and get your shots up to date and then start doing whatever you are going to do." As soon as Smith finished the sentence, he started to pull paperwork out of his inbox, put on his reading glasses and started to read. Clearly, Sue had been dismissed. She stood up and followed Massoni out of the room.

As they walked out, Massoni offered his views on this new job. For a change, his views were neither sarcastic nor ironic. He said, "Back in the age of steam when I was in Special Forces, we used to send pairs of operators out to the embassies in our area of responsibility. Their visits focused on what we called a needs survey. We wanted to see what our local allies needed before we sent a detachment to provide training. When I was on that circuit, I often met Klingon circuit riders who were doing what the CG wants you to do. It's grunt work, Sue. You are going to be on the road a lot and your diplomatic skills are going to be challenged because everyone in an embassy will hate you. Now, don't take it personal. They hate all visitors because visitors often cause trouble. Even if they don't cause trouble, they create extra work. Still, you will learn a lot. Now, won't that be nice?" The last line caught Sue by surprise, but she noticed that Massoni was offering his best sergeant major smirk as well as nodding.

"Yes, Sergeant Major, that will be nice."

Even with Massoni's warning, it sounded perfect to Sue. Live in the foothills of the Italian Alps waiting for "the call." Fly to a new location, debrief the volunteer, determine if he/she was of value, recruit them and handle the volunteer or turn him over to another HICU agent handler. And then, return to Italy for the next call. It fit Sue's acknowledged lack of patience in the standard intelligence work practiced by OGA and military case offices around the world. The new job meant she was always doing something different in some-place different. It definitely sounded nice.

WEARING A LITTLE THIN

October 2007 — December 2008

A fter her first six months on the job, Sue had changed her mind. Experience showed that most volunteers were either suffering from serious mental problems or were fabricators.

Nearly seven years after 9/11, the third world local grapevine announced there was money to be made by telling an American a story that linked at least two of the following four words: terrorism, Iran, drugs, nuclear weapons. Better still, link them all together because, from the perspective of the locals, Americans were easily fooled and very willing to give money for nothing. In six months, she had been on travel status for nearly twenty days a month, flying on military or commercial aircraft, landing, meeting with a local OGA point of contact or representative from the military attaché office, immediately debriefing the volunteer for hours, writing up the material (no matter how outrageous), waiting for the JIOC to respond — always a negative response — and then leaving. No beach holidays in Turkey or visits to the gold bazaar in Dubai. Just work, air travel and more work. Often the calls came back-to-back. When that happened, Sue didn't have any time at all back at HICU. Among other things, Sue's BOQ room began to gather piles of unwashed clothes. The TDY life didn't end up as nice as Sue expected.

As Massoni warned, Sue found that most embassies or military installations wanted no part of some hired gun from some mysterious part of SOF. Sue stayed on her best behavior and kept to herself when on her trips. The only real relaxation she had was a periodic visit to the Marine Detachment house where she could use their gym and drink a beer or a glass of wine with the embassy Marine guards. As to enjoying her time when she returned to Camp Ederle, Sue also came to realize that she had to be within two hours drive from post.

Since her injury, Sue hadn't been very social. Her only real colleague at HICU, Sarah Billings who went by the nickname Flash, called her the TDY hermit. It was not as if she had much time to do anything. Without fail, SOF HQS would call just as she was packing the Fiat for a trip into the Italian Alps. Holidays were the same. In December 2007, Sue had to cancel a planned Christmas trip to see her mother and brother in the US when a volunteer turned up in Tashkent. It took two full days of travel to get to the embassy, only to find out that while she was in transit, the Uzbek Intelligence Service had arrested the volunteer as part of a large drug smuggling ring. The irony was that the arrest was based on work that Sue and Jamie Shenk completed in early 2007. All Sue could do was accept the apologies from the military attaché and catch the next flight to Italy.

As the end of 2008 approached, Sue didn't even try to arrange any travel during the holidays. She stayed in Italy and did what she could to make her BOQ room as festive as possible. Most HICU collectors stayed in their duty stations and neither Smith nor Massoni made any attempt at all to celebrate the holidays. Sue did get an invitation to attend a Christmas Day meal at the Southern European Task Force Headquarters mess hall. She put on her ACUs, shined her jump boots, and headed to SETAF. The mess hall was filled with the smells of a classic American holiday meal. Sue was surprised to see Flash in attendance and even more surprised to see Flash wearing a military uniform. They sat together and moped for most of the meal. It was not exactly the best holiday. Hoping to generate at least a smile from her work colleague, Sue remarked to Flash, "At least I got all my laundry done before the next TDY."

Flash looked up from her plate of turkey, gravy and mashed potatoes. "Swell," was all she said.

AN INTERLUDE IN THE GULF

On New Year's Day, Sue finally received tasking on a volunteer who appeared to be neither a lunatic nor a fabricator. He walked into the US consulate in Dubai offering information on a complex Iranian computer hacking operation targeting the US military. Normally, the UAE would have been the responsibility of her colleague Sandy Tealor, assigned to Bahrain with responsibilities for the entire Persian Gulf. Sandy was still on holiday in the states with his wife and child, so Sue got the call. After 10 hours of travel including a train to Marco Polo International in Venice, a flight from Venice to Frankfurt and then a flight from Frankfurt to Dubai, Sue would have been the first one to admit, she was in no mood for another annoying fabricator. A member of the CIA station named David Sterling met Sue at the Dubai airport and drove her to a beach house on the Gulf.

As Sterling negotiated the Dubai traffic in the four-door Mitsubishi Pajero, he said, "Sue, I need to say this up front. The station wants me to participate in the debriefing of this guy. Iran is a high-profile target here. Hell, it's a high-profile target anywhere for the Agency and HQS wants a piece of the action."

Sue was sufficiently tired and jet-lagged that she had no emotion left nor any interest in arguing about who got credit. She said, "Look, David. I work for the SOF CG. This is his project and all I am is the guy who determines if the volunteer is a lead or not. If he is a lead, then your headquarters and SOF headquarters can sort out who gets what. I did twenty TDYs in 2008 going after targets and not one of them panned out. If this one does, then I will let your chief and the military attaché start the fight and they can kick it up to higher. I just want to do my job and I certainly don't mind having another person in the room. Is this guy a local or an Iranian?"

Sterling hit the brakes and swerved as a Ferrari supercar cut across two lanes and in front of the Pajero. After taking a deep breath, he answered. "An Iranian who is resident in Dubai. He claims to be running one piece of the network using the Dubai communications infrastructure as well as acquiring technology that he smuggles back to Iran using the Kish duty-free port as the intermediate stop."

"You spoke to him?"

"Nope. He was initially interviewed by the consulate security officer. Once we got the news, the MILATT engaged SOF and the consulate engaged me. We are scheduled to meet the guy tomorrow morning at 1030hrs at a cafe in Jumeirah."

"What languages does he speak?"

"He must speak some English. The consulate security officer doesn't speak any Arabic or Farsi."

"You an Arabist?"

"Nope, a Farsi speaker."

"Excellent. I am a Dari speaker. So, we start in English and if he seems to have trouble, we can switch to Farsi. I should be able to keep up with my Afghan Persian."

They pulled into the beach house which had an attached, two-car covered car port. There was a BMW 750 parked in the second space. As she got out of the car, Sue noticed the BMW was "up armored." Armored glass prevented a clear view into the car as it sat low on its suspension. Sue grabbed her suitcase and walked into another set of temporary digs. The sound of the surf captured her attention as she walked from the garage into the kitchen. It was most definitely the nicest TDY quarters she had occupied. The house had sliding glass doors that opened to the beach on both the kitchen and the small living room. Sitting in the living room were two men dressed in chinos and polo shirts. Sue immediately knew she was looking at seniors from the consulate. They stood up as Sue entered the room.

The taller and younger of the two men spoke first. He offered his hand and said, "Chief O'Connell, I'm Captain Jonah Barkley, the Naval Attaché in Abu Dhabi. Thanks for traveling so quickly. I suspect we messed up your New Year's celebration."

Sue shook his hand and said, "Sir, it's a pleasure. You may already know, I'm the SOF circuit rider so I do my best to get to the target location as soon as I can. Honestly, I wasn't upset that you interrupted the required, dress uniform, New Year's Day courtesy call on the Camp Ederle commander. I'm sure it would have been…swell, but work is certainly a better option."

Barkley smiled and said, "Chief, this is the local Agency senior, Mark Finestri."

Finestri was a good ten years older, two inches shorter, and about twenty pounds heavier than Barkley. Sue looked at a man in his early 50s who was probably a former wrestler or football player in college. Big shoulders, serious arm strength, a high and tight haircut, and a scar that ran from his right ear to his jaw. A few pounds overweight, but not a man who you would want to meet in a dark alley. Not unless you had a shotgun handy. He said, "O'Connell? I don't suppose you are related to Pete O'Connell? Or maybe, Barbara O'Connell?"

"Sir, I'm related to both. Peter and Barbara O'Connell are my parents."

"I doubt Pete O'Connell could be your father. He was a geezer when I knew him."

"That would be my grandfather."

"How is he?"

"He was murdered a couple of years ago. Russians. It's a long story."

"I'll bet. And your parents?"

"Dad was murdered by Russians as well. Mom is living in Western New York working as a troubleshooter for an international law firm."

"You probably hear this plenty, but your family made me smart."

Sue nodded. She wasn't about to be rude to an Agency senior, but in her mind she was ready for "Your grandfather…."

Instead, she heard, "You know your mother taught me plenty in a very short time. We were working an Iranian in Abu Dhabi in the last century," Finestri smiled. "In a few days, she taught me tradecraft I thought I knew, but didn't. She taught me handling skills I thought I knew, but didn't. I suspect that if we hadn't worked together, I would be selling used cars someplace in South Florida."

"Chief, it's worth noting that she is still using tradecraft and fire-arms."

"Even as a pensioner?"

"Well, it seems that O'Connells don't get to retire gracefully."

Finestri smiled and said with just a touch of sarcasm in his voice, "And here you are working the family business?"

"It's in the blood."

Barkley decided to help Sue out and interjected, "So I have heard. Now, I realize you just got in, but we wanted to talk to you about this walk-in."

"Yes sir. Just let me put my bag down and get a drink of water and I'll be ready to go."

Finestri shouted, "Sterling, get this lady a drink for heaven's sake. We are in the desert, she needs hydrating!"

Sterling walked into the living room with a tray of drinks. This was obviously staged from the beginning. He put a beer in front of Finestri, a glass with ice and a Diet Pepsi in front of Barkley and the same for himself. He said, "I brought water for you, but I can get a soda or a beer if you prefer."

"Water for now. Perhaps tea later. It's been a long day."

Over the next hour, they talked in detail about the volunteer. Both the Agency and SOF headquarters had conducted name traces on the volunteer, Ali Reza Khorasani. Hardly worth the effort since "Ali Reza" were the first two names of at least a third of all men in Iran and Khorasani simply meant "the guy from Khorasan" which was the entire northeastern third of Iran. Still, there were no reports linking the volunteer to any previous fabricators or registered sources inside the Intelligence Community. After that brief discussion, Finestri said, "I hope you realize this could be some sort of Iranian intelligence game. Perhaps to see how we handle a volunteer, perhaps just to get eyes on some American intelligence officers."

Sue said, "I think if we do a two on one, there shouldn't be too much trouble. Still, I wondered why you didn't have the second meeting at the consulate or even the embassy in Abu Dhabi."

Finestri said, "Blame the knucklehead security officer. It wouldn't have happened that way in Abu Dhabi. Our Regional Security Officer is one of the best in the world. His man down here just wanted the guy off the compound as soon as possible and he took the appointment as offered. I suspect he will be getting some wall-to-wall counseling the next time he visits the embassy, but for now, we have to live with what he left us. For goodness sake, we don't have any contact information for Agha Khorasani. If we wanted to meet the guy a second time, we had to play by these rules."

Sue noticed Finestri used the Persian honorific for Mr. Was he also a Farsi speaker? It would be good to know so she asked, "Chief, you speak Farsi?"

"A bit, Sue. A fair bit. After I did a tour here in Gulf and then I cut my teeth on Iranians doing what you are doing right now. Traveling the Gulf and the Eastern Med talking to volunteers and hoping for some big recruitment that would give us access to the Supreme Leader."

"Did you?"

"Did I what?"

"Get the big recruitment? I only ask because I have been working this circuit for over a year and all I have found are lunatics and fabricators."

Finestri erupted in a loud, deep laugh. "Ah, the good old days when all I had to worry about was lunatics and fabricators. Chief O'Connell, the answer to your question is I did get a decent recruitment eventually. A former Rev Guard intel type. Good reporter. Brave. Now dead."

Finestri rubbed the scar on his cheek. Sue figured there was more to the story, but she suspected today was not the day when she was going to get it. She knew that the Islamic Revolutionary Guards Corps had a military intelligence unit similar to the Russian GRU. And like the GRU, the IRGC had only one solution for traitors. Execution. This was another reason why Sue asked the next question.

"Chief, any chance we can get some body armor and some weapons for this meet?"

Sue heard Barkley draw in a deep breath. The Naval attaché was likely not real pleased that Sue might want firearms in his turf.

Finestri smiled and said, "You haven't checked your bedroom yet, but I think you will find everything you need there. One of the reasons that David is working with you is he has a bit of experience in…well, shall we say advanced security procedures?" He looked at Sterling.

"What the chief is trying to say is that I worked for a year on a SOF base in Qandahar meeting agents with some folks from Surveillance and Reconnaissance."

"S&R was my outfit before switching to the HUMINT side of the house."

Finestri stood up and said, "See Jonah, I told you this was all going to work out. We have a good team in place, O'Connell comes from a long line of case officers, she has a reputation from Cyprus and Zagreb of being a good partner, it's all going to be dandy."

Barkley stood up and said, "Dandy. Yup, I suppose it is going to be dandy."

As they walked out the side door, Finestri turned to Sterling and said, "David, don't dick this one up. If you do, I will choke you. Get it?"

Sterling smiled and said, "Yes, chief. Don't mess up. I got it."

Just as he got to the door, Finestri stopped as if he had forgotten something. He turned to Sue and said, "Please do your best to stay alive, okay? It's a lot of paperwork for me if you don't."

Sue couldn't think of anything to say except, "Yes, chief."

The next morning over a breakfast of oatmeal, flatbread and black tea, Sue reviewed the meeting plan with Sterling. She had a reasonable night's sleep, a shower and a brief workout on the deck overlooking the Persian Gulf. Sue figured that even if the volunteer didn't work out, she was living large on this TDY.

When Sterling arrived at the safe house, she waited until he made himself a cup of coffee and sat down at the table. She said, "So, we set up and watch for a bit before going to the cafe. If we see the volunteer heading to the location, we intercept him and tumble him into the Pajero, right?"

"That's what I recommend. I'm not real big on meeting some unknown guy in a place I can't control. If we are on the road in the Pajero, we have something resembling control. I will leave it to you to convince Agha Khorasani that it is in his best interest."

"Why me?"

Sterling looked at Sue and then looked down at himself. "OK, let's review. I'm about six foot, I weigh in at 200lbs and while I'm not as scary as Finestri, I can be pretty scary. Now, you are a woman, I'm guessing you weigh in at about 120lbs, and you are not scary. I'm sure when I get to know you, I will be scared, but first impressions are what we are talking about here. Make sense?"

"Just so long as you admit I might scare you."

"Oh, Sue. You already scare me. I've worked with S&R remember."

Sue smiled over her tea cup. Sterling was good to look at; about 30, fit, and wasn't wearing a wedding ring. She mentally shook her head and said to herself, "You are thinking like Flash. Like a shark, always looking for the next target." What she said to Sterling was, "Fair enough."

"You find everything you need in your room?"

"If you mean local women's clothes, a headscarf, a larger wool wrap known as an abaya, a set of body armor that fits perfectly, and a Glock pistol in a shoulder holster, yes, I found everything. I'm not going to ask how you got my measurements."

Sterling blushed and said, "Finestri reached out to the chief in Zagreb. She gave us your clothes sizes."

"It's a small world we live in."

"Yup. By the way, I just got a set of surveillance photos from our team covering the coffee shop. It looks like everything is cool for now."

"Let's hope it's cool at 1030."

Sue noticed Sterling smile for the first time since they met. He was definitely a good-looking guy. "From your lips to God's ears."

They set up in a covered parking lot two blocks from the outdoor coffee shop. Like much of Jumeirah, the café was a quick walk from the beach and in January it was filled with European tourists enjoying the warmth of the Gulf sun and waters while their countries were suffering through cold winter storms. Sterling and Sue listened through ear buds as the local surveillance team chatted about the various tourist couples. Sue knew the team had to be an OGA team. No military team would clog up the radio with such banter. Still, she found their caricatures of the Europeans amusing. Their ear buds filled with a brusque comment. *"Standby, standby. We have our package walking down the corniche. White shirt, black pants, leather sandals. He's wearing wrap-around sunglasses and he's carrying a laptop bag."*

Sterling keyed the microphone in the Pajero. "Roger, Keeper. Let us know when he is 100 meters from the shop. We will intercept at that point."

"Roger, Hawkeye."

Sue said, "Hawkeye?"

"I went to the University of Iowa. Finestri went to Michigan. He decided to label me Hawkeye since he is Wolverine. Not that I mind... much."

A minute later, a radio signal. Two clicks on the microphone. Keeper was on foot and behind the target. It was his signal that it was time to go. Sterling keyed the mic. "Standby, standby. We are underway."

Sterling gave himself a second to calm down before he proceeded. He started the Pajero and gently pulled out of the parking lot. No reason to drive in any manner other than a Westerner on holiday. They pulled up just as Khorasani crossed the street. Sue got out of the car. Khorasani took little notice of the woman as she left the car until she said to him in English, "Agha Khorasani, we are here to meet you. Please get in the car." Sue held the door open as Khorasani took a moment to decide if this was his appointment. In a split second, he decided it was and started to get in.

As soon as the volunteer and Sue were in the car, Sterling pulled gently away from the curb, did the first legal U-turn and headed toward the highway that connected Dubai and Abu Dhabi. The goal was to get on a limited access highway so that they could both debrief the Iranian.

From the back seat, Sue started first using her most polite Persian. "Agha Khorasani, would you like some tea? We also have a cola if you would prefer."

Khorasani turned to Sue and said in perfect English, "Tea would be very nice. Thank you."

As Sue poured the tea, she switched to English. She said, "I know this is an imposition, but could I see your identity documents. I need to copy them if we are going to make further progress." Sue expected trouble. Iranians could be exceptionally polite, but they could also take offense quickly.

Khorasani said, "I was surprised no one asked for my documents when I was at the consulate. Please, take whatever you need." He handed Sue a large portfolio-style wallet in exceptionally fine leather. In it, she found a UAE driver's license, an Iranian document that she recognized as proof of his completion of military service, and his business card. Printed on the card was his name and his business — Shamshir Import-Export. On the back of the card was an address in Dubai and a second address on the Iranian freeport island of Kish. In the wallet were both 10,000 UAE Dirhams and $2500 in hundred-dollar bills. Sue quickly photographed the documents, returned them to the wallet and then returned them to Khorasani.

He smiled and said, "I thought you might accept my gift."

Sue looked up to see Sterling's eyes watching her in the rear-view mirror. Sue said, "We hope your gift will be the information you have offered. It will be far more valuable to us than any money."

Khorasani turned to Sterling and said, "May I smoke?"

Sterling nodded and turned the air conditioner to recirculate so that he and Sue would not choke in the blue cloud he knew would follow.

After he finished the tea and his first cigarette, Khorasani said, "I wish to leave the UAE and go to America."

Sue laughed and said, "Agha Khorasani, so do I, but I have to accomplish things here before I can go home."

Khorasani laughed and said, "I can make you very important. I have very valuable information."

Sterling joined in the conversation and said in Persian, "Arzesh dar chashme ast, Agha Khorasani."

Khorasani smiled at the saying "value is in the eye of the beholder." He said, "Before we begin, may I know your names?"

Before they left, Sue and Sterling had agreed they would be Peter and Anna. Sue picked Anna in honor of one of her and her mother's most trusted agents, *DAREDEVIL,* murdered and buried in a Baghdad suburb two years ago.

Sterling started first and said, "My name is Major Peter and my colleague is Colonel Anna."

"Ah, a woman colonel in the secret service. It is so American."

Sue said, "Agha, we really don't have much time today. Can you tell us what is so valuable so we can tell you what it is worth?" The rules of the game with volunteers were simple. First, determine if they were really worth the effort and the security risk to continue to meet them. If so, make sure you had a communications plan that both kept them safe and did not compromise any tradecraft actually in use with established agents. Next, make no promises about what they get in return until you have something you can evaluate. Finally, if the volunteer was legitimate, make every effort to keep him in place so that he could be a long-term reporting source. So far, Khorasani had at least proven to some degree that he was who he said he was: an Iranian businessman in Dubai. A business card meant little until it was checked. Sue and Sterling needed more before they would agree to another meeting with this volunteer.

"Colonel, I am a logistics manager for the Revolutionary Guard intelligence service. I have helped them set up a computer network that they are using to conduct cyber attacks on your country, the British and the Saudis. The network has multiple spokes of a wheel so that it is difficult to identify, much less attack." He paused to take a long drag from his second cigarette that he had lit from the stub of the first one. He smiled and said, "But, the hub of the wheel is here in Dubai. I have the network diagrams for the centers in Dubai and in Turkey. I believe you will find those diagrams valuable. Will they be valuable enough to help me move away from here? For certain, if the old boys of the revolution find out there is a problem with their network, they will come to me first. I need to be out of the UAE."

Sue wasn't sure what the Agency protocol for this sort of strategic intelligence might be. She looked up into the rear-view mirror and into Sterling's eyes. This was his play.

He said, "Agha Khorasani, if the information is as valuable as you say, we can move you immediately out of the UAE. I cannot promise you the move would be directly to the US. That is not something I can know and I will not lie to you just to get you to agree. You will have to trust us to do our best."

Khorasani was now on his third cigarette and the air conditioner in the Pajero was not keeping up with the smoke. Sue opened her window in hope of clearing some of the air. She and Sterling waited for Khorasani to speak. Sometimes in an agent meeting, the best ploy was silence. It was up to the target to make the leap himself.

Khorasani said, "When we meet next, I will bring you enough information for you to evaluate my worth. After that we can talk."

Sue and Sterling were both relieved. This meant that they would acquire hard data at the next meeting and Khorasani was already agreeing to multiple meetings. It could be a real case.

During the rest of the drive, Sterling provided Khorasani with where and when they would meet in two days. He warned the Iranian to do what he could to make sure the meeting was not known to any colleagues and that it would be a natural for him to leave the office. Khorasani agreed to the location and said that it would be best if the meeting was mid-afternoon when most residents of Dubai were either in air-conditioned restaurants or had returned to their air-conditioned apartments for a mid-day rest. They dropped off Khorasani approximately a half mile from the original pickup point and headed back to the safe house.

Sterling keyed the onboard microphone and said, "Keeper, we are RTB."

The surveillance team leader said, "*Roger, Hawkeye. Returning to base. We look forward to your write up. The boss said to remind you that has to be RFN.*"

Sue was surprised to hear the surveillance team lead use Massoni terminology. RFN in MILSPEAK meant "right fucking now."

ALL HELL BREAKS LOOSE

Neither Sue nor Sterling were surprised that the next day the COS and the MILATT returned to the safe house at 0700hrs. Barkley was cautiously optimistic. Finestri was enthusiastic in his comments.

"IF, and of course it remains a big if, what he says in true, we have a huge case here. Headquarters has been on my ass for nearly a year asking me when we were going to find something about the Iranian cyber threat. They already know that the Russians and the Chinese are all over us so they assume the Iranians would be as well. Khorasani might be offering us details that show precisely the Iranian capabilities. They might be good, they might be bad, but if Khorasani isn't lying, we will have some data. That's all I need for now."

Barkley said, "Do we ask for help from the Fort?" Everyone in the room knew the MILATT was asking if the National Security Agency based in Fort Meade should be involved.

Finestri raised his hands in mock surrender and said, "Jonah, if we open that door now, they will send a dozen cyber gurus tonight and all of them are going to want to ride with Sterling and O'Connell on the next meeting. We would need a school bus to hold the meeting. I have no problem sharing the stuff with the entire IC once we know we have something to share. But I would like to know we actually have something to share before I invite Community interest. OK?"

Barkley was clearly not on board with Finestri's argument, but he was also not trained in HUMINT tradecraft. He knew it wasn't the time or the place to argue that the NSA had the experts that would be needed to make sense from whatever they got from the volunteer.

Finestri turned to the two case officers and said, "No pressure, now. After all, we are only talking about whether or not we go to cyberwar against the Iranians." He smiled and said, "Seriously, you need to be on your toes on this one. You need to play your best game next meeting so that we can get this guy on board. We still don't know what we have here, so I'm not saying you can recruit the guy in the car, but you need to refine the meeting tradecraft so we can keep him alive for a bit while we sort out what he is offering and decide if he is worth keeping. I brought down $5,000 you can give him if he delivers something tangible." Barkley's eyebrows almost hit his receding hairline. $5,000 was a good portion of his annual working budget as the Naval attaché. Finestri continued, "He gets the money as a down payment on further compensation, right? Make that clear to him that he is in the big leagues now and he needs to know we love him too much."

Sterling nodded and simply said, "Roger, Boss."

Finestri said, "I will have the full Keeper team deployed to support your meeting. We will go ghost quiet until your meeting so that anyone who is watching thinks we have gone on holiday. You are the only show in town, David."

Barkley said, "O'Connell, have you reported to your higher or to SOF?"

Sue said, "Sir, at this point, we don't know enough to engage SOF. You know what's going on and as far as my commander is concerned, you are my chain of command while I'm here. So, if you are good with the plan, I will proceed as outlined. If you want to engage HICU before we know more, that's your call."

Barkley responded to Sue's answer as if he had just won the lottery. He had expected some sort of back channel that he wouldn't hear about until he got some bad-news lightning bolt from SOF headquarters or the Defense Intelligence Agency. Instead, this SOF officer was playing it straight. He couldn't ask for more. All he said was, "Thanks, Chief."

The day of the meeting both Sterling and Sue checked and dou-ble-checked their plan. They would leave the safe house two hours in advance of the meeting. Their route would take them away from the meeting site for an hour. During that time, they would have a coffee at a coffee shop near the gold souk, walk through the souk and return to the car. One set of keepers would be watching their route from the time they left the safe house. The second set of watchers would be positioned in the area of the meeting site. Because of her background serving with SOF Surveillance and Reconnaissance, Sue had asked to meet with the senior team leader of the keepers to double-check their plan. While the team was pure Agency trained, Sue was pleasantly surprised that the tactics they intended to use were absolutely the same as those used in S&R.

At one hour in their run, they would double back and head to the meeting site — a café that Sterling picked. He had never used the site, but had cased the location multiple times in the past to ensure it was viable. Once they had the all-clear message from the Keepers, they would approach the site and, ideally, pick up their target 100 yards from where he expected to meet. As Sterling said to Sue, "You can never be too careful. If he is good to go, it's no big deal. If he is a provocation, we avoid the arrest by the service. And, if he is just bait that the Iranians are using to do us harm, well, we have done our best to avoid sitting on the x."

"Are you going to make a timing stop on the route or just roll up?"

Sterling smiled, "Sue, this is my town." He added with just a touch of sarcasm, "I can get us there on time."

Sue looked down at her hands. She wasn't used to working with anyone who had the same tradecraft skills, so she had jumped to a conclusion that was not fair. "Sorry, Dave."

"No dramas, Sue. It always is a good idea to double-check." His digital watch alarm went off. He said, "It's time to launch."

As soon as they got into the Pajero, Sterling set the countdown timer on his watch. He turned on the Pajero communications system and the onboard microphone. He handed Sue an ear bud and put one in his left ear. He said, "Keeper, we are ready to launch."

A female voice said, *"Roger, Hawkeye. All clear from our side."*

Over the next hour, Sue received a guided tour of the various parts of Dubai including the old port, the banking district, and the gold souk. She took the opportunity to buy a small bracelet for her analyst partner at HICU and a three-gold chain necklace for her mother. When they loaded back into the Pajero, Sterling keyed the microphone and said, "All good?"

The same detached female voice said, *"All good, Hawkeye. We will continue to sweep behind you until you are inside Keeper6's bubble."*

Sterling moved the Pajero through the Dubai streets at just the right pace so that he approached the meeting site minutes before the set meeting. Periodically, he looked down at his watch to check the amount of time remaining before the pickup. Keeper6 had already identified Khorasani walking toward the site, so they were ready to grab their target and move out. As promised, he was carrying a laptop bag. Sterling pulled up as he approached Khorasani. As with their first meeting, Sue jumped out of the passenger seat, opened her door so Khorasani could get in and then opened the rear door. Sue had her prosthetic leg inside the Pajero and her right hand on the pull handle when all hell broke loose.

The first shot hit Khorasani in the shoulder and sprayed blood over the passenger seat and Sterling. A half second later, the next shot hit Khorasani in the back of head. Sue immediately jumped back out of the Pajero, dropped to a crouch and began to scan the area as she reached under her abaya for the Glock. A flash of sunlight hitting a set of binoculars drew her attention to a rooftop to their rear. A rooftop that would have overlooked the meeting site as well as their current location. She identified two men on the rooftop. One with a set of binoculars and one with a suppressed bolt action rifle. In that slow motion time that comes with combat, Sue watched as the sniper worked the bolt on his rifle. He fired another round that missed Sue. The round peeled a part of the door and shattered the right-side mirror. It was too long a shot for Sue to return fire.

Sterling shouted at her, "Grab the bag and get in. We are not going to have a firefight here. Leave the body. He is very dead. Now, Sue!"

Sue realized that it made no sense to stand and fight, but it was just her nature. It was one of the reasons why she lost her leg in Jalalabad. She was naturally aggressive and when her blood was up, she often made the wrong decision. Sterling shouted again, "Now!"

The sound of police sirens coming up the corniche made the difference. Sue knew that they could not stand and fight. She knew that arrest by the local police would not be a good time. She grabbed the laptop bag from Khorasani's shoulder, pulled the body out of the Pajero and jumped into the blood-soaked seat. Before she had the door closed, they were gone.

At the safe house on the beach, Finestri and Barkley conducted a tag-team debriefing of their two officers. After they were both satisfied that Sterling and O'Connell had done everything by the book, they reviewed what happened next.

Sterling said, "We drove to the linkup point with the Keepers. They took us in one of their cars back to the house. Keeper6 said he would dispose of the Pajero and I suspect it is on fire someplace in the desert right now. Keeper4 took a photo of the shooter and his observer. Definitely not Arabs but he said it didn't look like Iranians either." He passed the printed photo over to Finestri and Barkley. It showed a pair of tall Europeans on the rooftop. One was taking down the rifle, the second was glassing the streets with his binoculars.

Sue said, "They were set up for the stated meeting site, but they still did the shot where we picked up Khorasani. It was a good 500m shot. Whoever those guys are, they are professional snipers."

Finestri and Barkley both nodded.

Sterling continued, "Keeper3 followed the two to a covered garage, but the Keepers didn't have the manpower to cover all the exits, so we don't know for sure when they left or what vehicle they used."

Finestri said, "Since this was a professional hit, these guys either left the garage on foot or inside some panel van. There is no way the Keepers could have sorted that out. We have a photo and that is very good news. Now, what was in the laptop bag?"

Sue said, "No surprises there, Chief. A laptop, a half-dozen CDs, and a power supply. We haven't touched the computer. I'm not a geek, but I know enough to know that a serious tech guy will have laid traps in a computer that starts to erase the hard drive as soon as a dope like me tries to access files."

Barkley said, "Mark, I'll get this to the cyber team in Bahrain this afternoon. If you have a team in Abu Dhabi, I'm more than willing to leave it to you, but the JIOC in Bahrain is a shared space and the cyber operators include folks from the Navy, SOF, and the Agency."

"Jonah, it's all yours. I look forward to seeing what you find, but I'm not in the least bit interested in how the cyber gurus find it. Meanwhile, I have to think about how I get this photo to the Dubai security service. They just might already have one of these faces on file. Of course, I have to think about how I explain the picture. Perhaps we fuzz it a little bit and then say we got it from a drone shot?" Finestri smiled. It was a weak joke, but all he could think of for now.

He continued, "I'm just glad the only dead guy is our walk-in. Now, Sue, as much as I would like to debrief you on the adventures of your parents and your own life as a super-secret SOF spy, I think you need to get out of Dubai today. Jonah and I will have the embassy admin folks buy you a ticket coming from the MILATT's office. You are traveling on an official passport, so that's no sweat. Jonah, would you be willing to make sure Sue gets out of our country without any drama? I honestly don't care where she ends up as long as she leaves today."

"Mark, you know I can do that. In fact, I already have the tickets waiting at the airport. A Lufthansa flight to Frankfurt leaving in three hours. I will use my airport pass to stay with Sue until she boards."

"Thanks, Jonah. Now I have to decide how to clean up Mr. Sterling's mess." He smiled at David Sterling.

Sterling wasn't sure if it was a good smile or a bad smile, so he just smiled back. He said to Sue, "Well, thanks for the memories of our time on the beach."

Sue shook Sterling's hand and said, "Always a pleasure, David. And if you are ever in northern Italy, look me up."

Finestri said, "Now that is an offer that you need to accept, young Sterling."

Sterling blushed through his tan.

BACK TO SCHOOL

January – March 2009

W hen Sue returned from Dubai, she suffered through another torturous debriefing from Smith and Massoni. Smith started by saying, "A gunfight on the corniche in Dubai? What were you thinking, O'Connell?"

"Boss, I wasn't in a gunfight. I mean, I wasn't shooting at anyone. Someone shot the volunteer and then I worked hard to un-ass the area. In fact, you could say I was never there because if you asked anyone, they would say I wasn't part of the problem, just an innocent bystander."

Massoni, ever helpful, said, "Boss, she did recover the laptop and the JIOC gurus in Bahrain think it is a huge gain for SOF on Iranian cyber operations."

Smith said, "I heard from Barkley and even from the COS in Abu Dhabi that you were nothing but helpful. So, I guess we can just say it was another case of O'Connell being a bullet magnet."

"Boss, not to put too fine a point on this, but is there any way I can get off this merry go round of chasing volunteers? The only one I have found that was any good is dead. Most of these guys are kooks or fabricators."

"O'Connell, do you remember what I said a year ago. What the CG wants..."

"Sir, I get it. But..."

"O'Connell, get back to your desk, write up the full report and give me a chance to engage SOF headquarters. You do know that capturing a trove of cyber intelligence isn't going to help your argument."

Sue didn't know what to say, so she simply said, "Wilco, Boss."

Never one to take no for an answer, Sue O'Connell began to pester her colleagues in the analytic shop, especially her friend Chief Warrant Officer 3 Sarah Billings who went by the nickname Flash. When she wore out her welcome with Flash, she approached Jim Massoni and pleaded for a new assignment. The sergeant major was not amused. Six weeks later and after two additional TDYs that led nowhere, Colonel Jedidiah Smith relented and gave Sue a new assignment. Flash apparently knew the details, but wouldn't reveal anything other than it was a counterintelligence investigation and that they would be working together. Sue was not even the least bit amused. The last time she was involved in a counterintelligence operation, she ended up in the trunk of a car rigged to explode and later in a sinking ship loaded with nuclear waste.

The briefing took place in Smith's office at 0800hrs. Individuals in attendance were Smith, Massoni, Flash and Sue. Smith opened by saying, "Let's start up front with a requirement for you to get this assignment, O'Connell." Before Sue could say anything, Smith said, "No whining. This is important."

"Yes, sir."

"This may sound less exciting than jet-setting around the Middle East, but it is a critical mission. In fact, it is the most critical mission you could do to protect our operational security. It is directly related to work that you and Flash accomplished a year ago in Afghanistan and to the work you just did in Dubai. So, when I tell you that you are going undercover as a student at the Defense Language Institute, I don't want to hear it. Check?"

"Yes sir." Sue tried not to make it sound like she was pouting even though she was.

"Hey, you might even learn something!" Massoni smiled his scary sergeant major smile. When he smiled like that you never knew if he was happy or about to eat you alive.

Smith shook his head. He had hoped that this wouldn't turn into another bit of banter between his sergeant major and his troops. He turned to Flash and said, "Flash, explain to O'Connell what you will be doing at DLI."

Flash spent the next few minutes speaking in her least amusing, most professorial way. She started by saying, "You remember that we seem to have been behind the curve every step of the way in almost all of the O'Connell operations. We track the Iranian and terrorist smuggling routes, find their suppliers are Russian criminal enterprises and then…poof, something goes wrong. In the case of our operation on the Afghan border where we freed Jameson, we ended up under attack by a Russian mercenary unit."

"Flash, I don't think we need to cover old ground. I remember our defector Beroslav shot in the back as we tried to escape. I remember the Russian mercenaries, with helicopter gunships, for goodness sake, destroying Jamie's safe house. That, by the way, is something he has never let me forget. So, the Russians or the Iranians or the terrorists must have a penetration of our outfit. I get that part."

"Did you know that your mom's work to find your distant cousin the assassin was also compromised? She used sterile communications provided by the Agency to contact your cousin. Instead, he responded by reaching out to her on her personal email address. It was only once she set up a separate, commercial operation that the assassin was captured."

"All I remember was how pissed I was last year when she was in Croatia at the same time we were taking down the Hizballah smuggling network."

"I think you were more than pissed off. You were so mad, you couldn't even speak."

"Yup."

"Well, luckily, your partner Flash was paying attention when I got a chance later to engage the COS. It turns out the Klingons think whatever problem we have is also a problem they have. In short, she thought the Russians have compromised all of our operational traffic."

"Shit, Flash. That means they are following all of our ops?"

Smith interjected, "You see, you can pay attention when you need to do so. Your most recent Dubai misadventure also argues that there is a Russian connection. But you also demonstrated your massive ego. It doesn't appear to be all of our ops. So far, it looks like it is only YOUR ops. Of course, like the saying goes, have you ever thought the single common denominator in all your bad relationships is you?"

Sue thought but did not say, "Always the critic."

At this point, Smith said, "Enough chit chat. Get out of my office, complete the briefing and when you have a plan for how to make this work, come back. Now, goodbye."

"Flash at your service, sir."

Later, and only after Sue delivered a mug of coffee to Flash's cubicle did the briefing continue. Sue said, "And does the Flash have something other than bad news to share?"

"Not only do I have bad news, I have a plan."

"Do you think you might tell me the plan?"

"How much time do you have?"

"Smith told me to learn about the new project, so I guess I have as long as it takes."

"Excellent. Go get your own caffeine and I will make you smart. While you are at it, you can fill this one up." Flash handed Sue a small, empty thermos.

"I have to bribe you to get the story?"

"Trust me, you are going to need the caffeine."

After several cups of coffee for Flash and tea for Sue, Flash completed her explanation of the problem. The level of compromise and, more importantly, the specificity of the compromise related to Iran, and Russian organized crime, suggested that there was not a human penetration of their SOF unit, or of the CIA channels that compromised her mother's operation. According to Flash, there had to be a sophisticated technical compromise of the shared communications network used in field operations. The operation had to be able to sort through data, identify traffic involved with some part of family O'Connell and/or HICU and then forward that traffic to some central node where the Russians would take action.

Flash started working with their mutual friend and cyber ops genius from the CIA, Melissa Nez, to uncover the nature of the communications network that they shared. According to Flash, that was the easy part because the Agency and SOF shared so little. There were only a few specific communications nodes where both Agency and SOF operational communications existed side by side, rather than independent, discrete networks.

Flash looked up from her third cup of coffee and said, "And then, Flash came through."

"As we expect her to do."

Flash did not appear to notice the sarcasm in Sue's comment. She continued, "I thought about some of the places that are not warzone locations. One was your alma mater, the Farm where Klingons train all case officers, their own and SOF officers. Melissa led a team to the Farm and they scrubbed the network clean. They found a worm loaded into the system by your former classmate, Stan Czyneski, who we all know turned out to be a Russian sleeper agent."

Sue nodded. She remembered how her classmate had compromised all of her early operations in Cyprus, tried to kill her brother, and was only caught because of a CI case that had its origins with her grandfather. Czyneski was now serving a life sentence in a federal penitentiary.

Flash continued, "OK, so we have one of the compromised networks identified, but that is primarily an Agency location. Melissa and her crew isolated the network so that it looks like it is still working, but it is operating inside a ghost network that the Klingon CI staff manage."

Flash looked at Sue to determine if she understood the effort involved in creating a ghost network that would appear real, but offered dead ends and misinformation to the end user. It was clear from the look on Sue's face that she had no idea how many thousands of lines of code had to be created and then monitored to make the ghost network look real. Flash shook her head and said, "Sue, go get another cup of tea. I would hate to have your little case-officer brain overheat."

For once, Sue didn't argue. The idea of creating multiple networks to track a hacker was in fact making her head hurt. She walked back to make herself a cup of tea.

When she returned, Flash continued, "Ready? OK, the next question was how do we find a similar DoD location? I knew one place where we share communications with the Agency. The Defense Language Institute in Monterey. Most Agency officers take language training at their own site, but some of their analysts are sent to DLI for refresher courses and some of their seniors attend the Naval Post Graduate School at the same location. It appears decades ago the Agency established a commo node there in the same comms center as the DLI network that links the Pentagon, the Defense Intelligence Agency and to the National Security Agency. Voila! We now know the location!"

"So, we shut the network down, scrub it, reboot it and all is well. What in the world does that have to do with me? I am, after all, a military case officer who handles SOF reporting sources and those sources are focused on the Middle East."

"Ah, well, that's where the CI gurus and Smith came in. In their collective wisdom, they decided that there must be an active penetration inside DLI willing periodically to reboot Russian spyware into the network. Otherwise, it would be impossible to use the DLI network the way they were working the Farm network. It is not, after all, a fire and forget mission. Melissa worked with the Agency CI gurus and they found their end by scrubbing personnel files. It turns out Czyneski recruited one of the permanent party at the Farm to keep feeding the software on a regular basis. It is something you have to fiddle with. The poor dope at the Farm thought he was loading defensive spyware from their CI shop. Instead, he was loading Russian malware. Once approached, he agreed to keep the malware updated — so long as he worked with the CI gurus. After all, the alternative was a cell next to Czyneski."

"And, the question remains: what does that have to with me?"

"It means you and I are going back to school."

"Eh?"

"Yup. Smith has requested and, no surprise, SOF headquarters approved, we serve as the hunters at DLI. We, well actually I, know more about this threat than anyone inside SOF. You, on the other hand, are pretty much my cover for being there." Flash smiled her most angelic smile. "And, Smith figured you might bear a grudge for all the problems generated by this cyber attack."

"The boss is right, but I don't know if it is enough of a grudge to get me to go back to school."

Flash took a sip from her mug with a yellow lightning bolt on the side. She ignored Sue's bleat and continued, "We are both due to get refresher training in our second languages anyhow and this gives us a chance to be on the ground working the target. You are getting what is called Dari to Farsi transition. It makes sense since our target set is becoming less about Afghans and more about Iranians. On the other hand, Flash gets refresher training in Russian. Oh, do I need to say what Massoni said to me? He said orders are orders. RTFU!"

Sue nodded. Command Sergeant Major Jim Massoni started his career as a shooter in both US Special Forces and in the Ranger Regiment. Before he served in S&R, he was a first sergeant in one of the Ranger battalions. He rarely used Ranger speak inside HICU, but when he said RTFU, meaning *Ruck the fuck up*, he was serious. It simply meant, stop complaining and get on with the job. It did not pay to get crossways with any sergeant major. Most especially, with Jim Massoni.

Flash continued, "Better get home and pack your bags. We leave on the next available military aircraft headed back to CONUS. Once we are in the continental US, we are authorized commercial travel to San Francisco and a rental car. Our report date is 07 April."

Sue shook her head and said, "Swell."

"I told Smith and Massoni you would love the idea. Northern California beaches, Napa Valley wine, Sonoma County cheese, jazz clubs in San Francisco. And a spy, or perhaps, spies to catch! What's not to like?"

"Language school. I hated language school."

"Spoil sport." Flash smiled and said, "Are you ready to return to Smith's office and tell him you are delighted with the plan?"

DEATH IN THE DUNES

06 April 2009, Abu Dhabi-Dubai Highway

Sandy Tealor was enjoying the ride. He started his military career as a SEAL and one of the best things about being a SEAL was flying low and fast over a body of water just before an insertion. The mix of speed and adrenaline rush while sitting near or in an open door of a helicopter was one of Tealor's favorite parts of the SOF world. In this case, an Osprey MV22 tilt rotor from the *USS Iwo Jima* was carrying Sandy and a dozen Marines toward an agent meeting in the desert. Not exactly the most clandestine method of insertion, but certainly one of the safest he had made for some time.

Sandy served in Iraq for 18 months after his training at the CIA training facility known as the Farm, and was then reassigned to work out of the US Navy facilities in the island nation of Bahrain. As the home of the US Navy Fifth Fleet, Bahrain was an easy place for a Navy chief petty officer to find a billet. From there it was a simple matter for a man in civilian clothes to leave the port facility and wander into the city or, if needed, to travel from Bahrain into the Kingdom of Saudi Arabia, the United Arab Emirates or even as far south as Qatar or Oman. This gave Sandy the ability to develop counterterrorism sources for SOF/HICU and to respond to any immediate tasking from the SOF operational units in Iraq or in the Horn of Africa. In the case of this operation, Sandy's source promised to provide information on an al-Qaida cell developing plans to

49

attack an unidentified US Navy ship during an upcoming port call in Dubai. That was about as important a report as possible given the large US military presence in the Persian Gulf.

Sandy's source, registered as 561, had a good track record of reporting on Revolutionary Guards smuggling operations between the UAE and Iran. This new reporting was a stretch on his access. He was a Sunni Gulf Arab who worked with the Iranians simply out of greed. Smuggling to Iran was the most profitable shipping and warehousing work around. His ties to al-Qaida were more than a little puzzling, made even more puzzling by 561's demand to meet at sunset in the sand dunes near highway marker 41, almost halfway from Dubai to Abu Dhabi. 561 said he wanted to be sure they met alone. Well, that wasn't going to happen. Sandy knew about the shooting three months earlier in Dubai involving a volunteer and his colleague Sue O'Connell. If he hadn't been home for the holidays at the time, he would have been the one at the ambush. For this meeting in the desert, Smith made it clear that Sandy would have serious backup. He wasn't upset in the least. If he had to choose shooters other than his old SEAL unit, a fire team of Marines would do very well.

The MV22 slowed as they approached the beach. During the transition from flying over the Gulf to flying over land, the heat from the beginning of the desert summer swept into the aircraft. Sandy could hear as well as feel the tilt rotors shifting from horizontal to vertical as they approached. The rear tailgate of the MV22 was open revealing azure blue water and a gray blue sky. Through the cockpit windows, Sandy could see the setting sun about a hand's width above the horizon. The crew chief turned to the Marines and raised one finger from each hand. One minute to landing. He then motioned that it was time to pull on their dust goggles and get ready to get off his airplane. The lead marine, Staff Sergeant Baker, turned back to his men and passed the one-minute warning, pulled down his goggles and pulled up his scarf. There would definitely be sand flying when the Osprey landed. Earlier, Baker had made it clear to Sandy that his Force Recon team would exit first, fan out to the left and right and then Sandy, "their package" as he had heard the Staff Sergeant say to his men, would follow. Sandy was dressed in a sand-colored flight suit without rank or name tag. Nothing to show Baker that Sandy was anything other than "some desk jockey." Well, Sandy figured it wouldn't actually make any difference if Baker knew he was a SEAL. He was just the package. Sandy pulled a sand-colored balaclava over his head and then his googles. He had a small backpack over his shoulder. Inside was his debriefing kit that included a camping stove, a canteen and a cup for brewing tea, a notebook, and an envelope with five hundred dollars. Sandy was wearing a SIG SAUER pistol in a drop holster and carrying his M4 rifle. Just about all you needed for a night of fun in the desert.

The Osprey landed with a slight bump and the Marines were off the tailgate in seconds and deployed in a V formation, each Marine in a prone position. The team positions covered 180 degrees toward the Gulf. Sandy waited until Baker gave him the thumbs up. He had barely cleared the gate when the Osprey took off and turned back toward the sea. A different tilt rotor would return to pick them up in two hours. As the noise disappeared and the dust settled, Sandy walked over to Baker and said, "Time to go."

"Check, chief. Follow me." It took them no time at all to cover the 400 meters to the meeting site. Sandy set up his stove and started to heat water so he could offer tea when 561 arrived. Baker dispersed his men along a sand dune that overlooked the meeting site. By the time the water was boiling on the stove, Sandy looked back toward the Marines. They had disappeared. They were perfectly camouflaged. In his ear bud, he heard Baker's voice say, *"1, 6. We have a target in sight. He just pulled off the road about 50 mikes in front of you. Driving a Discovery, Dubai plates."*

Sandy replied in the small microphone tucked in the front zipper of his flight suit. "Roger, 6. That's my man. Time to start the show."

561 arrived wearing a white dishdasha, the one-piece cotton garment worn by Arabs throughout the Gulf. He wore a red-and-white checkered headscarf. Over the dishdasha, he was wearing a worn tweed sport coat, and on his feet he had leather sandals. He was carrying a small prayer rug under his right arm. Timing was everything

in this meeting. Sandy and 561 could hold their meeting, have tea, and Sandy would leave. 561 would remain on the dune, spread out his prayer rug and conduct his sunset prayers. Anyone driving along the highway would see a devout Muslim.

Sandy said, "My friend, please come and join me. I have made tea for us."

"Shukran, Mr. Davies. It is always good to have tea with you."

Sandy poured hot tea into the cup and offered a small tin of sugar cubes. 561 took two of the cubes and tucked them into his mouth between his left cheek and teeth. He took the tea in both hands and drank slowly. When half the cup was empty, he handed it over to Sandy, who finished the cup. There wasn't much time for the meeting, so once the cup was empty, Sandy folded the cup over the cooling camp stove and set it aside. He said, "You have some information for me tonight?"

"Very important information. You have money? It is very valuable."

Sandy watched 561's face. There was something wrong tonight. He couldn't decide if it was fear on his face or determination. Either way, it was not a good sign. Sandy reached into his bag and pulled out the thick envelope with the money. He handed the envelope to 561. Ever the businessman, 561 opened the envelope to see how much was there. He smiled his broken-toothed smile and simply said. "Shukran." He nodded and then added, "I have the information here in my jacket. But first, I must sign something, correct? I always have to sign for the money."

This banter was more like 561 and Sandy relaxed for a moment as he reached into the top zip pocket of his flight suit to pull out the receipt. After all, the USG was not going to allow him to pass funds to 561 and not account for them. As he reached into his pocket, he heard the round hit 561 in the head with the hollow sound of a hammer hitting a pumpkin. A second one followed in the chest.

"6, 3. Target down."

"3, 6. Roger. 1, your pal was getting ready to cap you."

Sandy looked down at 561. When he used his right hand to pull out the receipt, 561 had pulled an ancient Browning Hi-Power with a three-inch suppressor. He had definitely planned to do Sandy harm. He spoke into his concealed microphone, "Thanks, gents. That was a close one."

Baker's voice came through Sandy's earbud, *"Not real close, chief. We had him targeted from the beginning. Just in case."*

Sandy looked around and said, "OK. I have about five minutes to clean up here and then I think we need to get going."

"Take all the time you need, chief. We are on schedule. Just come back towards us when you are ready."

Sandy nodded. He took a moment for a few deep breaths to wash out the adrenaline flooding his system after witnessing the few seconds of chaos. He figured if they could see 561 in the telescopic sight, they could see him as well. He looked over at 561. He started first by clearing his own material. He took the stove and the cup and put it in the backpack. Next, the envelope with 561's payment. Then, Sandy took the pistol, cleared the weapon and put it into his backpack. He worked methodically along the body: jacket pockets first, then pockets in the dishdasha and then under the dishdasha in 561's undergarments. There was a notebook and a mobile phone in the jacket. He put the notebook in a Ziploc bag and put the phone in a nylon Faraday bag that would prevent signals reaching the phone and prevent the GPS in the phone from reporting where it was. He was surprised to find body armor under the dishdasha. He worked the Velcro and elastic and took the body armor off the dead man.

Sandy rolled out the prayer rug and placed 561 on his knees facing Mecca. Whatever secrets he had, he carried with him to the grave. Sandy shouldered the backpack, now heavier with 561's materials. He picked up his rifle and walked along the edge of the dune for 100 meters before turning east toward the Marines' position. He hoped that by sunrise, the morning winds would have wiped out his trail. As he walked through the deep sand, he relived the entire operation and wondered where it had gone wrong. The only thing he knew for sure was 561 had come for a fight. 561 just hadn't expected to have a fight with the United States Marines.

SCHOOL'S OUT

S ue O'Connell sat in her cubicle repeating a series of Farsi verb conjugations. If there was one thing she realized after four months of language school, it was success at DLI standard proficiency in Farsi was not easy. She came to the school comfortable in the Afghan dialect of Persian known as Dari. She made it clear to the instructors that she was confident the transition to the new language would be a snap — perhaps a month, maybe two. Her instructors made it clear that they didn't think so. Her pronunciation of even the most basic words made the instructors howl. They called her a bumpkin. They said she would have been better starting from scratch. They were sufficiently rude that Sue often imagined how she might hurt them. But, as Massoni said, orders were orders.

After her injury and when SOF offered her the job as an intelligence collector, Sue realized that her new job often went counter to her natural impatience and her preferred method of action. It was what Massoni often called the O'Connell method of "ready, fire, aim." Now, she was involved in a counterintelligence investigation that required patience and a willingness to take abuse from language instructors who had no understanding of her job at HICU and no clue of her real job at DLI. Most of the language students at the school were going to be involved in signals intelligence. It didn't matter whether they were going to be posted at sea, in the air, or on the ground, they were simply going to be listeners. Sue wished she could spend an afternoon telling her instructors what her life was like and how she used her language skills. Getting your hands dirty was often not just a metaphor. Sometimes, she literally got her hands dirty and formal Persian was not useful when that happened.

Instead, Sue O'Connell decided to buckle down and prove the instructors wrong about her language skills for as long as the assignment lasted. Then, just before she left, she might just have to hurt one of them. After all, she was hunting one of the instructors. One of them was a traitor.

Now Flash was in the cubicle next to Sue, practicing her Russian. She pulled down her headset and tapped Sue on the shoulder. She whispered, "You about done?"

Sue looked around the language lab. Twenty cubicles, twenty students practicing various languages. The new Chinese language students were practicing the most basic tones of Chinese. The French and German students, most likely in refresher courses, were mimicking complete sentences. Sue shook her head and said, "I was done about an hour ago when my brain turned to mush. Even in the best of times, language school is like driving nails into my head. In this case, it's worse since it's only a complex, painful cover story."

"Stop moaning. You will be a better little case officer if you speak Iranian Farsi as well as Afghan Dari. We gotta go, we have a date."

"A date? When were you going to tell me?"

"How about now? Let's go." Flash took the CD out of the player in her cubicle, threw it into her laptop bag, tossed the headset on the desk and stood up. "No time to dilly-dally. We really do have a date."

"K," grumbled Sue. She knew that Flash was the point of contact for the operation. No one knew for sure if any of Sue's communications gear, phone or laptop, was compromised. Flash didn't seem to be the target, so HICU authorized her to buy a new phone and laptop with cash on their arrival in CONUS. She used these to communicate with Smith and Massoni using a commercial platform provided by Melissa Nez at the Agency. It might not be perfect, but it was better than using a compromised SOF network. And, it was certainly faster than sending letters.

Once they were outside the language lab and had their electronics secured in the trunk of their rental car, Flash finally revealed their "date." They were going to meet some of their local CI contacts. As they drove out the main gate manned by Navy contract guards, Flash said, "It turns out that one of the only US Army units left at the old Ft. Ord is a CI shop. They will eventually move to Hawaii, poor babies, but for now, they are in a building on the old post on the coast. We are going to meet three guys at Ord. One is our Army CI contact who owns the space, one is a Naval Criminal Investigative Service CI guru from San Diego and one is an FBI special agent from San Francisco. Smith says we are supposed to play nice with these guys. He also said not to get in their way. He pointed out that if/when we get a target sorted, we can't use the normal, O'Connell destructive method of finishing the target."

Sue smiled and said, "I resemble that remark."

As the car entered the main highway, Flash accelerated and said, "Indeed you do. Anyhow, that was Smith's way of saying that we are just the surveillance side of the equation. These CI gurus all have authority to arrest, detain, and question suspects. None of the techniques you learned from Jamie in Iraq or Afghanistan can be used. Check?"

"Jamie is really a sweetie when you get to know him."

"Would that be before or after he puts the sandbag over your head?"

"OK, so sometimes he gets creative."

"Yup. He is a very creative Klingon. So, we are agreed, no annoying O'Connell outbursts at the meeting? We just let them say their lawman piece, we agree like good little girls and then get back to doing the hard work. Check?"

"I will do my best."

"Massoni said you would say that. Then he said just do it."

"And whatever the sergeant major says is what we do."

Flash smiled and looked over at Sue and said, "Kinda, sorta."

Fort Ord was once the largest Army base in California. It was now mostly empty, but had been the home of the 7th Infantry Division and a large basic training facility from 1940 until the end of the Vietnam War. The base officially closed in 1994, but a small military contingent remained in one of the old base headquarters buildings. Fort Ord included miles of coastline. Access to the Pacific Ocean and proximity to San Francisco made it a very desired location in the 1950s through the 1980s. The Fort Ord that Flash and Sue drove on looked precisely like what it was — an abandoned industrial site, managed by the Bureau of Land Management awaiting someone in the US government to decide what to do with the property.

Sue was navigating off a digital map sent by the Army CI focal point. As they drove up to the only four-story building that didn't look like it was abandoned, Sue said, "Flash, I think we are here."

"What gave it away, Sue? The fencing and the armed guards or the big sign that says 'US Government Facility.'" Sue stuck her tongue out at Flash. Flash returned the favor.

After passing through the main gate, they parked in a slot identified as visitor parking. They called from the phone at the entrance door and waited for their focal point to meet them. They had their military ID cards out when he arrived. A tall man in Army Combat Uniform opened the cipher-locked door to the building and said, "Greetings to the last little bit of the Army at Fort Ord. Jasper Derry, Army CIC."

Sue thought Derry was probably at one time a very handsome man. Unfortunately, he had burn scars on the right side of his head and on the hand that he was offering. She took the hand without hesitation. She knew precisely how much it mattered to a wounded warrior to have a normal life. After all, Sue was one. She said, "Sue O'Connell."

Flash did the same and said, "Flash."

"Flash?"

"OK, Sarah Billings. I do prefer Flash."

"You got it, Flash."

As they walked into the building, through the obligatory entrance photos of the entire US chain of command, starting with the President, then the Secretary of Defense and then Secretary of the Army, Sue took a second look at Derry's uniform. He was a chief warrant officer like Sue and Flash. On his left sleeve was the insignia for I Corps. A black circle inscribed inside a second black circle. Above the unit patch was a Ranger Tab and a Special Forces Tab. I Corps was the Asia Pacific command and told Sue nothing about Derry's current unit. It was very much like the US Army Special Operations Command insignia on the left sleeve of Sue's uniform back in the barracks in Monterey. Thousands of service men and women were assigned to ARSOC and the same was true for I Corps. They included combat and support units in Washington State, Hawaii, and South Korea. The Special Forces insignia on the right sleeve identified his combat service. Derry was definitely the real deal. Sue felt more than a little under-dressed in her jeans, polo shirt and black fleece jacket.

Flash was never bothered by protocol or even manners: "So, Derry, Special Forces, eh? Which group?"

As the elevator door opened and Derry walked in, he said, "19th"

"Eh?"

He punched the button for the fourth floor and said, "Yeah, well, I was in law school and served with the National Guard SF unit since I was in college in Colorado. We were deployed a couple of times to Afghanistan."

"Right. Activated and deployed so that SF could rotate a full seven groups in and out of theatre. You ever return to law school?"

"Nope. Been on active duty since 2001. Never made it back to civilian life."

Sue finally decided to give Derry a break from the Flash interrogation technique. She said, "You know our background?"

"Some SOF intel unit supporting the Command, right?"

Before Flash could give an elevator speech on HICU and its role in hunting terrorists, the elevator doors opened on the fourth floor. Sue answered Derry by simply saying, "Yup. That's about it."

As they walked down the hall, Sue realized why the building was still in Army hands. Sometime in the past, the original office space had been modified to create a pair of sensitive compartmented information facilities or SCIFs on either side of the hallway. Each SCIF was accessed through a metal door with combination lock, a cipher lock on the door handle and a separate badge reader on the doorframe. It took real money to make a SCIF and once the military had one, they were loath to give it up.

Derry turned to the door on the right, used his ID card to trigger the first lock and then used the pin pad on the door handle to open the cipher. As they walked in, Sue noticed a small form on a magnetic clipboard on the door. The form identified who opened the vault each day. The form was initialed "JD" every day in the past month, opening precisely at 0600hrs and closing each day sometime after 1900hrs. This had to be Derry's office and he clearly had no life outside the office.

As they walked in, three men and a woman also in Army uniforms looked up. A female staff sergeant said, "Boss, the other two visitors are sitting in the conference room. Coffee and water are at the table."

Derry said, "Thanks, Judy." He headed into the conference room which was in the middle of the workspace. Sue thought, "A box inside a box, lovely."

As they walked in, a man and a woman stood up. Flash said, "Pretty easy to sort out which of you two is the FBI, no?"

The man in the gray suit smiled and said, "OK, my stunning good looks give it away? Or my excellent tailor?" He offered a very large, very calloused hand and said, "Walt Mitchem. San Francisco Field Office."

Flash shook it and said, "Flash, SOF Intel."

Since Flash had engaged the FBI special agent, Sue decided to introduce herself to the NCIS special agent. "Sue O'Connell. As Flash said, SOF Intel. What she didn't say was we are based out of Camp Ederle in Vincenza."

"Marla Vickers. I did a tour at Sigonella NAS. Life in Italy is nice, eh?"

"Can't say for sure. I'm on the TDY circuit. So far, I've seen the inside of my quarters a couple of times a month and then the inside of military aircraft headed someplace else."

Introductions concluded, Derry said, "There's coffee and water on the side table. Help yourself."

Flash walked over to the table and tossed a bottle of water to Sue while she made a cup of coffee for herself. "Amenities" such as they were completed, Derry took charge of the meeting.

"OK, there is no need for prologue, we all know the why and the how, what we need right now is an update from you. Any results?"

Sue hadn't expected quite the blunt introduction, but she jumped in. "So far, on my side, I have identified one instructor and one tech who could be targets. The instructor, Farhad Nisham, has been in the states about twenty years. He left Iran in the late 1980s as a student, spent five years in Germany and moved here in the '90s. He's careful when talking about himself which is hard since my refresher class is supposed to be all about conversational Farsi. Every time I try to get him to talk about Iran, or even about Germany for that matter, he dodges the conversation. I do know he has two generations of relatives still in Iran though one of his brothers splits his time between Kish Island and Dubai." Sue paused to see if they would ask more about Nisham before she moved to the DLI tech. They didn't so she continued.

"The DLI tech I identified is named Jack Nable. He's a Californian who was a computer tech in Silicon Valley for a while. He is an odd one. Certainly competent, but a screwy story when you figure working at DLI can't be as lucrative as working in Silicon Valley. He is not real friendly and not real helpful."

Flash chimed in, "Boy, that is the case. I did a run at him as well. I tried to engage him with geek talk and he just shut me down."

Derry turned to his counterparts and said, "Either of those names mean anything to you?"

Mitchem said, "Nable is someone we looked at some years back.

When I pulled the records of all the DLI folks we had on file, I think Nable was involved in some complaint on violating his NDA with a Silicon Valley firm. They canned him and he was blackballed from the tech firms in San Jose."

Sue said, "Violate a non-disclosure agreement and they exile you?"

"I guess it depends on the violation. This was right around the dotcom bubble in 2000 so I guess he thought he could score big and become a millionaire. Instead, he ended up making some money and losing his access to the community. Let me see what I can find about his finances."

Flash said, "Along with Nable and Nisham, I have found only one of the Russian instructors worth a second look. Nadya Bendalyani. First of all, I don't think that is her real name. Basically, Nadya Bendalyani is Jane Doe in the Georgian language. Of course, there are probably real Jane Doe's out there, but I'm guessing she isn't one of them."

Marla said, "Oh, I hope someone at DLI did a name trace when they hired her."

"Beats me. All I know is she is a part-time instructor, and she speaks excellent Russian without a Georgian accent. She claims to have been born and raised in New York City. That's my home town as well, so I tried to get her to offer up some personal information or her favorite haunts in the city. Nadya has worked hard to dodge all the questions. Maybe she saw in my bio that I'm from the city, maybe she just doesn't like small talk. She has an advantage because as a part timer, she is not the senior instructor. The senior, Sasha Merkovich, is a little bit of a tyrant in the classroom. I get slapped down every time I engage Nadya."

Derry said, "Hard to imagine you being slapped down, Flash."

"No fooling," was all Sue could add.

Flash said, "I'm trying to remain low profile."

This time it was Mitchem who said, "Hard to imagine."

Derry looked at Mitchem and Vickers and said, "Any information on Ms. Bendalyani?"

Both special agents shook their heads. Derry turned to Flash and Sue and said, "Any ideas on the way forward?"

Sue said, "I think we do our best to get our targets out of the class-room and into something resembling a social setting. If we can get something, anything, that supports our suspicions, then we get back to you and you get the authority to do some physical or electronic surveillance. Of course, if the name trace on Ms. Bendalyani aka Jane Doe turns up a blank, I think we have a good reason to focus our attention on her. She might be more open to an approach for a girls' night out than our two male targets. For now, I don't have a ton of ideas."

Flash said, "Given the fact that all three are working inside DLI and using DLI phones and DLI computers, is there any chance we can get some basic tech surveillance on them before we have probable cause for something outside DLI?"

Vickers said, "Their employment agreements will have included a warning that their government communications could be moni-tored. They have all been employed for some years without any sign of monitoring. I don't see why we can't do the needful at this point. The hard part is to get this accomplished through remote access."

Mitchem said, "If NCIS was to ask for FBI assistance, I think remote access would not be a problem. Just sayin'."

Flash said, "That's what is great about this country. Joint opera-tions at the troop level. No sand in the gears."

Mitchem said, "When was the last time you worked with the FBI?"

Sue said, "My brother is an FCI agent out of the Washington Field Office. He doesn't seem to complain much about his joint opera-tions."

"Working on…?"

"Iranians, I think. Though it might be Hizballah."

"That might be about the perfect way to bypass FBI bureaucracy. A link between Iranian spies and Lebanese terrorists."

Flash smiled and said, "Well, we have an Iranian in the mix here. What's not to like?"

Mitchem nodded, "Now you are thinking like a good field agent. There is always a way."

Derry said, "Hannibal said 'I will either find a way or make one.'"

Flash turned to Sue and whispered, "Derry is your kinda guy. Make sure you get his number before we leave."

For the first time in a very long time, Sue blushed.

WELL, ISN'T THAT CURIOUS?

T he FBI surveillance and raid teams waited outside the building. It was dark. It was late. It was a weekend and, best of all, it was raining. Annoying, but it was what they did for a living. The payoff would be when they broke down the doors.

Special Agent Bill O'Connell sat in the Ford Transit van with the two members of the Washington Field office cyber squad and his squad supervisor, Len Preacher. The interior of the van was packed with electronic gear that emanated a blue-green glow. The only other light in the van was a small red lamp just above the rear double doors, allowing sufficient visibility to see the door handles. It was a hot night for early fall and O'Connell and Preacher were sweating under their armored vests emblazoned front and back with yellow initials "FBI." This was not the first time the cyber gurus had spent the night in their van and they were dressed accordingly in FBI training gear — t-shirts, shorts, and trainers — all in the Quantico authorized navy blue.

The other foreign counterintelligence squads in the Washington Field Office referred to the Iran squad as "Reverend Preacher and his choir." No one on the squad thought that was funny. Particularly because Preacher was an exceptionally profane man when frustrated by FBI headquarters, other federal agencies, sloth, incompetence, lack of a professional demeanor, and, Bill thought, just about all life on the planet.

Still, Bill O'Connell liked working for Preacher, who ran the Iran FCI squad like a Marine platoon. Early morning squad PT at a local high school track followed by a shower and a team coffee and breakfast inside their squad bay at 0800hrs. Preacher used breakfast as a venue to get his first briefing of the day on their ongoing investigations. He passed that information on to the Washington Field Office SAC and the Iran Operations manager in FBI headquarters by 0900hrs. By 1000hrs, squad members were supposed to be on the street collecting new information on nefarious Iranian activities in the Washington Metropolitan Area (WMA), which included DC, Southern Maryland and Northern Virginia.

Iranian agents were known to approach Iranian exiles who had jobs in the WMA and coerce the exiles to work with the local Lebanese Hizballah operators. On the other hand, the second half of the target set, Hizballah operators, were villains both by nature and by trade. They self-funded their programs by low-level criminal activities. After three years on the squad, Bill was one of the old timers now. Preacher had him running a three-person team working a specific Hizballah target in Northern Virginia. Most days, Bill liked the structure and he liked working on the Iranian target. Today was not one of those days because he was the target of Preacher's frustration.

Preacher's face looked cadaverous in the blue-green light of the computer screens. He had a high and tight military style haircut and his thin, wrinkled face made him look precisely as dangerous as his reputation argued he was. Preacher had served on gang task forces, organized crime task forces, SWAT teams, and now an FCI team. Most FBI agents are well trained in firearms, but rarely have to use them more than once or twice in a full career. Preacher's reputation at the field office was a man who had more gunfights under his belt than most lawmen in the entire WMA. Like Bill's first squad supervisor, Jeremy Ferguson, Preacher's history as an FBI agent belonged in a movie script.

Preacher turned to Bill and said, "O'Connell, this intel of yours better have been right. Otherwise, I intend to choke you and then find your confidential informant and choke him." O'Connell was already nervous about the information his confidential informant or CI had provided. Normally, a straight up source on Hizballah criminal activities, the CI's most recent reporting was about a joint Hizballah-Islamic Revolutionary Guards Corps, IRGC, cyber operation. The CI said that the cyber operation was focused on two actions. First, the Hizballahis would steal the identities of low-level Department of Defense civilian employees. Once the identities were captured, Iranian hackers used the identities to gain access to the DoD unclassified servers located throughout the WMA and inside the Pentagon. Once inside the unclassified system, they could use a number of different techniques to gain access to the classified system. Or, they would use the unclassified services to steal more identity information and repeat the process.

When Bill provided this latest reporting in the FBI form 302 — the format used by special agents to document interviews — he worked hard to avoid creating expectations. The CI had been tasked by his Hizballah contacts to acquire high-end computer hardware and software for their building. In response to the requirement, he delivered very fast, very high-end gaming-style computers. The Hizballah contact made it very clear that the CI was never to come near the building or even Sterling at night. If they needed more equipment, he could purchase it and then drop it on the loading dock of the building by 1700hrs. A warehouse supervisor would sign for the equipment and, later, the Hizballah team using the equipment would evaluate his purchases and approve funds for the CI. They would do that at a time and place of their choosing. The CI ended his report by saying that they always passed the funds in a Maryland suburb, miles away from the warehouse.

No matter how hard Bill tried to downplay the lack of specificity, once the report arrived in the maw of the Hoover Building and across the river into the office of the Director of National Intelligence, it became the report of the day and ended up in the Presidential Daily Briefing at 0800hrs the next morning. By 1000hrs the same day, Preacher had his orders straight from the FBI director's office: "Put an end to this operation tonight!" Preacher knew that Bill's report was filled with unanswered questions, but orders were orders. At least they had a place and generally a time for the takedown, so that was something.

Preacher had well over twenty years with the FBI. He knew how to play the game to ensure he didn't end up squashed like a bug by either his SAC or some senior in the Hoover Building. Preacher's first call was to the Washington Field Office Special Surveillance Group chief. SSG provided sophisticated physical surveillance for the entire field office. He explained to the SSG supervisor what he knew, what he didn't know and the shitstorm that was raining down on him. Luckily, the SSG supervisor had a sense of humor and, more importantly, had an open night, so he authorized Preacher's use of his entire team. They would set up both fixed point and mobile surveillance rings around the warehouse identified as the center of the activity. SSG also had excellent relations with the Virginia State Police which meant they would have access to the Virginia traffic cameras nearby.

Next, Preacher called the cyber squad supervisor and the SWAT team leader. If he was going to raid a building manned by Hizballahis and possibly IRGC guys, he wanted to be sure he had both sufficient firepower and cyber horsepower. Since he had the director's email, resources were not a problem.

So, now they waited. Preacher looked at the tritium dial on his Luminox divers watch and said to no one in particular, "At least we know there are creeps in that warehouse. The surveillance team told us that much." He turned to O'Connell and said, "This better work out. You do realize SWAT has been out in this rainstorm now for thirty minutes. If they find an empty building, I'm not going to get in the way when they reach out to you." Bill O'Connell knew precisely what sort of wall-to-wall counseling he might face if this was a mess.

At 2315hrs, a loud beeping noise came out of the headphones of one of the cyber team. He smiled as he pulled the headphones off. He turned to Preacher. He said, "There is no doubt now. It is not clear who is doing the needful, but there are definitely computers using software to scrape data out of dozens of personal computers nearby. It looks like they are targeting kids playing online games. Plus, another set of computers are targeting the Pentagon ghost servers we set up this afternoon. I can't say who they are, but they are definitely committing crimes."

Now it was Preacher who smiled. As he stood up and headed toward the van door he said, "OK, O'Connell, let's get to work." They pushed open the van and stepped into a driving rain. Preacher walked over to a pair of black four-door pickup trucks parked out of sight of the building. As Preacher approached, the driver's window on the first truck came down. A woman with short brown hair said, "So Len, are we going to do this tonight?"

Preacher said, "Oh, you bet Nina. We are definitely going to do this."

She nodded and said, "Excellent." All four doors of the first pickup opened and four members of the Washington Field Office SWAT team climbed out. Dressed in olive Nomex jumpsuits and wearing body armor, three started to move toward the building. The fourth member climbed into the bed of the pickup truck and pulled a sniper rifle out of a waterproof case. The second truck started up and moved into position on the opposite side of the building. Three more members of SWAT deployed and, again, a fourth mounted the bed with his sniper rifle.

The SWAT leader said to Preacher, "You and O'Connell can join us, but wait until we have breached the door, K?"

Preacher said, "Nina, you get to do the tough guy stuff. All I want is the criminals and their kit. Ideally alive and unbroken."

"Can't promise," was all she said as her half of the team headed toward the front of the building. In the darkness, O'Connell could barely make out a second four-man team moving toward the loading dock. Earlier, the surveillance team identified the security cameras covering the front and back entrances. The SSG pulled off the site as they saw the SWAT team approach. They would disappear into the night and be back at the Field Office by the time the raid was completed. It never paid to allow surveillance specialists to be seen by villains.

The SWAT snipers in the back of the trucks were now aiming suppressed rifles at the cameras. In the van, the members of the cyber squad were watching the feed from the helmet cameras of the agents leading the two separate SWAT teams toward the door. They knew the same feed was playing in the SAC's office and, most probably, in the office of the director. The cameras had a night-vision setting, so all of the images were green with a slight grainy texture. The crew in the van also monitored the communications among the team.

Special Agent Nina Jacobs' voice came on first. *"5, Tell me when you are set."*

Her deputy's voice came through. *"6, We are in place."*

Jacobs voice again. *"Long guns, do the needful."*

A calm voice from one of the snipers. *"One done."*

"Two done."

Jacobs' voice now: *"Go, Go, Go."*

Inside the van, they watched as both teams used small explosive charges for forcible entry. The night-vision images turned white. The two sets of FBI agents entered through the collapsed doors. The helmet cameras had switched to normal setting as they entered a very well-lit warehouse with a dozen men working at picnic tables staring at computer screens. Some of the men were wearing headphones so they didn't realize what was happening until they were being detained. Several tried to run, which didn't make much sense given the size of the raid team, but human nature is such that when men with guns move toward you, the natural tendency is to run in the opposite direction. There was no place to run and no shots were fired. It was all over in seconds.

Preacher was the last man in the stack at the front of the building. O'Connell was the last man in the stack at the rear. They met in front of the bank of computers. The computers were running autonomous programs. They continued to run well after their owners were detained.

Preacher walked down the row of computers. He looked down at one of the screens and called O'Connell over to show him. "Now, isn't that interesting?"

O'Connell looked at one of the computers running a communications program back to some remote base. The information was all in Cyrillic.

RTB

I t was 0615hrs and Sue O'Connell was finishing a run on the DLI compound when her phone started to ring. After the loss of her left leg below the knee in 2005, it took a few years for the scar tissue on her leg to form such that the prosthetic didn't grind the skin when she ran. Now, Sue wouldn't win any sprints and she still couldn't run long distances, but she was pleased to see she could run two miles in 20 minutes and no longer follow the run with four ibuprofen, known in the SOF community as Ranger M&Ms.

The phone continued to ring as she dug it out of the nylon pouch at her waist and took a moment to catch her breath. The caller ID said UNKNOWN ID. It elicited the required response: "2615," the last four of this locally acquired phone. Her own phone remained in a Faraday cage container at RLSU until the techs determined the extent of compromise on their electronics.

Sue did not recognize the voice on the other end of the phone: "Chief, this is Bragg."

"Identify." Every day, SOF headquarters sent a set of challenge and password alpha-numeric which could be used in just this situation. "C145NT."

"Roger C145NT. I reply AB6511."

"Roger, Chief. We just got the word from your boss. Instructions are RTB. Confirm?"

"Roger, Bragg. RTB. I will tell my colleague."

"No need, Chief. We already called her. Stay safe."

"Roger, Bragg. Out here." Sue shut down the phone and headed for the BOQ room she was using while at school.

A shower and thirty minutes later, Sue was ready to leave. She had already informed her instructors by email that she was leaving. "Contingency requirement" was all she offered in the email. She also reached out to Jasper Derry by text to let him know she was out of the net. It was the last message she sent on the phone before she disabled the SIM card and pulled the battery on the phone. She met up with Flash at their rental car. Flash was already behind the steering wheel.

"You're late."

"Hey, it's just 07. How can I be late?"

"Because I'm ready to go."

"OK, so let's go."

"How was the date last night?"

"Date?"

"Come on, sister. Give."

"It was a very nice meal in Pacific Grove. We sat on the waterfront near the old canneries. Good conversation, coffee afterwards. He dropped me off at the BOQ at around 2200hrs."

"No mas?"

"No mas? We have work to do after all and a good bit of the conversation last night was about work. Still, it was nice to talk to a guy for a change instead of…well, instead of you. Now, let's change the subject. Are we going to get plane tickets at SFO?"

"I already took care of that, slowpoke. Hey, did you let Derry know that you love him?"

"I let him know we were leaving."

"Good enough for now. Once we get back to REAL SUE, you can get back in touch. But, of course, only after you let Flash do a deep dive trace on him."

"Really?"

"Trust no one."

"Not even me?"

Flash looked over at Sue as they drove out of the main gate at DLI.

"Well, OK, I trust you aren't the spy we are after. Let's see: getting locked in the trunk of a car, almost getting blown up in the Black Sea and fighting the good fight in the Konar more or less vets you."

"More or less?"

"Keep asking dumb questions and it will be less."

"Check. Did you get anything other than instructions to return to base?"

"Nope, just RTB. I assumed they authorized any cost tickets, so I booked us business class from San Francisco to Rome and then a hop to Marco Polo International into Venice. If they don't like it, then I will swear they were the only tickets available."

"Count on me to back up your story."

"Ya think?" Flash smiled. "Before I shut down the computer, I sent a note to Marconi's ghost account saying we would take the train from Venice to Vincenza. He needs to pick us up at the train station. I gave him approximate times for the pickup."

Sue nodded. Marconi was the tech guru for HICU. Before they left, he created a ghost account on an Italian server so that they could communicate with him outside of government channels. When he gave them the business card with the name Gino Marconi, *Maccanico di Gara* with a stylized open cockpit race car embossed on the card, Sue asked, "OK, what does that mean? I don't want to be carrying some card with a rude Italian pun created by Massoni."

"It just means race mechanic. When I was in college, I wanted to be a rally car driver. I ended up as a rally car mechanic for the Baja 1000. Not much money, but plenty of fun. Anyhow, Massoni said I could be anyone I wanted to be so long as I could spend 30 minutes talking about my job. Too easy. More importantly, the telephone number, the email address and the PO Box are all live, so you can use them if needed."

Sue smiled at the thought of Marconi picking them up in some sort of Italian rally car. She said to Flash, "It sounds like we are all set. I wonder why they pulled the plug on our op?"

"You realize it wasn't 'our' op anymore. After we gave Derry, Vickers and Mitchem the leads, we weren't going to be much help."

"I wanted to close the deal."

"Not in CONUS, my dear. You and I are *Out* of CONUS operators. No authority here, only trouble. Well, we are trouble OCONUS as well, but that's our job."

Sue had to agree. Inside the continental US, they were more trouble than it was worth. The targets were US citizens and only US law enforcement agents were going to be able to close the deal with an arrest, interrogation or creating a double agent. SOF's mission was for outside the US. DoD authorities were very ambiguous in a SOF mission, but those same authorities in a US based CI mission were very restrictive. Still, she wouldn't have minded seeing the operation through to its conclusion. If for no other reason than another dinner with Derry.

After twenty minutes of two-lane blacktop, Flash finally had the car on HWY 101 and she started to relax as they entered the traffic flow into the city. She looked at Sue and said, "I know you wanted more time with Derry. I get it. But orders are orders, no?"

Sue could feel the blush crawling up her collar. "What are you talking about?"

"Sister, it isn't like there wasn't some obvious chemistry. And your effort to provide a daily report to Derry since we last met was ever so cute, but not exactly subtle. And then dinner on cannery row. A real movie set."

"OK, so I think he is a nice guy. And, he's outside of the SOF community, and..."

"He's a hunk. An ugly hunk with those scars, but a hunk. I get it. And, once I have vetted him properly, I will give you the go ahead to make this work somehow."

"When did you become my warden?"

"Somehow you didn't realize that became my additional duty when you signed into HICU? Some trained observer you are."

"Orders from Massoni?"

"Well...yes. He said it was my responsibility to make sure you didn't do damage to yourself."

"He said that?"

"OK, he said don't let her fuck up."

"More like the Massoni I know."

"Anyhow, I think we make a good team and I'm not about to let you go all soft and mushy over a guy until I'm sure he isn't part of the opposition."

"The opposition?"

"Sue, what would be a better way to keep a source inside DLI safe than have a penetration of some part of the CI infrastructure in California? It might be Derry, it might be Vickers, it might be Mitchem, it might be someone else. Flash intuition says it might be one of them and I'm determined to find out which one."

As Flash argued the point, Sue had to admit she was right. And she was a little embarrassed that she hadn't thought the same thing. She said, "OK, I'm with you on this. I just got a little..."

"Distracted? Yeah, guys will do that to you. I remember this Ranger from First Bat I knew..."

Sue raised her hands in surrender and said, "Please, not another Flash adventure."

"Just saying, sister. Guys are fun to play with, but they also come with their challenges."

"Too true on that one, Flash."

---

12 September 2009, RLSU Warehouse

Massoni watched Flash and Sue O'Connell drag themselves into the RLSU warehouse. He was the only one present and he hadn't turned on the full set of ceiling lights. The warehouse was lit by the lights from his office and from the small gym that they had in the corner next to the cage where Marconi did his magic. Massoni had just finished his weight workout and was still in his black sweats and trainers. The warehouse was filled with the late fall sunrise creeping into the building when they opened the door.

Even after traveling in business class, Flash and Sue showed up with a gloomy disposition as well. It took them over 24 hours of travel from Monterey, California, to Camp Ederle, Italy. Even with a comfortable seat, jet lag from the time jump of nine hours coupled with over 20 hours in an aluminum tube of dry air takes a toll on the body. Flash was slightly better off than Sue on the flight simply because she didn't have the added complication of a prosthetic limb. The change in air pressure made Sue's prosthetic fit poorly and even in business class, all she could do during the flight was fidget every time the prosthetic moved against her leg. Even following the SOF protocol of drinking 8–10 ounces of water every hour and consuming no alcohol, they still looked and felt like they had been dragged backwards through a knot hole.

Massoni was his exceptionally cheerful sergeant major self as he said, "Well, good morning campers! I'm glad you decided to arrive at a decent hour. Of course, you missed morning PT, but I suppose an extra hour sleep was just what you weary travelers needed, eh?"

Flash just growled.

Sue said, "Marconi picked us up and we came directly here. Sergeant Major, it's 0630hrs, at least I think it is 0630hrs. My body clock says its 2130hrs yesterday."

"Sue, you need to get yourself a GMT watch. That way, you always know what time it is everywhere. Set the time for where you are going and live with it. Coffee helps, of course."

Sue said, "You know, my mother said that to me one time when I messed up time zones and called her early in the morning."

"She was sleeping?"

"No, she had just finished PT."

"As it should be! Now, get yourselves some caffeine and meet me in my office."

Flash finally decided to enter the conversation, even if it was an effort. "No Smith?"

"No Smith. Just me. That's why you need to meet me in the office. Drop your kit, get whatever you want to drink, and get into the office."

"Check, Sergeant Major."

After parking the HICU van, Marconi came into the warehouse. He said, "Good morning, Sergeant Major."

"Marconi, you missed PT. We will have to figure out a workout for you at lunchtime!"

Marconi nodded. There was no arguing with Massoni. "Swell," was all he said.

Sufficiently fortified from the coffee and tea station in the warehouse, Flash and Sue arrived at Massoni's office. Neither of them had ever been invited into his office. Meetings and debriefings took place in Smith's office pre-deployment and post-deployment. Massoni's office was designed to give the sergeant major a bit of privacy. It also allowed him to conduct periodic, face-to-face reviews with the HICU enlisted personnel. The majority of the members of HICU held non-commissioned ranks from the Army, Navy and the Marine Corps. Since both Flash and Sue were warrant officers and officially evaluated by Smith, the only time Flash and Sue would be expected to enter Massoni's lair was on invitation and, most likely, because they were facing an informal reprimand rather than a formal one from Smith. In short, Flash and Sue were not entirely certain this visit would be a happy one.

Sue learned well before she joined the military that people decorate their offices with reminders of what is important to them. As Sue entered the land of Massoni, she did a quick scan. There was an enlistment poster that looked to be from the 1960s showing the formation at Ft. Bragg when President Kennedy authorized the use of the Green Beret. There was another poster showing a Ranger in ancient jungle fatigues wading through waist deep water. There were team photos from Massoni's career including, Sue noticed, a picture of the Surveillance and Reconnaissance team lead by CW5 Jameson. That photo included a newly arrived CW2 Sue O'Connell. Otherwise, the only thing on the walls were maps of the various theatres where HICU officers were located. On the wall directly behind Massoni was a large whiteboard with everyone's name, their location and, if they were on TDY, when they were scheduled to return to HICU.

Massoni said, "O'Connell, if you are finished with your review of my 'I like me' walls, I think we can get started. Have a seat."

Sue blushed as she found a seat. Flash pulled up another classic Army olive drab metal folding chair. Flash said, "I was just about to offer some feng shui advice, Sergeant Major."

"Yeah well, I already did the needful, used my temple bells and my spirit knife to handle that requirement." He pointed over to a bookshelf filled with books on just about everything related to the history of US, UK and NATO Special Forces. Next to a pair of foreign language dictionaries, one French-to-English and the other Chinese-to-English, was a small bowl of black sand. Impaled in the center of the bowl was a brass ornamental knife with three carved ghoulish heads serving as the knife handle. Next to the bowl was a brass bell with the same iconography.

Sue tried not to let out a small gasp. Flash said, "Well, I didn't see that one coming."

Massoni smirked and said, "Just because I am this good looking doesn't mean I don't have a brain."

Sue finally got her mind wrapped around Jim Massoni as a scholar of Asian philosophy and said, "First Group?"

"If you must know, yes, I was on a couple of teams in First Group. Based in Okinawa. Along with picking up a black belt in Shoto-kan-ryu, I did some advanced language work using the Chinese I learned at DLI. I barely passed conversational Cantonese and had little success with Chinese logograms. This was all before the Brits decided to give up Hong Kong. When they did, we lost our infiltration routes into Southern China. Now, how about we talk about the future rather than the ancient past."

Flash said, "You don't want to know about our recent work at DLI. It's sorta the present, no?"

"Got all that briefing from SOF CI while you were enjoying your luxury travel back to REAL SUE." Massoni watched and smiled at Sue's grimace. "Flash, it turns out that you were right. Ms. Bendalyani was serving as the human interface for Russian malware periodically loaded into the Klingon network and our network as well. Where you were wrong was thinking there was a fink inside the CI community on the West Coast." Massoni offered a dramatic pause before he continued. He wanted to see how Sue would react. Once he noticed her discomfort, he continued, "We still haven't figured out who handled Bendalyani, but it wasn't anyone on the CI team that you met. Best guess is it is someone in the Russian consulate in San Francisco, but given this is a cyber op, it might be anywhere. I have no doubt that we will find out sooner or later since Bendalyani now is in the loving care of the NCIS office in San Diego. CI are trying to sort out if they can convince her to cooperate for a little bit until we determine the full scope of the problem."

Massoni paused again and said, "I know that disappoints Sue because there is no further reason to engage CI Special Agent Derry, but I'm sure Derry will find a way forward. He is after all a Ranger and Rangers lead the way."

Sue looked at Flash and said under her breath, "You had to tell him about Derry?"

Flash shrugged and said, "I had to tell Massoni what I thought, right?"

Massoni interjected before the conversation turned off topic, "Hey, it is my job to know everything. That's what a sergeant major does and it's a good thing, no? And, shouldn't I care about my people?" Massoni gave them his best effort at looking sincere.

Sue had to admit he was right even if he wasn't sincere, so she said, "Yes, Sergeant Major."

"Now, you did your jobs, mission accomplished. OK? If you want a pat on the back, I will do that as you leave the office."

Sue nodded and said, "A pat on the back or kick in the ass?"

"It entirely depends on whether you keep asking questions."

Both Sue and Flash nodded. Clearly, they were in the land of the sergeant major and that meant living by his rules. Simultaneously, they said, "Check, Sergeant Major."

"OK. While you were enjoying the beachfront property in California, your colleague Sandy was doing real work in Dubai. Well, in the desert between Abu Dhabi and Dubai. His asset tried to kill him, but Sandy's Marine security team handled that without any drama."

Sandy had been one of Sue's first friends at the Farm and, for a short while, he was a potential candidate for "the man for Sue." That potential never turned into reality. After graduation at the Farm, Sandy reconciled with his wife and they had been living at Ft. Bragg ever since. Sue assumed that they moved to Italy when HICU moved from Ft. Bragg to Camp Ederle.

Massoni said, "When we moved from Bragg, we assigned Sandy to Bahrain and took him off the TDY circuit. Even moved his family to that island paradise. All good. He's Navy after all so he got along with the Fifth Fleet leadership and, as a senior enlisted, he knew how to get things done."

Sue and Flash were used to Massoni being Massoni. They knew he would eventually get to the point.

"So, he has agents in Bahrain and in the UAE. One of his goobers, 561 to be exact, offered details on an AQ network."

Flash interceded, "Wait a second. Even I know that 561's access is to IRGC smuggling. How was he supposed to have access to AQ?"

"Flash, that was precisely what we said to Sandy. His answer was classic case officer: beats me but I will let you know when I see him. Smith insisted on overwatch. He smelled a rat, even from here. I suppose that's why he is a colonel and I am just a sergeant major." Massoni rolled his eyes. "Anyhow, Smith was right. 561 tried to cap Sandy. Problem was he met a Marine 5.56 round instead. Once the report came back here, Smith was out the door like a scalded cat. He has been in Bahrain ever since working with Sandy to sort out that problem. Leaving me…in charge!" Massoni waved his arms implying all of HICU was now his domain. Both Flash and Sue knew the HICU warehouse had always been Massoni's domain. Smith was just nominally in charge.

"So, Sergeant Major, what precisely do you want us to do now?" Flash didn't know Sandy as well as Sue, so she recovered more quickly from the story of a near miss against one of the team.

"So, we dispatched Ginger from Cyprus to Bahrain to help the boss and Sandy. They haven't come up with any solid leads, yet. It's only a matter of time. Someone is going to talk."

Finally, Sue recovered from the shock of hearing Sandy had just missed getting killed. She said, "What's the plan? Back to Cyprus?"

"Ah, the plan. Well, Cyprus was a good guess, but not correct. However, you are each traveling to places you have terrorized in the past." Massoni reached over to the thermos on his desk and poured another cup of jet-black coffee into his ceramic mug. The text on the side facing Sue said *Yes, I really do hate you.*

Flash shook her head and said, "OK, we find a set of traitors in California, Smith is hunting another set of traitors in the Persian Gulf, so it only makes sense to send us to Afghanistan…again."

Massoni smiled and said, "Nope. Not for you. Well, at least not yet. We have an intermediate stop we need you to do. You were so successful the last time you visited the Black Sea, we figured it was worth sending you back."

"Not again with Klingon Doug, the Fishman!"

"Flash, I understood you liked the guy and he liked you. And the answer is yes, another trip to the Klingon safe house on the Black Sea. Along with your pal, Melissa Nez."

Flash nodded. "At least I will have a smart partner."

Sue looked over and said, "And what have I been over the last two years?"

"Girl, you are one action chick, a real superhero, but you always roll your eyes when I start talking about advanced communications."

Massoni interjected, "Sue, you know you do that."

"And who wouldn't when the professor here starts to explain in painful detail the intricacies of her work while burying the lead. All I ask is to be pointed in the right direction."

Flash said, "You know when you compare yourself to a tank round, it doesn't help your argument."

Massoni interjected again, "I always thought of Sue as a blunt instrument but now that you mention it…"

Sue decided enough was enough. She was tired of playing

punching bag. "Sergeant Major, what in the world does a trip to the Black Sea have to do with anything a HUMINT collector like yours truly does for you?"

"Good, now you are asking smart questions. Let's start with the fact that you aren't going to be the Black Sea. You are going to Afghanistan to visit our very best Klingon friend, Jamie Shenk. But, let's start with why Flash is going to Turkey. The answer is that your work at DLI and even some FBI work is pointing to a direct connection to an electronic warfare ship in the Black Sea called *Bursa Chief*. Flagged as a Romanian cargo hauler but most probably Russian intelligence ownership. It certainly looks like *Vishnya* class collection ships except without quite as many antennas. According to maritime insurance information, it is supposed to be a commercial hauler from Sochi to Thessaloniki capable of handling two intermodal containers on deck and assorted cargo below decks. Most common route is it leaves Sochi, moors off the Turkish Coast to the entrance of the Black Sea for a bit, transits the Bosporus, moors out in the Sea of Marmara and then heads into the Adriatic."

"Just like the Beroslav ship."

"Well, except the electronic signature isn't the same and we don't think this one is hauling nuclear materials."

Flash said, "See, at least that's good news!" Both Flash and Sue remembered their last adventure in Turkey focused on hunting a WMD shipment coming out of the former Soviet Union. Except that the hunt was stage managed by a Russian spy and it nearly resulted in Sue at the bottom of the Black Sea.

Massoni said, "Since this is a joint CI mess, we are working with the Klingons, FBI and Army CI to sort this out. I don't quite understand why they asked for Flash, but SOF headquarters decided Flash was the woman for the job. So, that's all I need to know, no?"

Flash realized that if SOF headquarters wanted her to go to Turkey in this operation, there was nothing to say but "yes sir." So that's what she said, "Jim, please tell SOF Headquarters the answer is yes sir."

Massoni smiled and said, "Actually, I talk to the real power in SOF, the SOF command sergeant major. But, I'm sure he will be pleased to know that Billings is on the march."

Sue said, "And what about me?"

Massoni smiled and said, "Ah, what should we do with O'Connell? Well, there is at least one known end point for all this cyber nonsense. It is in a warehouse located just outside Dushanbe in Tajikistan. Not a big surprise. The Russians have had a military presence in Tajikistan for years and there is at least one Russian private contractor training facility there as well. If they wanted to hide a cyber operation in plain sight, why not hide it inside some Russian compound? Your job, O'Connell, is to work with our pal Jamie to figure out how to put an end to that side of the operation." He stopped to take a drink from his coffee cup. "Oh, and please do so without starting World War III."

Massoni took another sip of his coffee and nodded to them both. "Now, go back to your cubicles and read the traffic on this project code-named *Silicon Addiction.*" Massoni paused and commented, "And don't look at me that way, it was some genius at FBI headquarters decided the code name." Massoni continued, "And, by the way, since we can't trust our communications network, you have paper files that were transmitted by military courier. Old school stuff. So, read paper and when you are done, come back and tell me how you intend to do the job so I can tell the boss. My next scheduled call with him is 1500hrs local, so get hot."

Sue and Flash stood up and headed out the door. Before they got there, Massoni said, "And, you have admit the beauty of one final part of the story. I found it elegant that one bit of the puzzle came from an FBI operation managed by Special Agent William O'Connell."

Sue's head snapped as if she had been hit by an electric shock. "Bill?"

"Yes. Seems your intrepid brother was hunting an Iranian cyber operation and ended up uncovering a false flag job managed by the Russians. Small world, eh?"

Flash smiled and said, "All we need now is for Sue's mom to be involved and we will have a real party on our hands."

Massoni said, "That's precisely what I thought."

They returned to Massoni's office at 1300hrs. By this time, HICU bay was filled with analysts and a few HICU case officers either about to leave or just returned. Marconi was back in his workspace, a caged area set aside for his workbench, his tools and the admin shop partner, Marcus Bell, known to everyone instead as Alexander Graham given his last name and work as the network and communications officer for HICU.

As they walked through the bay, Sue realized how much she missed working with colleagues. Her work for HICU for the past few years had been always as a singleton someplace other than the warehouse at Camp Ederle. Her time on the TDY circuit translated into a week working someplace else, returning over a weekend to her BOQ, picking up a new assignment on Monday and heading back out on the circuit. Sue said, "You know, I could get used to working here."

Flash shook her head, "You would be bug nuts before a week was out. Anyhow, at some point, they are going to force you to be a manager. When they do, call me from wherever you are so I can remind you of your comment today."

They walked into Massoni's office. He was on the secure phone line but he waved them in and pointed to the two folding chairs they used that morning. Five minutes later, he said, "That was the boss. He got impatient and moved the call up by two hours. They are still trying to sort out who gave 561 the orders to cap Sandy. Right now, all they can say for sure is all the Sunni extremists in theatre, and as you know there are plenty, don't seem to have had any contact with our dead creep. Now, they are working back through 561's list of sub-sources. For once, I am beginning to understand why the Klingons do so much paperwork. We could have gone back through his reporting and pulled out the various names, but one of the forms that Sandy completed about a year ago had all of 561's sub-sources on one page. It's only a matter of time before they find the one who did the deed."

Massoni quickly transitioned to the new assignments: "So, what do you know about this operation and what are you going to do about it?"

Sue turned to Flash. She knew her colleague was just itching to tell Massoni what she thought about the project, so why get in the way?

Flash said, "OK, so this is an interesting challenge. It reminds me of some college research I did about what were called pirate radio stations. In the UK in the 1960s, outfits tried to bypass British broadcasting laws by setting up pirate stations on ships off the coast..."

"Flash, really? Do you think I know or care about pirate radio stations?" Massoni shook his head to emphasize that the answer was: No, he did not.

Flash looked hurt that Massoni wasn't interested in her prepared presentation. She said, "OK, if we have to work at O'Connell speed, I guess we just have to. Given what the files offered and the fact that I can't do any deep research on my computer, I only have a basic idea. What we have here is a modification of the electronic warfare trawler the Soviets and the Russians have used for years. The photos of the ship taken by a Navy P3 surveillance aircraft and the Reconnaissance office satellite show a modified cargo hauler with plenty of antennas on the top. Still conducting intercept operations, but as well as intercepting our communications, they are receiving and transmitting network communications from several dark web nodes."

"Dark web?" Massoni was well on his way toward being confused and he decided to slow Flash down. He hoped that this would not open up another complex discussion, so he said, "Just so we understand, OK? I'm assuming this dark web is something like the internet."

"Sergeant Major, the dark web is a part of the internet that is filled with nasties — people who don't want to be found and organizations that don't want folks to know what they are doing. In this case, the ship is simply using multiple identities to confound our efforts to locate their base that is stealing our stuff. And, since the ship is always on the move, it makes it plenty hard to pin down. The real question right now is whether this ship is the headquarters for the cyber effort or merely another cutout. We aren't going to know until we get closer or, better still, on board. But, Jim, now that we know where it is, why don't we just sink it?"

"Flash, what if it turns out that this is a Russian Navy vessel under a false flag?"

"Hmmm, probably not good if we sink it, eh?"

"World War III, not good."

"So, what do we do about it?"

"That's where you and your pal Nez come in."

Flash continued, "Given Klingon Doug's maritime platform and the brain trust of Melissa Nez and yours truly, it seems that you are looking at some sort of tech operation to disrupt this operation. Am I going in the right direction?"

"Flash, you are definitely tracking. Continue."

"I'm sure there are Klingon assets that Doug is running that might even get on board for a few minutes as they deliver cargo, food or fuel. First, we just design a widget that damages the download of the Agency and SOF communications. Next, we get an asset to emplace said widget."

"Once again, top marks. So, why are you still in my office?"

"Because I want to hear what you have planned for Sue."

"Fair. So, O'Connell, what do you intend to do for the nation?"

Sue made a tentative start. "I read the files including the FBI cyber material. It looks like another one of the nodes is in a warehouse outside Dushanbe. It might even be the primary location. Imagery shows the warehouse has multiple fiber optic lines feeding into the building, something that shouldn't be there given the economy of Tajikistan. The warehouse is owned by a Russian private military contractor known as SWORDFISH Group. No surprise, the CIA and Treasury files say this PMC is actually owned by a half dozen Russian oligarchs. Officially, the PMC focuses on airfield and port security and anti-piracy for Russian merchant ships. Unofficially, the PMC is affiliated with the Russian GRU and SPETSNAZ."

"Sue, I knew that much when you walked in this morning. My question is what do you intend to do about this?"

"I guess I get over to Afghanistan, match up with Jamie, and see what sort of cross-border agent network he has. If our commo net-work was clean, I would be able to do that from here, but I guess we can't rely on anything electronic at this point, so I have to go there and find out. Once I'm there, I do what I can to disrupt the network. Again, why isn't this an Agency mission? Their comms are less badly corrupted and they have the resources in place."

"Sue, I told you this morning, you are involved because the SOF Headquarters wants you involved. I suspect the CG wants one of our case officers working with Agency so that we can say we are all working together. The same goes for you, Flash. Let's not forget that the links to the Russian ship and the warehouse in Tajikistan are based on the DLI operation that you just finished. The CG is always playing about six moves ahead of the rest of the community, so there may be some other reason for it, but I reckon we aren't going to know that until we need to know it." Massoni paused and transitioned from collaborative peer to command sergeant major.

"So, you two, sort this out. Flash, check with Marconi and Bell on what sort of gizmo is needed. Is it software? Is it hardware? Is it both? You and your pal Nez have ten days to figure this out. She arrives here tomorrow on the CG's bird. The aircraft is taking a bunch of the SOF analytic team to match up with the CG in Iraq, and they offered to get her here pronto. The pouch included a landline contact for Mr. Doug Mornia in Istanbul. I'm assuming he is your Fishman contact. Get Marconi or Alexander Graham to go out, buy a phone for cash and then you give him a call. Tell him whatever you spies say when you want to link up."

Massoni looked at Sue and said, "You need to get to Afghanistan RFN and match up with Shenk. SOF Headquarters says you are already cleared hot for travel. So, travel! Flash and Ms. Nez might even catch up once they have done whatever tech magic they need to do. Now, get going."

As they headed out the door, Massoni said, "And when you pass Pluto's desk, tell him to wake up and get in here."

Flash smiled. She should have expected that Massoni knew Pluto usually dozed off in the early afternoon. As the focal point for Afghan operations, he regularly worked live communications with the HICU teams in Kabul and Jalalabad. While they were only two hours ahead of HICU, their operations were almost always at night. That meant Pluto's real working day started somewhere around near 2200hrs local time and ran pretty continuously until 0900hrs local when he started his HICU shift. Pluto had learned to avoid sleep deprivation by napping. "Yes, Sergeant Major."

KNOCK, KNOCK

B arbara O'Connell and Terry Reimer drove along the narrow streets of the resort town of Chautauqua. Small cottages built in the 19th century paired with townhouses that attempted to match the same design flavor of the town. For the better part of fifty years, the town council had been adamant that any development had to match the original design features that made Chautauqua a center for visitors for over a hundred years. The drive from the Buffalo airport to Chautauqua had included plenty of two-lane blacktop. As soon as they got off the Thruway, Terry had pulled down the canvas top of his Jeep and they enjoyed the dry fall weather and the mix of golds and reds from trees starting to change color. Terry Reimer, former Army Criminal Investigation Division special agent and retired Buffalo Police officer had offered to drive Barbara home from the airport before returning to his own house in East Aurora. Terry wasn't sure they were a couple...yet. Terry had a divorce in his past and Barbara had buried one husband and one lover already. They just enjoyed each other's company. So far, they had not shared each other's bedrooms. Terry still held out hope.

O'Connell and Reimer had been working for their colleague, Beth Parsons, a high profile "troubleshooter" for the Washington based firm, Stearns and Mandeville. Along with two colleagues who were former members of US Special Forces, Jake and Mutt, their job on this trip was to track down Serbian and Croatian criminals known in the intelligence community as PIFWCs — persons indicted for war crimes. Stearns and Mandeville had a number of US clients whose relatives were missing, presumed dead from the 1990s civil war. The US intelligence community had long since lost interest due to demands from the White House and the Pentagon for intelligence to support wars in Afghanistan, Iraq, and dozens of locations where al-Qaida and AQ splinter groups operated.

While Beth provided top cover for the investigation through her contacts in the US mission in Zagreb, Barbara and Terry used investigative skills to find sources that would help track the PIFWCs. Once they accomplished that mission, their special-forces colleagues conducted surveillance and covert entry operations at the target households. With the necessary material in hand, Beth's firm worked with several international banks to freeze the accounts of these war criminals. After that was accomplished, the firm provided all the details to INTERPOL so that they could issue what was known as a "red notice" that would guarantee the arrest of the targets if/when they should leave the country. Whether the PIFWCs would ever see jail time was something international courts would decide. In the meantime, Stearns and Mandeville would proceed in civil cases in the US court system that would force the bankers to provide compensation for the victims. From the perspective of the law firm and Beth Parson's private army, it was a good result. Plus, as Beth said to her team, they had a chance to enjoy Croatian wine at the company's expense.

As Terry and Barbara pulled into Barbara's neighborhood, they noticed a black Suburban parked on the street next to her driveway. As they approached the driveway, they saw a pair of black Ford Transit vans blocking the drive. Terry pulled his ancient jeep to the side of the street about a half block from Barbara's house. As he got out, he thought about Barbara's stories of her gunfight in Virginia and the more recent gunfight in Emery Park this past summer. He opened a small lock box under his seat. He pulled out his old backup pistol from his time as a lawman, a Colt Mustang. A little heavier than a Walther PPK, but like the Walther, chambered in .380. Enough for a "just in case" pistol. It was protected by an inside the waistband holster that Terry pushed into his jeans.

Barbara said, "What are you thinking?"

As Terry loaded the pistol, applied the safety and then put the weapon back into the holster, he said, "I'm thinking I have a legal permit to carry this gun and you have had more than your share of gunfights in the short time since we met. It might only have six rounds, but after that we can either run away or take a couple of real weapons from the villains."

Barbara shook her head. Terry was reverting to his lawman roots. There might be another option that was less…noisy. She pulled out her mobile phone. She had a number of different old colleagues on speed dial. She touched the screen under the name Mary and dialed Mary's mobile. The phone rang twice.

Mary Sanderson's voice came on the line. "Dear, I thought you were done with me."

"I never said I was done with you. I just said that I was done working for you, most especially now that you are the head spy-hunter at the Agency. But, I do need your help and I need it right now."

Mary Sanderson recognized the tone of voice at the other end of the line. She said, "What's happening?"

"Terry and I just came back from a trip working for Beth Parsons. When we arrived, we saw a number of vehicles around the Chautauqua house. All black, all bearing US government plates. We haven't confronted the visitors, yet. But I thought it might be a good thing to have you on the line."

"Wait a second. I will call Janice Macintosh and put her on the line as well. A conference call at this point in time might be useful."

Barbara reached over and touched Terry on the sleeve. Gently but firmly. She said, "We are going to wait here a second while I get the cavalry on the line."

"Washington? How can they help?"

"Well, they can't hurt, right? They might even tell us what is going on."

"I doubt it. The guys at your house are probably feds but, in my experience, local feds don't tell anyone what they were planning, especially Washington. Wait and see if I'm not right."

A voice came on the phone. "Barbara, it's a lovely Saturday in the Fall. I am working on my garden. I really hope you not causing trouble again?"

"Janice, I'm just back from doing very legal, very righteous work in Croatia for Stearns and Mandeville. With Beth Parsons, the former Ambassador..."

"Barbara, I know precisely what Beth and you pirates have been doing in Croatia. And I agree, righteous work, I've seen the court filing. Now, what's the problem?"

"Ladies, the story is Terry and I have just come home from a TDY and my place is crawling with folks who appear to be federal officers. I'm not saying they are, but they have all the markings: black vans, a black Suburban and all with USG plates. The only thing that isn't there is an armored SWAT truck and some crime scene tape. I'm not sure what is going on, but I figured it would be useful for you to hear it the same time I heard it. OK?"

Janice's voice said, "Sure, keep the phone on and let's see what happens next. I am assuming there won't be any gunfire."

"Well, if there is, we won't be the first to fire."

Mary's voice came on saying, "Swell."

Barbara tucked her phone in the top pocket of her jean jacket. She turned to Terry and said, "OK, let's see what is going on."

They walked up the driveway. Standing in front of the door were four men in black jumpsuits. One was holding a steel entry tool designed to pry the outer security door off its hinges. Behind the man with the pry bar was a second man with a steel battering ram designed to destroy the door lock on the main door. The other two jumpsuits had pistols drawn. Behind the assault team were two men with high and tight haircuts and gray suits. One of the men was using a handset to communicate with some other part of his team. As they walked up, Barbara heard him say, "OK, we breach in five. Five, four,..."

Barbara shouted, "Hey, why don't you just allow me to let you in?"

Terry almost laughed at the face the team leader made. Clearly, they hadn't thought to contain the area and he and Barbara were now within handshake distance.

The team leader hadn't recovered completely and his voice demonstrated that discomfort as he said, "And who the fuck are you?"

Barbara assumed her most motherly tone and said, "Sir, my name is Barbara O'Connell and I am the owner of this house. I've been away for a few weeks. By the way, there is no need to be crude. I recommend you take a deep breath and wash out some of that unused adrenaline. After you do that, I would like to know who you are and under what authority did you intend to damage my house."

The team leader finally regained some of his composure. He spoke into the handset. "Stand down, stand down. We have the perpetrators in custody."

He turned to Barbara and said, "Mrs. O'Connell or whoever you say you are, I am arresting you for violations under the Computer Fraud and Abuse act, US Code 1030." He started towards Barbara with a set of handcuffs. "You have the right to remain silent, if..."

"Hold on, partner. What is your predication for this arrest?" Terry Reimer had used his old lawman voice. He knew it wouldn't solve the problem, but it might slow down the process.

"And you are?"

"Terry Reimer, retired Buffalo Policeman, former Special Agent in the Army Criminal Investigation Division. And, by the way, you still haven't identified yourself to either this lady or myself. For all we know, you are criminals trying to steal from a couple of pensioners."

The other members of the raid team were perplexed. One minute, they were going to raid a house and the next, their team leader was in a dialogue with a pair of senior citizens, neither of whom were on the search warrant or the arrest warrant.

Barbara decided to take charge of the situation. She said in her most polite voice, "Sir, I am on a conference call right now with seniors at the CIA and the FBI. Would you like to talk to them?" She handed the phone over to the team leader.

The man in the gray suit looked for a minute like he would just throw the phone into an evidence bag and continue reading these two their Miranda rights. At the last second, he decided that it might be a worthwhile effort to find out if he was able to expand his search to other perpetrators. He said his best I'm in charge voice, "Yeah, who is this."

Janice Macintosh spoke first, "This is Janice Macintosh. I am the unit supervisor for all Russian foreign counterintelligence operations of the FBI. I'm talking to you from the Hoover Building in Washington, DC."

Mary Sanderson smiled as she heard Janice do her "I'm the FBI" thing even though she was in her garden. She decided to add to the equation, "This is Mary Sanderson. I am one of the directors of the CIA Counterintelligence Center. I'm talking to you from CIA headquarters in Northern Virginia."

Introductions completed, Janice continued the conversation, "Sir, I need you to identify yourself. I have already alerted the FBI Field Office in Buffalo that there is a potential hostage situation taking place threatening a former senior CIA officer. The Field Office has reported to me that they have launched their SWAT team in a Bureau helicopter and they expect to be on site in about twenty minutes. So, why don't we try to sort this out before they fast rope a team at your location."

Barbara couldn't hear what was being said, but she saw the color drain out of the face of the team leader. He paused and swallowed hard before answering. Terry whispered, "It must be nice to have friends in high places."

"Sometimes useful and sometimes not," was all Barbara said.

The team leader said, "Ma'am, my name is Special Agent William Thorpe of the Army Criminal Investigation Command. I am here investigating a cyber crime that is occurring at this location at this time. The cyber attack is focused on the Seneca Army Depot in Central New York. I don't believe I can say more than that on this line."

Barbara gently took the phone from Thorpe and spoke, "Ladies, what are we going to do about all of this?"

Janice said, "I will get in touch with the cyber team in Buffalo. They should be there in about 2 hours. Can you prevent them from tearing your house apart for that amount of time?"

"I think so."

"Also, please tell Special Agent Thorpe that we have recalled the SWAT team."

"Eh?"

"Well, I had to say something to get him to listen to me."

Mary Sanderson laughed and said, "I wondered about that. Nice line. I may use it someday."

Janice Macintosh said, "Well, I hope it works. Barbara, please put Special Agent Thorpe back on the phone. I think we can make this all better. And, thank you for calling me before you got into a gunfight."

Barbara handed the phone back to Thorpe, "Supervisor Macintosh wants to talk to you."

Barbara and Terry watched as Thorpe came to the position of attention and said, "Yes, Ma'am. No Ma'am." His responses ran for another minute. Suddenly, he switched to an even more stiff, "No, sir. No sir, we didn't do a coordination with the FBI. We didn't think it was needed. Yes, sir. I will make sure we have this covered soon. No sir, we will wait for the FBI cyber team. Yes sir, we will report to you as soon as we are finished here. Thank you, sir."

Thorpe handed the phone back to Barbara and said, "Ms. Macintosh said she would call later. Now, up front, I want to apologize for the confusion. One of the people who came on the line was Brigadier General Fitzroy. He is the senior Army officer assigned to the section Ms. Macintosh supervises. He wanted me to extend his apologies as well."

Barbara smiled at Thorpe and said, "Agent Thorpe, no harm done unless your team at the back of the house had already breached the door on the deck."

"Oh, no ma'am. No damage done there."

"Well, then. How about you send your raiders home, come into the house, have some tea. We wait until the FBI Cyber folks arrive. Sound good?"

"Yes ma'am." Thorpe spoke into the handset and said, "Stand down and return to base. I will give the details when we do the hot wash at home." He turned to the four men in the black jumpsuits behind him. He said, "You heard me. Head home. We can handle it from here."

A disgruntled team of raiders left the house, adrenaline slowly seeping out of their muscles. They all had headaches from the inability to wash the adrenaline out of their bodies through brisk action. They loaded into their black vans, backed out of the driveway and drove away. That left the two men in gray suits waiting at the door.

Barbara unlocked the security door and then the double locks on the main door of the house. She opened the door and said, "Gentlemen, please come in."

Terry smiled. He couldn't help himself when he said, "She is normally a good hostess but I don't think she was expecting guests. I'm not sure if there is any cake to go with the tea."

By the time they shared a pot of tea with the two Army Special Agents, a team of cyber specialists from the Buffalo Field Office of the FBI had arrived along with Barbara's most favorite local FBI agent, Special Agent Ellen Jones. The FBI agents from the Cyber Squad arrived in a silver Chevrolet Impala. Jones arrived in an electric blue Ford Mustang convertible. As Barbara watched Jones walk up to the door, she noted once again that Jones understood the concept of dressing for success. Even on a Saturday, Jones was dressed in very formal business attire, but that attire was hardly affordable on a federal salary. She was wearing gray wool slacks and a white silk blouse. A perfectly tailored black blazer and black Italian leather pumps completed the ensemble. Nothing in the ensemble revealed that she was carrying a firearm or had an FBI badge.

Barbara thought only Beth Parsons dressed in such a stylish

manner and still carried herself with such power. If Jones survived the FBI bureaucracy and learned how to play in the intelligence and law enforcement communities' sand boxes, she would be a very senior government player someday. She might have to give up the muscle car, but that would be for another day.

Jones was polite as she came in. Barbara expected she held a grudge from their previous encounter when she was the lead agent in an investigation of the assassination of a Russian sleeper agent in East Aurora. Barbara had done what she could to make sure that Jones got some credit for the capture of the assassin, but the capture took place in Croatia and there wasn't much credit to share. In fact, Jones seemed slightly more relaxed as she came in the house. Added to that baggage, Barbara could only imagine how much fun it had been for Jones to drop whatever she had planned for a Saturday afternoon and end up in Chautauqua.

After introducing her two colleagues from the cyber squad and determining where they should set up their equipment, Jones said to Barbara, "Mrs. O'Connell, it seems you simply can't stay out of trouble."

"Ellen, I will admit I seem to be a magnet for trouble. I suppose you already know, I am very happy you are here. Otherwise, the Army Special Agent in my kitchen would have put me in handcuffs and in the back of his Suburban and his crew would be using sledgehammers on my walls at this point searching for heaven only knows what."

"Sledgehammers, eh? I would have paid to see that."

"Droll."

"So, what exactly did he expect to find?"

"I have no idea. He wouldn't talk until you got here."

"Even using your CIA interrogation techniques?"

"We only use them overseas, Ellen. And I don't use them at all because..."

"I know, you are just a pensioner."

"Precisely. Would you like to come in and have some tea? I think Terry Reimer has made some coffee if you would prefer."

"Reimer is here as well." Jones paused and said, "What a bonus."

"Dear, sarcasm doesn't suit you. Follow me."

Once Jones and her team were in the kitchen and offered either tea or coffee, Thorpe finally realized that he was dealing with someone who really did have juice in the intelligence and law enforcement community. He finally relented to tell everyone in the house the story of why he was there.

"The story begins years ago. When the Army gave up the Seneca Army Depot as a nuclear weapons storage facility…"

Reimer couldn't help himself. He said, "Nuclear weapons? I thought all they had there was a rare herd of albino deer."

"That's still the case, *Mr.* Reimer." Thorpe emphasized the term Mister to make sure Terry Reimer understood that he was just a civilian. "The bunkers at the depot were demobilized some years ago and the facility turned over to the Bureau of Land Management. It will be completely demobilized in the next couple of years and the property sold. For now, the facility is run by the BLM, but it still has a Department of Defense purpose. It is the home of a small team of Army Special Agents focusing on cyber attacks on DoD facilities."

This time it was Jones who couldn't help herself. "That is the jurisdiction of the FBI with the assistance from the National Security Agency. What in the world is the Army doing working on this target set?"

Barbara noticed Thorpe looked at Jones like a boxer about to go 10 rounds with an unknown fighter. He chose his words carefully. After all, he already had one surprise today and he didn't want another. Barbara thought to herself, "He's learning."

Thorpe said, "Our jurisdiction is small. We are focused on cyber operations that are specifically targeting personnel and units of the US Army Commands and, especially Army sensitive activities. We know our adversaries, especially criminals but also state adversaries, terrorists and narco-traffickers, have focused their attention on our deployed troops. We have jurisdiction under our partnership with the Department of Homeland Security Cybersecurity and Infrastructure Security Agency. This is a Department of the Army operation."

Once again, Jones reminded Barbara of her daughter, Sue. Once she was on a subject, she didn't know when, or perhaps how, to be diplomatic. Before Barbara could intervene, Jones said, "And why is your office in the middle of the Finger Lakes?"

Barbara decided to try to help Thorpe. If nothing else, it might let him finish his explanation. She said, "Because who is going to look for an electronic footprint coming out of a demobilized Army base? It is actually a very clever idea." She paused and looked at Thorpe and said, "But, why did you end up at my house? At this point, you realize I am not an adversary, but certainly you must have done traces on me before you arrived?"

"Ma'am, we did do traces based on the location. Our open-source search showed this house was registered to one Alexandre Shotkin, a Georgian immigrant who moved from Brighton Beach to this location. That was consistent with the cyber tools showing this location was serving as a hub for some of the probes taking place at Ft. Bragg."

Jones smiled. She finally had leverage. She turned to her cyber teammates and said, "OK, we now know what we are looking for — some sort of network tool. Probably some sort of parasite on Mrs. O'Connell's internet connectivity and then bouncing a signal to another WiFi network. Let's start outside, check anything that connects to the house — power, gas lines, cable TV — and if we can't find hardware outside, we'll start to work on a software trojan horse." She turned to Barbara and said, "I think you can explain to Special Agent Thorpe how easy it was to load misinformation on the local property records. I will work with the folks outside."

Barbara nodded and said, "Thanks, Ellen. Would you be willing to take Agent Thorpe's partner with you so that I can have a private chat with him?"

Jones looked at Thorpe. He nodded. "Sure, we can do that. Gentlemen, let's go outside and see what we find."

Once the rest of the federal entourage let the kitchen, Barbara turned to Thorpe and said, "More tea?" He shook his head.

Reimer said, "I'm making another espresso. How about it?"

"No, thank you." Thorpe appeared to be looking for a reason, any reason to escape the conversation that he was about to have. He knew it would be nothing compared to the conversation he would have when he returned to his office and had to explain his actions to his supervisor. From his perspective, the sooner he could get out of Chautauqua, the better. He said, "So, what is this all about, Mrs. O'Connell?"

"Agent Thorpe, I have an idea, but it is a bit of a story. Are you sure you don't want some tea or coffee? After all, you are not going to get free of this place until your men are done." Reimer was already at the espresso machine. He raised an empty cup. Thorpe nodded.

Barbara decided to compress the story. Not because she thought it was secret, but because she expected Thorpe to be unwilling to believe it would start with a vendetta started in 1944. She said, "So, it starts with the murder of my father-in-law in this house. My father-in-law, my husband and myself were all members of the CIA and we worked counterintelligence and counterterrorism operations. It turns out that some of our operations ended up disrupting Russian criminal entities…"

Five minutes later, Barbara ended the highly edited tale by saying, "Most recently, Terry and I along with Special Agent Jones were involved in capturing a paid hitman who killed a Russian sleeper agent just north of here in East Aurora. So, there are plenty of people out there who might want to do me harm. And, regarding what Agent Jones said about property records, I think you now understand that any hostile cyber operation that is targeting the US Army would find changing Chautauqua county property records hardly a challenge. See?"

"Yes, ma'am. I see, but why? Why do this?"

Reimer had been quiet throughout Barbara's story. He wasn't sure what she wanted Thorpe to know, so he kept quiet. He found it interesting that Barbara had chosen not to reveal that her daughter was a SOF operator or that her son was an FBI Special Agent. Now that he understood the boundaries of what Barbara wanted Thorpe to know, he could add to the story.

"Agent Thorpe, I'm not saying I have a full understanding of why someone would do this. I do know that we put a hired gun, a successful Russian assassin, behind bars over a year ago. He had been their go-to man for what they used to call "active measures." Now, we know that before we completed that operation, the assassin knew Barbara's true name and her real email address. Knowing what you know about the current threat, don't you think they would make an effort to punish Barbara for our success? I know this isn't the same as an assassination or a capture, but if Barbara hadn't called her colleagues, what would you have done?"

"Probably arrested both of you and torn the house apart looking for her computer network attacking our computer network."

"And, it would have taken time and effort for us to get free and it would have distracted you from your real mission…at least for a bit. Plus, Barbara's house would have been a shambles and you would not have paid her a cent in compensation. A pretty good deal for the real villains, right?"

"Yes, sir. A pretty good deal."

Barbara added, "So, now what we need to do is figure out how we get back at them."

A voice from the hallway said, "What exactly do you mean by we?" Ellen Jones re-entered the room and the conversation.

Before there was anything resembling an exchange between Reimer and Jones or Jones and Thorpe, Barbara intervened. "I simply meant how will the USG proceed. We are not involved in this other than as potential victims. Terry and I have no part to play in this."

Reimer added, probably too quickly, "None at all. It's all your show, Agent Jones. Well, with the assistance of Agent Thorpe, of course."

Jones shook her head. She turned to Thorpe and said, "We found the repeater attached to the utility box outside. The gas meter has a small WiFi module that allows the gas company to read usage using a remote sensor. The parasite WiFi module was working off that utility feed to send and receive messages. We haven't been able to sort out the owner of the module, but it is definitely a high-end device. Agent

Thorpe, I've been instructed by my SAC to invite you back to the field office for a discussion on how to proceed. Does that sound good to you?

Thorpe swallowed hard and said, "Sure, that makes sense." He turned to Barbara and said, "No hard feelings?"

"None at all. Trust me, this isn't anything compared to the last time Terry, Agent Jones and I worked together."

Jones said, "Too true. The last time we worked together someone threw a grenade at Mrs. O'Connell. Having worked with her, I can almost understand why."

Barbara was pleased to see that Jones was smiling. Perhaps Agent Jones was beginning to understand the complexities of counterintelligence work and the importance of partnerships, including partnerships with civilians. She smiled and said, "It wasn't that bad was it?"

Jones looked at Barbara with a pained expression and said, "It was worse." Jones turned to the Army Special Agent and said, "Thorpe, shall we go?" With a brisk turn on her highly polished heel, Ellen Jones left the room.

At the last minute, Jones stopped and said, "I find it most curious that we end up with a cyber attack on you just after your son's team in Washington identified a cyber operation in Virginia going after the Pentagon. Odd, no?"

Barbara could only get out a "What?" before Jones left the house smiling all the way out to the street where her team was waiting.

FAMILY TIES

B ill O'Connell was still working on the reporting from the Sterling raid. The squad provided a basic summary to the SAC the morning after the raid and that information went to the director that evening. The fact that there were arrests as well as cascading high-profile National Security Division investigations meant that there was now a joint Cyber-CI task force focusing on both the Russian angle and the Iranian angle. Since the Iran team started the project, FBI headquarters decided the field end of the operation would be managed by Bill's boss, Len Preacher. That level of complexity was well above Bill's pay grade. For now, he was focused on handling about a ton of evidence acquired from the raid and the subsequent interrogations at the site.

The cyber squad had their own reporting formats that included reporting on coding, cryptography and routers. None of that material made any sense to Bill, but since he was the man who started the operation, he was responsible for turning the reports into a single document that would be delivered to the director and, eventually, to the rest of the intelligence community.

Preacher walked up to Bill's desk. He was in his navy FBI sweats. He had just finished his morning run. Bill was sorry he had missed it. PT with Preacher was always a terrific break from paperwork. However, today was not the day to lose focus. He had to finish the report. He had arrived at the office at 0330hrs, completed a short gym workout, showered and changed into his suit and was at his desk by 0430hrs. Preacher arrived at 0500hrs, offered Bill a cup of coffee and headed out for his run. Now he was ready to get something, anything that he could use when he reported to the SAC at 0700hrs.

"O'Connell, tell me you have the report completed."

Bill smiled and said, "Sir, I have the report completed."

Preacher was not amused. "Now, tell me the real status of the report."

"Sir, the actual report really is completed. I'm just compiling the various annexes that cover the evidence, the evidentiary chain, and whatever these cyber gurus call reporting."

"Excellent. So, I will have the full report ready when I get cleaned up and go see the SAC?"

"Yes, sir. Assuming you leave me to it, now."

"Hey, I can tell sarcasm when I hear it. I'm leaving now. But, let me leave you with this thought. Over the weekend, your mother was the subject of what looks to be a Russian cyberattack. Luckily, she has friends in high places and the FBI saved the day, as we always do."

"Huh?"

Preacher smiled and said, "Never mind. Stay focused. I will be back in 45 minutes with a cup of coffee for you. I expect to have a full report, two copies, with or without the annexes, ready to go when I return. I intend to give the SAC the report this AM. Check?"

"Yes, sir."

"And O'Connell, just so you know. Your mom is fine and she even was nice to everyone this time. No gunplay or hand grenades this time. All good."

Bill shook his head. Being part of the O'Connell family was never dull. At least until he finished this report, dull would be nice.

DEAD END

D oug and Flash were drinking coffee on the deck of the yali, the 19th century beach house converted into the CIA safehouse at the entrance to the Bosporus. Yalis were simply the beachside summer homes for the elite of first Ottoman and then Turkish society. They used them to escape the heat and the politics of life on the Golden Horn. When this house was placed on the market in the 1970s, the Agency used a local asset to purchase it, and then a second asset to renovate the house for the new owners. Once that cover story was in place, Doug came in and rebuilt the interior to make it a viable safehouse both for technical surveillance and for infiltration and exfiltration operations. The yali had a boat house attached to the lower deck and Doug's highly modified wooden-hulled speedboat was docked ready to go. Many of the nearby houses had collapsed from neglect over the years. Doug had saved this yali and lovingly repaired the various wooden structures. It was a safe house, but it was also Doug's home. He was proud of his work and, Flash had to admit, it was a very nice place to live.

Dawn light was extending long shadows over the Black Sea. It had been a warm fall and the mix of deciduous and pine trees offered a canvas of deep green and gold. Herons were hunting on the water along the coast. The previous evening while Melissa Nez was working on whatever it was that she did in the cyber world, Doug and Flash had used high-powered binoculars to watch herons fishing in the real world. This morning, they were watching groups of three and four of the great birds heading south and west along the Bosporus. Among other skills, Doug turned out to be an amateur ornithologist and he told Flash that the birds were on their migration route south from their summer range along the northwest coast of the Black Sea. "They will be heading toward warmer waters. No animal or man wants to be on the Russian Coast once winter comes in."

"You sound like you have some experience."

"Flash, you know that would be telling. After all, why would an Agency guy like me want to be on the Russian coast?"

"I can think of lots of reasons, but I'm thinking one of them might be to an exfiltration mission."

"OK, so I might have taken our little speedboat on a run up north. Of course, it would have been just an accident if I came close to the Russian coast."

"Of course. Accidents happen."

"You want another coffee?"

Flash could tell she was coming close to the edge of Doug's willingness to tell a story of the operation, but she couldn't help herself. She said, "Successful?"

"Yes. Now, coffee?"

"Sure. We need to fortify ourselves before Melissa wakes up."

Doug slapped his gnarled hands on the table and said, "Doug and two female spies in one place. What's not to like?" He headed into the kitchen to make more coffee.

As Flash sat watching birds, she noticed something else on the water. As she focused out into the shipping channel, she saw the clear outline of a submarine come to the surface and begin to enter the Bosporus. She turned back to the kitchen and said, "Doug, you need to see this."

Doug had heard the urgency in Flash's voice and came at a run. "What?"

"Look out at the shipping channel. It's a submarine."

Doug pulled his binoculars up to his eyes and said, "Yes, indeed. Looks like a *Kilo* class attack sub. You know, by international law, the

Russian Black Sea fleet is allowed to enter the Med. Subs have to run on the surface through the Bosporus into the Sea of Marmara and then out via the Dardanelles." Doug put his binoculars down. "This is good news indeed. We can expect a couple of *Grisha* class corvettes to come through today following the sub. After that, our ship should be transiting the Bosporus. It's a very predictable pattern designed to focus Turkish and our Navy attention on the serious Russian Navy ships. That allows the Russians to minimize interest in their…commercial ship."

Flash used the break to ask a question that she had wondered about since the first time they met, "Doug, has the singleton career out here worked for you? I mean, do you miss working with colleagues?"

Doug stopped for a moment, the two coffee cups in his hands. He shook his head and said, "Flash, the trade has good sides and bad. I happen to enjoy my own company more than I enjoy others. I like the work I do. I like meeting assets and producing intelligence. There are sacrifices made to make this work for a full career. I have no problem with the decisions I made. I didn't let a focus on advancement — or someone else's definition of what an intelligence officer should be — change who I wanted to be. It is a decision that every intelligence officer has to make. It was what you might not call career enhancing, but it worked for me. The secret to life is to acknowledge the good and the bad of your own decisions. Don't blame someone else for your decisions. Own them. Own the consequences."

It had been years since Flash had this kind of conversation. The last time was when she was serving in Afghanistan as an analyst forward deployed with a SOF assault unit. Days and nights of waiting and then a few hours of action. Flash had been allowed on raids because of her in-depth knowledge of both al-Qaida networks and computers. After the site was clear, she would enter with the second team to conduct site exploitation. One slow evening after a week of raids, she asked one of the raid team what it was like to be on the cutting edge for so long. He said nearly the same thing: Decide who you are going to be and then own your decision. It was a pretty clean philosophy but Flash suspected it wasn't necessarily an easy one.

Doug turned back to the kitchen. Over his shoulder he said, "You need to wake up Ms. Nez. It is going to be action stations soon enough."

Flash took one last look at the submarine as it headed toward the entrance of the Bosporus. With the sun rising almost directly across the Bosporus, the black hull nearly disappeared in the glare. She had little understanding of Navy operations, but she could easily understand why the sub would enter unfriendly territory at dawn. Just like any adversary, the sub commander wanted the advantage of the low light angle and sleepy watch standers as he entered Turkish waters. The herons paid no attention to the black shape in the water. They continued hunting for their breakfast.

Flash went up the creaky stairs of the old Turkish house. By the time Flash had reached the top of the stairs, Melissa's head appeared from one of the bedrooms. Flash laughed out loud looking at her friend's pillow face and chaotic halo of black hair. Melissa said, "What's all the noise about? I need my sleep."

"No time for sleep, kiddo. We got work to do."

"Oh, work. That's right. Isn't that what I did all night while you were sleeping?"

"No time to relate your genius. It's time to get going!"

As Flash came down the stairs, Doug shouted up the stairwell, "Breakfast will be ready in ten minutes. If you like your eggs warm, you need to get down here."

As she walked down the stairs, Flash said, "I'm not eating fish with my eggs again!"

Doug responded, "Too late." Doug was a good cook, but his meals always had the savory nature of the Eastern Mediterranean whether it was breakfast, lunch or dinner. Flash had to laugh as she heard Melissa upstairs groan and say, "Yuck!"

Doug and his two colleagues were out on the Black Sea by 9 a.m. The ladies were dressed in as close to "holiday boating attire" as Doug could find for them in the shops in Istanbul. It meant that they were wearing pastel colored long-sleeve shirts over their jeans, and long sheepskin vests over both. Equally colorful scarves covered their hair. On Melissa's lap was a small laptop linked to cables that disappeared into a wooden crate covered with picnic baskets and a cooler. Flash was in the cockpit with Doug. Melissa thought Flash was completely out of character wearing colorful clothes and covering her short black hair with a paisley scarf. Doug was wearing a clean turtleneck sweater and, for the first time since she met him, Melissa noticed he had shaved. Doug looked quite respectable compared to their first encounter when he looked like virtually every other dock rat at the Galatea Bridge.

Flash shouted over the engine noise and the crash of the waves against the hull of the speedboat, "OK, Captain Doug, what's the plan?"

"Flash, you know the plan since you were the one who came up with it."

"I know I know the plan, but do you know the plan?"

"You do know that mutineers are tossed off the ship and have to swim to shore?"

Flash put her hands on her hips and said, "I would like to see you try that one."

"It might be fun."

"For at least one of us."

Doug shook his head. "OK, so the plan. We cruise along the coast for a bit like any set of tourists. If we sight the target, we stop about a kilometer off and anchor. We have lunch. While enjoying our lunch, you and Melissa work your magic to intercept what you can. That should determine what we need to do once they anchor in the Sea of Marmara. It should give us some ideas on whether we even need to sort out an infiltration on board. Right?"

"Excellent. You didn't even ask silly questions like Sue does. You just accepted genius for what it is. Genius."

Doug said, "And I do miss Sue. Where is she now?"

Flash said in a stage whisper, "Too secret to tell."

"Afghanistan?"

Flash continued her stage whisper, "I guess it's not such a secret...."

Doug slowed the boat down by pulling on the pair of throttles between them. He turned his tanned and wrinkled face to Flash. "Flash, would you be surprised if I told you I'm friends with Jamie Shenk?"

Flash said, "It's a small Klingon world."

"Yup. Now, I've been in the Agency long enough to know that you tech guys really don't care what operators do or think. You just expect us to deliver you on target. Well, here you are."

Flash couldn't tell if Doug was joking or serious. She decided it didn't matter. As a way to avoid further conversation, she pulled out a set of large rubberized armor marine binoculars and started to scan the horizon in front of the boat. Nothing appeared in her search.

Melissa called from the back of the boat. "Flash, where is the ship?"

Flash looked back at Melissa and said, "There is no ship out there."

"Must be. The cyber signal is a full five bars. We have to be closing in on the ship."

Flash walked back toward her colleague. "Melissa, unless they have some sort of cloak of invisibility, I'm telling you there is no ship out there."

Doug pulled the throttles back to full stop. The boat settled into the water and began to rock in the waves. He reached over to his GPS receiver and set an electronic plot on the screen to his front. He checked his small onboard radar set. Nothing within 20 kilometers. He then checked his modified sonar set. It looked like any commercial fishing sonar display, but the Agency had modified it so that it was ten times more sensitive. He checked the sonar twice and then turned to the back of the boat. "Ladies, we have a challenge. Of course, with challenges come opportunities."

Flash turned to Melissa and said, "He sounds like Massoni."

From the bow Doug said, "Who's Massoni?"

"A sergeant major."

"Now that is a compliment."

Flash said, "I'm not sure, but I think you are better looking than Massoni."

Melissa said to both of them, "I don't know what she is talking about, but we are nearly on top of the ship, so where is it?"

Doug said, "We are sitting on top of it or darn close. There isn't a ship. There is an underwater buoy out there. About the size of one of the buoys they use to identify shipping channels, but the anchor chain keeps it about 30 feet underwater. There must be an antenna out there bobbing on the surface, but I suspect unless you were right next to it, you wouldn't see it."

"So, no ship."

Doug shrugged his shoulders. "Nope. I suppose *Bursa Chief* powered up the antenna system for an original test while it was anchored out here. Their likely cover was they were waiting clearance to enter the Bosporus shipping channel. While they were waiting, they used divers to place the buoy in a location away from normal shipping and unlikely to be found by any holiday boaters. Every time they come through, they move the buoy, check the electronics and the power. Pretty clever if you think of it. Hiding in plain sight. Well, more or less."

Flash shook her head. "Dead end."

Melissa looked up from her computer and said, "So, what do we do now?"

Flash said, "Sounds like we need some help from the Navy."

Doug said sarcastically, "Does SOF have Navy divers?"

Flash looked at Doug and, as if talking to a child, she said, "Yes, Doug. SOF has a couple of divers."

Doug smiled and said, "Well, let's go back to the yali. I've got the spot marked on the GPS, so we can come back anytime. You can whistle up your divers and figure out what you want to do on the tech side. Based on the sonar signature, there probably isn't some sort of computer that you are going to access. It is another relay station." He walked back to the cockpit and started up the twin diesels. In less than a minute, they were returning along the coast.

Flash was sitting in the back with her colleague and said, "You know, for a Klingon, Doug isn't a bad sort."

Melissa said, "I heard that. Don't forget I'm a Klingon too!"

Flash nodded. She said, "You are a tech Klingon. Totally different. I meant an operator Klingon."

Melissa said, "Like Jamie."

Flash looked up at the sky and said, "Ah, Jamie. Now, he is one different sort of cat altogether."

---

27 October 2009, CIA safehouse, Black Sea

Doug drove the speedboat out from the covered dock with four passengers. This time instead of Doug and two women, it was Doug, two men and two women. The two new occupants were members of the Special Boat Service from the British airbase in Akrotiri. After Flash called Massoni and described the underwater buoy, Massoni reached out to SOF HQS and learned all of the SOF SEALs were deployed in Afghanistan. They could fly a team out from the East Coast, but offered instead a team from UKSF. Ten days later, Doug in his local fisherman identity picked up two very fit young SBS operators from Galatea Bridge.

After a day of briefings, the two SBS divers, who identified themselves only as Flipper and Mick, offered a simple plan: Dive on the buoy, collect both underwater photography and electronic emissions, and if possible, determine what, if anything could be accomplished in an effort to gain access to the electronics. Not quite the commando mission that they had hoped for, but certainly better than working out in the cramped gym space in an aircraft hangar on a Royal Air Force base on Cyprus. And, it didn't hurt that there were women, a picnic lunch and a very nice, very fast speedboat in the mix. Flipper said, "I heard from some of our mates that working with you Americans can be amusing, but I didn't realize it was going to be a holiday."

Flash smiled and said, "You have no idea how much fun it can be to work with us."

Doug watched the GPS as he approached the buoy. The Brits recommended stopping 100m away to ensure that wave action or sound would not trigger any anti-tampering devices. The boat settled into the water, rocking gently in the late fall breeze. After a quick 360 degree check for observers on other ships or even from the coast, they donned their dive gear and silently slipped into the water. Melissa leaned over the side of the boat and passed Flipper a watertight box with a sensor array designed to capture any emanations that might be on site. She then passed Mick a high-definition video camera. In seconds they disappeared into the inky black waters.

A half hour later, they reappeared and joined their counterparts on the boat. After ditching their wetsuits and returning to tourist clothes, everyone settled down to a picnic lunch of cold meats, cheese, Turkish breads, and very cold white wine.

Mick started the discussion. "The buoy is right strange. It is surrounded by an anti-tampering cage that extends out about 2 meters. More or less looks like the cages oceanographers use when they are observing schools of sharks. Just far enough that you would need very specialized gear to touch the buoy and not trigger any alarm that might be associated with it. It really looks old school, painted flat black, like the contact mines you see in the World War II movies."

Mick continued, "That was the first thing I thought as we approached. I thought we were looking at some World War II relic that could blow up any time. I changed my mind as soon as I heard the sensor start to collect. That buoy is sending traffic at a high rate, it's like something you would expect from an underwater cable."

Flash had to probe, "Not that you would have ever been near some adversary underwater cable..."

Mick said, "Well, if we had, but of course we haven't, then yes, it would have been just like working a sensor near an underwater cable. We aren't going to do much with this unless we want to blow it out of the water. Basically, it's a dead end."

Melissa had been completely captured by the video and sensor feeds throughout lunch. She finally said, "Well, we now know what it is. A repeater in the Black Sea. We can also say for sure that it is accepting data from hundreds, perhaps thousands of sources in the region. One curious thing: the output signal is bi-polar. It is repeating signals from the east and the west."

Doug said, "So, it is sending stuff west as well as forwarding stuff from the west? What does that mean?"

Flash said, "And that means we have another puzzle to solve."

Flipper said, "You know, if we wanted to disrupt this little operation we could."

Doug and Flash looked at the SBS diver. He had been fairly quiet since coming out of the water. Melissa was the first to react. "How?"

Flipper said, "I'm assuming the location of this repeater is fairly critical to its capability."

Melissa said, "Yes..."

"Well, what if the anchor cable broke? The repeater would float to the surface and then be subject to tides and currents. It might even float into the shipping channel or wash up on the Turkish Coast. Don't you think that would be a mess for whoever owns the equipment?"

Doug finally recovered. He smiled and said, "I just happen to have a hacksaw in my tool box here."

Mick said, "Mate, no need to work that hard. We brought a small bit of detonation cord with us when we came over on our RAF aircraft. Not enough to do real damage to the device or the cage, but just enough to cut through the anchor chain." The two SBS swimmers were already pulling on their wetsuits.

"Brilliant!" Flash said. "Now I know why Sue loves you guys from the SBS."

Flipper said, "Who's Sue?"

Doug said, "I'm offering a lovely meal and drinks at the yali tonight, so I reckon you better get to work."

Flash said, "Fish, again."

Mick and Flipper were already in the water and didn't respond.

The two divers approached the buoy. They were living in a silent world where only the noise from their regulators passed through the thick rubber hoods on their wet suits. Mick was carrying a large waterproof lamp and Flipper carried a small satchel with the detonation cord, a chemical timed detonator, and a set of engineers' tools. They approached the buoy, keeping watch for any additional anti-tampering devices that might cause them harm. They circled the buoy twice using both the waterproof lamp and their own headlamps to check the device. At the end of the recce, they stopped and came up face to face. They both used hand signals for OK.

Once they agreed that it was all clear, Flipper released some air from his buoyancy compensator and headed down the chain. Before they entered the water, they agreed that the most clandestine way to cut the chain was as near to the anchor as they could get. The most likely source of wear and tear would be where the sea anchor rubbed against the buoy chain. That was where they would plant the detonation cord. As Flipper finned further down, the Black Sea surrendered surface light. By 50 feet, he was operating entirely by headlamp.

At 60 feet and in complete darkness, Flipper found the joint between chain and anchor. He opened the satchel and pulled out a small roll of detonation cord. He wrapped the cord around the chain, attached the chemical detonator and fired the plunger. On the surface, that would mean he had 15 minutes to get clear before the detonator fired. At nearly two atmospheres, he wasn't entirely certain how much time he had, so he finned away from the chain at a brisk pace. As he passed Mick, they turned and headed to the boat. Neither diver had been under pressure for long enough to require a decompression stop, so they angled to the surface just as the detonator fired and the cord wrapped around the chain burned at 6500m/second.

Before the SBS divers were back in the boat, Doug observed through binoculars the buoy and its anti-tampering cage bob to the surface. Still watching the buoy, he heard rather than saw the divers climb back into the boat. He looked back at the divers and said, "Gentlemen, that was a nice piece of work. Now, we need to get back to the yali. I will need to report a hazard to shipping to the Turkish Coast Guard." Doug fired up the engines of the speed boat, spun the wheel of the craft and headed back down the coast. Mick and Flipper were out of their dive gear and back in civilian clothes well before anyone might have observed the five people on holiday.

THE SILICON ADDICTION

While she remained careful about her security, Barbara O'Connell was not about to be a prisoner in her own home. She had just returned from jogging along the lake front. It was a perfect late-fall morning, the trees had turned to a mix of gold and red depending on whether they were oaks or maples. It was cool but not cold and the sunrise had been a perfect orange globe rising behind the cottage as she headed out the door. Barbara had never been a serious runner, but recently she found that an hour outside at dawn, whether at a jog or walking, was just the thing to clear her head.

This morning she had once again wondered why her house had been targeted for a cyber operation. After the first ten minutes of a slow jog while she limbered her muscles, an idea formed in her head. The recent revelation about her home security was simply another gambit in the long-term conflict between the O'Connell family and Russian intelligence. If that was the case, it was entirely possible that the device planted on the exterior of the house had been there for years. After all, who would have checked?

When she took over the house, she didn't make any effort to conduct an electronic sweep. It would take a very paranoid person to spend time and money hiring a team to do this sort of sophisticated work. If the device had been operating for the long term, it might help explain the death of Peter Senior and the fact that the Russian assassin, Michael O'Connell, had known her personal email address.

After all, if the limpet was redirecting sensitive electronic traffic from Seneca Army Depot, why couldn't it capture her personal traffic?

The Agency was just starting cyber operations when Barbara retired. She had read enough open-source material on criminal cyber threats that she could imagine some sort of electronic parasite residing on her house had enough capability to do more than one thing at a time. And, if the adversary went to the trouble to target her father-in-law, why would that adversary remove the device when another O'Connell moved in?

As she rounded the last turn and headed home, Barbara decided that she would need to call Jake Longstreet, former Green Beret and another of Beth Parson's contractors. Long before he took on the contract with Stearns and Mandeville, Longstreet managed a small team of former special operators named *Condotierri Maletesta* or CM. CM made a good living conducting penetration testing, or "pen testing" in industrial security parlance. His work, and most especially the work of one of his partners named Mark, included technical surveillance counter-measures. If anyone could do a sweep of her house, Mark could.

While in the shower, Barbara worked out how she would engage Longstreet. The mobile phone rang just as Barbara was getting out of the shower. The phone call interrupted her planning. Barbara picked up the pay-as-you-go phone that she had used ever since her confrontation with Michael O'Connell. Only her closest friends knew the number. She looked at the caller ID. Only three numbers on the screen: 571. The area code issued to mobile phones in Northern Virginia. She decided to answer the call by using the last four numbers of her mobile.

"9237."

Janice Macintosh's voice came through the digital speaker. "And good morning to you, dear."

"Janice, it is Sunday morning. I haven't had my tea yet and I doubt this is a social call."

"The FBI never rests."

"So I have been told."

"I am calling you from my own pay as you go."

"That explains the number, or lack of it."

"We do what we can."

"So, shall I make some tea and sit down?"

"Would you be interested in a visit?"

"Your place or mine?"

"Preferably yours. Can you put me up for a night?"

"Absolutely. I love pajama parties. Dinner and wine are included in my bed-and-breakfast plan."

"See you this afternoon."

"Ciao." Janice had already hung up.

Barbara finished toweling off and put on a pair of jeans and a long-sleeved polo shirt. She kept the shirt untucked. After slipping on a pair of well-worn boat shoes, she walked over to her bed where she placed her running pack when she came upstairs. She pulled out her Smith and Wesson Model 60 revolver in nylon pocket holster. After some months of legal wrangling, she had eventually recovered the pistol from the FBI. After the confrontation in Emery Park last summer, when Barbara used the revolver to bring down her attacker, the FBI confiscated the pistol as evidence in the arrest of Jason Macalvey for his attack on Barbara. They decided that it wasn't crucial to their prosecution when Macalvey quickly agreed to a lesser sentence in exchange for his cooperation on the Michael O'Connell prosecution for the murder of an East Aurora resident. Barbara's favorite local FBI agent, Ellen Jones, delivered the pistol with a less-than-subtle warning that she hoped she didn't see the pistol again.

She opened up the top drawer of the nightstand and pulled out a leather holster and slipped the holster onto her belt, put the revolver in the holster and pulled the shirt over the top. Barbara had never been one to wear a firearm full time, especially in her house. Still, after the past three years of danger, she figured it was worth the annoyance until something resembling safety returned to her life. Barbara looked in the mirror and said to herself, "Well, I hope she won't see it again."

She went downstairs to the kitchen and started the electric kettle. A pot of black tea was in order along with a bowl of oatmeal and some fruit. Since Janice would be visiting soon, Barbara took the next hour to tidy up the guest bedroom and make a plan for dinner. She welcomed the small bit of domestic normalcy in what was certain to be interrupted by whatever Janice was coming to tell her. Life had not been the same since the death of her husband a half dozen years ago. When Russians killed the Beroslav crime family who were central to the entire drama, Barbara thought that was the end of her worries. Then the story of another family member, Michael O'Connell, Irish terrorist and Russian assassin for hire, arrived on her doorstep and a new threat arrived with him. After his arrest, and with his trial due to start in the next month, once again Barbara thought the days of personal vendettas against herself and her family were over and done.

The recent confrontation with Thorpe and the revelation that there was a Russian cyber parasite attached to her house was almost too much to bear. When would this madness end? A small voice inside her head answered. "Never." Barbara did her best to ignore that voice as she ran the vacuum cleaner around the house. Vacuuming, dusting and baking filled the rest of the day. Very domestic, even if she was wearing a revolver on her hip.

Janice Macintosh arrived at the Chautauqua House late afternoon as the sun was setting over the lake. The low light angle in the fall turned everything a golden brown. Barbara was sitting on the small deck off the living room, drinking a cup of tea while watching a chevron of Canada geese circle the lake and finally settle on the water surface. They paddled into the shoreline for the night. When she moved into the Chautauqua House, one of the few additions she made to the property was a set of discrete security cameras that covered her driveway and the approach from the lake. The driveway camera sent an alarm to a small base station in her kitchen. The beeping pulled Barbara away from her calming view of the geese on the lake. Janice Macintosh and the links to Barbara's other world had arrived.

Barbara watched on the camera as Janice got out of a ten-year-old, navy blue Chevy Tahoe. Given Janice's small stature, she first took a step on the running board of the truck and then down onto the macadam driveway. Barbara and Janice had been friends for almost twenty years and other than a few gray streaks in her pageboy haircut, Janice still looked like the gymnast that she was in college. Barbara knew Janice was absolutely tough as nails and scary fit, but she could imagine how easy it would have been twenty years ago for Janice's male colleagues in the FBI to just assume she was a "girl lawyer" trying to be a lawman. As Janice told her some years ago, it wasn't until she passed selection for the San Antonio Field Office SWAT that she began to get some acceptance in the field as more than just the "cute brain."

After settling Janice into the spare bedroom and pouring them both a glass of crisp, New York State Riesling, Barbara ushered her guest out on the deck to finish watching the sun go down. Barbara could hear Janice's breathing change as she began to relax from the six-hour drive from DC and, perhaps, from the stress and strain of her day job as a senior FBI supervisor in the National Security Division. Barbara knew it was only a matter of time before Janice would speak, but she allowed her friend a bit of peace before asking the question.

"So, while I really love having you here, since company is not something I have often, I suspect there is more to your visit than a desire to break out of the Washington Metro and drink a glass of New York wine."

"Could it be your cooking?"

"Well, it might be, but without a ton of warning, you are going to have to live with a dinner of broccoli garlic pasta and some fresh bread from the local bakery."

Janice smiled, "No caviar?"

"Not on a pensioner's salary."

"I suspect there is a little money for nice things courtesy of Stearns and Mandeville."

"Mostly I'm saving up for a trip to see Sue in Italy. My Agency experiences in Italy were all work and that meant no trips to enjoy the country, the food or the museums."

"Yup. I know what you mean. You get a work trip scheduled to someplace nice and then the government expects you to work. Most likely in an isolated embassy office and, if you are lucky, out on the street, in the dark. Once the job is done, you get called back to work your own isolated office. It is swell."

"Except when you can visit a friend who lives on a lake."

"A house on the lake. Pretty nice."

Barbara corrected her friend. "Here in Western New York, they say a cottage on a lake. If it is small, as this house is, you have a cabin in the woods, a bungalow in the town, or a cottage on a lake. And, honestly, I could never have afforded this place. Peter's father invested very wisely in property in the 1960s and 1970s. He bought this place, a townhouse that Bill owns in Georgetown and the farmhouse on the Potomac that is Sue's place. All three are out of the reach of civil servants today, but back then, I suppose it was just how he spent his salary. He was downrange for years. Single father, no real outside interests except some first edition books. I think he understood that if he was going to have a legacy, it would be property."

"Well, based on your tales of your father-in-law, I suppose regular travel to war zones probably augmented the salary."

"Too true. And, to think that he was gunned down here after living through it all is hard to take."

"A good long life and, from what I have read of the file, a quick ticket out. Not a bad way to go." Janice took a drink from her wine glass and stared at the horizon. They were both quiet as the sky changed from orange to red to mauve.

Barbara smiled at Janice as she poured another glass of wine. "So, that's a dark thought. I hope your technique for engaging old friends is better than that."

Janice shook her head. "Sorry, it's been a week."

Barbara said, "Well, actually for me it's been a lot longer than that."

"Too true." Janice knew that over the past years Barbara had watched her husband die of poisoning, her daughter recover from a below-the-knee amputation, had been involved in uncovering a Russian sleeper agent who tried to kill her daughter and successfully killed Max Creeter at the O'Connell Potomac House, and more recently survived a grenade attack sponsored by a distant cousin of her husband. Barbara had more than her share of chaos the past couple of years. "So, now I'm here to add to your troubles."

"Oh, great. Can we at least have dinner before that? Anyhow, it's going to get pretty chilly out here soon and I need to get cooking in the kitchen."

"Deal. Need a sous chef?"

Barbara smiled, "Not for this meal. But you can cork the white and uncork a bottle of red in the pantry that will go with the meal."

Two hours later, with the main meal completed, over coffee and a bowl of chopped fruit from the local farmers' market, Barbara said, "OK. Spill. Why are you here?"

Janice looked up over the rim of her coffee mug, "How about we clean up and then we talk this through, OK?"

Dining room table cleared and dishes washed, Barbara and Janice moved to the small living room that opened through French doors onto the deck. The view from the room was of the lake and the lights of other cottages along the shore. It was very peaceful.

"Any cognac in the larder?"

"Hmmm, probably not. I stopped filling the liquor cabinet some years ago. It's wine or coffee or wine and coffee or wine and tea. Your call."

"Wine and chocolate?"

"Ah, now you are talking. I have some dark German chocolate and a Shiraz that just might do the trick." Barbara walked back into the galley kitchen and returned carrying two wine glasses and the bottle of Shiraz. She handed Janice a box of chocolates.

Janice said, "And when exactly did you start carrying a firearm in your own house?"

"The pistol printed?"

"Not so a civilian would notice, but I certainly noticed as we were doing the dishes."

Barbara smirked, "Ever had a grenade thrown at you?"

Janice laughed, "Nope."

"How about a bunch of villains break into your house hell bent on killing you."

"Not yet."

"Well, I've checked both boxes and I'm still not quite sure when I will decide I don't need to have a firearm handy."

"Fair enough."

"So, are you going to tell me what you want to tell me?"

"Wine and chocolate?"

"Does this count as bribing an FBI agent?"

"I don't think so since I am the one who is going to ask you to do the FBI a favor."

"I'm a good citizen. I will do my part."

"Then pour the wine."

As Barbara poured the Shiraz and Janice opened the box of chocolates, the fragrances filled the living room. They sat across from each other on two of the four Roycroft wood and leather chairs that Peter Senior purchased at a garage sale in the 1980s. It was most pleasant.

Janice took a deep breath and said, "Would you turn on some music?"

Barbara said, "Does it matter what kind?"

"Nope."

Barbara understood immediately. Janice was looking for some sound masking. It reminded her that she needed to get someone from *Condotierri Malatesta* up to do a TSCM sweep. She walked to the corner of the room. The radio was an old table top model in quarter-sawn oak. An original multi-band radio from the 1930s that had been lovingly restored by Peter Senior. It took a minute for the tubes to warm up and then the wood cabinet and old speakers offered a deep bass tone as Barbara tuned to the Buffalo Jazz station. Once the music started to play, Barbara returned and sat next to Janice. If Janice was worried about a tech device in the Chautauqua House, Barbara knew the conversation was serious.

"Let's start with the electronics mounted on your house. They had been in place for years. Relatively old technology, but reliable. It is all part of a much larger program, or maybe..." Janice took a sip of her wine, "programs…managed by several adversaries. The FBI has been working for nearly ten years on tracking internet crimes. We have a separate division called the internet crime complaint center that focuses on criminals who are running wild on the internet. In my shop, we look at the counterintelligence side of the equation. The intelligence community used to feel safe from computer attack because they were not linked to the outside word. It turns out they are completely wrong. Post 9/11, the IC spent time and effort creating an intelligence and special operations intranet so that the various parts of the community could share information and share it quickly. The downside to that is once you have a breach in one part of the community, you have a breach in the entire community."

Barbara nodded and said, "And, I suppose you have found a breach."

"More than one, to be precise."

"Russians?"

"Well, the first breach is related to the Czyneski case."

Barbara nodded. Cyzneski was at the center of the death of her father-in-law and her lover, Max Creeter. He was a Russian sleeper agent buried deep inside the counterintelligence center of the CIA. When he was arrested, he confessed to his crimes out of sheer ego and, perhaps, to avoid the death penalty for his conspiracy to kill US citizens. Barbara assumed he was buried deep in some supermax prison.

Janice continued, "Czyneski worked with a number of unwitting members of the IC. He had them load what he called virus protection programs on the internal network. Those programs were designed to pull data from the network."

"But if the network is not tied to the internet, how do they exfiltrate the data?"

"The computer wizards explained and I still don't understand. I think it has two steps. First, the periodic loading of virus programs designed to scrape data off the network. Obviously, that was only periodic access. Dangerous, but only periodic. It seems that there was also some software loaded to allow the Russians to access a computer through a keystroke logger. It wouldn't work with a computer located in a secure facility, but post 9/11, the IC has provisional bases all over the world that are not as secure as the various headquarters. We need folks out there in these bases and those folks need access to the network, but it turns out their computers are exceptionally vulnerable."

Barbara captured the point and said, "And the exfiltration of the data required various intermediate points along the way. Those points included the repeater located at this house."

"Well, not exactly." Janice stopped to take a bite of chocolate and a sip of wine. She sighed at the pleasure of the moment. Eventually, reality intruded. "The Czyneski threat was fairly contained and managed through accessing data directly from these provisional locations in Afghanistan, Iraq, and wherever else we had a computer portal. Your little parasite was part of another program. And, you'll appreciate this, a program that was partially uncovered through work by your very own FBI Special Agent."

"Bill? I thought he was working on an FCI squad in Washington focused on Iranians."

"Indeed, he was and is. His team busted a warehouse in the DC suburbs that was supposed to be an Iranian cyber team stealing identities and credit card information. Those identities belonged to individuals working in the Pentagon and the identities of their families. What was curious about that network was the actual criminal activities were passed along two channels. The expected one pushed data to a known server farm in Dubai owned by the Islamic Revolutionary Guards Corps. The second channel went out to a series of servers that eventually ends up in Central Asia at a location that the Agency says is owned and operated by a Russian private military contractor."

"IRGC and a Russian PMC working together?"

"Beats me, but we think the Hizballahis were profiteering."

Barbara said, "Hizballahis have always been partial to self-funding their work through criminal action. I suppose it is a very short step to imagine they would work with a Russian PMC or Russian organized crime or both."

"Exactly. Their plan was scraping identities from unwary Pentagon employees and, it seems, giving those identities to their primary patron inside the IRGC. But, they seem to have decided there were others who might pay for both the identities they offered to the IRGC and any others that looked vulnerable. There didn't appear to be any IRGC direct supervision for this operation, so the Hizballahis were doing what they do best: making money. According to the interrogations, they told the IRGC each month they had acquired a set number of identities. Every month, they also offered a different set of identities on the dark web. We know for sure that a Russian PMC bought some and we suspect, but haven't proven yet, that the Chinese Ministry of State Security bought others. There were others that were sold to standard cyber criminals. Sadly, there aren't many civilians inside the IC other than the counterintelligence and cyber ops folks who understand cyber security. We suspect the warehouse was capturing and curating about two dozen identities a month for the past year."

Barbara finished her tea and looked at Janice. "What a can of worms! I suppose you have come here just to commiserate with your pal, a wretched federal pensioner?"

"Well, not exactly."

"No, I suspected not. Every time I see you or Mary, I figure I am about to get into something that is, shall we say, challenging."

"And, we know you like a challenge."

"And, does this mean another grenade attack?"

"I certainly hope not."

"Overseas?"

"Nope, right here in your backyard." Janice paused to measure Barbara's reaction. She decided to proceed. "I suspect Special Agent Jones did not tell you that she left the internet parasite in place."

Barbara tried hard not to shout. Her comment came out just short of a growl. "No, she did not."

"And she hasn't reached out to you since."

"No, she has not. Am I serving as a tethered goat?"

"Well, not exactly."

"What...exactly?"

Janice took a sip of wine and popped one of the dark chocolates into her mouth. Barbara wasn't certain if it was a stalling technique or Janice simply enjoying the mix of red wine and chocolate. It took Janice some time to finally speak. "So, I told you that we are tracking the links from the warehouse in Northern Virginia to the various end users. The IRGC connection was pretty easy. More or less a straight shot to Dubai, then to Kish Island and then to a server farm in Esfahan. We are working on that one with the military. They have the resources in the Gulf."

"I would guess so after nearly five years in Iraq."

"So, the other link is more complicated. The Russians have demonstrated a far more difficult target. Their signals bounce all over the world. Right now, our best guess is the end point is in Dushanbe, Tajikistan."

"Janice, let me say up front, for me Dushanbe is a BTDTNA."

"Eh?"

"Been there, done that, never again. It was my first experience living in a civil war and I definitely didn't like it. It was in the early '90s and it was a civil war. Every citizen of Tajikistan was picking sides. We were in the middle trying to sort out what was happening. It was no fun."

"Well, I am not asking you to have big fun in Tajikistan."

"Good." Barbara raised her glass in a mock toast.

"We need you to do something right here in upstate New York."

"Now I am really confused. What do you want me to do here?"

"Let's start with what you already know."

"Which isn't much. So, spill."

"The guy you met, Special Agent Thorpe."

"Tall guy, high and tight haircut, threatened to break down my doors. That guy. I didn't like him."

"Well, neither did Ellen Jones. In fact, she really didn't like him and took it on herself to do a deep dive on this guy. He isn't exactly what he said he was."

"As in, an alias?"

"Well, no. He is an Army guy and he does work at Seneca Army

Depot. He just may be an asset for somebody as well. At this point, we don't know who he is working for other than the United States Army."

Barbara smiled and said, "Special Agent Ellen Jones is showing real potential, don't you think?"

"Indeed. And her boss, Chason, recognizes her potential and gives her plenty of leeway to follow leads that another supervisor might consider frivolous. This time, she appears to have been successful."

"Tell me more."

"Well, Agent Thorpe seems to have taken it on his own initiative to come to Chautauqua. There was no warrant, there was no lead named Shotkin, at least no lead in our databases. Jones has more data on his background, but I figure we will let her brag about that work. After she decided to dig a little further and with the help of our cyber guys, she found a connection between the parasite on your outside wall and a parasite inside the Seneca Army Depot. Both are feeding into a stream that seems to end in Dushanbe. I say seems because cyber operations turn out to be filled with…misdirection."

"So, Thorpe is a villain?"

"Well, we don't know yet and we want your help to find out."

"How?"

"Drink your wine and have a piece of chocolate. It will be good for you."

Barbara did as she was told and repeated, "How?"

"Well, let's talk about what we think happened. We think the Russians realized that once the link in Northern Virginia was compromised, they needed to shut down some of their electronic nodes used in the past to obscure their operation. Plus, they needed to make sure any agents they had inside the cyber community were not compromised. Jones thinks Thorpe was tasked to recover the repeater on your house so that the connection to Seneca Army Depot stayed safe. That way, they had a safe repeater site in the Northeast that they could use for any other cyber operations or any future operations that they might design. I have talked to my counterparts in the Pentagon. I haven't revealed our interest in Thorpe, but I did ask them if the

Seneca facility is legitimate. Indeed, it is. The truth is that if Thorpe is a penetration of the Russians or the Iranians or who knows who, they would probably do whatever they could to keep him safe so that they could continue to use the facility as access to the Army cyber community."

"And, what does Barbara O'Connell do other than serve as a tethered goat?"

Janice smiled and said, "Just be a tethered goat."

"Doesn't the tethered goat end up eaten by the tiger just before the hunter shoots the tiger?"

"Not in my stories."

"So, what are the details?"

"You agree?"

"In principle, who wouldn't agree? We are working on a threat to our national security. I already have this repeater attached to my house like some nasty little parasite. Of course, I agree. At least, so long as I am completely in the loop."

Janice smiled and used a stage whisper to say "You can count on the FBI."

"If you remember, that wasn't how Special Agent Jones thought it should work out."

"Jones learned her lesson. She isn't thrilled with the idea, but she is willing to accept that this is going to make her look good. Very, very good. I suspect you already realized Jones is ambitious."

"And rich. Where does her money come from for all the high style clothes and that car?"

"She's the daughter of a corporate lawyer from New York City. Attended all the right schools and decided she needed to serve her country."

"I can certainly appreciate that sentiment."

"Her parents didn't. They thought she should return to the house on the Hamptons and either take a job with one of several family businesses or get married and make grandchildren. I think you know she has a science PhD. I suspect the family wanted her to rise in the corporate ranks of some Beltway bandit in the military industrial complex."

"Can't blame the parents for wanting the best for their daughter. And, I suspect she is an only child, right?"

"Yes, indeed."

"So, if Jones plays nice, she gets to join the big FCI leagues in New York or in DC?"

"Exactly."

"Hmmm, she might even work with my son."

"Well, as I understand it, Bill has his own plans for keeping his love life in the family."

"You seem intent on avoiding the rest of that story. Do tell!"

"Pour another glass of that excellent Shiraz and I will reveal some DC gossip. Then we call it a night and tomorrow, we invite Special Agent Jones down for a meeting of the minds here in Chez O'Connell."

"Deal."

———

The next morning, FBI Special Agent Jones arrived just as Barbara and Janice were cleaning up breakfast dishes. Barbara's surveillance cameras alarmed up as the electric blue Mustang pulled into the driveway. Jones arrived dressed once again in FBI business wear — a dark wool pants suit, white shirt, and flats. Of course, on closer inspection, you could see the suit was not off the shelf and the shirt was silk. Barbara wasn't sure if Jones was just arriving after Sunday church or if she dressed in business armor because she was meeting with a senior from the FBI. Either way, Barbara was pleased to see that Jones' demeanor did not reveal any anger or concern. Jones' previous visits to the Chautauqua house had started with this young special agent striding up the driveway in a very aggressive manner as if to say "I'm here to serve a warrant. Don't get in my way."

Barbara opened the door before Jones could knock.

"Under surveillance?"

"And good morning to you as well, Ellen. And, yes, there are security cameras here and there."

"Better safe than sorry, eh?"

"You know my story, Ellen. Can you blame me?"

"I suppose not."

"So, are we going to keep this conversation at the front door or would you like to come in for some coffee or tea?"

For the first time, Barbara noticed a gentle smile on Jones' face. "Tea would be splendid."

"Then please come in. Janice and I are working on the last of our morning tea and coffee out on the deck."

Jones' demeanor shifted as if she just remembered that a very senior FBI officer was in the equation. She stiffened and put on whatever she thought should be her game face for an interview with an FBI senior. Still, she walked in, up three steps in the entranceway and into the main living room that overlooked the lake. The morning sun was reflecting off the lake. Blue skies were already filled with chevrons of geese lifting off the lake and heading south. They knew it was nearly winter and time to go.

Janice walked over to Jones, coffee cup in her left hand, right hand extended and a smile on her face. "Special Agent Jones, it is good to meet you face to face."

"Yes, ma'am. After our previous conversation over the O'Connell case, I am happy to see that you are still willing to talk to me."

Barbara smiled as she thought about her first contact with Ellen Jones when Jones tried to play the "I'm in charge" card and had to be introduced "the sisterhood" of senior women in the intelligence community. It was a painful lesson for the new FBI special agent, but hopefully, Jones learned it wasn't personal.

"Ellen, we all learn through experience. I hope you and I can work together on this new case without any baggage."

"No, ma'am. I am good with working on this case."

"Excellent. Let's sit outside and talk about it."

Barbara arrived at the table with a tray with a new pot of coffee for Janice and a pot of Earl Gray tea for Jones and herself. She quickly "played mother" pouring out the coffee into Janice's cobalt blue mug and the tea into a white ceramic mug for Ellen. She topped off her cup of tea and said, "I don't take anything with my tea, but there is some sugar there if you like."

"No, thanks, Mrs. O'Connell."

"Barbara, please."

"Yes, ma'am."

Janice stole a glance at Barbara and gently rolled her eyes. Janice turned to Jones and said, "Let's start. First, while I know how FBI protocol works, here in Chez O'Connell and inside our circle of trust, we are going on a first-name basis. Does that work for you, Ellen?"

Ellen was clearly perplexed. She had received instructions directly from the Buffalo Special Agent in Charge or SAC to meet with an FBI senior at Barbara O'Connell's residence to work on the cyber case that started with identifying the repeater outside the house on the lake. Instead, she was being treated as an equal in what felt like a conspiracy. It made her uncomfortable and she wasn't entirely certain how to respond. She said, "Janice and Barbara, I need to know what we are up to before I join up."

"Fair enough, Ellen." Janice paused to look at Barbara who gave her a nod. "Let's start with why we are here."

Barbara stood up, walked back into the living room and over to the radio. It took a minute for the tubes in the back to warm up. Barbara tuned the radio to the local classical station out of Buffalo. Baroque chamber music washed over the room and out the door at a volume that was just above a comfortable setting.

Janice continued, "First off, apologies for the music. Barbara hasn't had a chance to hire a TSCM sweep yet."

"And that is needed?"

Janice shrugged her shoulders and said, "At this point, we don't know."

Ellen said, "And we are doing this here instead of the field office because…?"

Janice said, "Because the only thing we know for sure is that some if not all of the IC communications networks could be compromised.

If that is the case, then our Quantico tech specialists have told me that it is just possible to turn about any piece of electronics into a surveillance system. You will notice that Barbara's place is not exactly a technology hub."

Barbara decided to answer, "I have a laptop and a printer!"

"Which I noticed last night is not visible anywhere. In the closet? In a concealment somewhere?"

"That would be telling."

Ellen Jones was not used to this type of back-and-forth banter. She came directly from academia into the FBI and as a first-tour agent, her engagement with colleagues and especially with supervisors was always under scrutiny. She kept herself to herself. She decided it was time to ask some hard questions. Her voice revealed the tentative nature of her commitment to this special project as partially described by her squad supervisor. "Can I ask a direct question?"

Barbara was still in a slightly playful mood so she answered, "Of course. You can't expect a direct answer though."

Janice shook her head. She said, "OK, so ignore our Agency colleague for a moment…"

"Retired Agency."

Janice looked across the table at Barbara and said, "Whatever." She turned to Ellen and said, "Your investigation into Thorpe raised more questions than answers. I asked your SAC and SSA Chason if you could help on a nationwide CI project. They were kind enough to say yes. So, here we are." Janice raised her hands pointing to the deck, the blue sky, and Chautauqua Lake. "Now, before I go into the details of the plan, I think Barbara would benefit from details of your investigation into Army Special Agent Thorpe."

Ellen nodded and pulled out a notebook from her jacket. She flipped to a bookmarked page and started, "Army Criminal Investigation Command Special Agent William Andrew Thorpe. Born 04 June 1965, Wiesbaden, West Germany. Father was an Army helicopter pilot with a stay-at-home wife and one child. They moved four times and settled at Ft. Knox, Kentucky for Thorpe's high school years. Thorpe joined the army in 1987 after two years of college at

Eastern Kentucky University. He started as a military police officer and transferred into the Criminal Investigation Command in 1990. After attending the Army schools, he served in Germany from 1990 to 2001, as a Special Agent. Reassigned to an Army force protection at Bagram Airbase in Afghanistan in 2002. He returned to the US in 2003 and took the job as the Chief CIC investigator at the Seneca Army Depot at the Army Cyber Center. Basically, he has had a pretty quiet career. Not a lot of success as a CIC investigator. In fact, no success based on the Army CIC records. He was careful in Afghanistan to focus on the internal threat from the Afghan direct hires at the base. It meant he didn't travel much outside the wire. I suppose that makes sense if your job is to protect the largest US base in country, but I know of friends involved in Army force protection who were deployed to various forward operating bases. Not a great career, but no problem areas identified either. He started as a chief warrant officer one and after twenty years he is now a chief warrant officer three."

Barbara followed the details as she thought of her daughter who was a CW3 after about ten years in the service. Of course, she had opted for SOF and specialized MI training and had been severely wounded in combat, but still twenty years and only two promotions seemed a little slow even by Army standards. She said, "Ellen, what raised your suspicions?"

Ellen looked up from the notebook. She took a moment to decide what she was going to say as if determining what, if anything, Barbara O'Connell needed to know. Eventually, she relented and said, "Barbara, the fact that we couldn't find any legal justification in the system for their trip to your house started me down a path looking for anomalies throughout Thorpe's career. I noticed that his cases in Germany focused primarily on building source networks that were not linked to any specific criminal investigations. I contacted a couple of his former supervisors who were all retired. They said that Thorpe seemed to them to be a guy coasting along rather than really working hard."

"They found that odd because in their experiences, the guys in

CIC of the Army during the early days of German unification and then the fall of the Soviet Union were usually really hard chargers. There were former Stasi agents trying their hands at criminal enterprises, established Russian mafia networks trying to steal US equipment as our bases closed, and there were lots of GIs who were trying to make a fortune selling military equipment, including weapons and ammunition, to some of these same villains. Thorpe never seemed much interested in those cases. No one could figure out why." Ellen paused to take a drink of her tea.

Barbara looked at her and said, "A warm up?"

"No, thanks." Another sip.

Janice finally said, "Ellen, I know the value of a dramatic pause, but please stop hiding the lead. Tell Barbara why Thorpe is now a target of our investigation."

"Sorry, I just thought background was useful."

Barbara decided a little encouragement was always a good thing in a debriefing, so she said, "And I needed that background. What's the key?"

"Based on the fact that Thorpe lied to us about why he was interested in this property and in general about why he mobilized a team to go after a location when it would have been very clear to any federal investigator that there was no Shotkin at this residence, in fact no Shotkin in all of western New York State. That made me wonder what could possibly be the predication for the raid. I looked a little harder at Thorpe's federal connections. He had no known contact with the FBI, but he did have a contact with the Agency Counterintelligence Center."

Barbara said, "Czyneski."

"Yes. Buried deep in some files from 2002 and while Thorpe was in Afghanistan, I found multiple email chains between Czyneski and Thorpe. All referring to investigations that on the surface look normal but had no Agency, FBI or even Army file numbers. I figured this was some sort of open code communication between these two men. Based on this connection, I was able to get a warrant to look at his bank accounts. Thorpe has many of them. He has a bank account in Geneva, NY which is where his Army pay goes. He has a bank account in Delaware which receives regular electronic deposits. And the Delaware bank automatically sends funds offshore to an account in Berlin which he appears to have opened in 1991 as a joint account with a German citizen, Hilda Schmidt."

"Also, he has disguised the accounts using different versions of his name linked to different addresses in the US. He avoided any Treasury scrutiny because he always used his true social security number. He hasn't reported any of these accounts on his periodic security reinvestigations. The deposits and EFTs to the offshore account were always in different increments and well under the maximum limit of $10,000 so they didn't come up on any Treasury checks. So far, we haven't linked these accounts to anything specifically illegal, but his actions are certainly suspicious for an Army criminal investigator. Best guess is that Thorpe has been receiving regular payments from someone for something for about ten years that he wants to hide from his organization and from the USG. Of course, the German account will be hard to investigate unless we engage INTERPOL and, for right now, we don't want to do that and show our hand to anyone who might be protecting Thorpe."

Barbara shook her head and said, "Damn. And if I hadn't come home when I did, he would have been wandering around this house. If he knew the repeater was outside the house, what was he looking for inside the house?"

Ellen said, "What indeed?"

Janice said, "Or what did he want to place inside the house under the cover of a federal raid? That is what this operation is going to find out."

Barbara shook her head and said, "I'm really not going to like this, am I?"

Ellen smiled and said in a stage whisper, "I already don't like this."

Janice smiled at her new partners and said, "Think of it as an opportunity to excel!"

Over dinner, Janice explained her plan. Jones would reach out to Thorpe and tell him that the Buffalo Field Office had no further interest in the parasite because they determined it was an old and dead piece of technology. There was no way to move forward on the project. Ellen's job was to make that as convincing as possible. Once that happened, Barbara was to be on alert. Janice expected Thorpe to have very specific instructions to recover the device and, perhaps do something inside the house. What no one knew at this point was whether he had other instructions related to the Chautauqua House or Barbara O'Connell. That was the most complicated aspect of the operation. Janice was confident that Ellen could draw Thorpe out, but would he just sneak in and recover the parasite or did he have other instructions? It would be up to Barbara to keep watch and stay safe during that part of the operation.

Once Thorpe recovered the device, the FBI would surveil Thorpe looking for his handler or co-conspirator. Janice presumed was a Russian sleeper agent operating somewhere in central New York. This part of the operation was classic counterintelligence work. Find the target, surveil the target, identify the handler, and, ideally, catch the target and the handler together.

Janice said she wanted Ellen and her supervisor Chason to focus on that part of the equation. Not as easy as it might sound because the surveillance bubble would have to be loose enough that Thorpe would enter and leave Chautauqua thinking he was surveillance-free, while tight enough that the team would not lose him regardless of the direction he went. Janice said she intended to travel on Monday morning to the Buffalo field office to reinforce the importance of the program. In advance of that trip, she offered Ellen a sealed envelope with a set of written instructions to pass to her SAC and Chason. Janice said the documents were requesting this assistance and a request to keep the entire project, code named *Silicon Addiction*, off any FBI servers.

Ellen couldn't help herself. She looked at the two women who were past her mother's age. They seemed so...matronly. And yet they were talking about actions that seemed closer to what you might expect in 1950s film noir. She said, "I have no problem being a part of this operation, but why don't we just roll on Thorpe now and get him to tell all. After all, he must have some plans for the future and those plans probably don't include spending time in a supermax prison."

Janice nodded and said, "In a normal espionage case, that's exactly what we would do. But, Ellen, this is a different world we are dealing with now. It is a multi-faceted cyber case. Quantico cyber teams are looking at a number of hostile, redundant systems. They have told me that many of these systems are semi-autonomous. I'm not certain what that means exactly, but they have said to me that if we just shut down Thorpe, we wouldn't find some of the parasites running on servers inside the Intelligence Community or the Defense Department. We need to play this out for as long as possible so that the cyber warriors involved in this case can build a better picture of the entire network."

Janice paused and drank the last of her coffee. She said, "Think of this as a complex white-collar crime operation. If you just get one of the villains and don't know the network, by the time you get him to roll on the enterprise, the villains will have had time to make their cash and possibly themselves disappear. It is even more complicated when you are talking about software and digital memory across multiple continents. We need Thorpe in play for as long as possible before we throw cuffs on him. That gives your cyber squad and the Quantico team time to build up an electronic surveillance record that helps us understand the entire enterprise. Make sense now?"

Ellen realized that arguing with a unit supervisor from FBI headquarters was not wise. She might not agree with the program, but if Janice Macintosh was in charge and her SAC and Chason were on board, then there was nothing sensible about making a fuss. She put on her most sincere face and said, "Got it. I'll make sure I deliver the material and look forward to seeing you tomorrow."

Janice closed by saying, "As part of this operation, we had to agree to Army Counterintelligence participation. I didn't have a choice on that, but I did have a choice on who. I read about a DoD cyber operation in Northern California. Totally separate operation but with some of the same Russian connections. The CI special agent, a guy named Jasper Derry, will be monitoring the case from California. As we get closer to an arrest, he will fly to Buffalo and work with you and Chason. Ellen, when that happens, I would appreciate it if you would pick him up, introduce him to your SAC and Chason and then bring him down here to meet Barbara."

Ellen wasn't thrilled with the idea of adding yet another person to what she could only call a conspiracy of seniors. And, worse still, an Army guy with a hick first name like Jasper sounded like a real treat. However, that part of the operation might not ever happen if she had anything to do with the program. She could keep him on the West Coast for some time while she sorted out what should be done in this case, her case. That said, Ellen understood that no matter how collegial Janice had been over the past two hours, she was still a very senior FBI supervisor and she had just delivered a very polite order. She said, "Absolutely."

Barbara stood up and said, "Excellent. So, do we start making dinner or start drinking wine or both?"

Ellen stood up and said, "I will leave the evening to you two. I need to get back to my apartment."

Barbara smiled and said, "And your cat."

Ellen said, "You remembered! Yes, I need to get back to my cat."

As Barbara and Janice watched Ellen Jones get into her Mustang and drive away, Janice said, "She isn't on board, is she?"

"Not even a little bit, dear. But, she is ambitious enough to know that swimming upstream on this project is a bad idea. We'll get her on board as things develop. She sees this as her big case. Of that, I am absolutely certain."

Janice was quiet for a moment. She wasn't sure if she needed to tell Barbara that Derry and her daughter were...something. Instead, she said, "So, did you say wine?"

"A well-chilled dry Riesling will be dandy, don't you think?"

RETURN TO AFGHANISTAN

F lash was once again in the sergeant major's office. She spent the first half hour explaining the events as they unfolded in the Black Sea. After their day of sabotage, Flash and her colleagues returned to the yali. On arrival, Doug turned on a radio that looked like a relic from some World War II ship and contacted what he called "colleagues" at the Turkish Coast Guard Command. He reported seeing what looked to him like a sea mine floating in the waters just off the shipping lane entering the Bosporus. His contacts said they would mobilize an air search and then intercept whatever threat there might be.

Flash continued, "It was less than an hour later that we saw one of their helos racing out to the search area. Followed by a Coast Guard cutter. Fishman Doug and I sat on the deck of the yali watching as a second fast boat from the Turkish Navy followed about thirty minutes later. It wasn't long before we heard the explosion. I don't know if the Russians had anti-tampering explosives on their buoy or the Turks just blew it out of the water. Either way, it was nice to see a plan come together."

"Outstanding, Flash. And no international incident! I like the way you work. Do you think you could use your influence on your pal O'Connell and prevent further gunfights?"

"Jim, that is a pretty heavy lift. Especially since I'm here and Sue is in Afghanistan."

Massoni smiled and Flash knew she had fallen into his trap. "Well, if that's the case, we need to get you to Afghanistan as soon as possible. I hope you enjoyed the life of a pirate on the Black Sea. I suspect it won't be as...nice living in Jamie's world."

Flash knew she shouldn't say something rude or stick her tongue out at the sergeant major. She also knew that she had been the one who stepped willingly into his trap. All she could say was, "Check, Sergeant Major. When do I get there?"

Massoni smiled and said, "Well, it just so happens that the CG's bird is heading to Bagram the day after tomorrow. I might be able to get a seat on the bird if you can stand the luxury of a VIP jet."

Flash nodded and said, "I suppose that means I need to travel in a uniform."

Massoni used his most sarcastic tone, "Well yes, Flash, and I will expect you to salute all the seniors you see as well. You are still in the Army. I think a flight suit, boots and a beret will be good enough. Get your kit packed tonight just in case they change the schedule. We don't want REAL SUE to be the cause of any delays, do we?"

Flash was already at the door. She turned and said, "Nope." She was gone before the tennis ball Massoni threw at her hit the wall. She turned back to Massoni and smiled. She said, "By the way, Sergeant Major, what is the news from the boss out in Bahrain."

Massoni said, "The news is the boss is pissed and he is trapped on a Navy ship and can't get the answers he needs. He's hating life."

Flash said, "Just like us."

Massoni said, "Except we aren't trapped on a ship."

THIS AIN'T GONNA BE EASY

Ginger had never seen Smith angry. Smith was never friendly. He never seemed to get angry no matter what the circumstances. But now, Smith was angry. Actually, Smith was ballistic. He was pacing inside the safe room that the ship captain had set aside temporarily for the three HICU officers. When he and Smith arrived in Bahrain, they had initially set up in Sandy's small office at the embassy and they had stayed in the spare bedrooms in the townhouse that Sandy and his wife, Janet, and their toddler, Malcolm, had on the Bahraini economy. During the first month, they had scrubbed all of the records from 561, and explored all available information from the Navy and the embassy, as well as any technical intelligence they could get from DIA. They worked twelve-hour days trying to sort through facts, rumors and misinformation from these searches. They reviewed the case file on the murder of the Dubai-based volunteer. They met with anyone in the intel community in the region who might be able to help.

As October ended, Ginger grew progressively more nervous about how long he was going to be on this assignment. He had a stable of his own assets in Cyprus who were tracking Hizballah operations in the Eastern Mediterranean, as well as sources reporting on the rising threat of Sunni extremists in Libya. He knew that Smith was aware his cases were critical to the situational awareness that CG/SOF demanded. Ginger also knew that Smith wanted to solve the puzzle

143

of how 561 ended up trying to kill Sandy. Now it was November and Ginger needed to get back to Cyprus if he was going to make any of the meetings with his assets. They could only go on ice for so long before they stopped responding to any contact with their HICU handler.

Ten days ago, they had transited by helicopter to the *USS Iwo Jima* which was still on station in the Gulf. In those ten days, Sandy and Ginger and another squad of Marines had made four different attempts to meet with Sandy's other assets in various locations along the Dubai-Abu Dhabi highway. Normally, Sandy would just fly to Dubai, rent a car and roll out on the highway, hold the meeting, camp overnight somewhere in the desert, return the car and fly back to Dubai the next day. The pattern, except for the desert camp, was not inconsistent with the various Americans and Europeans that transited Dubai to hold business meetings. Smith had insisted that Sandy would not hold another "standard" meeting until they sorted out what had gone wrong. The captain of the *Iwo Jima* and the onboard Marine commander were more than happy to support a SOF mission, at least for the first two times. Unfortunately, they had made four trips and not seen a single agent. Two of Sandy's principal agents, file numbers 267 and 925, had not shown up for either their set meeting times or the backup meeting times. While he was waiting for Sandy and Ginger to return from their most recent foray into the desert, Smith received a "personal for" message in SOF channels. P4 messages were never a good sign because it meant a SOF senior wanted to send an "unvarnished" message to a subordinate. This message included a paragraph from CIA headquarters sent to the senior SOF intelligence officers or J2, an Army major general. The reports stated that Agency liaison with the UAE intelligence and security offices had identified four suspicious deaths in country in the previous four weeks. The intelligence community shared databases showed that two of the victims were registered as agents of HICU, one was registered as a force protection asset handled by NCIS, and one was registered as an Agency source. The J2 ended the P4 message by asking Smith to provide any details he could about the HICU cases.

After he received the message, Smith walked up to the command deck of the ship and politely asked the captain if it would be possible for the three HICU officers to get back to Bahrain on the next available resupply bird. The captain of the ship, a senior Navy captain who was nearing the end of his career, had treated Smith, an officer of equal rank from the Army, with courtesy throughout the ten days. He was done being polite. He said, "Colonel Smith, we have been pushing the envelope here with multiple insertions on the UAE coast. I had my orders to support your mission, but now we are done. My ship is returning to its Gulf patrol mission. Our next resupply mission will be an underway resupply ship-to-ship scheduled for tomorrow. I know that won't work for you. I will arrange one of my Ospreys to take you back to Bahrain, but you will have to wait a day or so while we sort out the mission profile. Will that work?"

Smith knew that the captain was not asking for agreement, he was just telling Smith what he was going to do. Smith smiled and offered his hand saying, "Captain, that will be great. Please let me know when that mission is set. In the meantime, I will be in our quarters working with my two men and staying out of the way. And, thanks again for your flexibility." As he left the command deck, Smith's temper was on a slow simmer. By the time he got back to their quarters, his temper was at a boil. When Sandy and Ginger returned from the latest unsuccessful mission, he exploded.

Smith's voice bounced around the metal walls in their quarters in what could only be described as parade-ground volume. "Gentlemen, what is going on? I am asking you as politely as I can, because I leave profanity to my sergeant major. I want to know what is going on!" He slammed his hand on the P4 message that was sitting in the middle of the table that served as their work station. "The J2 wants to know why two of our assets are dead in the UAE. Of course, the J2 already knows about the dead volunteer earlier this year and the death of 561, so the reality is that we have three dead assets and one dead volunteer." He took a breath and said in a menacing, but much quieter voice, "Any thoughts?"

Ginger knew that Sandy was the target of Smith's anger, so for case officer solidarity he decided to take a stab at answering Smith's demand. "Sir, given the nature of Sandy's work here in the UAE and the fact that all three of these assets were killed within a short time period, I think it argues for a compromise of our communications rather than Sandy's tradecraft. After all, if his tradecraft was shit, the assets wouldn't have been killed all at once. They would have been killed over the space of months. Plus, the earlier murder of the volunteer, which had nothing to do with Sandy, argues that this is not something Sandy did or failed to do."

Sandy looked at Ginger and said, "Thanks, I guess."

Smith's temper storm had passed and he looked at his two case officers. He said, "If that is the case, it means our entire network is compromised. None of our assets, anywhere in theatre, are safe. And, it means none of your peers are safe. We are going to have to regroup and start from scratch."

Sandy queried, "From scratch? You mean rebuild the entire HICU network?"

Smith shook his head. He was imagining how hard it would be to start from scratch in Afghanistan and Iraq. He said, "I don't know the answer to that question. What I do know, Sandy, is you need to face the fact that all of your assets in the UAE have been killed. No telling how long your assets in Bahrain will stay alive. Your mission for now is to warn your Bahrain assets, put them on ice, and then find out who killed your assets in the UAE. And, all the while keeping you and your family safe. Not easy, but easier than your colleagues in warzones. Ginger, you need to get back to Cyprus RFN. As soon as you get back, you need to do the same for your assets in Cyprus."

He turned back to the worktable and sat down. "Gentlemen, you need to leave me alone for a few minutes while I figure out how to reach out to our team without the use of any of our standard communications. We leave on the next Osprey heading to Bahrain. That isn't for a couple of days. We have worn out our welcome on the *Iwo Jima*. I don't blame the skipper a bit. He needs to do his own mission before he ferries us back to dry land. For now, imagine that we could be tasked to get out anytime from now until a week from now."

Sandy and Ginger walked over to the bunks against the far wall and sat down on the lower bunk. Ginger whispered to Sandy, "This ain't gonna be easy, cuz."

"No shit, Sherlock," was all Sandy whispered back.

TEA IN THE PAMIRS

lash arrived at Bagram Airbase in Afghanistan on 11 November. The only other time Flash had traveled on the CG's Gulfstream Jet had been two years ago when the HICU team traveled to Afghanistan to find and free a kidnapped SOF officer. That flight had been filled with dread, as none of the passengers on board knew for sure if their colleague was alive or dead. This time, Flash was simply another passenger, and per Jim Massoni's instructions, she made herself as invisible as possible. Invisible in a Flash way of course meant wearing a Nomex flight suit with a leather nametag that identified her as Sarah Billings with the rank of CW3. She found a seat as far away from the seniors as possible on the small aircraft, put on a set of headphones, opened her computer and worked. She hoped that none of the seniors would ask the hard questions related to the security problems at HICU or what her mission might be in Afghanistan. After a few hours flight, Flash fell asleep and did not wake until the aircraft banked over the Hindu Kush mountains and headed into Bagram.

Massoni had pulled some strings inside the sergeants major network and Flash was on the ground for less than thirty minutes when a German Air Force officer pulled up in a Mercedes Gelandewagen SUV and took her to a twin-engine Dornier headed to Mazar-e-Sharif. She sat in the back of the aircraft filled with German officers traveling together to German Army headquarters in Mazar-e-Sharif.

They didn't want to talk to her and she was unwilling to unleash her less than perfect German on her hosts. The German Air Force aircraft landed in Mazar-e-Sharif just as the sun was setting to the west. Flash had been in Afghanistan on multiple TDYs but mostly working out of the SOF headquarters in Bagram. This was only the second time she had flown into Mazar-e-Sharif and the first time that she was in an aircraft with real windows rather than a cargo aircraft with small portholes. She watched as her aircraft climbed over the snow-capped range of the Hindu Kush and then settled into a more sensible altitude of 10,000 feet over the plains of Samangan and Balkh provinces. Afghanistan rarely seemed inviting, but in November and already in the grip of winter, the land below looked bleak.

When the aircraft landed, Sue was waiting for her in one of a dozen four-door Toyota pickups running back and forth along the taxiways and hangars of the airfield. Sue had been in country for nearly two weeks with a basic set of orders: work with their CIA counterpart to disrupt by any means necessary the cyber operation in Tajikistan. It was nothing more than a vague outline of a mission when she arrived. By the end of two weeks, it wasn't more developed.

"So, how was the visit with Fishman?"

"It was exceptionally productive. No gunfights, no exploding ships, no nuclear waste. A small bit of det cord and a lovely evening with some of your SBS pals. Do you think the lack of drama might be because there was no O'Connell?"

"Cute. We have a bit of a drive, why don't you entertain me with the tale."

Flash's recounting of the Black Sea operation took nearly an hour, and ended with a question for Sue: "So, did you get anything accomplished?"

"I got a chance to look at the target location from a UAV shot that OGA took using one of their birds running along the border. And, I got a chance to watch Jamie at his best working the system to figure out how we are going to disrupt the Dushanbe end of this."

"Amusing?"

"Ever so much." Sue had to concentrate on her driving as she joined the convoys of cargo trucks headed north toward the Afghan-Uzbek border towns of Hairatan and Termez. Their Toyota was dwarfed by a mix of tractor-trailer trucks, flatbed trucks carrying shipping containers, and stake-bed trucks hauling Afghan produce and livestock. Periodically Sue would creep out to see if she could pass, only to be forced back when exactly the same sorts of trucks rushed by heading south.

After the third near miss, Flash commented, "I'm in no hurry to end up in a ditch."

"Chicken."

"Take your time and tell me what you know about this end of the project."

Sue settled in and accepted that they were going to travel at 30 mph for the rest of the trip. "It turns out Jamie knows a fair bit about cyber operations. He won't tell me much other than he worked on disrupting fiber optic transmissions in Iraq during Desert Storm in the early '90s."

"As a Klingon or one of us?"

"He didn't say, but I think as one of us working with OGA. He said he was sheep dipped as a detailee to OGA."

"Quaint."

"Anyhow, he has been in secure telephone dialogue with OGA headquarters deciding whether we want to disrupt or simply tap the cyber traffic. He said he was in contact with Melissa and her crew, so I guess that's a good thing."

"Since we really don't know who is running this show, I can see why he is thinking about making it an intelligence op first. Does he have any assets in play?"

"We are supposed to meet one tomorrow. We were waiting for you to arrive so you can join us in the meeting."

Flash laid on the sarcasm thick as she said, "Oh, how exciting."

"Hey, do you want to earn your TDY pay or not?"

"Flash is always ready to fight on the ramparts of democracy."

"Yup. That's what I told Jamie."

"And he said?"

"I think I will pass on what he said."

"Spoil sport."

Jamie was sitting in a swivel chair in the middle of the command-and-control room in the safe house. It was a "box within a box" plexiglass construction that filled what was probably a large dining room for the previous owner — an Afghan warlord/smuggler. The owner made the error of siding with the Taliban in the Spring of 2001 and by December 2001, he was no longer a warlord. Jamie hadn't said what happened to the owner. Sue assumed he was dead.

Normally, three of Jamie's team would have been in the room: watching feeds from Agency and military UAVs; monitoring intercepts from local smugglers telephones; and planning the next set of raids that they would conduct with help of the Afghan commando team that Jamie created in the past two years. Instead, the room was quiet and the computers were shut down. Jamie was looking at Sue and Flash.

"Flash, the geniuses in Headquarters told me to make sure your mission was successful. Nothing more. Really? As if it was too secret for me to know? Sue has already told me the target, so what's so secret?"

Flash smiled her most genuine smile, which only warned Sue that Flash's answer was going to be sarcastic. "It isn't too secret for you to know. Well, maybe it is. I may have to check."

After Jamie growled, Flash continued in a more polite manner, "Big Chief, it's too secret to put in regular communications because we don't know which of our communications have been compromised."

"Eh?"

"Remember the attack in Konar?"

"How could I forget. You two drove me out of house and home."

Flash said, "I wouldn't have called that home."

"I get nostalgic. OK, so this is a better place, but what does the Konar operation have to do with anything?"

"It turns out that one of the things that Beroslav gave us was a lead to a large compromise of both Agency and SOF communications. And, it turns out that one of the nodes, if not the major node of the compromise, is in Dushanbe."

"So, they didn't tell me anything more than to help because they were afraid it would end up on some server in Dushanbe."

Flash smiled and said, "And Massoni said you were dim."

"I'm not taking that bait, Flash. I know Massoni is not going to say that. He isn't smart enough to use the term dim. Coffee?"

"So, no hard feelings?"

"I didn't say that. I just asked if you wanted coffee." Jamie stood and walked to a table that served as their coffee and tea bar.

Flash nodded. Jet lag was starting to attack her brain and her bones. Sue walked over to Flash and said, "You know, we could wait until tomorrow."

Flash looked at her analog/digital dive watch. The analog face was set to Afghan time, the smaller, digital screen set to European time, GMT +1 and HICU headquarters. She said, "I am probably okay for another hour," she changed the volume from normal Flash loud to real loud, "BUT IT WOULD BE NICE TO HAVE SOME COFFEE."

Jamie sauntered over with a tray. There was a cup, a small French press, a sugar bowl and some milk. A small plate of tea biscuits completed the delivery. "It takes time to serve guests properly."

Flash started to laugh as he put the tray down next to her and handed her a paper napkin. She said, "No linen napkins?"

"We save them for VIPs."

Sue decided to jump in, "And we are?"

"Deadbeat cousins who have come to mooch and ask favors." He sat down in the swivel chair and turned to Sue. "Your tea is brewing up. So, don't feel neglected. And when you come back, can you bring me a cup of tea as well?"

Flash laughed and said, "I knew it was going to be fun working with you two again, I just didn't guess how much fun. Big fun. Jamie, let me bring you up to speed on what we know, what we think, and the large gaps we don't understand at all."

"Sweet. I will take notes."

An hour later and a delivery of another cup of coffee for Flash, Jamie said, "So, what do you and the cyber gurus think we are we supposed to do? Blow up the building?"

Flash answered, "I suspect that's Sue's plan. I reckon it was just her way of asking 'why don't we just use a drone and a couple of hellfire missiles?'"

Sue replied, "Sounded good to me."

Jamie interceded in this ongoing feud. He said, "Subtle it is not. Plus, we really don't want to declare war on both Tajikistan and the Russian Federation. And, based on what you just said, we don't know for sure that it is the Russians."

Flash looked at Jamie as if he had just said the earth was flat. "Really? You don't think it is a Russian operation?"

Jamie said, "What I think is that it is probably a Russian operation using a Private Military Contractor as cover. But that's just what I think. You said part of the story is focused on an IRGC collection operation and that you guys have lost several assets that were reporting on the IRGC. Plus, in case you are interested, the IRGC has had a presence in Dushanbe going back to the early days of Tajik independence from the USSR. So, before we all assume we know something, don't you think we might consider alternative scenarios. For example, maybe the PMC in Dushanbe is working for themselves and the Iranians are paying for a product?"

For a change, Sue realized that Flash was the one who had jumped the gun. She said, "Flash, what say you to the Klingon's argument?"

Flash sat back in her chair and finished her coffee. She put the mug down on the tray and said, "Flash says it is time to sleep. I need a clear head to work through Jamie's argument."

Jamie nodded and said, "Take any open room, Flash. We'll see you bright and early for PT and then breakfast. Set that fancy watch alarm for 0600hrs local and we'll get you properly set on this time zone." For once, Jamie's smile reminded both Sue and Flash of Jim Massoni. It was friendly with just a slight edge of menace. Flash nodded and left the room.

Jamie turned to Sue and said, "All I'm saying is that we might want to do some spying before we decide to do some sabotage."

Sue said, "I'm not arguing at all. I'm just amazed because I've never seen anyone outsmart Flash."

"It helps that she was jet lagged."

"So, you decided to pick on her when she was weak."

"I've made a successful career of picking on the weak. Don't knock it until you've tried it. Now, can I invite my guys back to work? We do have other responsibilities other than serving as your minions."

"But you are so good at being a minion."

"Don't confuse politeness with weakness."

"A quote from some Chinese scholar?"

"Just another Jamie quote. Ask the guys, I'm full of them."

Early the next morning, they sat outside on a patio drinking coffee and tea. The November sun filled the small courtyard. Jamie admitted he had taken on the challenge of serving as the safe house gardener and the area where they were sitting was surrounded by rose bushes and a marigold vine that crawled up the side of the house wall. A large Mulberry tree served as the only shade tree on the compound and, most probably, the only real shade tree in many miles. It was too late in the year to have flowers, but Sue could imagine what the patio might look like in the spring.

"The previous owner wanted something resembling a Persian garden and while I did my best to do him harm, I can appreciate his sensibilities. It takes a fair bit of water, but we have a deep well. So, I keep this little garden alive."

Flash looked up from her steaming coffee cup. "A gentleman barbarian, then?"

"Thank you."

Sue had been up for longer than the other two and was slightly impatient. She said, "It is a very pleasant place to plot and scheme. So, Jamie, what do you have in mind."

Flash looked at Sue. "Always the spoil sport. Just when I was beginning to absorb Jamie's Sufi vibes."

Jamie chuckled and said, "You two are like a married couple."

"I've learned traveling with Sue is always a joy."

Sue looked at Jamie and said, "See?"

"OK, so back to work. Here's what I have in mind. I have a smuggling asset who runs across the Afghan border to both Uzbekistan and Tajikistan. Mostly bringing cheap Russian and Chinese trade goods into Afghanistan avoiding the customs duties at Termez. He might even smuggle the occasional case of liquor for some of the Afghan mullahs who wouldn't want to be accused of hypocrisy."

Flash smiled and said, "And who would? Plus, it just might give a Klingon some leverage."

"Perhaps. But, that's another story. My guy is familiar with the Russian military presence in Dushanbe as well as the Iranian Embassy. It seems that even Iranian diplomats have a taste for vodka. Who knew?"

"So, that's the guy we are meeting tonight?"

"Right. His code name is *TIMESHARE*, he goes by Aziz and he knows me as Baradar Peter. We can meet him tonight...well, zero dark thirty tomorrow, debrief him and even task him to get us more information on Dushanbe."

"Oh, take me, take me," Flash said with her most sarcastic voice.

Jamie shook his head and continued, "Once we match that with our UAV imagery, we may have enough to figure out what we need to accomplish here. Hopefully, by Christmas."

Flash moaned and said, "I'm going to miss Christmas in Venice?"

"Brilliant operations take time. By the way, you don't get to join us."

"What?"

"Well, you can join us virtually since we will be sending a sound feed back here, but there isn't a good reason to expose you to *TIME-SHARE*. Just sayin'."

Flash offered her best pout.

Sue said, "Well, let's see what we can get from *TIMESHARE* before we lament a Christmas in this outpost of democracy." Jamie said, "I do have a Christmas tree. Haven't planned for you, so no stockings for Flash and Sue, but you never know what Santa Claus might bring."

Sue shook her head and said, "OK, so what's the meeting plan?"

"It's a rural meeting on the Afghan-Tajik border. We drive to the site and wait. He arrives, we talk, we go home."

Sue nodded.

Flash said, "Swell. So, I have a live feed? Can I give Sue prompts?"

Jamie said, "Sure. You speak Dari?"

Flash said, "Not in my job description. I do speak Russian in case that helps."

"Not much. *TIMESHARE's* Russian is about as good as my Chinese."

"Which is...?"

"Not much more than greetings and an apology for not speaking Chinese. I've always wondered if Massoni taught me those two phrases just to get me into trouble."

"Count on it," was all Flash said.

QUOTES FROM A SUFI SCHOLAR

Sue and Jamie left the compound just as the sun was setting on the mountains to the southwest. The mountains were already snow-capped, so the last few minutes before the sun dipped behind them, they glowed blood red. Sue wondered if that was some sort of omen.

Her travels to Afghanistan had been filled with danger. She lost her leg in Jalalabad. She and Jamie were attacked by a Russian PMC in the Konar and narco-traffickers tried to kill them in an ambush on the streets of Hairatan. It wasn't as if Sue thought often about omens or luck — good or bad. She lived in a world where you made your own luck through skills and situational awareness. Still, she had been in combat enough to know that the first person killed usually dies before even realizing he is in a gunfight or a minefield.

She looked over at Jamie. He was Massoni's age. A full SF career and now years working for OGA. During her travels with him over the past two years, she had seen that his level of preparation and care was as good if not better than most SOF operators. Still, there was always that first time. That thought created a hollow in her stomach. She took a few deep breaths to wash away the concern.

"Don't worry, Sue. We aren't going into this meeting on our own."

"Eh?"

"I could feel that concern. It's just one of my superpowers."

"And what do your superpowers say?"

"That you never know when your time is up."

Sue was surprised that Jamie had captured her thoughts in one sentence. She said, "And that's the truth."

"Indeed, but you can make your own luck. Plan for the worst-case scenario and then plan for an even worse case than that scenario. Then, get the resources you need to keep yourself alive. Don't trust anyone's plan but your own. It's not rocket science."

Sue smiled and said, "You are starting to sound like Massoni."

"Well, I'll admit Massoni and I grew up together and learned the same lessons."

"Where and when?"

"Here and there and a long time ago."

Sue felt that door shut. Gently perhaps, but shut.

Jamie said, "Now, first we are going to review what you already know and then we'll review what you don't know and I didn't say inside the compound because...well, you were the one who said we had an OPSEC problem. So, here are the details." Jamie turned on the CD player. The speakers in the armored Ford Ranger offered a strange mix of what sounded like a roomful of people all talking at once. "It's a mumble tape I got from an audiologist. They use it to test hearing aids, but it also makes any audio surveillance super difficult."

Sue realized once again that Jamie operated at a different level than any tradecraft she was taught at the Farm. She said, "Clever."

"Keep smart, learn new things, stay alive." Jamie looked at her and smiled his most friendly smile. It looked to Sue more like what she imagined from the Cheshire Cat in *Alice in Wonderland.* "So, we are going to drive south on the Mazar-Hairatan highway for about ten miles and then head east on a track. Not a high-speed motorway, but it cuts across to the highway that runs north out of Kholm. We meet up with our escort there. We turn north toward the Afghan-Tajik border and meet *TIMESHARE* about 20km south of the border. We should be there around 2330hrs and the meeting is set for 0030hrs. I meet him on a ridge line."

"Our escorts are the Tomahawks?"

Another Cheshire Cat smile. "Learning quickly, young Sue. Two trucks of Tomahawks who will precede us to the meeting site, set up and be ready to kill anyone other than *TIMESHARE.* "

"Not a technique they teach at the Farm."

"They teach the principles of meeting security. This technique might not be taught at the Farm, but it certainly is consistent with the principles of meeting security."

"It doesn't hurt that you have your own mercenary army."

"It never hurts to have a mercenary army. You should know that from your grandfather's stories."

This comment caught Sue completely unawares. She had never mentioned her grandfather and had no idea that Jamie even knew about her family history. She said, "What is that supposed to mean?"

"Long before I went to the Farm, I attended a number of different Army Special Warfare schools. They actually give you time to read stuff in those schools, unlike the Farm, and I found archival material about OSS operations in Europe and in Asia. One of the more interesting ones was a mention in one report of this Major Peter O'Connell and his small band of Shan tribal mercenaries who operated in Northern Thailand. The file focused more on the Free Thai movement, but I decided to explore the Kachin story. Members of the OSS trained and ran Kachin Ranger units. They were made up of Burmese and Thai tribals. Most were used for strategic reconnaissance and some for classic guerrilla warfare. Major O'Connell used his band of Shan for more...shall we say...*personal* action against the Japanese. He also used those same bandits when he served in Laos over twenty years later. Old bandits at that point, but I suspect just as lethal."

"And when were you going to tell me about this family history?"

Jamie looked hurt. "I thought I just did. "

The truck rumbled off the road and started on a smooth dirt lane that quickly transitioned to a rutted track. Jamie was quiet for a half hour as he negotiated the rough track that once again transitioned into a smoother ride.

Sue was lost in her own thoughts. Every time she thought she had a grip on her family history, some unexpected revelation arrived. Her grandfather was kind to her and when he hosted Sue at his Potomac House, now her Potomac House, they shared their mutual interests of music, novels, and chess. It really wasn't until she joined the Army and started working in military intelligence that her parents revealed the full extent of the family connections to the intelligence community. Recently, her mother said that she found her grandfather's diaries in the Chautauqua house. Those diaries revealed history that even her mother never knew. Secrets seemed to be as common in her family as green eyes.

Jamie interrupted her thoughts. "We are finally back on a smuggler's road. It should be relatively smooth going until we meet up with the Tomahawks. However, please keep awake. I'm relying on you to track your side of the vehicle. Smuggler's road can mean ambush country as well."

Sue had her M4 loaded and on safe. Up until now, it had been barrel down between her legs. She shifted her left leg prosthesis, pulled the rifle up and angled it just slightly so that it would be easier to put into action if needed. Of course, in an armored vehicle, that would only happen if they were forced to dismount, but over the past few years, Sue learned that if her prosthesis could get in the way in a crisis, it would get in the way.

Jamie continued, "So, *TIMESHARE's* standard tasking is on Iranian and Russian activities on the border. He has reported on IRGC al-Qods running a safe house on the south side of Dushanbe near the airport and a Russian private military compound outside of the Tajik military airbase that the Tajiks share with a battalion of Russian VDV."

Sue nodded. She wasn't surprised that al Qods, the IRGC special forces, were in Tajikistan. Al Qods forces were the core trainers for Lebanese Hizballah, Palestinian terrorists, and Shia dissidents in the Gulf States. The Russian airborne unit — VDV stood for

Vozdushno Desantnye Voyska or air landing force — was probably a quick reaction force for any Russian base in Tajikistan. Given the North-South unrest that had plagued the country since independence from the USSR and the regular border skirmishes between Tajikistan and Uzbekistan, a QRF would be very useful to protect Russian interests.

Jamie continued, "I meet *TIMESHARE* once a month and he delivers two or three intels per month on the activities of these various organizations. He smuggles contraband into Tajikistan for the Russians and smuggles Russian consumer products into Afghanistan." Jamie laughed, "You haven't seen kitchen products until you've seen an old Soviet microwave. Definitely scary."

Jamie stopped his discussion as he slowed to negotiate a switchback on a sand dune. He said, "As we come over the top here, we should see the Tomahawk signal. One long dash from a red-filter flashlight about a mile to our front. T in Morse code. Reply with J using the SureFire with the blue filter. They do still teach Morse code, right?"

Sue didn't want to admit to Jamie that she had never received any Morse code training either in SOF or at the Farm. Still, one relic of her time with her grandfather was her memory of the Morse code alphabet. It was one of those curious pastimes at the Potomac House. Sue wondered if even then he was preparing her for a life of secrets.

As they crested the hill, about a mile to their east, a red filter flashlight flashed one dash. Once the signal repeated, Sue replied with a dot and three dashes. When she repeated the signal, the red filter replied with dot dash dot twice.

Jamie said, "They just sent Roger Roger. Long range recognition completed." The road smoothed, Jamie downshifted and accelerated toward the linkup.

Once they arrived at the rendezvous, Jamie got out of the Ranger and greeted each of the Tomahawks with a bear hug. As they offered him tea, Jamie shouted at Sue, "Come, join my people. We must have tea!"

The Tomahawks were Afghan Shia trained by Jamie in the early days of the war in Afghanistan. As the war became more focused on conventional force-on-force between the US troops and the Taliban, Jamie convinced Kabul station that there would always be a benefit in a small force of well-trained guerrillas, especially guerrillas who had lost homes and family during the Taliban ethnic cleansing and genocide of the North from 1999-2001. Most were young men who had no ties to any family. The Tomahawks became their family and Jamie was their surrogate father. Sue witnessed their loyalty when they worked in the Konar together to save Chief Jameson and when they worked the previous year to disrupt narco-traffickers and human smugglers operating out of Termez. If the Tomahawks were involved, Sue was confident they could handle any trouble short of a B52 attack.

They sat on the ridge line in the dark. Jamie used the time to brew up tea and pour it into a thermos. One hundred yards away, the Tomahawks watched for any threats. In the darkness, they were completely invisible in their hide locations. Sue thought that many of her SOF colleagues would be hard pressed to match their hide skills or their silence. Jamie had a large night-vision scope mounted on a tripod as he watched for the arrival of his asset. Sue looked at the luminous dial on her dive watch. It was just past midnight.

Jamie whispered, "I know. He's late. He's always late. His alternate is 0100hrs. He almost always splits the difference and arrives at 0045hrs. Patience, grasshopper."

Sue smiled at the reference to a long-ago TV show. Jamie and Massoni were cut from the same mold, but Massoni had to maintain some degree of formality as the unit sergeant major. Jamie had none of those restrictions and that meant he could be as rude or as kind to her as he chose to be. So far, the mix was in Sue's favor.

As Jamie predicted, at 0040hrs they watched as the moonlight caught a Soviet era Lada sedan arrive and a single figure exit a vehicle. He started walking toward the ridge line. Sue noticed he walked with a distinct limp favoring his right leg.

Jamie whispered, "Imprisoned by the Russians during the Tajik Civil War, released and then tortured by the Iranians working with the Islamist revolutionaries. They thought he was a Russian stooge. The man has a serious bag of hate for both."

At *TIMESHARE* approached, Jamie stood up and greeted his source in Dari. "Dust-e-Aziz. Greetings!"

In the moonlight, Sue could see a smile break on *TIMESHARE's* face. Then he saw Sue and frowned. "Another person, Pieyter. I don't like it."

Jamie said, "My friend, this is my little sister Mariam. She and I work together sometimes. The Russians killed her family. She hates them."

TIMESHARE smiled again. "Mariam, I know we will be friends. Shared hatred makes good friends."

Sue nodded and spoke a Persian couplet, "You who blame injustice on mankind, it is but an image of your own dark mind."

TIMESHARE laughed, "An ally and a scholar of Jalaluddin Rumi! Our enemies have no chance."

Jamie nodded and said, "So, my friend. Sit and have some tea. We have much to talk about tonight."

Sue expected the meeting to proceed slowly, but not as slowly as it developed. Jamie and *TIMESHARE* focused nearly the entire first hour on the weather, family — which in Jamie's case was entirely fictitious — and poetry. Sue had little to offer in any of the three categories. She watched as Jamie demonstrated why he was such a good case officer. He showed interest in *TIMESHARE's* life, asked questions that demonstrated to his source that he remembered previous personal stories, and generally worked hard to make the relationship more personal than professional. Sue wondered if she would ever become as good at the trade. She had heard over and over again that both her mother and her father were very good at agent handling. As she looked back on her own experience since graduating from the Farm, Sue thought her work in a post 9/11 counterterrorism world left little time for the sort of care that Jamie used. Still, here they were working on the side of a sand dune spending time talking about family. Sue decided then and there that she would work harder at the trade if she ever got another chance to be just an agent runner assigned PCS somewhere.

When the thermos was almost empty, Jamie switched to business mode. "My friend, what do you know about the Russian mercenaries living near the airbase?"

TIMESHARE paused and took a sip of tea. "This is the first time you have asked that question, Pieyter. It is interesting because in my reports I have written out for you, I mention these mercenaries. They are a curious group, even for Russians. I found out about them earlier this month and decided to put one of my men outside their walled compound to watch what they do. They never seem to go outside their walls. I thought there might be some business there, but they don't seem to want anything from my salesmen. The Russians on the airbase are always asking for something: fresh fruits and vegetables, carpets, vodka, hashish, even women. The VDV troops and, I think, some of the mercenaries travel back and forth every day by helicopter to some part of the country and return at night. The Russians living in the compound near the airbase are exactly the opposite. They never answer our queries at their gate. Most strange."

"Am I right they are Russians?"

"Oh, truly they are Russians and they are definitely mercenaries. They have a company name on the gate. In Cyrillic it says *SWORD-FISH* and it has a picture of some sea creature. Their only visitors are the mercenaries from the airfield. Well, not their *only* visitors." *TIMESHARE* smiled with his mouth of broken teeth.

Sue decided to join the conversation, "Uncle, you have a joke for us?"

He said, "I just find it curious that at least once a week, my man reports that a car from the Iranian Embassy visits the compound. What business could the Iranians have with these Russians who live inside all day? And, if it is a secret, why drive an embassy car to the compound?"

Jamie said, "What business indeed?"

TIMESHARE said, "Do you think they are making poisons to kill Tajiks?"

Sue said, "Uncle, does the building look like a chemical factory?"

"No, it does not. But it has no windows. Just a metal building surrounded by a dirt wall with barbed wire on top of the wall. What could be so valuable that you have to protect it with no windows? That is why I think they are making poisons."

Jamie countered, "Would they truly share poisons with the Iranians?"

"No, Pieyter. That is why they are so strange. What is it?"

Sue was about to push the conversation toward their real interest. A hard look from Jamie stopped her just after she said, "Uncle..."

TIMESHARE looked her way. "Yes, sister...?"

Sue decided to change her approach. "Do you think your man is in danger from these men?"

TIMESHARE laughed and said, "My man looks like a Sufi beggar. In fact, he is a Sufi beggar. Everyone knows him. They think he is witless. Only I know he is not."

Jamie offered, "Mariam is simply concerned because she knows what Russians can do."

"As do I, Pieyter. Now, do you want to know more about them?"

"I do, my friend. But most of all, I want to know why the Iranians visit."

"Ah, that is too easy for me. I will simply ask them."

"Ask them?"

"You know my Iranian contacts like my deliveries of vodka. I will just ask them why they are going to the Russians. I will make it sound like I am worried they are buying their vodka there. I will warn them that the Russians will not keep their secrets." *TIMESHARE* broke into a laugh that sounded more like a cackle to Sue.

Jamie let out a guffaw slapped him on the back and said, "That is a good joke, Aziz. Yes, please ask them. Can we meet again after you ask them?"

"Why not? I meet them this week. Shall we meet again on Friday night? I will have an answer for you. Of course, you know it will be a Persian answer. We both know..."

Jamie completed the sentence, "Somewhere in the answer may be the truth. We just will have to decide where the truth hides inside the lies."

TIMESHARE stood up. He rubbed his right leg as he straightened up. He said, "It is time for me to go, my friends. I will see you on Friday."

Both Jamie and Sue stood up and said, "Inshallah. Remain safe."

TIMESHARE smiled. He rubbed his leg again and turned toward his car. Before he left, he said, "I learned my lesson years ago, Pieyter. I know how to stay safe."

WHAT'S NEXT?

After the meeting in the desert, Jamie and Sue and their Tomahawk escorts drove back along the smuggler's trail until they reached the main Hairatan highway. At that point, the two Tomahawk pickup trucks flashed their lights and turned back toward their nearby compound. Sue was behind the wheel as they rolled into the safe house compound just as the sun was coming up. They dumped their gear in the ops center and headed up to their respective rooms for a shower and some sleep.

By 1400hrs, they were back in the ops center with a very frustrated Flash. Based on the high risk of compromise in their communications, the only thing Flash had worked all morning was a set of maps and scale drawings of the suspected PMC location. Important, painstaking work, but agonizingly slow compared to her usual pace.

"So, what happened? What do we know?" It was early afternoon and Flash was nearly standing on tip-toes waiting to hear about the previous night's meeting.

"Flash, *TIMESHARE* liked Sue."

"Dandy, what else?"

"Sheesh, will you let it go already? I'm working on translating his notes and putting them on paper. I thought Sue was in the impatient one, but you are really a peach."

Sue jumped into this back and forth. "I don't think I ever used that description."

Jamie was sitting at one of the long tables in the center looking over pages of *TIMESHARE*'s reports. Next to him was a pair of dic-

tionaries, a Dari-English dictionary and a second Tajik-English dictionary that according to its cover had originally been a Russian-Tajik
dictionary then translated to English by the Russian instructors at
DLI. Jamie had a pair of reading glasses perched precariously on
the end of his nose and a cup of tea near his left hand. He looked up
again and said, "OK, Flash. You want to help, how about translating
some of these Russian phrases."

"They are written in some oddball script."

"Yup. That's what you get when you have a guy who grew up
in the Soviet Union education system, was taught both Russian and
Tajik in Cyrillic and now writes in Persian script. So, you can help,
or..."

Sue jumped in, "Or, you can debrief me on what *TIMESHARE*
said. I think we can accomplish that outside and leave Mr. Grumpy
to his translation."

Jamie growled. That was enough of an instruction for both Flash
and Sue to fill their mugs and head out to the patio.

An hour later, they peered into the ops center to see if Jamie was
done deciphering the written reports. Apparently, he had completed
his tasks because he was wandering around the ops center offering
annoying guidance to the rest of his team. Since he seemed in better
humor, Sue opened the door and asked, "Is it safe to come in?"

All three of Jamie's officers looked up and said "NO!"

Jamie turned and said, "They just don't like direct supervision.
Let's leave them to their work. We can go outside and I will tell you
what *TIMESHARE*'s reports said. Of course, it all starts with my brilliant ability to decipher his chicken scratching."

Sue offered, "Tea for the brilliant one?"

"Indeed."

Sue grabbed the mug out of Flash's hand and walked over to the
coffee station as Jamie and Flash walked outside.

Jamie drank his tea quietly as they sat in the November sun. Sue wasn't sure if this was simply an effort on Jamie's part to annoy Flash. Whether it was or wasn't, Flash was nearly apoplectic when Jamie put down his mug.

"Really? Like you really needed a refreshing cup of tea?"

Jamie looked up at Flash with what appeared to be a hurt expression. "What makes you Ms. Cranky this morning?"

"I'm used to having data, lots of data. Coffee and data are my two joys...well, other than men."

"And because we can't receive data from SOF or OGA headquarters, you are cranky? We don't have enough men around here for you?"

"Exactly."

Sue decided this could go on all afternoon. Once again, she decided to intervene. "Jamie, why don't you give us some data from the reports?"

Jamie smiled and started to relate the results of his translations. "*TIMESHARE*'s reports focused on multiple subjects. I tasked him some time ago to give me information on possible vulnerabilities of the Iranian diplomats. One of those reports was a detailed report on a member of the Iranian intelligence service and how he both uses and distributes black tar opium. Now, opium use is not as significant as you might imagine among the Iranian hypocrites. But distribution is not something you want to admit, especially when you are using the diplomatic pouch to send your product back to Tehran. I think that has some real potential." He paused and said, "More tea?"

Flash said, "Not yet, you creep. I know you are hiding something."

"OK, well if you intend to call me names..." Jamie folded his arms across his large chest.

Sue could see that Jamie was enjoying himself too much. It was time for her to serve as the adult in the meeting. "Please give us the rest of the story."

Jamie looked at Sue and said, "Since you are being so polite, I will. *TIMESHARE*'s three other reports focused on the warehouse we are targeting. It looks to be just as we suspected. The PMC working at the airbase would like the locals to think that it is simply a storage facility for their weapons and equipment, but *TIMESHARE* reports that the Dushanbe power authority reports the warehouse uses more power than the entire Dushanbe International Airport. He went by the place and heard air conditioners running full blast. The facility also has an 1800 KW generator which looks to be simply for backup. I looked up the purpose of that type of generator. The answer is any facility that needs uninterrupted power, like..."

Flash jumped in, "A data center."

"Yes, Madame. A data center with racks and racks of servers. *TIMESHARE* found a guy who delivers fuel and other basic supplies into the compound. His sub source says he is not allowed near the building. He delivers the fuel to an underground tank outside the wall. Any other materials such as metal racks, tools, conduit, cables are all off-loaded by Russians at the front gate. They pay him in cash and escort him off the property. But the best part was in the third report. Can I have some tea now?"

"Not yet. I may choke you."

"That would be amusing."

Sue said, "I'll go get you some tea. You two have to promise not to fight until I get back."

Flash said, "Maybe." Jamie just raised his hands skyward as if appealing to some Central Asian earth spirit.

Sue came back five minutes later with Jamie's mug and a tea bag floating in the steaming hot water. She put it down on the arm of his lawn chair and said, "OK, let's continue."

Jamie nodded and said, "Thank you. So, as I said, *TIMESHARE*'s last report talks about a pipeline that runs out of the warehouse and heads west towards Uzbekistan. He doesn't know where it goes, but he did say it follows the highway that heads toward Termez. *TIME-SHARE* said it is not a natural gas or electrical pipeline. He thinks it is some sort of fiber optic conduit and he knows there are access ports to the pipeline about every 25km. Something to consider, eh?"

Sue said, "A pipeline going to Termez?"

Flash had given up her crankiness and offered, "During the days of the USSR, the roads north out of Dushanbe were closed half the year or more because of snows in the Pamirs. The main road taking cotton, Tajikistan's primary cash crop, went west to Uzbekistan and at Tashkent, cotton and whatever else Tajiks produced was loaded onto freight cars and shipped north by rail. I suspect somewhere west of the Tajik-Uzbek border, the pipeline leaves the main road and heads either directly to Tashkent or north along the rail line. It means we have to look at this pipeline. It should be easy to find on imagery."

"See, you are happy and we haven't told you what he said last night!" Jamie's white teeth and mustache smiled over his tea mug.

"Flash, before you explode," Sue interjected, "the only thing TIMESHARE said last night on this subject was he sees Iranian diplomats visiting the warehouse. He doesn't know why, but I suspect we do."

"Now it's my turn to be grumpy," Jamie said. "What do you know that I don't know?"

Flash said, "It turns out the FBI found a cyber operation that was selling data both to the Russians and to the Iranians. They looked at it as an identity theft effort, but..." After a pause, Flash completed her sentence, "It could be all part of this larger cyber op. I don't know enough about the Russian intelligence links to the Iranians, but I can see a Russian PMC selling services to the Iranians just as a different finance stream. Cyber is complicated enough that the PMC might figure their primary client — FSB, SVR, GRU, or whatever Russian intel organization is paying them — probably wouldn't or possibly couldn't audit their work. It's all zeros and ones after all. Millions of lines of code."

Sue shook her head. "This seems way too complicated for me. Are you saying that the PMC might run multiple operations along a single data pipe? They ship the data Russia wants to Moscow and somehow pass the data to the Iranians in Dushanbe?"

Jamie smiled and said, "And remember, that data pipe works both ways. What if they are also shipping some sort of data product back to CONUS?"

Flash looked at Jamie, "You are one twisted cat. Are you thinking that along with stealing data they are also feeding some sort of false data inside CONUS?"

Jamie said, "Why not? And all at the speed of light. Better still, if the disinformation is inside your cyber firewall, you would believe it is true, right? Think about what the Russians did to Estonia in 2007. Basically, they shut down the electronic networks of an entire country. The most important Estonian bank was hit with denial-of-service attacks. And, all because the Estonians wanted to remove a statue of Russian "liberators." Now think about how much damage you can do if you reside inside a cyber network. Not only denial-of-service, but serious disinformation. And, once you do figure there is disinformation inside your system, how do you sort out what is real and what is false? It is just the gift that keeps on giving."

Sue said, "No wonder the code name for this op is *Silicon Addiction.*"

Flash brought both hands up to her temples. "Now this is making my head hurt."

Over the next three days, Jamie, Sue and Flash spent hours on secure video teleconferences or SVTCs. It started with Jamie talking to Kabul station and CIA headquarters reporting on *TIMESHARE's* information and the imagery obtained from the UAV working the Afghan-Tajik border. Sue and Flash held a SVTC with Massoni at HICU and Smith sitting in his cabin in the *USS Iwo Jima.* After they passed the information to their respective leadership, they had to wait for decisions to come from both CIA and SOF headquarters. It was a relatively painful delay for Jamie because of the impatience of his two SOF houseguests.

Two days before Thanksgiving, Jamie walked upstairs just after midnight and knocked on the door of the room Sue and Flash shared. "Wake up sleepy heads. We have work to do." He walked away knowing that at a minimum they would be shouting invectives and might actually throw something at him. Just before he reached the end of the hallway and headed down the stairs, he saw Sue's head pop out of her room. "You knocked?"

Jamie answered in a stage whisper, "Shush. You'll wake up the guys."

"You woke me up."

"Yes, and you and Flash need to come downstairs, we have work to do." Before Sue could say anything else, Jamie was down the stairs.

Sue returned to the bedroom and threw a pillow across the room at Flash. It landed with a thump at the foot of her bed. Flash popped straight up. "What?"

"Get dressed. We have to go downstairs."

"I need my sleep."

Sue was busy attaching her prosthetic as she said, "And I need to get out of here, but I don't think either of those needs are going to happen anytime soon."

"You sure this isn't one of your dreams?" Over the past few days, Flash had experienced Sue's nightmares and knew how disruptive they could be. She looked at her dive watch through sleep-fogged eyes. "It is 0100hrs. Why now?"

Sue's second pillow headed towards Flash's head. "Because Jamie said now. I suspect he got something from Headquarters."

"Makes sense." She looked closer at her watch, hit the backlight button for the digital time set for HICU headquarters. "0100hrs here is midday in DC."

Sue was pulling on her sweatpants, "Whatever. We aren't going to find out until we get downstairs."

"I'll be there is a second. Start the coffee."

Sue now was as dressed as she was going to be in her black sweatshirt and sweatpants and black trainers. "Ghorban-e-shma."

"Eh?"

"Persian for I am your slave."

"Rightly so." Flash ducked as Sue tossed a previously used pair of socks at her roommate.

After a full pot of coffee just for Flash and a pot of tea for Jamie and Sue, they sat down at one of the worktables in the ops center.

Jamie started by saying, "OK, now just remember I am the messenger here not the guy who thought this up."

Flash said, "I woke up to talk to a messenger?"

Sue said, "Jamie, we got it. You just got the guidance from HQS."

"Actually, I got the guidance from a three-screen SVTC from the Agency, the FBI, and your CG. If I had known it was going to be that much fun, I would have been better dressed and roused you earlier so the CG could see your pillow faces." He took a sip from his tea and continued, "So, here are the basics. The HQS gurus figure the Russian GRU outsourced their cyber operation to a PMC called SWORDFISH Group so that if there was any pushback from the West, the Russian government could deny everything. Of course, the HQS deep dive of SWORDFISH shows a company leadership made up of retired SPETSNAZ so for all intents and purposes it is a GRU outfit."

Flash said, "Once a Chekist always a Chekist."

Jamie nodded, drank some tea and continued, "HQS is convinced the PMC management decided to make more money by selling their capability to the Iranians as well. HQS reported there was an unknown level of cooperation in Syria between this same PMC and IRGC. And, as we know from Sue's work in Cyprus and the data you collected from Beroslav, there have been Russian mafia links to Iran for a while. They figure SWORDFISH decided there was enough bandwidth for both clients. The only reason we know some of this is because the Iranians subsequently outsourced their side of the operation to a Hizballah cell in Northern Virginia who sold some of the results of their data scraping back to the Russian FSB. We can only speculate on what the FSB intended to do with personal data scraped from the Pentagon..."

Flash interrupted, "But it wouldn't be good. I get that, please move on at a faster data rate. I know you are keeping it slow for Sue but I would like to know how this affects us before I fall asleep."

Sue gave Flash a one fingered salute.

Jamie shook his head and continued as if he hadn't been interrupted, "...but the FSB is always after data for their operations — both recruitment and influence operations. They are especially interested in compromising material, *kompromat* in Russian intel-speak. I suspect there are more than a few US politicians worrying right now based on the results of the FBI investigation. Which...as I heard earlier was stage-managed by another O'Connell."

Sue wanted to avoid a discussion of her family business. She said, "I'm with Flash, what does this have to do with us."

"Patience for goodness sake. I've already compressed nearly a half hour of SVTC time. And remember, I'm the one who suffered as the Agency, FBI and your headquarters gave me a lecture on things I already knew. So, from their Olympian perspective, we need to get a better understanding of the data streams that are flowing to Dushanbe. Step one will be Friday when we meet *TIMESHARE*. Step two will be some sort of technical operation that they are still designing. Meanwhile, with the data they have, they are creating a series of shadow networks that will give the Russian network false information for both the Agency and SOF. As to the Iranians, I think your team in the UAE is going to shut that network down on a more... permanent basis. After all, the Iranian effort is focused exclusively on capturing SOF data and using it to destroy or disrupt your operations in the Gulf."

Flash said, "Oh, great. It's simple. We just tap a fiber optic line in the middle of bad guy country and make sure we don't trigger the arrival of some large security force ready to smush us."

Sue laughed, "Smush? Really?"

Flash looked up from her coffee cup. "Hey, it's the middle of the night. My vocabulary is limited."

Jamie said, "It seems the eggheads back in CONUS are already assembling a simple technical solution for us. All we have to do is deliver that solution somewhere on the data pipe. It looks as if the plan is to disrupt but not destroy the data pipe. If we time the disruption properly, both of our HQS will switch to the ghost networks and the Russians will be none the wiser."

"How long before they figured they can deliver the kit?"

"Let's just say I hope you like my Thanksgiving dinner menu."

A beleaguered Flash looked at them both and said, "Swell."

THANKSGIVING IN JAMIE'S HOUSE

26 November 2009

Holidays away from home are never especially joyful. Thanksgiving is especially hard for Americans deployed overseas because of fond memories of large family gatherings, excessive meals, and football on TV. Sue noticed in the past that amazingly tough shooters in SOF would get nostalgic at the very thought of Thanksgivings past. Many of her own Thanksgivings while in college were spent with her grandfather while her parents were assigned abroad. Peter O'Connell Senior was a reasonable cook and he worked hard to keep both of his grandchildren amused, but it nearly always fell short. Her brother would leave for University of Virginia on Friday and Sue would make her excuses to leave Saturday morning. She didn't have a lot of nostalgic memories to work on, so for her Thanksgiving with friends and colleagues was about as good as any she had as young adult.

Jamie and his team did their best to make Sue and Flash feel welcome. Kabul station flew in three turkeys and a ham from the US. Jamie had the Tomahawks shop in local markets for the ingredients for his recipes that included an okra-and-tomato stew, carrot-and-raisin pilau and multiple desserts including a fig tart and two apple pies. The Tomahawks also received a visit from Jamie and his deputy Mitch with one of the turkeys and a second set of desserts so that every member of the Tomahawks had a chance to sample Jamie's cooking.

What Sue hadn't expected was Flash's response. Flash had yet to come down for the evening meal with the team so Sue went up to see what was the matter. She found Flash lying on her bunk staring at the ceiling.

"Thinking big thoughts before you get the dopamine drag from too much turkey?"

"Nope."

"Care to explain why you are going to be the last one at the party?"

"Nope."

Sue shook her head. "Alright then. If you don't want to talk, I'm certainly not going to try to make you talk. The meal is ready, the guys are waiting, Jamie is wearing a ridiculous chef toque and I am hungry."

As Sue turned toward the door, Flash said, "Really, you are just going to leave me here to mope?"

"Yup. If you won't be even the least bit civil with your pal and comrade-in-arms for the last couple of years, I'm not going to worry about you."

"OK, so I was being a creep. I would like to talk."

"Make it snappy, I'm hungry!"

"The Billings family gathering for Thanksgiving was always magnificent. We lived in NJ and my folks worked in the City. That meant that just about anything you could imagine from any culture on earth could end up on our table. There wasn't a bodega or deli in Manhattan that didn't know my mother or my father by their first name. Thanksgiving was the family gathering. My mother would make enough food for a dozen even though it was just my mom and pop and yours truly. I miss them."

"Flash, you haven't told me zilch about your family. Where are they now?"

"I missed my last Thanksgiving with them in 2000. I was on my first deployment with SOF. They were super proud of their commando daughter." Sue could see Flash was tearing up. Flash stopped for a second, sniffed back tears, and continued. "We all agreed that I would make sure I had leave in 2001. I put in the paperwork on 1 September to be sure I locked in the weekend. It never happened. 9/11 happened instead and both of my folks never made it past that day. Mom was a broker working in tower one of the World Trade Center." Flash smiled at the memory, "As a kid, I actually visited the Roof at the Top of the World restaurant for a milkshake and hamburger. Not standard fare on their menu, but Mom knew the lunch chef and arranged it so I could have the meal after the lunch crowd was gone. Dad was a Fire Department of New York captain in one of the hook-and-ladder companies in the Bronx. Mom never made it out of WTC1 and Dad was one of the firefighters killed when WTC2 collapsed. The only good thing, I suppose is that neither of them knew the other died that day." Flash looked at Sue. She was quietly crying. "We never found their bodies."

Sue was stunned. She knew several of those killed at the Pentagon, but no one in New York. Bad enough to lose family members on that day but to never find their remains was too horrible to imagine. She didn't know what to say. Eventually she asked, "Does anyone in the unit know?"

"Massoni. He makes sure I have dinner with him on the anniversary of 9/11. He lost a pal at the Pentagon. We drink whiskey and cry."

Sue couldn't imagine what she could possibly say to help. So, instead, she said, "Well, kid. Right now, we need to show up for Jamie's dinner. If nothing else, you need to see him in the toque."

Flash pulled out a black handkerchief and blew her nose. "You don't need to share this, right?"

"I suspect by now you know I'm good at keeping a secret."

Flash smiled and said, "Yup. Like you kept me in the dark about your BTK for nearly a year."

"It wasn't that important."

Flash shook her head. "So, you thought revealing the secret when you hopped toward me after that night in the Black Sea was good enough? I almost had a cow."

Finally, Flash said, "Let's go downstairs before we both start...
bawling."

"Fair."

THANKSGIVING IN CHAUTAUQUA

T he FBI watch on the Chautauqua house turned into boring days and nights, with Barbara O'Connell doing her best to entertain her FBI minder. At first, Ellen Jones stayed in the guest room in the Chautauqua house. That only lasted for two days when over breakfast she said to Barbara, "Any chance you can manage this without my supervision?"

Barbara smiled as she looked up from her mug of tea, thinking about how she was under supervision by a junior special agent. It was a rainy, dreary day and Barbara could imagine how Sue might feel serving on "geezer watch" with no action day after day. Barbara had at least a little sympathy for Ellen. "I hope you don't take offense Ellen, but I never actually wanted you to be my houseguest. I don't know if that was your choice, your supervisor's choice or the SAC's choice. It certainly wasn't my choice. So, to answer your question: yes, I can manage watching over my own house. If it will make you or your bosses any happier, I can set up the WiFi network running my surveillance cameras so you can watch the house and still keep track of your work and…" she smiled, "your cat."

Special Agent Ellen Jones might have grown comfortable with working on this project, but she wasn't about to take the bait on Barbara's question of her living arrangements. She said, "That sounds great. I will call the boss and see what he says."

An hour later, Ellen had loaded her overnight bag into her Mustang and left. Barbara could hear the exhaust rumble from the Mustang's V8 as it left the neighborhood. She said to no one in particular, "I guess she has had enough of life with a pensioner."

As the days approached the holiday season, Barbara was pleased to hear that her son Bill was able to get leave and visit for the Thanksgiving weekend. Barbara willingly agreed to let Bill bring what he carefully called a colleague to visit. Bill had never been willing to introduce Barbara to any of his previous female friends. This sounded serious and Barbara was pleased to hear it. Janice had hinted that Bill and a special agent named Molly Hansen were a couple. Barbara could imagine how hard it would be to balance a relationship with two jobs in the FBI.

The day before Thanksgiving, Barbara finished her grocery shopping and started on one of the many pies she planned. She made up the guest bedroom and set up a cot and sleeping bag in the small study upstairs just in case Bill and his "colleague" didn't want to share a room. Barbara was fairly certain that it would never be used, but she didn't want to presume anything.

That evening, Bill and Molly rolled into the driveway in Bill's ancient Jeep Cherokee. After he left the Marines and joined the FBI, Barbara had expected Bill to give up the square two-door beast for a newer vehicle. Bill's explanation was simple. "Mom, I go to work on the Washington Metro. The FBI gives me a government car to work in. Granddad's house in Georgetown is within walking distance of everything and I'm a half mile from a bicycle trail if I want to see something other than my neighborhood. Why in the world would I invest in a new vehicle when the Cherokee continues to run?"

Barbara didn't argue at the time. Now, she thought how a six-hour drive in a fifteen-year-old Jeep from DC to Western New York might be a true test of friendship. Barbara's experience with Terry Reimer's ancient Jeep had been enough to convince her that the Range Rover had better survive for a while. Still, Bill and Molly didn't seem any the worse for wear when they climbed out of the Jeep.

As Bill walked into the cottage he said, "Mom, thanks for hosting us for the holidays. This is..."

"Yes, dear. Molly Hansen. How are you and how did you survive the rock and roll associated with ancient springs in Bill's Jeep?"

Molly offered her hand and got a strong handshake in return. Janice told Barbara that Molly came to the Bureau from the Texas Department of Public Safety, so she had expected a Texas accent. The only evidence of Texas was the handshake and the look into her eyes and the slight smirk as Molly said, "Mrs. O'Connell, it is a pleasure to meet you. You do realize you are one scary person to meet? After all, just about everyone at Washington Field has seen the video of your adventure with a hand grenade."

"Molly, by now you must know that was just a one-off. I'm just a mere, wretched federal pensioner trying to enjoy a quiet life at a cottage by the lake."

Bill shook his head as he carried the bags into the house. "See what I mean?"

Molly said, "You know Bill has been dodging telling tales of family O'Connell for as long as I have known him. Any chance I will get some tales of adventure this weekend?"

Bill and Barbara said in unison, "Nope."

Barbara focused on preparing dinner as Bill and Molly settled in. Given the standard Thanksgiving fare the following day, Barbara had made a simple vegetable soup and matched it with fresh bread from the local bakery and cheese from an artisan cheese maker who lived south of town. Matched with a New York State Dry Riesling, she figured it was just about right for weary travelers.

Dinner conversation focused on amusing tales of Bill's youth and Molly's time as a patrol officer on Texas roads. Barbara served as the facilitator of the back and forth. The last thing she wanted to do was delve into her life which even she admitted was...complicated. Fairly soon after dinner was completed, both of her guests looked to be close to falling asleep. Barbara took the lead and said, "OK, you two. I suspect you had to work a full eight-hour shift today before six hours of travel. Off to bed. I will do the cleanup. Tomorrow, I will have coffee and tea ready by 7 a.m., but probably not before since I like to do my exercise routine early. A friend of mine named Terry Reimer will come by around 2 and we will plan to have dinner at 4. So, go away!"

Molly said, "Dishes? I am exceptionally good at drying dishes."

"We will test those skills tomorrow. Tonight's dishes are just going into the dishwasher. Shoo!"

Barbara watched as her son and what appeared to be more than just a colleague walked up the stairs. She was pleased to see Bill had found a partner, perhaps the partner. She thought at least one of her children just might have a normal life. Thanksgiving was going to prove that "normal" for the O'Connell's wasn't exactly the same as normal for most people.

ON THE RUN

T hanksgiving Day began with a dusting of white snow that covered the ground and coated Bill's white Cherokee with a layer of frost. Barbara's normal routine was a quick walk on a trail along the lake followed by a stop at a local bakery to pick up fresh bread. The bakery would be closed for the holiday, but she still went out for her walk, taking care on the snow-covered trail. She noticed that her footsteps were not the only ones on the trail. She often met other runners and walkers on the trail, so it did not seem important as she pushed herself to complete her normal two miles in the freezing temperature made even colder by the breeze off the lake.

By the time she returned home at 6:30, she could smell coffee already brewing. Molly was at the counter working the espresso machine and the electric kettle. "Good morning! Bill says you take tea in the morning. Right?"

"Yes, please. There are builders' tea bags in the tin. And, where is my son?"

"Builders?"

"It's just a generic term. In the UK, there are a number of tea companies that make very generic, very fast brewing teas. Instead of a coffee break, English blue-collar workers get a tea break. Not much time allowed, so they need a tea bag that brews up quickly. Hence, builders' tea. You didn't answer my question. Where is my son?"

"Still under the covers. I figured a cup of espresso might change that."

"Excellent. You make the espresso and I'll make the tea. We'll do a light breakfast at 9. OK? That will give us all a chance to use the only shower in the place. Apologies but this is a cottage after all."

"No worries, Mrs. O'Connell. I've already done a quick workout and showered. You go next and sleepy head can just wait."

"Deal. Tea can wait. I'll head to the shower right now." As Barbara climbed the stairs, she noticed the cot and sleeping bag were untouched. She smiled as she headed into the bathroom.

By late afternoon, Barbara and her three guests were nearly comatose from a classic Thanksgiving meal of turkey, bread stuffing, mashed and sweet potatoes, a salad, a fruit bowl, and fresh-baked rolls. Chilled New York State white wine matched the meal perfectly. Coffee and tea followed. All at the table agreed dessert would have to wait few hours.

They watched the winter sun set over the lake. Canada geese were touching down on the lake for the night. As with many of their peers earlier in the month, these birds would be heading south before winter closed in and Great Lake storms promised to freeze the surface of Chautauqua Lake. Terry Reimer was the only one at the table who grew up in western New York, so he spent a bit of time reminding everyone why Buffalo winters were so dire and why any bird that could fly the distance would do so.

Barbara was pleased to see Terry was on his best behavior over the meal, telling amusing stories from his time as a patrolman in Buffalo and avoiding any adventure tales related to their recent work in Croatia. Molly replied by telling her own tales of what it was like to serve on patrol on lonely Texas roads. Between the two storytellers, Barbara and her son focused on filling wine glasses and coffee cups. It was a wonderful moment as they laughed at amusing tales and watched the sunset turn from gold to auburn to mauve to blue black.

Eventually they all moved from the dining room into the living area to crowd around Barbara's small TV set and watch football. Barbara accepted the healthy criticism that her TV reflected her age. "At least it's a color TV," was all Barbara could offer in her defense.

Terry said, "I don't think that is going to mean much to these guys who don't remember a time when TVs were black and white."

Bill said, "I do so remember black and white TVs! When we lived in India and in Moscow. Little tiny sets with rabbit-ear antennas. Of course, there was nothing to watch, so it hardly mattered."

Molly elbowed Bill in the ribs and said, "Hush, we are trying to watch the game!"

Barbara stood behind her three guests and smiled. It had been a long time since she had enjoyed a domestic scene like this one. It was definitely worth all the work in the days before the holiday shopping and preparing the meals. Her thoughts were interrupted by a small buzzing noise coming from the kitchen. Terry looked up from the couch. He knew the noise was the surveillance camera alarm and he had a feeling that nothing good could follow.

The whoosh from the firebomb shook the cottage. Barbara was the first to reach the front door. She opened it to find the front of her house and both Jeeps in flames. She also saw a dark figure running away wearing a small backpack. Terry reached her just as she turned back into the house. "What the heck? My Jeep?" At that moment, the ancient Jeep Wrangler exploded in full flames. Bill's Cherokee followed.

Barbara took charge: "There are three fire extinguishers on this floor and one in the garage. I will get the one in the garage. One is here in the closet and two are in the kitchen. Let's get going." She disappeared through a side door that led downstairs to the garage below the house. Terry ran into the living room and said, "Someone just firebombed our vehicles and the house. Two fire extinguishers in the kitchen. Meet me outside!" Bill and Molly were already on their feet. They headed into the kitchen.

Barbara knew there was little they could do to save Reimer's Jeep, but she did want to prevent the fire from doing serious damage to the house. As she came out of the garage, she saw the damage from a different angle. It looked as if a Molotov cocktail hit the front door and spread fire along the wall on the side of the house where the Russian cyber tool had been mounted. Barbara rushed over and began spraying that side of the house with fire suppressant. The main natural gas feed was there and if the fire or even excessive heat reached the meter, the house was finished. Luckily, Barbara reached the wall before the mix of gasoline and dishwashing liquid reached the meter. The suppressant did its job and the only damage was black scorching. One thing was certain. The Russian tool was gone.

Barbara returned to the front of the house to see her three guests putting out the last of the fires. She turned to Reimer and said, "They took the parasite."

Reimer said, "You know, hanging out with you is a real treat."

Bill and Molly walked up. Molly said, "Parasite?"

Bill nodded. "There was a Russian cyber tool on the exterior of the house. It seems it was part of a larger operation that I exposed in DC. Buffalo Field Office left the tool in place to see what would happen next."

"And, now we know," Molly observed.

Barbara said, "OK, here's what we need to do right now. We need to find the creep who did this."

Reimer said, "And how exactly are we supposed to do that?"

"We use the GPS tag that the FBI put on the tool. I might just have the GPS tracker on my iPad."

"Mother!?"

"Hey, we can either do this or sit around and eat pie and cry," Barbara said. "Whatdya' think I'm going to do?"

"They bombed our vehicles!"

Barbara looked over her shoulder into the garage. "Not all of them." She turned back to Bill and Molly: "I suspect you brought your badge, creds and sidearms, no?"

Molly smiled and said, "Of course."

"Then go get them. Terry and I will get the vehicles ready."

After the two agents left, Terry said, "You willing to open your arsenal?"

"I already opened the concealment before I opened the garage door. You can't be too careful."

"Not if your last name is O'Connell."

"Follow me."

They walked into the garage. Barbara turned on the light and walked over to a workbench where a leather holster was sitting. Barbara said to Terry, "You familiar with a 1911?"

"Ya think?"

"OK, here is your piece."

"And yours?"

"I said I opened the arsenal before I opened the door. Mine is already on my hip." Barbara pointed to a small bulge just behind her right hip. "Now, let's get the vehicles ready." She tossed Reimer a set of keys to the Range Rover. "You and Bill go in the Rover."

"And you?"

Barbara pulled a canvas car cover off the second vehicle. The neon light from the garage ceiling revealed a vintage, red and white Austin Healy 3000. Barbara jumped into the driver's seat. Just before the weather turned foul, Barbara had Peter Senior's sports car tuned. She hadn't expected to use it, but figured it needed care before winter. Now, she was happy she did. "Molly and I will be traveling a little faster and, admittedly colder."

"Nice…" was all Barbara heard from Reimer as she started the sports car.

They left the cottage after gathering jackets and locking the doors. Both Jeeps were still smoldering, but the fires were out. Barbara was pleased that on Thanksgiving Day, with her nearest neighbors on holiday and the rest of the street gazing at their TV screens, no one had noticed the fires. Even with two FBI agents on hand, it would have been impossible to begin the chase if the fire department and local police had arrived as first responders. As they pulled out of the driveway, Barbara handed Molly her cellphone and an iPad with the tracking software mapping the location of the Russian cyber device.

It was clear the device was already on the Southern Tier Expressway heading east.

Barbara joined the interstate at Beamus Point. She could see the Range Rover struggling to keep up. That would not matter too much once they were on the highway. She would have Molly call Bill and let him know where they were headed. The open cockpit of the Austin Healy was noisy even at a slow speed, at higher speeds conversation became a shouting match. Barbara said "ON MY PHONE I HAVE ELLEN JONES ON SPEED DIAL. CALL HER."

"ELLEN?"

"JONES."

"Check. What do I say when she answers."

"WHAT?"

"WHAT DO I SAY?"

"SHE IS FBI. TELL HER WHO YOU ARE AND WHAT WE ARE DOING."

"CHECK." Molly found the number and dialed it.

"Jones."

"Jones, this is FBI Special Agent Hansen from Washington Field. I'm with Barbara O'Connell."

"And you are in hot pursuit."

"How did you know?"

"I'm tracking the same GPS beacon that Mrs. O'Connell clearly tapped. I received the alarm when it moved. Where are you?"

Molly looked at a road sign as they blasted past it at well over the speed limit. "I-86 headed east."

"OK. I'm mobilizing the surveillance team including the office helicopter. Try not to get into a gunfight until I get there, okay?"

"Gunfight?"

"You don't know Barbara O'Connell, do you?"

"Just met her yesterday. I'm dating her son."

"OK. Just realize that she is one dangerous woman."

"Saw that with the grenade film."

"That's not the half of it. Do your best to control her instincts."

"The perpetrator just firebombed her house and two cars in the driveway. I suspect she is a little pissed off."

"Swell. I'm on my way. And Hansen, we really want to take him alive."

"Who?"

"Whoever took the device. I reckon it is an Army guy we already met, but I didn't expect the attack. No telling who or how many are in the vehicle. Out."

Barbara looked over at Molly. The large, ancient dials on the instrument panel made her face glow a mix of green-blue. She shouted, "WHAT DID SHE SAY?"

"SHE SAID YOU WERE DANGEROUS."

Barbara smiled. "ANYTHING ELSE?"

"SHE'S BRINGING THE CAVALRY."

"GOOD. WE MAY NEED IT."

Bill had been quiet for the first part of the drive until they pulled on I-86. Finally, he asked, "Are you and mom…a couple?"

Reimer smiled and said, "A couple of what?"

"Come on, Terry. Are you dating?"

Reimer was concentrating on keeping the ancient Range Rover on the highway. It was definitely not made for speed. "Nope. We are working together. Every once in a while we go out. So far, that's about as much as I can say. Not that I wouldn't like to be…dating as you said. I just don't know enough about your mom to know what's coming next."

"If you think she's a puzzle, wait until you meet my sister."

"I heard. Quite the character."

"I wouldn't use that word, but she is something. Now, what the heck to you think is going on right now? I mean most folks would have stayed at home and called the fire department. Instead, we load into two vehicles and decide to chase down a villain."

Reimer smiled. He said, "As if you don't want to catch the guy who just destroyed your Jeep?"

"OK, I will admit I would like to catch him myself. I would like to express my displeasure."

"Yeah, well displeasure isn't the word I would use. That Jeep of mine has been through a lot and now it's finished. I definitely want to see the guy who did this."

"I take it mom had a GPS tag on the Russian device?"

"I think it was an FBI tag, but I suspect she decided to be sure she could follow the tag. Some sort of secret squirrel stuff that I don't understand and, honestly, don't want to understand. I'm just a simple cop."

"I doubt that, Terry. Now the real question I need to ask is: Are you armed?"

"Yes, sir. And since I'm a retired lawman, I'm even street legal."

"Excellent. Do you think we can prevent mom from starting a gunfight?"

"Hard to say. I'm thinking...not. I suspect it is going to be Biblical when we get there." Reimer looked over at the young FBI agent. The man in the passenger seat looked rock hard. He also looked concerned.

"As in an eye for an eye?"

"More like as in a pillar of salt."

Jones called Barbara's mobile. Molly answered, "Yes?"

The voice at the other end echoed as if the caller was inside a large metal drum. There was also a vibration that was clearly not from a car. "Hansen, I am in the Bureau bird headed to your location. We figure he is headed back to the Seneca Army Depot. That's where he is based. Expect him to take the exit at Horseheads for Watkins Glen. From there he will head north toward Romulus. We are going straight there to set up a roadblock south of the base. I have a SWAT section with me. The SAC decided we don't want to engage the Army because we don't know who else is working for the Russians. Keep on his tail and report, OK?"

"Sure, Jones."

"And remember, we want him alive."

"Check."

"Out."

Barbara looked over at Molly. "WHAT DID SHE SAY."

"SHE SAID DON'T KILL HIM."

"I'll DO MY BEST."

Molly nodded as they passed yet another highway overpass at just above the speed limit. Given their ability to follow the tag and the fact that the FBI would be set up in front of the target, Molly figured Barbara was keeping to the speed limit so that she didn't run afoul of a State Police patrol. Molly shouted, "YOU HAVE DONE THIS A COUPLE OF TIMES, EH?"

"WHAT?"

"FOLLOW."

"YUP, A COUPLE OF TIMES. HAVING THE TAG HELPS A LOT. KEEP WATCHING THE TAG. I DON'T THINK THE TARGET IS GOING TO JUST DRIVE BACK HOME. JONES IS WRONG."

Molly looked down at the iPad. So far, the tag was staying on course. She wasn't about to argue with Barbara, but she didn't see any reason to doubt her FBI colleague.

They had just crossed over the Allegheny River when Molly saw a blue highway road sign that said OLEAN 5mi. Molly noticed the tag moving off the highway. She shouted, "IT'S MOVING OFF THE INTERSTATE. NO, WAIT, IT'S NOT. YES, IT IS."

"CHECK. EXPAND THE MAP. SEE IF THERE IS A PARALLEL ROAD."

Molly looked down at the map. She said "YES, IT'S NY16. THE TARGET GOT OFF AND IS HEADING NORTH ON NY16.

IT RUNS PARALLEL FOR A WHILE AND THEN TURNS NORTHWEST."

"WHERE DOES IT GO?"

"TOWARD A BUNCH OF SMALL TOWNS."

"ANY AIRFIELDS?"

"A LITTLE ONE."

"OK. LAST MAP QUESTION: CAN WE STAY ON THE INTERSTATE AND EXIT SOMEPLACE FARTHER ALONG 16 OR DO WE GET OFF AT OLEAN? LOOK QUICK BECAUSE THE EXIT IS IN TWO MILES."

Molly ran her finger along the map. "WE CAN EXIT AT HINSDALE. THAT'S THE LAST TIME 16 CROSSES THE HIGHWAY."

"OK. NOW, CALL BILL AND TELL HIM WHAT'S HAPPENING."

Molly reached for her own phone. She called Bill and said, "How are you doing?"

"Oh, just great. Terry and I are really enjoying life following taillights."

Molly smiled and said, "Don't pout. FBI Agents don't pout."

Bill said, "You have some news?"

"Yes, the target is off the highway and on a parallel road. We are going to exit at Hinsdale. We may be able to cut him off. At least we won't lose him."

"Roger. Do you want us to exit now or follow you?"

Molly thought for a minute and said, "Exit now. Get on 16 and track north. We still don't know what the target vehicle looks like so don't pass anyone. K?"

"In this Range Rover, that is not likely."

"See you soon."

Bill turned to Terry and said, "The target has jumped off the interstate. We need to take the follow. Exit here and turn north on 16."

"OK. Do we have any idea what our rabbit looks like?" "Rabbit?"

"As in the kid's game of hare and hounds. We are the hounds. He is the rabbit. Now please answer the question. I don't want to get too close to anyone who has Molotov cocktails in his car."

"Fair enough. For now, we don't know. Our instructions are not to pass anyone. Mom and Molly are going to stay on the interstate and exit at the last time that 16 crosses the highway. With a little luck, we may box him in."

"Sounds like a plan. The good news is on Thanksgiving evening, it's not like there is a lot of traffic." Reimer took the Olean exit and followed the signs to NY16. In a mile he was headed north again not more than a quarter mile from the interstate. "Clever little bastard. He must have assumed there is some sort of tag on either his car or the device. It looks like 16 parallels the highway for a while. If Molly and your mom hadn't been paying attention, they would have stayed on the highway until it was too late. This is not some simple villain. The guys knows how to duck surveillance."

"Well, he didn't duck us."

"At least not yet."

In the Austin Healy, Molly looked up at Barbara. She was concentrating on driving, but it was clear she was also thinking, and thinking hard. Molly shouted, "DO WE CALL JONES?"

Barbara shook her head. "NOT YET. WE DON'T KNOW IF THE TARGET IS JUST DROPPING OFF THE HIGHWAY TO DETERMINE HIS SURVEILLANCE STATUS. HE MIGHT JUMP BACK ON THE HIGHWAY AT HINSDALE. PATIENCE IS THE WATCHWORD IN SURVEILLANCE."

"I'M NOT ALL THAT GOOD AT PATIENCE."

"YOU AND MY DAUGHTER."

Ten minutes later, Molly watched as the target on the iPad passed under the interstate and headed northwest. "HE'S STILL IN FRONT OF US."

"WELL, IT WAS TOO GOOD TO BE TRUE THAT WE WOULD BOX HIM IN. OK, TRACK HIM CLOSELY NOW. THERE ARE PROBABLY PLENTY OF ROADS HE CAN USE."

"CHECK."

They didn't have to wait long. The target on the map left NY16 two miles ahead of them. Now that the Austin was not traveling at super-highway speeds, the cockpit seemed almost livable. Slightly warmer and certainly quieter. At least they didn't have to shout. Molly said, "Turn right at the next road."

Barbara reached down on the dashboard and flipped a toggle switch. A pair of rally-style headlights doubled the illumination on the pitch-black highway. Even with the extra lights, they barely saw the sign. HATCH HILL RD. Barbara said, "Call Bill. Tell him the turn is Hatch Hill Road. About two miles past the junction with the interstate. Molly nodded and made the call. Barbara toggled off the lights as she turned on the macadam highway walled in by old oaks and maples that had long since lost their leaves. When Barbara turned off the Austin's headlights, she slowed down since they were running on just the marker lights. She said to Molly, "This could be a little tricky now. Let me know when and where you see the target stop."

"Molly said, "The target turned left about a half mile ahead. It's stopped."

"OK, call in the cavalry now. Let Jones know where we are."

Molly nodded, picked up Barbara's phone and called Jones.

The echoed voice answered, "Jones."

"Jones, its Hansen. Change in plan. The target has gone off the highway at Olean and is stopped at a regional airport north of the city. We are headed there now."

"Hansen, do not take any action until we arrive." Jones paused and Molly could imagine she was checking her map. "OK, so we are about five minutes out."

"Got it. We will standby and block the highway entrance to the airfield."

"Out."

Barbara looked at Molly. She said, "I noticed you didn't tell her we are already here."

Molly smiled. "She says she's five minutes out. Why should I waste my time telling her anything but the location?"

"A lot can happen in five minutes."

"A lot."

"Call Bill and tell him we are waiting for him and Reimer. Tell them to approach the airfield with their lights off."

"Got it."

Molly made the call as Barbara used first gear to creep up to the turn to the airfield. As soon as they turned on the airfield access road, they could see a twin-engine Beechcraft parked on the taxiway with its engines running. Next to the aircraft was a late model, gray four-door sedan. They watched as the driver got out of the car with a briefcase. A man walked down the stairs at the rear of the aircraft. They exchanged greetings. As they walked toward each other, the man from the aircraft pulled out a pistol and shot the driver three times at point blank range. The shooter picked up the briefcase and walked back toward the aircraft.

Barbara said, "I'm not waiting for the cavalry." She put the car in gear, turned on both the headlamps and the driving lamps and accelerated toward the aircraft.

The man from the aircraft heard the growl from the Austin's engine. He spun around, dropped to one knee and opened fire. It was exceptionally accurate pistol work. Two rounds splintered the Austin's windshield.

At the same time, all four of the car's tires exploded. Barbara had a hard time controlling the car as it slid on the collapsed rubber toward the sedan. As the Austin came to a stop, Barbara was out of the car with her pistol drawn. Molly was just few seconds behind her. She took cover behind the sedan while Barbara stood up and took careful aim. The first two rounds did not appear to hit anything. The next three rounds of .357 crashed into the left engine of the Beechcraft. Smoke started to engulf the engine as the pilot started his takeoff roll. The shooter on the tarmac caught up to the stairway, climbed into the aircraft and pulled the door shut as the Beechcraft accelerated down the taxiway, spun onto the active runway and took off, belching smoke from the left engine. The crippled aircraft dipped a hard left and headed north.

Barbara walked over to their now dead target. As she expected, it was Thorne. She heard Molly on the phone. The noise from the

.357 was still ringing in her ears, but she heard Molly saying, "Yes, it took off heading north. The left engine is damaged. First three digits on the number is VP-C. I didn't get the rest. No, we don't need any help here right now so you can pursue the aircraft. We will secure the scene. NO, I SAID WE WILL SECURE THE SCENE. OUT."

"Ellen being Ellen?"

"I do want to meet her. I think we might have a chat someday. Perhaps in a gym. She definitely needs some wall-to-wall counseling."

Barbara smiled and said, "Jones is just way young and trying hard to be in charge. So far, I have been…shall we say, problematic?"

"She warned me about gunfights."

"Hey, did it look to you like I was looking for a fight?"

"Nope, but you sure ran into one. Hey, by the way, what happened with your first two rounds?"

"I load birdshot into the first two rounds. It is a reasonable deterrent for any normal problem. I suspect when they find the aircraft there will be a few dents near the engine. The second three were full power .357. They certainly did some damage." As she talked to Molly, Barbara walked over to the Austin Healy. She noted the windscreen was a complete loss. She walked back toward the driveway just as her Range Rover arrived. She stopped Riemer in time as she stepped over a series of caltrop road nails spread across the road. It explained why she now had four flat tires and four bent rims.

Riemer got out of the Range Rover. He said, "Are we too late?"

"We were all too late. The target is dead and, before you ask, I didn't shoot him."

Bill stepped out of the passenger door of the Rover. He said, "Mom, are you okay?"

"Yes, dear. Just fine. The Austin is going to need some serious work." She smiled and said, "Oh, Molly is fine as well."

Bill walked over to Molly. "Did you have a nice Thanksgiving?"

"Oh, it was lovely. Is it always this much fun with the O'Connells?"

"You have no idea."

CONTINGENCY PLANS

A fter what was the best possible Thanksgiving under the circum-stances, Sue and Jamie spent the next evening on the same sand dune waiting for *TIMESHARE*. Sue praised Jamie for the fantastic dinner the previous night. Jamie was justifiably proud of his efforts.

He said, "You know, I can't tell you how many Thanksgivings I have spent OCONUS. Probably my first one was in a training camp in El Salvador in the 1980s. I was the commo NCO on my SF detach-ment and I rigged up an antenna so we could hear a radio broadcast from the States. The meal wasn't exactly grand, but just being able to listen to a football game on the radio helped. I swore at that point that if I had any way to do so, wherever I was and whoever was on my team, I would always make sure we had a way to celebrate Thanksgiving. The best one while in uniform was Thanksgiving of 1990. My team was preparing to do a forward watch mission on the Saudi-Iraq border for Desert Shield, but the team leader heard that President and Mrs. Bush were going to visit the troops. He made sure we were there." Jamie laughed, "Along with about a couple thousand other mugs from the 82nd. Still, it was pretty special."

Just before it was Sue's turn to share a Thanksgiving story, Jamie's radio link to the Tomahawks came alive. He picked up his headset and started a brisk conversation with one of his men. He completed the conversation and said, "We've got a bit of a challenge. It appears

TIMESHARE is on his way. The bugger is way early. Worse still, it looks like he is being followed."

"What's the plan?"

"We have a contingency plan for this sort of thing. The Tomahawks will let *TIMESHARE* through and then they will set up what looks like a police road traffic stop. They have the necessary resources to handle the trailing vehicle. It may be just another smuggler or it may be something else. We hold the meeting and the 'Hawks will contact us once they sort things out on the road."

"If it is trouble?"

Jamie smiled a humorless smile. "Oh, we'll hear trouble well before they report anything."

TIMESHARE arrived in no condition to be debriefed. He was scared and frantic. Sue watched as Jamie did his best to calm him down. He offered him strong black tea with three lumps of sugar. He made *TIMESHARE* sit down, take some deep breaths and finish the first mug of tea before he said anything. Finally, he said, "Pieyter, it is trouble. I need your help."

"Of course, my friend. We are always ready. Tell me what happened and what you need. Take your time. Start at the beginning so I know everything."

Sue decided it would help for *TIMESHARE* to hear a woman's voice. She reached out and gently touched his arm. She said, "We will help, uncle. Do not worry."

Jamie filled *TIMESHARE's* mug and said, "Please, brother. Trust us."

He started slowly. "It all started because I asked too many questions of the Iranians. They did not like my questions and they offered no answers. I did not argue with them and tried to make a joke. They didn't laugh, but they seemed to accept my explanation. Then today when I was working at my warehouse, I noticed there were Russians in a Landcruiser watching my shop. I decided not to go home. I did not want to show them where I lived and where my family lives. I drove around Dushanbe and then took the ferry across the Amu Darya and came here. They followed me all evening."

Just as *TIMESHARE* finished his story, there was the sound of a very short, very violent firefight. He looked up at Jamie. "Pieyter, are we under attack."

Jamie smiled and said, "No, brother. But the Russian followers are."

The radio squawked and Jamie put on the headset. He listened for a few seconds and then said, "Shabash!" He turned to *TIMESHARE* and said, "The Russians are no more."

TIMESHARE said, "What about my family?"

"Do the Iranians or the Russians know where you live?"

"I do not think so. I am very careful to only meet clients at my warehouse."

Jamie offered almost parental guidance in slow, deliberate formal Persian. "Then we will move you and your family as soon as we can. We need you to return to Dushanbe and gather your family. Take them out of town. Be sure you are not followed. We will meet on the Termez highway tomorrow night at 20hrs at the kilometer marker 110. You and your family will be safe. Do you have anyplace you can stay in Afghanistan?"

TIMESHARE nodded. "My wife's family lives in Kholm. I have used my profits over the years to create a farm for them. We can live there if you get us out of Tajikistan."

Sue had no idea what Jamie was considering but she used this moment to touch *TIMESHARE* once again on the forearm. She said, "Uncle, we will take care of you. This is my promise."

"Maryam, I believe you."

Jamie continued in his most formal Persian. He said, "Brother, you need to leave now. You must go home and gather your family. Leave the house before dawn. Do not go back to your warehouse when you leave your home. Take the family on a drive into the mountains. The Iranians and the Russians will not know where you have gone. The Ismailis in the mountains will not talk to them, so you will be safe. Find a tea house and enjoy your last day in Tajikistan. Remember, come down after dark. Talk to no one. Stop nowhere. Take the Termez Road and stop at marker 110. Wait for me there."

"And my men? What should I do about them?"

"How do you contact them?"

"Many ways. Most are locals who I call. They serve as couriers."

"Can you call them using the local payphones."

"Of course, Pieyter. That is how I do it."

"Then call the couriers and use whatever code you have that tells them to go to ground. Do this first before you go home to your family. I know you must have a code like that in case the police got too close to your work."

"Of course."

"Tell them you will be in touch. Inshallah, you will. Now, brother repeat the instructions."

Sue listened carefully as *TIMESHARE* repeated the instructions. He did so without error.

Jamie reached into his rucksack and handed *TIMESHARE* a mobile phone and a parcel. He said, "Brother, this is for only one call. That is the call I will make to you when you are at marker 110. Do not turn on the phone until 19hrs. I will contact you between 19 and 20hrs. Use the parcel as you see fit to make sure you, your family and your men are safe. Trust me."

TIMESHARE reached out and grabbed Jamie's hand. Sue could see there were tears in his eyes. "You are my brother. I trust you with my life." He stood up slowly, rubbing his right leg as if to get the blood flowing back into his old wounds. *TIMESHARE* turned and walked down the hill.

Sue shook her head and said, "That was amazing. How did you come up with all of that on the spur of the moment?"

Jamie let out a deep breath. He looked directly into Sue's eyes. "Always plan for the worst. In this part of the world, that means always plan for an exfiltration. I've had this plan in place for the better part of a year. He always lived on the edge. I was determined not to let him fall off the edge." Jamie poured himself a cup of tea and said, "Of course, now he has to follow instructions. He has five thousand dollars in Tajik currency. That's his part of the bargain. We need to get going." Jamie looked at the tritium dial on his military watch. "There is a lot of work that needs to be accomplished before tomorrow night. If you don't mind, I need you to drive us home. I have some calls to make."

Sue nodded as they stood up and packed their kit. Sue walked toward the truck while Jamie checked the area with a blue-filtered flashlight to be sure nothing remained of their time with their agent. They loaded into the truck and started toward the dirt highway. Sue said, "You never said what the Tomahawks reported. "

"Dangerous country to be driving at night. Easy to come upon a smuggler's ambush. Real easy."

"Too bad, eh?"

"Too bad for whoever was in the Land Cruiser, that's for sure."

"Russians?"

"The Tomahawks thought they were Central Asians. I suspect the Russians are too careful to come across the Amu Darya just to follow TIMESHARE."

"Then it will be a while before anyone in Dushanbe expects to hear a report."

"Inshallah. Now, please drive carefully. This is not the autostrada in Italy and this truck isn't your FIAT."

"Flash?"

"Massoni."

Sue looked over at Jamie's face bathed in the green glow of the Ranger's instrument panel. He looked as serious as she had ever seen him.

EXFIL FLIGHT

When they arrived at the safe house in Hairatan just before 0200hrs, Jamie said to Sue, "Get some sleep. I will wake you in a couple of hours. This is going to be a long run and you need to get some sleep now because you won't get any until we have *TIMESHARE* and his family safe and sound. I will grab some later today after I get the wheels in motion for the exfiltration. I will need you as fresh as possible this afternoon when we are checking everything. I said I have this planned out, but that doesn't mean I have everything ready to go. We will need to check and double check stuff. Now, get lost!"

Sue knew that Jamie was right. She wanted to help, but right now, the way she could help most was to be as fresh as possible later in the day. Sleep was something that tough guys pretended they didn't need. Old warriors knew it was something you had to plan for and grab whenever you could. Sue was no old warrior, but she knew Jamie, just like Massoni, had been through enough bad times that his advice made sense.

As she crept into the room she shared with Flash, she heard a voice from inside a sleeping bag say, "How'd it go?"

"Not as well as can be expected. It is going to be crazy tomorrow so get your beauty sleep now. Jamie gave order for me to get a few hours sleep. I suspect you are going to need your beauty sleep as well."

"Now after that little prologue, you know you have to tell me something, anything. Remember, Flash demands data."

"*TIMESHARE* has been compromised. We are going to exfil him and his family tomorrow night. I don't know how, Jamie didn't say."

Flash was already up and pulling on black sweatpants and a black hooded sweatshirt.

Sue said, "Where do you think you are going?"

"Downstairs to help. Tomorrow, you are going to be focused on action hero stuff. I suspect tonight Jamie just might need a super genius like the Flash."

Sue pulled the sleeping bag over her head and said, "Wake me at dawn, super genius."

"Check, action hero."

Flash found Jamie making himself some tea. She could see he was worried and not up for any comic relief. Just like Massoni, when the joking stopped you knew it was deadly business. She padded silently over to Jamie wearing black tai chi shoes. She started making coffee.

"What are you doing here?"

"Making coffee."

"And then?"

"And then I am going to do whatever you need me to do. Make you tea, make you food, assemble any sort of data you need, whatever it takes. I'm not one of your commandos..."

Jamie smiled and said, "Until you are. I seem to remember a night in Pakistan and a chick with a sniper rifle..."

"Yeah, well okay. Think of me as a Demi-Commando. Sort of like a Demi-Sec wine."

"OK, here's what we need. I need all the data you can pull from SIGINT and UAV imagery on Dushanbe and on the highway heading west out of the city for the last 48 hours. I suspect Sue told you we have lives to save."

Flash filled her coffee cup, added two healthy scoops of sugar and headed to the table with the workstations. "What's the logon? Remember, we don't want to use the SOF net."

Jamie walked over to where Flash was sitting and typed in *SOFGE-NIUS1*. "I created a shadow account just for you."

Flash smiled her most gentle smile and said, "You shouldn't have."

"Let's just say, I know my limitations and I know your capabilities."

"Only some."

"Enough! Get to work. Meanwhile, I have to get the rest of the rescue team assembled."

Flash threw a pillow at Sue's head at 0700hrs. Sue shot upright like she had just received an electric shock.

"Why did you do that?"

"Because I have seen you thrash around when you have your dreams. I figured a gentle wake up nudge might result in some danger. Long range pillow launch seemed just right."

Sue rubbed her face and said, "What time is it?"

"0700hrs. Jamie instructed me to let you sleep until now. He just crashed. He said we are going to regroup at noon and review the plan."

"The plan?"

"Beats me. I spent the night preparing situational awareness for all the threats I could think of, assembled imagery, maps and general info on the city and the highway heading west. I figured it wouldn't go to waste because it's the same area we are going to work in when we conduct the SWORDFISH op."

"OK, so what do I do between now and noon?"

"Well, a shower might be a good start."

"Smelly?"

"Yup. After that, Jamie gave me a file that you need to read. I read it and I think you definitely need to read it."

Twenty minutes later, Sue came down the stairs in her sweats and black trainers. This was the sort of day when she would have preferred to wear shorts and a t-shirt, but she still wasn't comfortable with the stares she knew she would get from Jamie's teammates when they saw her prosthetic.

Flash looked up from a workstation. She said, "While you are getting your tea, some coffee would be nice."

"Check." Sue returned in a minute with Flash's coffee and a mug of hot water with a tea bag floating on the surface. "You said I had something to read?"

"Yup. You have to hand it to these OGA guys. They are definitely members of the Department of Redundancy Department. They still have a secure fax capability so even though they are also under this CI threat, they have the ability to send and receive data. We could learn something from that. I found out Jamie's commo guy still knows how to send and receive Morse code and they still have a book of ciphers so that if all else fails, they can communicate the same way your granddad did in the OSS. Amazing."

Sue opened the file as she said, "Yeah, amazing." There were about 50 pages in the file with various reports from CIA, DIA, and the FBI. She knew there was a reason why Jamie wanted her to read the file, but she also knew that her tolerance for HQS speak, no matter whose headquarters, was limited. She looked up at Flash and said, "Any chance of a Cliff Notes version of this?"

Flash shook her head. "Really? Your little case officer brain can't handle 50 pages?"

"Not on less than five hours sleep."

"You got five hours."

"I got about five hours in the rack. That doesn't mean I got five hours sleep."

"Poor baby. OK, if you want the basics, I will give you the basics. I will even give you some tape so you can tab the parts of the file you absolutely need to read."

Sue said sincerely, "Thanks."

Flash started at the beginning of the file. "This is a joint intelligence community operation now. Everyone is still calling it *Silicon Addiction*. The primary threat is to our communications channels. The

Agency has the capability to disrupt the threat by creating a ghost network. Our pal Melissa Nez has been the team lead on creating the network. The hard part is filling the ghost net with stuff that looks like real material. I figure the Agency has the manpower..."

Sue said, "Or the cyber power..."

"Yup. It is also critical that when they deploy the ghost network there isn't a clear delay that would reveal the change. That's where we come in. More on that later. SOF doesn't have any of those sorts of resources. And, it looks like our threats are coming from the Iranian use of the material anyhow, so shutting down that part of the net is something we don't need to worry about because our boss intends to design a serious kinetic disruption in the UAE to disrupt if not destroy that angle."

"So, what are we expected to do?"

"Luckily, as Jamie said, we are no longer expected to tap the line. We are just supposed to disrupt the data going into Dushanbe for about an hour. That will give the geniuses back in CONUS enough time to stand up the ghost network and start feeding the Russians false data."

"I saw a part of the file was from the FBI."

"Now, here's where it gets interesting. We were part of the CONUS based investigation when we were at DLI. You do remember DLI, right?"

"Yes, dear."

"And that CI dish of an investigator?"

"Yes, dear. Please move on."

"I just wanted to be sure..."

"If you continue down this route, I may jam a pencil into your head."

"You could try." Flash smiled a less-than-friendly smile. "OK, so that part of the investigation and your brother's part of the investigation dovetailed into a separate set of operations that has the FBI all over the US taking apart the Russian and Hizballah networks. Honestly, I found that fascinating but I doubt you would except for one little piece."

"And?"

"Well, there is this operation taking place in Chautauqua, NY."

Sue felt her stomach churn. "Not again."

"Yup. Except this time, no gunfights and no grenades." Flash smiled and said, "At least not yet. The Russians seem to have put some sort of cyber parasite on your Grandfather's house. It was just one of many in CONUS designed to obscure the network. They are still working on that one."

"My mom doesn't seem to be able to stay out of trouble."

Flash smiled and said, "I need to meet her."

Sue looked up. All she could think to say was "Inshallah." She took a sip of tea and said, "So what are we doing now?"

"Well, your super genius pal is designing something that will disrupt the data pipe. Since we are going into bad guy country tonight anyhow, I figured we might as well do something for our mission while helping Jamie with his mission."

"What's the plan?"

"I haven't quite figured one out yet."

"Perfect."

"Hey, give me some credit. I have to think up this stuff all on my own. It's not like you are an engineering wizard."

"I didn't think you were either."

Flash smiled and pointed to the other side of the work room. "Nope, but he is."

"Who is?"

"Barry is Jamie's commo dude. The same guy who can do old-school stuff so we can communicate. He just happens to have a masters in electrical engineering. He and I have been scheming since 06 this morning. He says he will have a plan by noon."

"Charmed him, eh?"

"Flash is good at lots of stuff in case you hadn't figured that out."

Sue shook her head. She said, "Any chance for breakfast?"

"All the oatmeal you can eat, but not near the workstations."

"You want some?"

"Why not."

They left the control room and headed to the kitchen. Tea and porridge sounded just about right to Sue. Flash had been looking at the frozen bagels and decided to see what a mix of microwave and toaster would do for her breakfast.

***

At 1130hrs, Sue and Flash returned to the ops center. The rest of Jamie's team were at the far side of the room addressing other operations. The LED screens on the walls showed video feeds from two separate drone operations in the area. Jamie's commo tech, Barry, and a new Agency officer were sitting in another corner of the room working over a map and a yellow legal pad. They seemed to be working on a series of calculations.

The new Agency officer had arrived while they were eating and working through the details of the file. Sue noticed immediately the newcomer was unlike any of the other Agency officers she had ever met. First, he was older. Flash whispered "Who is the geezer? Some visitor from a country western band?"

Sue guessed he was nearly 60. Hardly a geezer by normal standards, but a very old man by SOF standards where mandatory retirement age was after 30 years in service. That usually meant well before 55 years old. He had a flat top haircut and a slight paunch. He was about two inches shorter than Flash. Blue jeans, cowboy boots and a well-worn short-sleeved khaki field shirt. An ancient Rolex GMT Master on his left wrist and a heavy gold bracelet on his right wrist. Peeking out from under the shirttail was a worn, leather holster that looked like it held a Browning Hi-Power. On the chair next to him was a very old, well used, shearling-lined flight jacket. In a room full of big personalities, the final thing that made Tony out of place was he was very quiet. Sue whispered back to Flash, "I reckon he is some senior come to tell us not to screw this up."

"A Headquarters geezer on Jamie's turf? I'm doubting that guess. I mean, really, just look at his clothes. It's like he just stepped out of a time machine." Flash nodded and walked over to find out.

Just as Flash started to engage, Jamie walked in wearing a t-shirt,

Ranger panties and crocs on his feet. He looked like he hadn't slept all night and, as both Sue and Flash knew, that was because he hadn't slept all night. He said, "Tony, thanks for coming up to visit. I hope you haven't been too bored talking to Barry."

Tony's baritone voice, tempered by years of whiskey and cigarettes, was just above a whisper. He responded to Jamie's jibe, "Shenk, the only reason I'm here is because the chief ordered me up here. I knew as soon as I got the instructions that I was in deep shit if you were planning a mission."

Jamie looked hurt. "As if I would put you in harm's way."

"Like Ramadi in 2005?"

"OK, so things didn't go exactly as planned."

"I guess. Who are the ladies?"

"Sue and Flash. They are our SOF partners."

Sue decided to add to the amusement. She offered her hand and said, "He did get me blown up in Baghdad."

Tony walked over and shook her hand. "At least one of you has suffered under Jamie's yoke before."

Flash said, "Hey, he made me ride over the Hindu Kush in the middle of the night…in winter."

Jamie said, "And did you complain? No. Did I give you coffee when you woke up?"

Flash said, "No! You offered tepid tea."

"It was tepid because you were a late riser."

Sue realized this could go on forever if she didn't intervene. "Tony, what part do you play in Jamie's world?"

"My job is to get you in and out of Tajikistan."

"Land or air?"

"Air."

Jamie said, "And wait until you see how! You are going to love it."

An hour later they loaded into two of Jamie's Rangers. Tony was in the lead vehicle with one of the mechanics that flew in with him.

Jamie drove Sue and Flash in the second vehicle. They pulled out of the compound and immediately turned and headed east, away from the main highway. Flash was the first to ask the question, "Where the heck are we going? I don't see anything but a set of truck tracks in the sand."

Jamie smiled. "It is my secret airstrip. It is also where the Tomahawks live. Relax, it's not too far."

They hit a substantial rut in the road. Even though they were belted in, Sue and Flash and their kit were thrown around the truck interior like marbles in a blender. Sue suffered the bone jarring ruts in silence, but Flash couldn't let it go. She said, "So, am I going to be both deaf and a cripple by the time we arrive?"

Jamie said, "Did someone in the back seat ask for music? Excellent." He turned on the radio and another of Jamie's CDs of 1970s rock music came out of the speakers.

Sue turned to look back at Flash and said, "You had to make it worse, didn't you?"

Flash shrugged.

Eventually, they drove up to a fenced compound that held three sets of double-wide trailers and a large military-style hangar. The Tomahawks at the gate recognized the two Rangers and let them in. On arrival, they drove onto an improvised runway which looked to be made of some type of steel mesh and crushed gravel. Nearly as noisy as the previous dirt track but mercifully level. The two trucks pulled up in front of the main door of the hangar.

Tony had already arrived and was talking to his ground crew. Jamie said, "Don't be surprised about how Tony's ground crew treats him. He is their hero. Been flying for the Agency for nearly forty years. Licensed to fly anything from a C130 to a crop duster. Cut his teeth flying Porters and old B25s in Laos. The Kabul hangar has the station helicopters, a couple of special purpose fixed wing aircraft and this wonderful beast!"

Sue and Flash got out of the Ranger and faced an aircraft that looked to be something out of a World War II newsreel. As always,

Flash had the first word. "What sort of aircraft is that? Are we wing-walking to Tajikistan?"

Before Jamie could say a word, Tony spoke in a defensive tone. "That is my aircraft. It is an AN2 Colt. It was manufactured in the 1950s. Completely tuned by my mechanics down south and hardly any parts from the 1950s. Well, some parts are original since we couldn't find replacements."

Sue started to walk around the aircraft. At some point in its history, the aircraft had been painted a bright red similar to the red used in search and rescue aircraft and Coast Guard patrol craft. Nearly sixty years of exposure to the elements meant the exterior was now a faded rust color. The feature that had captured Flash's attention was that the Colt was a biplane. The top wing was both wide and long, fairly typical of any short takeoff and landing aircraft, but longer and wider than any US military STOL aircraft. A lower wing extended out from the bottom of the fuselage. It was only about half as long, but just as wide. The landing gear looked to be modified with a heavy-duty frame and a pair of tires that looked like the tires on the front axle of a tractor. Under the engine cowling was another throwback from the last century: a radial engine with a four-bladed propeller.

Jamie looked at Flash as she walked around the aircraft with a frown on her face. "Ah, you are just a spoiled sport. The Air Branch guys have transformed the aircraft. New engine, new cockpit, bigger fuel tanks. They checked the wing spars. Nothing is going to fall off. Even a little radar jammer in case we do get found. What's not to like?"

Flash said, "How about entering a hostile country, going after a set of even more hostile mercenaries, recovering an asset and his family, and doing the entire thing with winter on the way."

"If it was easy, they would send the Army to do this."

"Wait a second, we are the Army."

"Not any more my friends. Didn't I tell you? To make sure the Department of Defense lawyers didn't get their panties in a knot, SOF officially detailed you guys to me. Just like in the movies, that allows the Secretary of Defense to disavow any association with you. Right now, you are on the books as two more of Jamie's minions. Sue, remember when I said I had been sheep dipped? Well, you are officially sheep dipped."

"Dandy," was all Sue could think to say. Sue turned to Tony and said, "I notice there isn't any tail number or other markings."

"We can add those depending on where we go. For tonight's job, we are just going to be…anonymous."

Flash walked up to Tony: "With that radial engine, you are going to be anonymous?"

"Depends on where you fly and how low you fly."

Jamie said, "See, I told you it was special. That's the sheer genius of the operation. If we are going to infiltrate into Tajikistan and exfil my guy and his family, the only solution is to fly. Uzbekistan and Tajikistan have been on the edge of war since the fall of the USSR. The only place we can cross the Amu Darya is at the Termez bridge or the Termez ferry. That's the easy part. Then we would have to cross a well-defended border with Uzbek, Tajik and Russian guards and most of the border is mined. I'm not liking that option. Now we could parachute in, but then we might have to walk out. Remember what I said about border guards and minefields?" Jamie had a thermos cup in his hand and took a sip that to Sue smelled suspiciously like her mother's favorite tea, Earl Gray.

"So, here we have an AN-2 Colt that was used by the Soviet Air Force for just about anything when they needed a STOL aircraft. According to the overhead, there are a half dozen of these sitting on the Dushanbe airfield in different states of decay. At least two of them are still used by the Tajik National Police to move their guys around the country. The STOL capability allows them to land on roads or farm fields. And, the best deal is none of the AN-2s ever made had any other electronics that allow air defense to identify them. It has a twelve-passenger payload which should cover us and *TIMESHARE's* family." Jamie smiled and said, "Plus, I've always wanted to use a Lysander for an operation. The Colt is no Lysander, but it is pretty darn close."

"Lysander?" Sue wasn't familiar with the word.

Finally Tony spoke up. His voice was just above a whisper, "Really, you don't know about the Lysander? Ms. O' Connell, I'll bet your granddad used one in the OSS. Great STOL aircraft from World War II. Delivered spies and saboteurs all over France. Plus, it was a dream to fly."

Sue said, "My granddad?"

"Flew him in and out of a bunch of Laotian airstrips. He was a senior, I was a punk pilot who gave up a dandy bush-pilot job in Alaska to fly for Air America. Of course, in those days we used Pilatus Porters, but we didn't care who knew we were flying."

Sue shook her head, "Another set of stories that I never heard."

Jamie said, "Enough reminisces, we actually came out here to see the aircraft so we can load plan for tonight." He turned to Tony, "I reckon we will have about 150lbs of kit for the fiber optic sabotage and then four of us. That leaves us with more than enough room for the folks we are pulling out of Tajikistan, right?"

Tony nodded. He said, "We need to keep the heavier weight near the wing struts. When we leave Tajikistan, put the passengers in the back. I suspect they won't weigh much."

Flash said, "What he's saying is you need to be as far forward as possible."

Jamie looked hurt. "Are you saying I'm fat?"

Sue wasn't in the mood, so she said, "Just heavy, not fat. After all, muscle is more dense than fat."

Jamie turned to Flash. "What she said." He turned to Tony: "We need to be on the ground for about an hour before the linkup with the asset at 2000hrs. So, when do we need to be here to load up?"

"OK. It's going to take us about a little over an hour to get there given my flight route. So, we need to leave around 1700hrs. You need to be here at 1600hrs so there is no delay. It should be plenty dark, so I'm not worried about either our takeoff or landing on the highway in Tajikistan."

"Check, Tony. OK, you two, let's get back home and see what my super genius has concocted for the sabotage part of this operation."

Flash was already walking to the Ranger. She said, "Just when did we start calling your place home and, by the way, super genius is my job."

Jamie loaded into the driver's seat, started the truck and more 1970s rock music throbbed in the speakers. "Whatever."

They returned to the airfield at 1600hrs. Sue and Flash were in the rear two seats with Jamie driving and Barry in the front. They were all wearing black watch caps, olive green flight suits and black boots. The sabotage equipment had been cross loaded into the three rucksacks making each weigh a little over 40lbs. Flash and Barry explained the purpose of the equipment, but Sue barely understood their deep dive into fiber optics and electronics. Eventually Jamie explained, "They have created an electronic pulse machine. Think of it as a microwave that we are going to wrap around the fiber optic line." He watched as Sue offered her best impression of someone dazed and confused. "OK, let's just say, they are going to access one of the inspection ports, do whatever magic they are going to do, and we are going to keep watch while they do it. Got it?" Sue nodded.

Now, as they walked to the aircraft with rucks on their backs, Flash turned to Sue and said, "You okay with carrying one of these?"

"You think I have a choice?"

"Nope. I guess we just have to embrace the suck once we get on the ground."

Sue's comment was lost in the sound of the large radial engine firing up.

Jamie walked over to Flash and said, "You can't come."

"I don't weigh much. In fact, I weigh less than Sue."

"That's not the reason why you can't come. I need someone here to monitor the comms and manage our infil and exfil. We don't need three operators on the ground doing the needful in Tajikistan. In fact, if I didn't need Sue to handle *TIMESHARE's* family, I wouldn't take her. I knew you would be a creep about this. Let me show you why I need you here."

Jamie took a crestfallen Flash into a small office in back of the hangar. He turned on the lights and revealed his reasoning. "I have a Soviet built, stand-alone radar modified to modern standards. I have two download screens for the two drones we have flying in support of this mission. They don't have reach to see the landing site, but they do have coverage about twenty klicks into Tajikistan. I also have a separate, commercial link set up between you and your pal Melissa Nez back at the Agency. You won't be able to talk classified shop, but you will be able to serve as our link to the Agency when they start to switch over to the ghost network. No one on my team but Barry is cleared to *Silicon Addiction*. Finally, I need you managing the connection to Tony. Flat out, I need your brains here rather than lugging another rucksack in the desert." Jamie paused and said, "Please?"

Flash was already sitting in the nylon swivel chair in front of the multiple screens. She started to work the keyboard serving as the link to the Agency. She put on the headset with the boom microphone and looked at Jamie. "You need me here. I get it. Now get out of here."

Jamie left with a smile on his face. They loaded their rucks through the crew door, climbed in and secured the rucks. Sue looked at Jamie and said, "Where's Flash?"

"She's doing what only Flash can do. She's going to manage the entire operation for us. I will carry the last rucksack to the target. No dramas, so load up."

Barry and Sue belted into the primitive sling seats on opposite sides of the fuselage. Jamie climbed up front with Tony in the co-pilot seat. Sue and Barry put on sound suppression headsets so that when they did finally land in Tajikistan, there would be no temporary or permanent hearing loss from the industrial sound of the Colt's radial engine. As they settled into for the ride, Sue noticed the interior of the aircraft smelled of aviation fuel and industrial lubricant. She hoped the fuel smell was simply a remnant of the fueling process and not some sort of fuel leak. Jamie looked back into the hold of the aircraft, smiled and gave them a thumbs up. Sue used that moment to offer a different hand signal in reply. The aircraft taxied out to the metal runway and lifted off into the darkness.

A SIMPLE MEETING IN A VAN

Once Smith and his two HUMINT operators got off the *Iwo Jima*, Smith immediately dispatched Ginger back to Cyprus to maintain contact with his assets. He warned Ginger to watch for any CI signs that might argue that his assets were also compromised. Smith closed by saying, "For God's sake, stay safe. If it means a less productive meeting, so be it. But we already know that one set of our operations has been compromised and at least one asset tried to kill Sandy. Build in whatever security measures you need. If you need guardian angels, I can get you an ODA from the 10th Special Forces FOB in Germany. Just let me know." Ginger left on the next available commercial flight to Cyprus.

The next day, Smith held a secure video teleconference with his sergeant major to catch up on all HICU operations and specifically on the operations related to their compromised communications. Massoni reported that none of the other HICU operations had shown any degree of compromise and SOF Headquarters recommended a cautious restart. He also provided additional information from both the CIA and the FBI on the links between the Russian cyber operation and the Iranian cyber-scraping effort in Northern Virginia. Finally, he offered the latest information from Flash on both the buoy operation in the Black Sea and the developing situation in Afghanistan.

Smith looked up at the screen in Sandy's small office on the US

Navy compound in Manama. Massoni had never quite captured how the video camera and the microphone worked in SVTCs. His face moved back and forth between filling the whole screen and disappearing completely. His sergeant major voice roared out of the speakers in the office and Smith spent some time adjusting the volume so that he could stand the noise. After Massoni delivered his updates, Smith asked "So what are we supposed to do here in the Gulf?"

Massoni shook his head and offered what little he knew. "Boss, the SOF HQS has identified a number of warehouses on the outskirts of Dubai that might serve as the delivery points for the Iranian cyber operation. They should have the details soonest. If they send them to me, I'll get them to you RFN. It looks to me like we are talking about a little bit of sabotage to disrupt the Iranian operation. I don't know how much capability you have out there, but the SOF staff offered to provide any resources you need to get the job done."

Smith said, "Roger, Jim. I will ask Sandy about that. If it is a small job, we may be able to do it ourselves or possibly borrow some operators assigned to the Fleet. I guess we are just going to have to wait and see. The best news today is that our problems seem to be limited to Sandy's patch and, perhaps, some of the operations we have in Afghanistan. Let me know as soon as you can. Out here."

Smith hit the close button on the keyboard and stood up. He stretched and thought about the current situation. After a less-than-positive experience in the first part of this trip, it looked as if there might be some closure. He wasn't looking forward to another trip to the UAE. Especially since it would have to be a trip using US Navy assets.

Before they could make another run to Dubai, Sandy had a meeting to complete. From a pure US force protection perspective during the upcoming holiday, he absolutely needed to meet his asset. The asset, with the HICU identifier 227, was a Bahraini dock worker in Manama. Sandy recruited him in 2007 after 227 walked into the US Embassy and requested a meeting with someone from security. 227 had proven to be a reasonable source on the efforts by IRGC collaborators to identify fleet activities and US Navy headquarters security measures. His motivations were relatively simple: he liked his job, he needed the money to support his family and even though he was a devout Shia Muslim, he did not want the US Navy to leave and take with it all the work that made his life better than when he was working at a dock owned by a cousin to the Bahraini emir.

Smith and Sandy decided to conduct the established car meeting with 227 together. In a two-up meeting, the handler usually stayed in the back with the asset and the driver focused on physical security. A moving car meeting was always difficult for a case officer. By using a driver, the case officer could focus on nothing more than the asset and the meeting and the car was never in one place for more than a few moments. It was about as safe an agent-handling method as could be expected outside a secure US facility. Smith asked, "What sort of vehicle can we use for this?"

Sandy smiled and said, "I bought a Korean micro-van last year from a fruit vendor here. Still has fruit advertisements on the side of the van. At the time, I thought it might be useful for an exfiltration van if I needed to get myself and the family out of town. It seems to me it would work perfectly so long as you think you can squeeze yourself into the driver's seat."

"Don't push it, Sandy. If it has wheels and an engine, I can drive it."

"Excellent, Boss. I recommend we do a little area familiarization for you over the next couple of days. Our meeting is Saturday night, 28 November at 1930hrs."

"Then let's get to work."

Smith and Sandy drove around the island for two days focusing on the various Manama streets near the commercial port. At the end of each day, Smith had two very pleasant evening meals with Sandy and his family in their quarters on the Navy post. While he never quite forgot the problems facing HICU during this time period, it was a very pleasant respite from what could easily be called the loneliness of command. Smith had a long career as an intelligence officer preceded by his first few years as an enlisted man in the Ranger Regiment. Except for Sergeant Major Massoni, he had no family, few friends, and no confidants.

Thanksgiving with a family was something he hadn't experienced in years. They talked about everything but work. Books, music, travel and Sandy's early life at sea all filled the evening with fun conversation. At the end of the meal, Smith said to Sandy's wife, Janet, "I want to thank you both for the hospitality. It has been great. We will be working on Saturday night and, assuming all goes well, we may need to make a short trip to Dubai. After that, I will get back to Italy depending on what sort of military hop I can catch and you can have a family back."

Sandy hadn't ever seen Smith demonstrate any degree of humanity and was shocked by it. Janet smiled and said, "Jed, it has been our pleasure. I know you have plenty to worry about right now, but I hope this has been a little break from those worries. Come visit us anytime."

Smith nodded. He wasn't quite sure what to say and figured the best he could do was to say nothing. He stood up, shook Janet's hand, and headed out the door. His BOQ room inside the Navy compound was waiting. As he left, Janet turned to Sandy and said, "That is one sad man. You have any idea why?"

"Beats me. These last couple of nights were the first time I have had non-work conversations with Smith. It's not like he has a real social nature."

"Sandy, you keep him safe. He is a softy at heart."

Sandy smiled and said, "If you think Smith is a softy, you should see our sergeant major. He is a real teddy bear."

Janet heard the sarcasm in his voice and punched Sandy in the arm before returning to the kitchen and the dishes.

On Saturday afternoon, Smith and Sandy prepared the van for the meeting. It was located in a small warehouse space inside the Navy facility. They completed an internal communications check, reviewed the concealments that held a medical kit, flashlight, pepper spray, pistols and other tools of the trade. Smith took his place behind the wheel and Sandy his place in the back seat. Smith keyed the radio linked to the US contractors managing the security perimeter: "Nighthawk, nighthawk. Two two leaving base. Confirm."

"Roger, two two. We will have the back gate open. Please give us at least 2 mikes before you return so we can make sure we have the gate open."

"Roger, Nighthawk. Out."

They drove for an hour along a set route to confirm that they were clean of any surveillance. The micro-van had a small four-cylinder engine that probably belonged in a small two-seat car rather than a van, but the engine had enough low-end torque that Sandy promised that they could scoot if need be. Sandy's voice came in Smith's earbud, "The engine will redline pretty quickly, Boss. You need to be careful on the accelerator."

"Thank you, Dr. Obvious. You just focus on what you are going to do tonight and I will do the driving."

"Check."

The pickup site was in a short alleyway just behind a fast-food stand advertising "*The best shawarma in Bahrain.*" It was close enough to the commercial port that 227 could walk to the site, but far enough away that he was unlikely to see any work colleagues. Smith approached the site at speed, downshifted rather than using his brakes, cut the lights and the van disappeared into the alley. Smith dropped down his night-vision goggles and looked into the green glow of the light-enhancing device. Standing at the end of the alley was a man in western clothes. He fit 227's description and was carrying a red nylon bag in his right hand. That was the safe signal. Smith said, "Looks like our man is ready."

Sandy said, "I will open the door and we'll get working."

As Sandy opened the door, he heard the whoosh of an RPG fired from behind the van. All he got out before it hit was, "Boss..."

The shooter was either inexperienced or had misjudged the size of the micro-van. The rocket propelled grenade skimmed off the riveted aluminum top of the van and continued down the alley toward 227. Either by plan or with common sense, 227 disappeared just as the round exploded on the far wall of an adjacent building.

The flash blinded Smith for a minute. The concussion from the grenade imploded the entire windshield, striking Smith with shards of tempered glass. He felt shrapnel hit his right shoulder and his ribs. A final piece of shrapnel struck the night vision goggles and broke them in half. Smith jammed the accelerator to the floor and headed toward the end of the alley and, he hoped, escape. He was deaf from the RPG concussion but he could feel bullets impacting the rear of the vehicle. He shouted, "Sandy, you okay?"

Sandy said, "Kinda busy right now, Boss." Sandy was leaning out of the van where there used to be a sliding door, firing an MP5 sub-machine gun in the direction of their attackers. Either the concussion or some pieces of shrapnel had peeled the door completely off the van.

Smith said, "Right turn. Hang on." He downshifted, and the whine of the little four-cylinder filled the cabin. The van made it around the corner and toward a side street that would connect to the main highway back to the Navy base. As they made the turn, another set of gunfire opened up from the roof of the building to their right. Rounds passed through the roof of the van creating rough flower petals in the aluminum. Again, the shooters did not seem to be terribly expert and the sprays of lead seemed to have missed both the driver and passenger. Sandy reached into one of the conceal-ments and pulled out a red smoke grenade. He released the spoon, reached out the open van door and threw the grenade as far in front of the van as he could. The van disappeared into the red smoke while rounds continued into the street. None hit the van.

Smith switched to the base radio and shouted, "Nighthawk, two two. We are RTB in two mikes. We have wounded and the vehicle is damaged. Confirm."

"Two two. Confirm you are RTB. Do we need to launch a QRF?"

"No need to launch a quick reaction force. We are near enough we can limp into base. We do not appear to be followed and have cleared off the x of the ambush."

"*Roger, Two two. We will have medics standing by.*"

"Thanks."

Later, neither Smith nor Sandy could say for sure how Smith made it back to base. Smith argued it was simply adrenaline; Sandy said it was sheer cussedness that saved them. Either way, they arrived at the back gate of the base and stopped just short of the ambulance that the security team called. Smith was suffering from blood loss from the two shrapnel wounds and a concussion from the shock of the shrapnel hitting his NVGs. Sandy hadn't noticed, but he had a gunshot wound in his left shoulder from the rooftop attack. They were both in the Navy hospital in minutes.

Two hours later, Sandy called his wife. He told her he was fine, which they both knew was a lie, but Smith was still in the operating room. He said he would be home as soon as possible. As soon as he hung up, he used the satellite phone he always carried in his meeting "go-bag." He called Massoni.

"Sandy, what sort of mess are you in now?"

"No time for jokes, Sergeant Major. The boss and I just ran into an ambush. I'm okay, well sorta okay. The boss is still in surgery. They told me that he will be fine, but that's just the shit that doctors always say when they don't know for sure."

"Sandy, I can be there in the morning. I'll catch the first military flight I can. You need more reinforcements or will I do?"

"Jim, I think you and I can do the needful. I certainly will appreciate your company."

"Check. I'm on it. I will call back as soon as I have an ETA. Out here."

Sandy sat back in the hospital chair and finally let himself accept the adrenaline wash that always followed a firefight. Between the adrenaline wash and the painkillers, he felt cold. He shivered and a nurse saw him. She came up with a blue blanket with an embroidered US NAVY insignia. She said, "Petty Officer, you need to get home or you need to get admitted. Which is it?"

Sandy looked up at the nurse. A lieutenant. He decided to be as polite as possible. He slowly stood up and said, "Ma'am, I need to stay until I find out how my CO is doing. I have to report to higher as soon as I know. My wife is on her way. I will go home then. OK?"

The nurse said, "Petty Officer Tealor, Colonel Smith is out of the operating room and in the ICU. He will make it. We know how to treat trauma, Tealor. Please report that much to your higher and then get out of here. You wound was superficial, but it was still a gunshot wound. No need to hang out here. Come back in the AM. That's an order."

"Yes, ma'am. And thanks. As soon as my wife gets here, I'll be gone."

As the lieutenant left, Sandy redialed Massoni's number. It wasn't great news, but it was about as good as could be expected.

EXFIL!

Sue made sure she had a seat near one of the portholes in the fuselage of the Colt. She wanted to see as much as possible before they landed in a location where she might need to make an immediate, life-or-death decision. The full moon had just risen on the eastern horizon as they took off, bathing the barren desert landscape in silver light. What Sue might not have expected was how low Tony flew as they headed north and east toward the Afghan-Tajik border. He seemed to be not much more than 200 feet off the ground as they skimmed the rolling fields and dunes of eastern Balkh province. Once, she looked away from the porthole to view Tony and Jamie in the front of the aircraft. Both were wearing advanced night-vision googles similar to the ones she had seen worn by pilots from the 160th Special Operations Aviation Regiment. Sue knew that even walking with night-vision googles was a challenge. Flying at 150 miles an hour at 200 feet required a level of skill she had never seen in any pilot except of those in SOAR. No wonder Tony's ground team thought him special.

Sue recognized the terrain for the first thirty minutes of the flight, as Tony followed the smugglers' track that Jamie used to get to their meetings with *TIMESHARE*. During this part of the trip, she couldn't help but wonder how *TIMESHARE* and his family were surviving their ordeal. Everyone on the plane had long experience in life-threatening operations. *TIMESHARE's* family would have had their normal life completely disrupted in the last 24 hours. They wouldn't know what was going to happen next. They would have to trust his judgment and pray. Jamie said *TIMESHARE* had a son and a daughter and both were in their teens. What would a teenager think when father said we are leaving our home for good?

Sue's own experience of moving every two or three years had been difficult enough. But at least in her case, the move was structured, predictable and included moving all their belongings to someplace new. They weren't running for their lives. Sue's thoughts returned to her travel with her mom after her grandfather was killed and her mom's house was under surveillance. At least when she was running for her life, she knew why. She made a mental note to be sure to engage *TIMESHARE*'s family once they were on board.

The aircraft did a hard bank north. Sue looked out the porthole and saw nothing but stars in a silver-gray sky. They leveled out and she heard the engine increase pitch as they dropped even lower to the ground. For a brief moment, Sue saw the glow of the Amu Darya. At this time of year, the river was barely 100 meters across so the crossing into Tajikistan was simply a flash of river and then more of the same dunes and a few farm fields that used the river water for irrigation. There were no lights all the way to the horizon, which was framed by a series of black mountains to the east.

A few minutes later, Jamie looked back from the co-pilot seat. He shouted and gave a familiar set of hand signals. "One minute!" Jamie held up both hands with forefingers extended. Sue wondered if Jamie was enjoying playing the role of jumpmaster again. She looked across the fuselage at Barry. He acknowledged the signal with a thumbs up as they prepared their weapons and equipment to leave the aircraft as soon as it landed. Sue took one last look out the porthole and thought she saw movement on the ground below. A reception committee or enemies? They would know soon enough.

The landing was as smooth as any Sue had experienced. As soon as the aircraft slowed to taxi speed, Tony hit one of the wheel brakes and the plane spun around facing back the way it had come. Jamie walked back into the passenger area and said, "Welcome to Tajikistan. We will be here for a little less than an hour. I believe it is in our best interest to get hot on mission one — disrupting the fiber optic network." He looked at his watch. The tritium dial glowed nearly as bright as a flashlight. Sue noticed his watch was set for Zulu time — Greenwich Mean Time. Their flight was synchronized with both the arrival of *TIMESHARE* and the planned CIA HQS shift to the ghost network. There was no time to spare, so they opened the door on the left side of the aircraft and jumped out on the pavement of the highway that had served as their landing zone.

Jamie pulled one of the rucksacks over his shoulder and said, "OK, let's follow the little green chemlights to the inspection hatch for the fiber optic line." He smiled and said to Barry, "The Tomahawks have done all the work for you. The hatch is open so all you have to do is emplace the gizmo and turn it on," he looked at his watch, "in precisely ten minutes. Leave it on for ten minutes and then come back here. The Tomahawks will close the hatch, recover the chemlights and disappear into the night."

Jamie, Sue, and Barry headed toward the open hatch. Sue carried the power supply, Jamie carried the microwave generator, and Barry carried the actual disruption device to be placed on the fiber optic line. As promised, the Tomahawks had marked their way and opened the hatch. As they approached, Sue saw two of Jamie's team standing next to the hatch, smiling from ear to ear. Clearly, this was just another night's adventure for his team. Once at the hatch, Sue and Barry turned on the red-filtered headlamps they were wearing, opened their rucks and assembled the electronic device that would be used to disrupt the fiber optic signal. After dropping his ruck, Jamie walked over to the Tomahawks and started a conversation.

Barry jumped through the hatch. Once he was in place, Sue passed him the device. In the red glow of his headlamp, Sue saw him place the device on the conduit. The device looked like a gray cuff around the large white conduit piping that protected the actual fiber optics from any water or rodent damage. However, it would not prevent the microwave energy from disrupting the signal. Barry matched the timer with his own tritium-dialed watch and climbed out of the hatch.

As he reached the surface, he said, "All we have to do is wait. The device will do the rest."

Sue smiled. "Will we be able to heat a coffee from the microwave energy?"

"Let's hope not. When I built the device from the stuff in our warehouse, I did my best to shield the system so the energy is directed specifically into the pipeline."

"Just joking, you knucklehead. If we were going to have leakage, I would already have walked back to the aircraft to make sure I didn't lose my hair."

Jamie finally joined the conversation, "Though a bald O'Connell might be even more terrifying."

"It's a curse to be so beautiful, no?"

"So I've been told."

Jamie reached into a cargo pocket and pulled out an Iridium satellite phone. He dialed a number and said, "You awake?"

Flash's initial response was clearly less than polite. What she did say was, *"The client is in countdown."*

Sue heard Jamie say, "Roger."

Barry shook his head. He looked at his watch and said, "Here we go."

Sue said, "I don't hear anything."

Jamie whispered in her ear, "It's not supposed to make any noise, Sue."

"Oh." Sue looked over at the three Tomahawks standing just outside the range of their headlamps. All she could see was the white of their teeth as they smiled at the operators.

Jamie told Flash, "We are operational."

"Roger. The client is working on it."

"Tell us when they are good to go."

"Patience."

The ten minutes passed quickly. Jamie asked Flash if it was enough time.

"More than enough. The client says they are pleased with the delivery."

Jamie nodded and Barry jumped back down into the hatch and

recovered the device. They disassembled it, reloaded it into their rucksacks and headed back toward the aircraft. Sue looked over her shoulder as she walked away. The Tomahawks had already secured the hatch and were walking backwards away from the location recovering the chemlights and using brush to obscure their footprints. Jamie had trained them well.

When they reached the aircraft, Jamie said, "OK, load the kit into the airplane and then rejoin me out here. I'm not expecting any trouble, but if there is, we will need to get *TIMESHARE* and his family loaded while the Tomahawks do the needful against any unwanted guests."

⁓⁓⁓⁓⁓⁓⁓⁓⁓⁓⁓⁓⁓⁓⁓⁓⁓⁓⁓⁓⁓⁓⁓

They saw *TIMESHARE* before they heard his arrival. The lonely stretch of road had been empty for the entire time they were there and now they saw the headlights of a car heading their way. Jamie said, "I am going out to meet the car at the traffic control point that the Tomahawks have set up. He is going to need to see a friendly face."

Jamie jogged the 100 meters along the road up to the TCP. He watched as the car first slowed and eventually came to a stop. Jamie confirmed it was *TIMESHARE* and his family and walked them back to the aircraft. Tony already had the engine running as they approached. By the time they had reached the plane, the Tomahawks had disassembled the TCP, loaded into their trucks and driven into the desert with *TIMESHARE*'s car at the end of the convoy. Sue helped *TIMESHARE*'s wife and children climb into the aircraft and buckled them into their sling seats in the rear of the aircraft. She used her best Persian to assure them that everything would be okay. They didn't look convinced and neither was Sue.

Jamie shook his agent's hand and, with Barry's help, loaded *TIMESHARE* into the aircraft. Barry and Jamie jumped in and secured the door. Before Jamie could make it to the co-pilot's seat, the Colt had started to roll. Once Jamie was seated, Tony pulled the throttle back, the radial engine screamed, and in less than 200 meters, they were airborne. Jamie looked back into the darkened cabin and gave everyone a thumbs up.

Shortly after Tony had pointed the aircraft south, Flash's voice came through Tony and Jamie's headsets. *"Just so you know, this is going to be a bit of a challenge. You have company. Radar shows you have at least one, no two, rotary wing aircraft in pursuit. I don't know if they have located you yet. If you intend to make yourself invisible, now would be the time to start."*

Tony keyed his microphone and said, "Roger." He reached down to a set of toggle switches on the instrument panel and pushed both down until a red light appeared on both. He said to Jamie, "It may get a little uncomfortable for the folks in the back. You might want to warn them. You have a couple of minutes and then we start evasive maneuvers."

"Check." Jamie unbelted from his seat and worked his way back.

As Jamie started to the back of the aircraft, Tony heard Flash's voice in his headset. *"Neat trick, Klingon. Cloaking device appears to be working well."*

Tony smiled. He said, "We do our best."

Jamie came up to *TIMESHARE* and his family. He whispered in his agent's ear, received a nod and then headed back to Sue and Barry. They leaned forward as he squatted in between them. "Going to be a little bumpy for a bit. Turns out someone is trying to find us or at least trying to find *TIMESHARE*. Tony says he intends to lose them, but that will mean some serious flying. Got it?"

Sue said, "So, we are going to be riding the vomit comet."

"Exactly. But please do not barf in Tony's airplane. He will definitely be pissed off if you do."

Barry said, "Is there anything we can do?"

"Not unless you think you can hang out the door of the aircraft and shoot at our pursuers while Tony does a bit of dodge and run."

Sue shook her head, "Not in my job description."

Barry said, "Not mine, either."

"Then just stay belted in, keep your eyes on the portholes so you don't get airsick, and let Tony do his magic. If it looks like our guests are getting sick…"

Sue said, "I used to be a jumpmaster. I know…push their face to the window so they see the horizon. And, if at all possible, avoid getting sick yourself."

"Check, Sue. OK, I'm going to get back to the cockpit to see if I can help."

"You know how to fly?"

"Nope. But I do know how to navigate. He may need some help on that front." With that comment, Jamie started back to his seat just as the aircraft dropped in altitude. As he walked by *TIMESHARE*'s wife, she started to cry. Jamie reached down and touched his asset on the shoulder and smiled. He used his best Tajik to say "All will be well, my friend. I promise."

In her SOF career, Sue had flown with some of the best pilots in military service. The pilots from 160th SOAR were famous for delivering SOF operators anywhere, anytime, and in any conditions, almost always at night. The pilots in the USAF Special Operations Squadrons were equally well known for their willingness to deliver personnel and cargo on time and in exceptionally rough terrain. Still, Sue had never flown in an Agency aircraft piloted by a pilot as experienced as Tony. She watched as he brought the aircraft down and began to hug the terrain. Terrain-following radar and other military skills were commonplace. Flying at full speed at twenty-five feet above the ground was something entirely different. Flying at that altitude for any amount of time was hard on Sue's combat-expe- rienced composure. The bright moonlight made it easy for Sue to see every impending obstacle. As soon as one was avoided, the next one appeared first in shadows and then bathed in silver light. Her stomach was in knots for the entire time. Sue could not imagine what it must be like for Tony where any loss of concentration would mean catastrophe.

When the Colt crossed the Amu Darya, Tony keyed the micro- phone. He asked Flash, "What's the story?"

Flash's voice echoed in both Tony and Jamie's headsets, *"They hovered near your LZ and then headed directly south rather than along your flight route. Drone coverage shows now they are running a recce patrol west along the river. If they are Tajik government birds, that should be it."*

Jamie keyed his microphone, "If they are not Tajik birds, we can expect them to cross the river. Keep on them, K?"

"As if I was going to do anything else."

Tony continued to concentrate on his flying. Now that he was in Afghanistan airspace, he raised the Colt to a more comfortable 500 feet above ground. He turned on the transponder that identified the aircraft as friendly so that USAF fast movers and various helicopter gunships on air patrol did not scramble against an intruder. He said, "Flash, we are about twenty minutes out. Please let my crew know."

"WILCO."

Twenty minutes later, Sue could see the glow of the airfield lights and began to relax. The aircraft passed over the runway once, Tony banked the Colt and then settled it gently on the improvised runway. Unlike the landing in Tajikistan, Tony let the aircraft slow on its own and then taxied to the front of the hangar. They had made it.

JUST THE PERSON TO HAVE IN A GUNFIGHT

J amie walked back into the passenger compartment. He shook hands with *TIMESHARE* and then continued back to the aft passenger door. He opened the door, kicked out the hinged stairwell and walked out on the tarmac. Tony's ground team were already working on the aircraft. A small team of Jamie's Tomahawks were waiting with a van and one of the four-door Rangers to take *TIMESHARE* and his family to their relations in Kholm. After helping the family out and wishing them a quiet farewell, Jamie waved as the Tomahawks headed out.

Sue and Barry waited until Tony climbed out of his seat and headed to the door. Sue said, "That was some flying, Mister."

"Yup. It's what I do," Tony said. He climbed out of the aircraft, stretched a bit and then shouted to his team, "Let's get this bird in the hangar. She needs a quick check before we head back to Kabul. Come on. It's not as if we have the rest of the night off."

Barry turned to Sue and said, "I thought I would barf every time he made one of his jumps over some sand dune."

"Barry, it's all about keeping your eyes on the horizon. To be clear, it wasn't easy for me either. Let's offload the gizmo and get out of this contraption."

Sue got up slowly. She had learned that prolonged sitting paid havoc with her prosthetic. The tension related to the flight hadn't helped. She pushed off from the wall of the fuselage and stumbled slightly. Luckily, Barry was heading for the door so he didn't see her difficulty. She worked hard to avoid anyone outside family and her small circle of trust to know she was a BTK. By the time Barry was standing at the door, she was walking normally.

Barry stopped and said, "I'll pull out the rucksacks and toss them to you."

"At fifty pounds each, let's agree there won't be any tossing, OK?"

Barry smiled and turned back into the aircraft. Sue used that moment to climb carefully down the stairs leading with her prosthetic. When she got to the bottom of the stairs, Jamie was waiting. "Where's your pal, Flash?"

Sue shrugged. "Hey Jamie, I just got here, remember?"

The likely back and forth was interrupted by the distant, but unmistakable sound of the twin turbines of the Soviet-era helicopters. Slowly coming in from the east. Jamie looked at Sue and said, "Oh, that's not good."

Sue turned toward the aircraft and said, "Hey Barry. You need to get outside, now!"

Barry's muffled voice said, "What?"

Jamie stuck his head inside the crew door and said, "Get out here you silly tech geek! We may have a fight on our hands!"

Even in the moonlight, it was impossible to identify the approaching aircraft at that distance. They couldn't even be sure if there was one or two. Worse still, they didn't know if the aircraft they heard was friend or foe. After all, the Afghan Army was flying old Soviet-era helicopters. It could be the local security service or the local Balkh government militia investigating the airfield lights that suddenly illuminated in the middle of the night. Of course, there was a more sinister option — that they were about to be visited by SWORDFISH mercenaries.

Jamie looked at Sue and said, "You realize it might be some time before we get the Tomahawks back from their sojourn in Tajikistan. I reckon it's only us kids for a bit. I have a couple of RPGs in the hangar, but otherwise it is going to be a gunfight with what we have right now."

Sue said, "Swell. Go get the RPGs. Let Tony and his crew know what is happening and Barry and I will get behind some cover. Can he shoot?"

Barry was climbing down the stairs when he said, "Shoot what?"

Sue grabbed Barry by the hand and they trotted over toward a concrete structure that in some distant past probably served as a revetment for exhaust blasts when Soviet-era aircraft scrambled from the airfield. Tony's crew shut off the airfield lights and all the lights in the hangar as they manhandled the Colt inside. Now, the airfield had taken on a surreal nature as the full moon setting behind them backlit the hangar and the runway with long shadows. Sue remembered moonlit games of hide and seek with her brother when they would visit her grandfather at the Potomac River house. Now, the game was deadly serious. If they were careful, they would see their adversary long before they were seen. That might be their only hope of survival.

Jamie walked up to them carrying two RPG launchers and a ruck-sack full of RPG rockets. Around his neck was a set of blue hearing protectors. He was pleased to see that Sue and Barry were still carrying theirs from the flight. He said, "OK, this is all we have to play with for now. Tony and his guys are setting up a M2 .50 caliber machine gun on a tripod at the hangar door. They have some line of sight to the runway, but I'm hoping that a few RPGs may dissuade any visitors."

Barry said, "I don't know how to use one of those."

Sue smiled and said, "I don't think Jamie was going to let you use one anyhow."

Jamie turned to Barry and said, "I think you need to get back to the hangar and help Tony. Someone is going to have to make sure the .50 belt feeds properly and that's the sort of skill that an engineer will understand. Tony will be the gunner, but honestly, I'm not sure his mechanics will be much help. OK?"

Barry nodded and headed back to the hangar. Sue said, "That was an especially gentle way of getting Barry out of the way."

Jamie said, "Or, you might think it was my way of getting more one-on-one time with my favorite SOF superwoman."

Sue smiled. "Oh, Jamie. You really know how to talk to a girl."

"That's what they all say."

As the helicopter noise grew louder, Jamie and Sue moved to opposite sides of the concrete blast wall. They agreed that if there was more than one helicopter, Sue would fire first at the trailing aircraft and then Jamie would engage the lead aircraft. Jamie offered what Sue thought was a bit of unsolicited advice: "Try to hit the tail of the aircraft. If we can disable the tail rotor…"

"Thank you, General Shenk. I know enough about helicopters to know that if the tail rotor is disabled, the torque from the main engines will beat the helicopter to death all by itself."

As the helicopters approached, Sue checked her M4 and pistol after loading a rocket propelled grenade into the launcher. Their resources looked fairly puny, but Sue figured the maximum number of troops that they would face would be thirty. If they could take out one of the birds and if Tony engaged the other bird with the M2, they had a better-than-even chance to survive. Sue remembered some data from her days as a military intelligence officer at the 18th Airborne Corps. Direct attacks against a fixed defensive position required at least a four to one advantage. Those odds were not in Sue's favor right now. They had to reduce the odds early in the fight or they were finished. One of the reasons Sue left the conventional army was that her nature was to work alone, using stealth and skill. SOF was the best place in the army for those skills and she had proven capable. She also knew from real experience when she lost her left leg, that combat was not fair. She intended this fight to be as unfair as she could make it.

After what seemed to be forever staring into the darkness, Sue could finally see the two MI-8 troop-carrying helicopters. Painted black with a red commercial logo, they were most definitely not friendlies. Sue looked over at Jamie and he nodded to her. They would have one chance to win and it would be just as the helicopters nosed up, flared their props and prepared to land. They had to wait until the last minute before using their most powerful weapons. The helicopters arrived in trail traveling at 50 feet along the modified runway. They intended to land directly in front of the hangar.

Just before they landed the first helicopter launched a series of rockets from pods attached to the MI-8 landing gear. The rockets flew over Sue and Jamie's head and exploded on the runway just short of the hangar. Having fired what must have been rockets designed to keep any adversaries' heads down, they hovered and landed.

The rotor wash from the helicopters threw dust in all directions. Sue was temporarily blinded as sand billowed around her. When her vision began to clear, the first thing she saw was a flood of green tracers. The tracers were coming from behind the hangar and hitting the trail aircraft. Sue armed her RPG and fired at the same aircraft. The round hit the tail boom of the helicopter where it joined the main fuselage. The explosion was deafening. The flood of the tracers now moved up the length of the fuselage. Sue was close enough to see the cockpit glass shattering. The helicopter began to swirl, whether because of the loss of the tail rotor or the death of the pilot. As it swung in an unpredictable manner, the tail boom hit the first helicopter along the fuselage. The rear rotor became a saw that cut through the fuselage from bottom to top just in front of the twin turbine engines. The fuel tanks in the lead helicopter exploded and threw shrapnel in every direction. The two helicopters landed in a single mass of twisted and burning metal. Jamie fired his RPG at the lead helicopter as it landed. Sue was certain there would be no survivors.

Jamie walked up to her. He pulled down his ear protectors and pulled up his sand goggles. He said, "Hey, how did you make that shot? You didn't have any goggles!"

Sue admitted, "I just aimed in the general direction and let loose."

"Well, it did the job. Where did the green tracers come from?"

"Beats me. I always figured green tracers meant Soviet ammo. I expected the M2 tracers to be red."

From the shadows behind them, a voice said, "Well, that's because the tracers were Soviet. Just like the gun."

Jamie said, "Where were you in all of this?"

Flash said, "It turns out a couple of the Tomahawks showed me an old Soviet era anti-aircraft gun. A ZSU-23/2. They maintained it and had the ammunition. We pulled behind the hangar and waited. All I had to do was aim the two barrels of the 23mm gun and pull the trigger. Mighty impressive if I say so myself."

Jamie nodded. "Just the thing to have in a gunfight."

Sue smiled and said, "I think what you meant to say was Flash is just the person to have on your side in a gunfight."

Flash nodded and said, "What she said."

RECOVERY

Massoni arrived late. He used the power of the SOF Command Master Chief, the senior NCO for all of SOF, to get a seat on a P3 Orion flight from Sigonella Naval Air Station to the Navy airfield in Bahrain. Sandy picked him up and they went directly to the Navy hospital. Unlike his previous trip to the hospital when he was just another patient, Sandy began to realize quickly that sergeants major command serious influence no matter the service uniform. Massoni arrived in his Army Combat Uniform and highly polished jump boots. Almost immediately, the enlisted staff did everything they could to make sure his desires were met. Sandy traveled in Massoni's wake, arm in a sling and walking slowly due to the multiple scrapes and bruises from the previous night's attack.

The first stop was at the senior nurses' station in the ICU. Massoni did a masterful mix of senior NCO engagement and charm and the nurses responded in kind. The senior nurse on duty, a Navy lieutenant, said, "Sergeant Major, I'm afraid there is very little I can tell you right now about your commander, other than he is stable. His first trip into the operating room was reasonably short. However, early this morning, he had to be taken back into the operating room. The tissue damage related to his chest wound was more extensive than we thought and he suffered a collapsed lung. We treated that and now we have him under close watch. His wounds are not life threatening, but the next 24 hours are going to be critical for his overall recovery. The

241

good news is he is exceptionally fit. You folks in SOF always are. But, he is not a young man and that means there will be a slow recovery."

"When can I see him?"

"You can see him now, but he needs to be quiet, so please don't get him too excited."

Massoni smiled his most innocent smile. "Do I look like someone who would cause excitement?"

"Sergeant Major Massoni, you look exactly like someone who might cause excitement. I am just asking for you to keep the colonel calm. He needs to rest. We don't want his blood pressure to crash. You can only have about ten minutes. Clear?"

"Check, Lieutenant. And thanks." Massoni turned to Sandy and said, "Wait here, Sandy. I need to see the boss alone. After that, we can return to your office and I will get in touch with SOF headquarters. After that, we'll just have to see."

Sandy was disappointed but nodded, "Check, Jim."

Thirty minutes later, they drove back to Sandy's office in the Fleet headquarters. Massoni was very quiet and Sandy was not about to press. Finally, Massoni said, "About the only thing the boss focused on was your health. I told him you were fine. Just a little bruised. He doesn't need to know right now that you have a GSW, OK?"

Sandy could understand why Smith didn't need to know about his gunshot wound. It didn't matter one way or the other. He said, "What do you think, Jim?"

"Sandy, here's the deal. The boss is going to be fine eventually. I'm not sure how much internal damage was done by the various wounds. I'm not entirely sure even the doctors know at this point. For certain, nothing that is on his charts is life threatening. Everything I saw suggests he is in for a long recovery. For now, he is in good hands and we just have to let the Navy do their job while we do ours."

"And that is?"

Massoni looked over at Sandy. Sandy had not seen Massoni this determined. Massoni replied, "Find the bastards who did this and make them pay."

"Check, Sergeant Major."

30 NOVEMBER 2009, HAIRATAN SAFE HOUSE

S ue didn't hear about Smith until she and Flash were back in Jamie's compound outside Hairatan the next morning. They had spent a full day at the airfield sorting out any information that they could from the wrecked SWORDFISH aircraft. As expected, there were no survivors and, much to Barry and Flash's annoyance, very little recognizable equipment that might offer intelligence. The only thing they could say for certain was the aircraft were hostiles and not associated with any government — Tajik, Uzbek, Russian or Iranian. That was a relief for Jamie. While he was certain that their actions were righteous, he didn't want to think these actions would start yet another war in theatre.

Both the Agency and SOF Headquarters were confident that the ghost networks were working as planned, so a flood of regular traffic started to fill the in-boxes for Jamie's team and the SOF workstation. The first piece of traffic was a simple note from Massoni. It said: CALL ME.

Sue walked outside in the morning sun. She used the RLSU-issued satellite phone to call Massoni's phone. She assumed he was still in Italy. After establishing a secure connection Sue said, "Sergeant Major, are you checking up on us? We actually accomplished our job here and plan to head home tomorrow. There is a German Air Force cargo aircraft leaving Mazar heading back to Ramstein. We should be back RLSU on 02 December."

The secure combat satellite communication network generally

removed any emotions from a conversation. Voices were flat and barely recognizable. Still, Sue could hear a troubled Massoni as he said, *"Sue, we have trouble here in Bahrain. I need you to get here ASAP."*

"Jim, what's wrong?"

"I will explain when I see you. Short answer is the boss is in the hospital and Sandy is recovering from a GSW. Pack up and see if you can get a bird to Manama. SOF HQS will do the expedited travel. Just engage the folks at Bagram. We need you and Flash here. Out."

The connection ended abruptly. Sue was dumbfounded. Smith in the hospital? Sandy wounded? Massoni picking up the pieces in Bahrain? She walked into the command room in a daze.

Flash looked up from her workstation. She was preparing the report for SOF headquarters. She could see Sue was worried. It was not time for the normal back and forth she and Sue had shared for the last few years. "Sue, what's up?"

Sue said, "Pull Jamie outside. We need to talk."

Flash shut down her workstation and, grabbing Jamie by the arm, followed Sue out the door.

Sue told them all she knew. Massoni in Bahrain. Smith in a hospital there. Sandy WIA. Massoni's instructions for them to get to Manama on the next available military aircraft. Jamie was the first one to recover. "Do we know anything else?"

"I don't. Massoni was not his usual self."

"No doubt. He's close to Smith." Jamie paused and said, "How about I engage the folks in Manama…informally of course. They should know something."

"Jamie, that would help. Right now, all I know is Flash and I need to get to Bagram RFN. Massoni said SOF headquarters there would get us on a bird to Manama."

"After last night's adventure, Tony hasn't left yet. How about I put you on his bird to Bagram. It would be a shorter hop than going to Mazar and trying to find a bird heading south."

"Thanks. Flash and I will pack up while you get in touch with Tony."

Flash had recovered from the initial shock. She said, "I will contact

Bagram and sort out how soon we can get out of Afghanistan and get to Bahrain."

Jamie looked at the two operators. He said, "If there is anything I can do, you know you only need to ask."

Flash said, "Jamie, don't go all sappy on us. We know how you feel. If you can get us to Bagram, that would be great. Oh, and you can do the reporting on the mess at your airfield."

Jamie smiled and said, "What mess? It seems no one wants to hear about any trouble with some rogue mercenaries from God knows where. Afghanistan is a dangerous place. All I got this morning from Kabul was congratulations. I'm sticking with that as good enough."

RETURN TO THE GULF

Sue and Flash got to Manama as fast as humanly possible. As expected, Massoni's links inside the senior non-commissioned officer network worked like magic. As they climbed off Tony's aircraft in Bagram, a Suburban pulled up. An Air Force Security Police NCO called from the front seat, "Are you Chiefs O'Connell and Billings?"

Dressed in their military unmarked flight suits, it made sense that the SP would be puzzled as they got off what was obviously an OGA bird. Flash responded first, "Yes, that's us."

"OK. Please jump in. I have to take you down the flight line right now."

Once they were in the Suburban, they headed down the flight line toward a C130 Hercules with engines already running. The SP pulled up to the tailgate and said, "Good luck you two. I don't know who you are or where you are going, but you definitely have some juice. This aircraft was supposed to be out of here a half hour ago."

Sue said, "Sergeant, it's not us that has the juice. It's our sergeant major."

He smiled and said, "Well, now it makes sense. No offense, but I didn't think two Warrant Officers were controlling the USAF. At least not today."

Flash said, "Thanks for the ride. We'll see you on the other side."

There was a crew chief sitting on the tailgate, wearing his helmet tethered to the aircraft communications system. He motioned for Sue and Flash to board the aircraft. Before they were even off the ramp and into the aircraft, the crew chief started to close the ramp. They sat in the nearest red sling seats and belted up. Surrounded by cargo pallets heading out of theatre, they didn't expect a comfortable ride to Manama, but it would be as fast as possible.

As soon as the aircraft reached its cruising altitude, the crew chief returned, this time without his helmet. He said, "Chief O'Connell and Chief Billings. My sergeant major told me to take care of you. Anything you need?"

Sue said, "Any chance of a box lunch? We haven't eaten in about a day and a half."

"You got it." He turned to Flash and said, "Chief Billings?"

"Coffee. I need coffee."

The crew chief smiled and said, "I have coffee, but you need to know it's a long flight and our comfort station isn't all that comfortable."

Flash smiled and said, "Trust me. After squat toilets in Afghanistan, I'm guessing it will be okay."

The C130 touched down at the US military side of the Manama airport, dropped off the two SOF operators, fueled up and left before anyone picked them up. Sue and Flash shouldered their rucksacks and, carrying their long gun cases and helmet bags that served as their combat briefcases, they headed toward what seemed to be the flight operations building. When they arrived, they saw Sandy waiting in the lobby, arm in a sling, dressed in Navy combat utilities. It had been some time since Sue had seen Sandy in anything resembling a uniform. The utilities were in a blue-and-gray computer-generated pattern with his petty officer rank on his collar and his SEAL Trident sewn on his chest. He looked tired and sad. Sue was not excited to see her tough-guy colleague in anything resembling an emotional state.

"Ladies, follow me. I have the vehicle waiting."

Flash couldn't help herself. "Ladies?"

As they closed within whispering distance, Sandy said, "We are on blue water Navy turf right now. You are Warrant Officers and I am a Navy NCO. Protocol, my friends. Protocol, please, until we get into the truck."

Sue had spent far more time in the conventional forces than Flash, so she fully understood the drill. Conventional forces were all about rank structure and protocol in public. In private, it might be different, but in public it was "Yes, sir. No, Ma'am." She followed Sandy out to a navyblue Suburban with the back hatch open. They threw their kit into the back and climbed into the vehicle. Sandy closed the door and drove away.

"Apologies about not meeting you on the flight line, but I don't have any of the necessary clearances from the base to do so. Anyhow, it wasn't a long walk."

Flash said, "And I apologize if I said the wrong thing. You need to know, I've never served in any unit other than a SOF unit. Rank is not exactly something I think about…ever."

"No dramas, Flash. We are a small, hopefully invisible, minority here in Manama and I just didn't want some young Navy ensign dressing me down for not treating you properly."

Sue said, "So, what gives? All we know is the boss is in the hospital and you apparently served as a bullet magnet."

Sandy started the story from the beginning and finished just as they were approaching one of a dozen trailers inside a gated and guarded compound. He finished by saying, "They say the boss will recover, but they intend to evac him back to Italy tomorrow on one of the Nightingale flights. He is considered an ambulatory patient, but just barely. It turns out his wounds were more severe than the docs thought at first. It doesn't help that the shrapnel wounds were from a very rusty truck. He's on pain killers, antibiotics, and will likely need a couple of more operations back home before he can really start to heal. It's a mess."

Flash said, "Is this home for now? Do we have connectivity? Can I get to work?"

"I take it you are on the sergeant major's wavelength. We need to find, fix and finish the assholes who did this."

"Exactly."

"OK, well this is our little bit of RLSU. Jim is inside. If you like, I can take you to the BOQ or we can just get to work."

"Work!" was what Sue and Flash said in unison.

They grabbed their long gun cases and their computers from the back of the Suburban and walked into the trailer. The transition was dramatic, from bright sunlight to the dark interior lighted by a pair of neon bulbs and two computer screens. Sue stumbled on the doorstep as her prosthetic caught the door frame. She bumped into Flash who then bumped into Jim Massoni who was hunched over a computer screen filled with two different sets of graphics: a map of Manama and an overlaid map of the digital footprint of a mobile phone.

Massoni said, "Flash, put your shit down and come tell me if I have this right. It looks like we have data that helps us track 227. Sue, lock up your long guns and pistols in the safe over there, K?"

Flash grabbed a rolling office chair and gently nudged Massoni out of the way. "Jim, let me see what you have. Please tell me why we want to track 227."

"Because he was supposed to be at the meeting that ended up being an ambush. I want to know if he was part of the ambush, a tethered goat, or dead. I'm assuming that if his phone is still moving around, he was part of the ambush."

"OK, let me see what you have. Let's remember, anyone could be carrying his phone."

"In the meantime, I'm going to talk to Sue over here." Massoni pointed to the opposite end of the trailer, where a folding table and four folding chairs served as an informal office. Sue followed Massoni. In the small space, Massoni looked like a caged tiger in a zoo. Angry and trapped.

They sat down at opposite ends of the table. Covering the table was a detailed air graphic map of the area from Basra, Iraq to Doha, Qatar. Normally, Sue would have expected Massoni to spend the first few minutes in what might be called sergeant major banter. Instead, he opened in a style more common to Smith — direct and blunt.

"So, we have two missions here. One, to find out who did this to the boss and Sandy and to make them pay. Two, we have to disrupt or destroy the IRGC cyber network in Dubai. I know you want to do the first mission. But we need you to do the second. If we don't do the second, we run the risk of more trouble in the Gulf. I have talked to the boss and he is very clear about our priorities…I should say, your priorities."

"But, Jim. You need me here."

Massoni put a very large hand on the map on the table. The hand covered the entire UAE. "We need you there. You worked with the defense attaché, you worked with OGA there. In the long run, we are going to need their assistance or, at the very least, their approval to do whatever it takes to shut down the IRGC cyber operation there. The CG wants it to happen, the boss wants it to happen, and we absolutely need it to happen if HICU is going to continue working in the Gulf. Sandy, Flash and I can do the necessary spade work at this end. The CG is sending a team from S&R to help. If you get going, you might be done in time for any 'finish' work we need to do here. Just so you know, this isn't me asking a favor. This is the CG and the boss giving you an order."

Sue knew Massoni's argument made sense. With three HICU folks on the ground and a team, probably a four-man section, from Surveillance and Reconnaissance to help them build the necessary target package, they didn't need another RLSU case officer. *And*, there was no doubt that the IRGC cyber network needed to be taken out of the picture as soon as possible. *And*, she did know the players in Dubai. Logic wasn't part of the equation right now. She wanted to punish the people who attacked her SOF family. She wanted to be there when whoever did this to her family was "finished." Unfortunately, she didn't have a ton of options. When the CG and Smith issued orders, there was only one adult thing to do. She said to her sergeant major, "Roger that, Jim. Of course, there will be a bit of a delay while I get my civilian kit, my passport and…"

"Already here, Sue. I brought them with me." Massoni pointed to a duffle bag and a suit bag in the corner. "I went into your BOQ and got three sets of civilian clothes and a set of class Bs, just in case. You keep a clean household, so it was easy enough. I even polished your jump boots for you just in case. You have to keep up a standard."

Sue finally saw a small bit of the old Massoni peeking through the serious discussion. She knew he knew she knew that he had considered two moves ahead. She said, "I suppose there is a plane ticket already purchased?"

"Yup. And I reached out to the Navy attaché, a Navy Captain Jonah Barkley. Well, I reached out to the real power in the defense attaché office, Master Sergeant Stoner. Stoner and I served together in the Ranger Regiment. So, he squared the trip with his boss. He will pick you up at the Dubai airport and take you to the consulate. Anything else you want me to do? I could arrange a tour of the gold souk? A camel safari?" Massoni smiled his dangerous sergeant major smile.

"No, Sergeant Major. I think all I need to know is when I leave."

Massoni looked at his ancient, military-issued watch. "You have three hours to get clean, get changed and get to the airport. Luckily, Sandy already knows the plan, so he offered to take you to his house and let you change there. Do I need to say anything other than you need to get hot?"

"Nope." Sue reached into her helmet bag. She pulled out her holster and Glock 19 and handed it to Massoni. "I'm assuming you will take care of this and my long gun. I don't think I will need it in Dubai. They have their own arms locker."

"So I heard from Stoner. Good luck, Sue. Get it done and get back here."

"Roger, Jim." Sue grabbed her helmet bag and the two suitcases and walked back toward the door.

"Bye, Flash."

A distracted Flash said, "Bye, Sue. Have a good trip wherever you are going. We'll take care of this trouble before you get back."

Sue smiled and nodded to Sandy. "I take it you are taking me home for a shower and a change of clothes."

Sandy smiled and said, "I hope so. You need both."

WHO DOESN'T LIKE A LITTLE BIT OF SABOTAGE?

A three-hour Gulf Air flight brought Sue from Manama to Dubai. Waiting in front of the Customs and Immigration counters was a large man in a blazer and khakis wearing a lanyard with two different laminated identification badges. One was a US Embassy photo ID identifying the man as Michael Stoner. The second was a similar photo ID from the UAE Ministry of Defense which clearly served as an airport pass allowing him special access through Customs and Immigration. He walked up and shook Sue's hand. "Ma'am, I'm Master Sergeant Stoner. I'm here to expedite your passage through this small bit of Emirati bureaucracy. Please give me your bags and your passport."

Sue nodded and said, "Any friend of Jim Massoni's is a friend of mine."

Stoner smiled and said, "Did he actually say we were friends?"

"Something like that."

"OK, well, let's get over to the VIP lane and get out of here."

In less than ten minutes, Stoner had used his excellent Arabic to get Sue and her bags through customs and her official passport stamped with a 30-day visa. After that, they were on their way. Waiting curbside was an armored Suburban with another American behind the wheel. Stoner shouted, "Kirby, get your lazy bones out here and help the chief with her bags."

They arrived at the same safe house that Sue had used in January. Once again, the armored BMW was in the garage. The Suburban pulled in behind the BMW and Stoner got out to help Sue with her luggage. He said, "I'll just check with the skipper to see if he needs anything else. If not, Kirby and I will get lost."

Sue nodded and said, "Thanks for the help, Michael. Hey, can you tell me something about Captain Barkley? On my last trip, I only saw him in civilian clothes. What's his story? I could use a little help as I sort out this new operation."

Stoner smiled and said, "Quiet one, the skipper. Here's what I know for sure. Captain Jonah Barkley, a graduate of Annapolis, but he never wears his ring. On his dress uniform, he wears the Trident, but he never talks about what unit he was in. Medals include a Silver Star with V device and a Purple Heart. Just like with the Trident, he doesn't say anything about that. I do know he did something to his back. He can't run or swim much anymore. Works out like a demon. You definitely don't want to arm wrestle him."

Sue laughed, "Never intended to take on a Navy captain in any competition! But that helps plenty. I do think there may be some trouble and I just wanted to know his tolerance for…ambiguity."

Now it was Stoner who laughed. "I think his tolerance for ambiguity is pretty high, chief. As in off the scale if you want to know. We haven't been following the defense attaché playbook. And, in case you wanted to know, you can count me in if you need a strong back and a weak mind."

"Count on it, Michael. Let's go in and see what sort of plan is waiting for us."

Sue and her Ranger escort entered the beach house. Waiting for them were the same three officers who she last saw in January. Sue smiled and said, "Gentlemen, have you ever left this delightful house since January?"

Finestri smiled, raised his hands toward the ceiling and said, "Once you find paradise, why would you leave?"

Stoner turned to his boss and said, "Skipper, do you need me or do I go back to the shop?"

Barkley was balancing a mug of coffee on his knee. He said, "Michael, send Kirby back to the office and tell him to come back here in three hours. I would like your views on the subject we are going to discuss."

"Check, sir." Stoner turned and told Kirby to get lost. He returned and took a chair next to the Navy attaché.

Finestri played the host and said, "Michael, we have beers and sodas in the fridge and coffee on the stove. Help yourself. And, please ditch the tie. You are making me nervous."

Stoner looked over at Barkley and once he got the nod from his boss, he stripped off the tie and headed into the kitchen.

Finestri motioned to Sue and said, "Same goes with you, Sue. Go to the kitchen, get what you want to drink and come back here. We are going to be getting serious, so you might as well get comfortable."

Once Stoner and Sue each returned with a Diet Pepsi, the meeting started in earnest. Finestri opened by describing the current situation including, the Manama attack on Sue's colleagues and the intelligence on the IRGC cyber operation in Dubai. Once he finished, he turned to Sterling and asked, "David, what can you add?"

"Chief, I used our local sources to identify the likely IRGC warehouse. HQS narrowed it down to two on the docks and *RINGSET* sorted the rest. The warehouse in question is the only one that has sufficient power to manage a data farm. The other warehouse is IRGC all right, but it is where they store their black-market acquisitions. According to *RINGSET*, the black-market storehouse is guarded 24/7. The other warehouse has security cameras, but no guards."

Barkley interrupted, "David, how does *RINGSET* know all this?"

Sterling smiled and said, "Because he runs the docks. He's a Pakistani. Former Pak Navy commander who retired and moved to the Gulf to make money. He finds it amusing that he is getting paid by the dock company, by the IRGC and by us. He brought ground photography for us to use along with the electricity bills that show the difference between the two buildings."

Finestri said, "I think David has earned his pay, don't you Jonah?"

The Navy attaché nodded.

Sterling continued, "*RINGSET* can also get us access to the docks from a side entrance to the port. Or, he said he could help us approach the warehouse from the water side if we can do it with low-profile craft. He just wants to be sure he isn't the one ending up in an Emirati jail for the rest of his days."

Barkley said, "RIBs would be easy enough to use. And, we don't have to worry as much about the Emirati video coverage of the roads to and from the port. I have met the captain in charge of the Dubai Port Authority. He's an Emirati Coast Guard captain and we hit it off pretty well. They have a very sophisticated level of video surveillance on the road entry points and along the exterior wire surrounding the port. They bought it from a UK company and they purchased the maintenance contract as well. Pretty hard to beat. They use Coast Guard cutters to patrol the waterfront. The docks themselves don't have much in the way of video coverage, only because the salt water and storms just make video surveillance a maintenance nightmare."

Sterling said, "RIBs?"

Finestri shook his head. "Apologies for my young spy. HIs combat ops were all in Afghanistan and not a lot of use for rigid inflatable boats in Afghanistan."

Sue said, "I just got here and have been out of the net for the last couple of days working on part of this op in Afghanistan. Out there, our job was to disrupt the cyber operation long enough for the gurus back in Washington to set up a ghost network filled with disinformation. What is our goal here? Disrupt or destroy?"

Finestri laughed. "Right to the point, eh? Sue, the answer is whatever we can do. HQS has given me carte blanche on this one. What about you, Jonah? What are your orders?"

"My HQS just wants us to fix the problem. They do want to know up front, so they can manage the consequences. It seems to me that a little fire on the docks might serve both options. First to destroy their current equipment and, if they decide to rebuild, give Washington time to work their cyber magic."

Stoner finally decided to add something to the equation as he agreed with his boss. "You know, docks are dangerous places. Lots of flammable materials, plus fuel oil, and some of the big fork lifts are run on propane. If a fire started, it might be really hard to put it out before a building was completely destroyed."

Finestri rubbed his very large, heavily scarred hands. "And who doesn't like a little bit of sabotage?"

It took the better part of a week to get the various pieces in place. Finestri brought in a tech officer named Mark to manage the actual sabotage. While Sue would have simply put a small charge on the wall of the warehouse and surrounded it with flammables, neither Finestri nor Barkley were impressed with her direct approach. Barkley said, "Sue, it is important to remember that we live here and have other missions in the UAE other than this one. Mark has a plan that will work, more or less, the way you want, but any effort after the fact to investigate the fire will point toward either something or someone else. Since 9/11, we have trained the Emiratis both in Abu Dhabi and Dubai on multiple counterterrorism skills. We work with them against their own and other regional extremists. They are good at what they do and we don't want a forensics team trained by us or by the Brits to figure out we are the perpetrators of this operation."

Sue nodded and said, "Sir, I'm still pretty green when it comes to disguising operations. In SOF, we rarely care if the enemy knows that we are the ones who conducted the operation."

Barkley said, "Sue, you may not know, but I served in SOF for a long while. I get the fact that the best skills SOF has are skills at breaking things and killing people. But, in this case, there is a good reason not to plant the US flag on this operation."

"Blowback?"

Finestri said, "Well, of course, we don't want to piss off the Dubai authorities. Actually, what I meant was Mark and I have a plan to make sure that when the Dubai authorities investigate, they will find evidence of a plot pointing to Iranians themselves. The Rev Guard is powerful back in Iran, but the IRGC isn't a monolithic organization. Lots of internal rivalries. So, you could imagine one part of the IRGC hating the fact that another part of the IRGC is gaining power just because they have computer skills. After all, IRGC Special Forces, al-Qods, is fighting all over the Middle East. They might not find it amusing that the computer geeks are getting all the praise."

Sue hadn't even considered this level of complexity. She simply expected to help the local team engage in some sort of disruption. Instead, Finestri was talking about creating an operation which would have secondary and possibly tertiary effects. The Iranians might start looking for saboteurs in their own house. The Emiratis wouldn't be too pleased that some Iranian feud was spilling over into their port facility. And, after the fact, Barkley and Finestri could even offer to help their liaison colleagues solve the crime. It reminded her of when she would play chess with her grandfather. Most of the time he would win, but even when he lost, his play was elegant, complicated and very confusing to a college student who thought she was playing a simple game.

"Sir, how are we going to do this?"

Finestri said, "Well, to start with, you and Sterling are going to meet with *RINGSET* and load some ideas into his head. Meanwhile, we are going to sort out what other evidence we need to leave behind so that the investigators come to the proper conclusion."

Barkley smiled and concluded, "Of course, we have to actually accomplish the sabotage for all of this to work."

BALANCING ACT

David Sterling sat at the dining room table in the safe house. Across from Sterling, Sue was studying a set of papers that he just dropped off. He said, "This is the script for tonight. I need you to sell this to *RINGSET*. He needs to believe you are a HQS expert on this subject and that you are here to protect the safety of the port. While we are hosting him on a long car ride into the desert, our guys are going to be starting the fire."

"I think I am better suited for the sabotage operation."

"And I always wanted to be an astronaut. But, that's not how this is going to work. We are case officers and tonight we have to both debrief an asset and set him up for success. I don't think you get a choice in this. My chief, your boss here, and all of our higher head-quarters types have made it pretty clear who does what and when we will do it. And, I reckon it's worth pointing out that the Agency has specialists in sabotage. Before you arrived, I heard Finestri talking to HQS about sending a full team to support Mark. So, study hard because this is going to be a very important balancing act. We get *RINGSET* to believe our story and he does the rest once he sees what happens. Everyone in the equation wins."

"Except the IRGC."

"Well, yes. We intend to make it difficult for the IRGC. Sorry, Sue. No gunfights tonight." Sterling looked over at his SOF partner. "Don't pout. It isn't something spies do."

Sue studied hard all afternoon. Her role in the meeting was to serve as a senior from Washington who was an expert in Iran and, most specifically, the IRGC. During their meeting with *RINGSET*, she had to convince him that there was trouble inside the IRGC between some of the players he knew in Dubai and an entirely different faction in Tehran. The "briefing" was to be a gift to *RINGSET* for his collaboration and to help him understand the state of play in Dubai. While the meeting was taking place, the Agency team would set off an explosion and a fire at the warehouse. Sterling pointed out that any forensics evidence left behind would point to Iran. The hope was that *RINGSET* would use the information to push the subsequent investigation toward IRGC tensions in Dubai. Ideally, that would disrupt other IRGC operations in Dubai and possibly throughout the UAE. At worst, it would certainly direct attention away from the real perpetrators.

An hour before they needed to leave for the meeting, Sterling sat down with Sue for a rehearsal. After 30 minutes, he pronounced Sue an expert who almost fooled him. In an effort to just give her brain a rest, Sue asked, "Did you ever sort out the assassins of our walk-in?"

Sterling shook his head. "Nope. Our contacts inside the police and security services used just about every high-tech tool they had to sort it out. After all, murder on the streets of Dubai is not good for the reputation of this banking, trading and tourist capitol of the Gulf. One thing they did say was cameras that focused on areas around the incident were spoofed and had shut down an hour prior to the event and for two hours after the event. Someone was serious about making a clean getaway."

Sue was annoyed at Sterling's report and interrupted: "David, are you telling me that you guys gave up after that?"

"Hey, if you let me finish, maybe you would know the rest of the story."

Sue said, "Sorry. I've always been a little impatient."

"Ya think? Anyhow, we used a couple of our local assets to determine possible suspects who traveled to our little city on the Gulf. The police had already checked that as well, but they didn't know what they were looking for since they only had our complaint that an American vehicle was attacked and an innocent Dubai resident was killed because he happened to be walking by our vehicle." Sterling shook his head and said, "Don't blame me. That's the story that Finestri used to get information from his contacts." He took a drink from his Diet Pepsi and continued. "We checked the airline manifests out of Dubai International and found four individuals from a Russian security firm called..."

Sue interrupted again and said, "SWORDFISH."

Sterling smiled and said, "You've heard of them, eh?"

"Just a little. It's a long story and we don't have time tonight."

"OK. So, the SWORDFISH team were nominally here for business development with other Russian corporations that use Dubai as their entry point into business in Iran. HQS traces showed that the four guys were former Russian Special Forces..."

"SPETSNAZ."

"If you keep interrupting, I'm never going to get through this story."

"Sorry."

"We don't have any proof, but we did put their names on an international travel list that the entire IC uses to track spies, terrorists and organized crime figures. If they travel by air again using the same names, we will know in advance. Hopefully, some future station somewhere will then have the capability to find, fix and disrupt them."

"So, they got away with the assassination."

"Sue, in case you are interested, there are lots of stories like this. We do what we can where we are and hope that it builds a case for the future."

"I said I am impatient."

"Well, the advantage I have is Finestri keeps me on a short leash and makes me smart every time I get...impatient."

Sue thought about Sterling's comment as they started their circuitous route to the meeting. She was pleased to be working with Smith, Massoni, and Flash, but she wondered what it would be like to have the sort of day-to-day mentoring that Sterling received from Finestri. It wasn't really in the structure of the SOF HUMINT program to have real stations and bases like OGA. First, there weren't that many SOF collectors like Sue. Secondly, even if there were enough collectors, she suspected there weren't many US Embassies in the world that would accept a SOF unit and a station. If the conditions were right, Sue was certain that she would be a better officer with that sort of mentoring.

Her silent deliberations were interrupted as Sterling said, "Thinking about your role?"

"Thinking about the big picture."

"I try not to spend much time on the big picture. Too busy thinking about my little picture."

"That's how it's been for me for the last few years. But, this last set of TDYs has made me wonder if my little picture is all that successful."

"Well, let's focus on our little picture tonight. It just might have a big impact. K?"

Sue smiled and said, "Right you are, David. I will get my game face on."

Sterling pulled over to the side of the road and said, "Good to hear. Now please get in the back of the truck. *RINGSET* gets to ride in the front until we get to our meeting site."

"In the desert?"

"In the desert. Folks go out into the desert all the time to have little campfires and watch the stars. Plus, it gives them a degree of privacy that doesn't exist in the city."

"And women ride in the back."

"Don't be silly. The second case officer always rides in the back so that they can do harm to the agent if he gets...dangerous."

"Sorry, you are right. I'm just not used to two-up meetings."

"Two-up?"

"MILSPEAK for any meeting where there are two operators in a car."

"Well, I haven't done a lot of two-up meetings either, but the last time I brought a HQS egghead to meet with *RINGSET*, the egghead was more than happy to ride in the back."

Sue nodded and said, "Got it. Be quiet, ride in the back until the meeting and then amaze the asset with my brain."

"Now you are talking like a real expert. Here we go."

The meeting in the desert with *RINGSET* was uneventful. As Sue expected, RINGSET was reticent to hold a meeting with two officers, especially when one was both new to him and a woman. Still, Sterling was successful in convincing *RINGSET* that it was in his interest to hold the meeting with the "expert from headquarters." Sterling offered two incentives: first, a bonus for taking the time to listen and, second, a warning that the information that Sue had would certainly make him safer and possibly more successful in his job.

Sue looked at *RINGSET* while Sterling served tea from a thermos and talked to his asset. The source was in his late 50s. A small, fit man with military bearing. A clipped mustache in a style more commonly seen on British movie actors of the 1960s than seen on any men's faces in the 21st century. He was polite but used to being in command. She watched as Sterling used multiple means to bring *RINGSET* onside, including appealing to his ego, his family and even his loyalty to their "partnership" in fighting terrorism. In the end, RINGSET agreed to listen to what Sue had to say.

Sue opened with her own effort to build some sort of rapport with this asset. "Commander, I want to thank you for taking the time tonight to see us. I hope what I am going to provide to you will be useful to our mutual program to keep Dubai harbor safe."

RINGSET nodded and said, "You are welcome. Where do you come from exactly?"

Sue decided on the spot to keep as close to the truth as possible. She simply assumed the character of her best friend at work, Sarah Billings aka Flash. "Captain, I am a senior analyst from the US Special Operations Forces. I spend my time tracking terrorists who are operating in both the Eastern Mediterranean and in the Persian Gulf. I started my career providing direct support to our Navy commandos. Eventually, I was reassigned to our SOF headquarters."

"You have worked at sea?"

"Yes, sir. Of course, not directly with the commandos but on the mother ships they use as their bases."

"Then you know something about the maritime threat?"

"Yes, sir. My work has focused on both terrorist smuggling operations and piracy off the Horn of Africa. We have worked to interdict these threats. I use many different sources to find and fix the targets and then my colleagues work on finishing the targets."

"Finishing?"

"Most times, we say the finishing piece is conducted…kinetically."

"I do like that turn of phrase, Miss…"

"I am a Navy lieutenant commander. My name is Sue Maxwell."

RINGSET turned to Sterling and said, "I believe this will be a most interesting conversation." As he said this, Sue quietly let out a sigh of relief.

Sterling nodded, "Commander, I hope so."

Sue decided to take control of the meeting. "Commander, as you well know, we are concerned about both the al-Qaida activities in the Gulf as well as Iranian surrogates. Based on your previous reporting, I spent the better part of the last month focusing on the activities of the Islamic Revolutionary Guards Corps in Dubai."

"You have followed my reporting?"

"Extensively. You are such an important partner in the region. We consider your reporting as the most reliable insight we have."

RINGSET reached up and touched his mustache. He looked like a cat who had just had his back scratched. Sue was convinced that inside his head, he was purring.

"Commander, normally, I would pass information through our office here, but the recent information seemed so important that I wanted to give it to you directly."

Sue could see she had set the hook. She needed to be careful not to pull to hard. She waited until he said, "Please continue."

"Sir, our concern has to do with a threat to your port from internal jealousies taking place between the IRGC contingent here and the IRGC contingent on Kish Island."

RINGSET nodded and said, "My own sources have said the same thing. I am required by my Emirate masters to allow IRGC activities on my docks. I do my best to make it as hard as possible for them to conduct any smuggling, but I have my orders. I know the IRGC leadership has been frustrated with the delays we create."

Sterling couldn't help himself, he said, "Sir, precisely how do you know this?"

RINGSET turned to Sue and said, "You see. He's always so impatient. He wants to know the who, what, where, and when and he wants to know it now."

Sue decided to further engage in selling the story. "Commander, I'm sure you have the same view as we do that intelligence delayed is intelligence denied. My colleague is less impatient than he is diligent."

RINGSET laughed and said, "I have told him many times the same thing. I accept that he is simply diligent." He turned to Sterling and said, "So, my sub-source working the Iranian warehouse district, Ali Hashemi, told me about these tensions last month. He said we needed to accommodate the senior IRGC officer at the port if we didn't want trouble. I took the news to my Emirati supervisor. He told me to ignore this reporting. He was convinced that it was just Iranian efforts to extract more concessions. I was not so sure."

Sue was ready at this point to close in for the pitch. "Sir, you are right and your supervisor was wrong. We have other sources, special sources, that have outlined a serious feud between your Iranian contacts and those in Kish. The IRGC contingent in Kish are connected to the IRGC leadership and they have made it clear that there needs to be some sort of example made in Dubai to make sure the IRGC contingent on your docks understand their failures. We do not know, but we think it might include some action against the IRGC members. We don't have full details on this, but I took it upon myself to make sure you knew what little we did know."

RINGSET nodded and was about to speak when a series of beeps erupted from his briefcase. Sterling looked at his source and said, "I hope that is not your phone, Commander. We always say it is important for neither of us to have a phone on when we hold our meetings."

RINGSET offered a dismissive wave. "It is not my phone. I gave you my word and fully understand why I shouldn't have it on. I have a very old pager system linked to the fire station at the port. It is an alarm system that links me directly to my counterparts in the port fire brigade. My friends, I have to call to find out what is going on. They would not contact me except in an emergency and if I don't respond, they will wonder why."

Sterling started to pack up the thermos and blanket as *RINGSET* stood up. He said, "Commander, can we wait until we are closer to the city? I really don't want the GPS on your phone showing where you are right now."

"Peter, we need to hurry. I am supposed to answer this page in five minutes or less."

The three rushed back to the car. *RINGSET* said, "Lieutenant Commander, I noticed you are limping."

Sue nodded. She hoped in the darkness he didn't see her blush. "Sir, I was injured some years back in an accident on the ship we used for our commandos. It never quite healed."

RINGSET nodded. "Ships are dangerous places. Even on normal patrols, I often had men injured while we were underway."

With that, they loaded into the vehicle and headed into the city. As soon as they were a mile away from the site, Sterling stopped and said, "Commander, you can use your phone now." *RINGSET* got out of the vehicle and made the call. When he got back in, he said, "There is a fire on the docks. I need to return immediately."

The rest of the drive was filled with *RINGSET* receiving one call after another and mobilizing his own team. Just before they reached the drop-off site, he said, "It is at one of the two Iranian warehouses. The one filled with material headed for Kish was not damaged. The one that is empty except for the IRGC communications system is the one on fire. So, you see the warehouse with valuables is fine, the second building is a complete loss."

He turned to Sue in the back seat, "I think your reporting on the feud was correct. It looks like arson. The Iranians from Kish have sent their warning to the Iranians here. If the Iranians do not listen, there is no telling what might happen next." *RINGSET* smiled and said, "The fire has expanded to include a warehouse owned by one of the Emirati princes. I wonder what my supervisor will think now."

After they dropped off *RINGSET* and drove home from the meeting, Sterling said, "That was great. I almost believed the story myself. And the addition of the Navy rank closed the deal."

"Just don't tell Captain Barkley that I decided to frock myself by about four different ranks."

"I think he will find it just as amusing as I did."

Sue said, "So, you really think we sold the story?"

"You sold the story, Sue. And yes, I do think this is going to work in our favor. You didn't oversell the story. You just said there was a feud with the IRGC in Kish. You didn't say anything about actions in Dubai. *RINGSET* will put the pieces together on his own."

Sue let out a long sigh of relief. This was probably the hardest meeting she had since her time with Jamie in Baghdad when they had to convince an asset to collect on the nexus between terrorists and Russians. It didn't end well for that asset. She hoped *RINGSET* had better luck.

---

12 December 2009, Dubai

The next morning, Finestri and Barkley arrived at the safe house to debrief their two case officers. Finestri was in good humor as he made himself a cup of strong coffee from the espresso maker in the kitchen. He shouted, "The team from headquarters were brilliant. Bypassed the security systems, entered the warehouse and blew the shit out of the servers and the datapipe. Set fire to the entire building and left little forensic hints of Iranian perfidy that our Emirati colleagues are sure to find. How about you guys?"

Sterling said, "Boss, you should have seen O'Connell in action. She had *RINGSET* convinced that he was going to be the smartest man on the docks today. Just enough information to get him thinking about the feud between the Rev Guard guys here and their counterparts in Kish and Tehran. Then, boom, he gets a call that says the dock is on fire. I honestly think he was just as pleased to have the fire as he was to have our information. Apparently, his bosses have been ignoring his warnings about the Iranians. He implied they had been paid off. Now, he has proof or, at least once they do the needful, he will have proof that he was right all along. By the way, he loves O'Connell."

Sue blushed and Finestri said, "We all love O'Connell."

Barkley said, "Even Stoner loves O'Connell and he doesn't like anyone." Barkley looked over at Sue and said, "By the way, I have your next set of orders."

"Sir, I expect they are return to Manama."

"No, Sue. They are return to Italy. The instructions came from Manama this morning. Apparently, your sergeant major and your analyst are flying back to Italy on the Nightingale that is carrying your commander. They didn't say anything other than you need to get back to HICU as soon as you can catch a commercial flight from Dubai to Venice."

Sue was taken aback. When she left a week ago, they still hadn't sorted out who attacked Sandy and Smith. It seemed hard to imagine they had identified, surveilled, and finished the target in that amount of time. Still, if Massoni and Flash were headed home, there was no other explanation. Sue said, "Yes, sir. I will check flights and see what I can catch."

Finestri said, "The least we could do was help on that front. When Jonah told me your instructions, he and I worked with the embassy travel folks to get you the first flight out of here. It leaves today at 18hrs. It is Alitalia which is not my favorite airline, but we did get you a free upgrade to first class. Even I haven't traveled first class for a while. Pretty slick, no?"

Sue smiled and said, "As long as I don't get into admin trouble back home."

Barkley said, "I checked the regs. My office paid full-fare economy. Nothing more, nothing less. The upgrade might have been Stoner's work. He plays tennis with the Alitalia station commander. Anyhow, this is one of those times when all's well that ends well."

Finestri shook his head. "Stoner plays tennis? Really? It must look like they allowed a bear on the court."

Barkley said, "Mark, don't be fooled. He is one of the best players in the foreign community. He and I are a mixed doubles team. He has a powerful serve and he is terrifying at the net."

"Now, that I can believe. OK, Sterling. You need to get back to the office and start writing up how brilliant you and O'Connell were. I will add the finishing touches and we will put this bit of Iranian threat to bed for the time being."

Barkley said, "Sue, I will have Stoner pick you up at 1500hrs. That will give you time to get through security and even time to shop in the Dubai Duty Free."

Finestri said, "Or, hang out in the Alitalia lounge and drink cappuccinos."

Sue smiled and said, "Thanks. My mom has always told me I need to buy a GMT watch. Maybe this is the time and place."

Finestri nodded. "A little reward for doing good work. Not a bad idea."

MISSION NOT AT ALL ACCOMPLISHED

13 December 2009, RLSU, Camp Ederle

S ue arrived at the HICU warehouse exhausted. It wasn't that first-class travel on Alitalia wasn't very nice, it was that she couldn't concentrate on the luxury because she had no idea what she would face when she arrived in Italy. The train to Vincenza was late. As she rode into the mountains in the middle of a winter rainstorm, she did nothing but fret about her boss, the actions of the team in Bahrain and what might be the next step in *Silicon Addiction*. While each piece of the operation had accomplished what it set out to do, there were so many moving parts to the cyber aspects of the operation that Sue didn't feel as if she or anyone else in the equation had accomplished anything. And, once again, she had faced an implacable adversary with the Russian mercenaries at SWORDFISH.

Sue joined the Army after the Cold War ended. Her early days in military intelligence at the 18th Airborne Corps focused on a peacemaking mission in the Balkans and the hunt for war criminals who committed atrocities during that civil war. That was both an easy mission to understand and an easy mission to accept as righteous. It was also a mission that involved working with the Russians. Generally, it had been productive. Once she transitioned to SOF, Sue had a single target: terrorists. Now, terrorists came in all shapes, sizes and ideologies, but in Sue's mind, they were easy to understand. They were the enemy. As this operation unfolded, it seemed to her that there were no good guys and bad guys. Just shadowy threats that seemed just out of reach every time the team tried to "finish" the target. It was a world that made Sue uncomfortable. When she went through selection for Surveillance and Reconnaissance, her instructors emphasized the importance of patience. At the Farm, her Agency instructors emphasized the importance of accepting ambiguity. As she looked out the rain-streaked train window, Sue realized she had a shortage of both patience and acceptance.

She walked into the RLSU warehouse soaked to the skin, carrying her bags, and definitely in no mood for any happy talk from her sergeant major. She shouldn't have worried. There was no happiness to be found inside. Flash was dressed in her usual warehouse uniform: black sweatshirt, black sweatpants, black trainers. Her general demeanor was even more black than usual. Sue dropped her bag at her desk next to Flash and said, "I'm back."

"We need to go see Massoni. By the way, he's in a mood."

"Me too."

"So, let's all get morose together."

Sue and Flash walked up to Massoni's office. For the first time since Sue moved to Italy, the door was closed. Flash knocked and said quietly, "Jim, Sue is back."

"Enter." The response took Sue completely by surprise. That was Smith's normal instruction, but again Massoni never used that tone. Sue had known Jim Massoni for ten years. He might be threatening, he might be jocular, but he had never been blunt. Sue prepared for the worst.

As she walked in, she noticed a desk covered with brown military-style files. Some were opened and others were stacked on the left side of the desk. Massoni was wearing an OD green Army nylon shirt, called a sleep shirt in Army parlance but never actually used for anything more than a long-sleeve undershirt. Over the sleep shirt was a very old sweatshirt with cut off sleeves. The sweatshirt probably had a Ranger Regiment Scroll some years ago, but years of use meant the yellow and red imprints were barely visible. Like Flash, Massoni was wearing black sweats and black trainers. He looked as if he hadn't slept in days.

"Jim, what's the news on the boss?"

"He's recovering, but it's far worse than we thought. He got some sort of secondary infection related to the shrapnel they pulled out of him. Good news is the doctors are confident the antibiotics they are giving him will work…eventually. For now, he's in isolation. You can only see him if you dress out in a moon suit so that you don't bring any bugs into his room. His morale is good. He's a tough guy and will get through this, but it isn't going to be this week or next."

"When can I go see him?"

"Maybe in a day or so. I went there yesterday, tried to use my sergeant major magic and they told me to get lost. I waited until the senior NCO at the hospital told me that. Imagine. Him telling me to get lost. It was definitely not fun." He poured more coffee from the thermos into his cup and took a drink. "Do you bring good news?"

"Well, the IRGC data center has burned to the ground and the Emiratis are investigating the Iranian consulate convinced they did the deed themselves."

Massoni smiled, "Well, that is good news. Did you light the fuse?"

"The Klingons did that themselves. They told me I had to focus on the disinformation side of the equation. Apparently, I did a convincing job of focusing attention on Iranian internal rivalries. That should put some pressure on the locals to prevent or at least delay the rebuild." Sue decided to change the subject. "What happened in Manama?"

"Precious little." Flash was clearly disappointed.

Massoni nodded and said, "The trail went cold. Sandy's agent, 227, disappeared and the only thing we found was a discarded cellphone in a dumpster near Manama port. We suspect 227 is in Manama harbor wearing cement shoes. Flash did her magic, hacked into the Bahraini customs and immigration and found nothing to point to suspects who might have arrived and departed around the time of the attack. It was nothing but mission not accomplished. Pissed off the S&R team, that's for sure. They did what they could but, without a lead, that wasn't much."

"Were the Klingons any help?"

Flash shook her head. "They were not. They don't have assets focused on port. That's supposed to be Sandy's job or the Navy's job or someone else's job."

Massoni said, "Flash was not pleased with their cooperation."

Sue nodded, "Sounds like it. So, what do we do?"

Massoni said, "Sandy is expanding his network right now. You never know what sort of leads he will find. The good news is that between the work with Jamie in Afghanistan and the work in Dubai, SOF Headquarters and the Agency are convinced we have put an end to our cyber threat…at least for now. We are back in business."

"So, what's next for me?"

Massoni looked up from his desk. "Sue, I think you and Flash have both earned some leave. Why don't you take some time now and return just after Christmas. By that time, we will have regrouped, the boss will be on the mend, and we will start 2010 focused on the normal set of villains."

Flash said, "Are you actually authorizing leave?"

Massoni nodded and said, "Well, it's the boss who authorized the leave. If it was up to me, I would keep you here to get back in shape and to clean this warehouse. You two and Pluto are the only folks available other than Marconi and Alexander Graham and they keep telling me they have work to do rebuilding our commo system."

Sue said, "Can we visit the boss?"

Massoni nodded. "He's at the Hospital on Aviano Air Base. I think once he is better able to travel, he may end up at Wiesbaden or even Walter Reed. Call to sort out visiting hours and, Sue, wear your uniform. I tried to visit in civilian clothes and no one took me seriously."

Flash said, "That must have been a mistake."

Massoni smiled and said, "Yes."

Sue nodded and said, "I'll give them a call right now."

Flash grabbed Sue by the arm and said, "Sue, I think we need to get out of here before he changes his mind about leave."

Sue nodded and said, "Too true. Jim, we will let you know our plans soonest."

Massoni was already looking down at a file on his desk. He said, "I don't know how the boss keeps his sense of humor given all this crap he has to read."

Sue said over her shoulder, "I didn't know the boss had a sense of humor."

Massoni grumbled, "Yup. He's a laugh a minute and even more so from his hospital bed."

BEDSIDE BRIEFING

Massoni told her they should arrive at the hospital in their army combat uniform. ACUs were not the most comfortable of apparel, but they did allow their owners to show rank and unit designator. It was raining and cold, so Sue put on an Army wool sweater under her ACU blouse and then pulled on her Gore-Tex jacket. Shined jump boots and her red beret completed the uniform for the day. Massoni showed up at the BOQ at 0750hrs after telling her he would pick her up at 0800hrs. Sue knew the drill, and she had been waiting since 0745hrs. She knew if you were anything less than 10 minutes early to a meeting with a sergeant major, you were late.

Massoni pulled up in an ancient Mercedes sedan. When the car left the assembly line in Germany, sometime in the 1970s, it was probably leaf green. Years of Italian sun had bleached the car to a mix of green and light brown. Massoni rolled down the passenger side window and said, "Don't stand out there in the rain, Sue. Get in."

Sue jumped into a leather-and-wood cockpit that did not look like it belonged to the beleaguered exterior of the Mercedes. She belted in and they were off to the hospital. Massoni was wearing his ACUs and a pale green Army fleece. He had his green beret tucked into the cargo pocket of his right leg. Sue said, "Is the boss going to be okay? I know what you said in the office, but between us, how is he?"

"Sue, I don't know for sure. His room is one of the few at Aviano Air Base designed for patient care. He is going to be transferred to Landstuhl Hospital in Germany tomorrow on a medevac bird. The nurses on his floor are pretty protective of his privacy. I think he is in for a long recovery, but you know how that is."

Sue nodded. She knew very well how that was. She wasn't looking forward to a trip to a hospital. She had more than enough bad memories of her time recovering from the gunshot wound that took her left leg.

Prior to entering the room, Sue and Massoni had to dress out in full hospital personal protective kit over their uniforms. Again, that was part of the memory of her stay in Walter Reed. Every time her mother and brother visited, they were dressed in blue smocks and head coverings and wearing blue nitrile gloves. It served as a warning that Smith's injuries were serious. Even so, Sue was shocked when she saw Smith in his hospital bed. He seemed to have shrunken since she last saw him. His skin had a gray tone and he had dark circles under his eyes. Still, he brightened when she entered. "Sorry I can't get up to give you a hug."

Massoni smiled and said, "Boss, as your sergeant major, I need to remind you that you can't fraternize with the troops." Smith grinned and settled back on his pillow.

"I'm going to Landstuhl tomorrow," he said, after pausing for breath. "Probably going to be there for a couple of weeks. After that, they say I can come back here and do outpatient recovery." Sue sat down at the chair next to the hospital bed. "Boss, you just relax. I'm here to say hi and then get lost."

"No dice. You need to relate all of your adventures."

Sue spent the next twenty minutes outlining her work in Afghanistan and then in Dubai. She kept the stories short on details and long on amusing anecdotes. Smith followed carefully and asked pointed questions when Sue strayed too far from the five Ws and an H or who, what, where, when, why, and how. When she was finished, Sue said, "Boss, I really don't know if we had any real success in these missions. We certainly disrupted the Iranians and we supported OGA and SOF in Tajikistan, but I don't know if we can call either of those operations a win."

As Smith pondered Sue's comment, Massoni broke the momentary silence. He had obviously been thinking hard about the same things: "This cyber stuff is hard. We can't use the term 'winning.' This isn't like our counterterrorism operations. CT ops are like karate, the winner is always the one who is fastest and with the best strikes. This is more like judo. Our adversaries are using our own strength, our own capabilities against us. There are bad actors out there who are burying their actions inside the millions of lines of code that we rely on every day inside our own networks. Since our successes are based on our networked operations, these networks have become our greatest vulnerabilities. We just have to live with the reality of these new threats and be ready to fight with our minds as well as our technology. And, we have to recognize that these bad actors will hide behind civilian and quasi-civilian entities, including PMCs like *SWORDFISH*. It means we have to get smarter. It means we have more work to do."

Sue and Smith both looked astonished. The sergeant major had captured all their work during 2009 in a few sentences.

Massoni said, "What?! Just because I'm this good looking doesn't mean I can't come up with smart answers."

After Sue and Smith finished laughing, Smith said, "Sue, did Massoni tell you I authorized you and Flash some leave?"

"Yes, sir. I think I will go home for Christmas. The last time I tried that it didn't work out so well. I'm hoping this will be a quiet time in CONUS."

"If you are willing to do so, can I ask you to take Flash with you? I think she could use some family time and she doesn't have one of her own."

"I was thinking the same thing. Of course, I'm not sure Flash will give up time chasing men from Ederle, Camp Darby and Aviano."

Smith smiled. "I think you will be surprised." He paused and drew a pained breath.

Clearly his wounds were troubling him and he was tiring. He continued, "Sue, when you come back, I want you to consider taking a bit of time to serve as my XO. Jim is good at what he does, but I am going to need someone in our trade to help me manage things until I'm back on my feet. Will you do that? I don't think it means more than about six months. You are my senior collector. I will need someone willing to keep track of things as I recover. I have already checked with the CG. He agrees and is recommending you for promotion to CW4 so that you have the rank to do the needful."

Sue was dumbfounded. She hadn't thought about anything but the next TDY for so long. Now, Smith was asking her to take a greater responsibility for all HICU operations. It would mean giving up all of the things that she liked about her work, but it would also mean she could "settle in" to HICU for a while. She said, "Sir, if you think I am up to it, I'm in."

"Excellent. I will let the CG know." He paused for another moment and said, "Jim already agreed with the plan, just in case you are interested. Actually, like any good sergeant major, he made me realize that his plan was a good plan that I should support." Again, a brief smile from Smith and a nod from Massoni. He said, "Now, get out of here. Go home for a couple of weeks. Rest, eat too much, enjoy your family and then be prepared to work like crazy in 2010. OK?"

"Sir, can we stay in touch while I'm back in CONUS?"

"Of course. They won't let me have any electronics in here...yet. Jim has promised to give me a smart phone from the shop before they load me on the Nightingale flight tomorrow. Stay in contact with him and he'll keep me informed. Now, get lost."

Sue stood up and rendered her best salute. "See you on the other side, Boss."

Smith nodded and said, "Roger that, Sue."

As they got back into Massoni's car, Sue said, "He's not real good."

"Sue, the boss is a fighter, but I think right now he is fighting secondary infections. It is going to take longer than he thinks to get back on his feet. That's why you and I have to keep REAL SUE operational for a while."

"Sergeant Major, I hate it when you call the shop REAL SUE."

Massoni smiled and said, "Yup. I know."

HOLIDAY HOTEL

S ue, Flash and Barbara O'Connell were working in three of the four corners of the kitchen in the Potomac River house. Smith had been right about Flash. As soon as Sue offered to host her in Virginia, Flash jumped at the chance. When they arrived at Dulles and headed down to the Potomac River House, Sue called her mom. After a brief discussion, Sue agreed to host the family gathering at her place. Barbara explained on the phone, "Chautauqua house is just too small for everyone. We need the sort of space and the sort of security that Potomac River House offers. Bill will be bringing his girlfriend Molly for Christmas and I would like to invite my colleague Terry Reimer."

When Flash heard the plan, she said, "Colleague, eh? I have to remember to use that noun in the future. So... meaningless."

Sue said, "She deserves some friendship, don't you think? After all that she has been through?"

"Sue, I didn't mean it that way. I just meant it was a great OGA sort of descriptor."

"Whatever."

When Barbara arrived, Sue and Flash joined her in the living room. Barbara related the full tale of the chase across the southern tier of New York State. Barbara ended the story by saying, "We never did sort out who Thorpe was working for, but I suppose the FBI wasn't surprised when they did ballistics on the bullet that killed him.

A 9mm short used in a Makarov pistol. By the way, they found the plane. It crashed in a field in Ontario. By the time the RCMP and the Canadian Security and Intelligence Service arrived, the aircraft was on fire. Nobody was in the aircraft. They had all disappeared."

Sue said, "Disappeared into the Russian consulate in Toronto, no doubt."

"Sadly, we don't even know that much." Barbara continued, "I suspect so, but there weren't a ton of leads no matter where the FBI and CSIS looked. I honestly can't say that the entire operation was a government adversary. There were too many twists and turns in this story to know anything."

Sue was tempted to offer a brief summary of their actions in Afghanistan and the Gulf, but she realized that if she got started she would eventually relate the entire tale. It was time for her to be the member of the family to keep the dark secrets. It didn't feel right, but she couldn't see any good way to justify the telling. So, when her mom asked how things were for her since they last talked, Sue said, "Busy."

Flash nodded and added, "Very busy."

Barbara asked, "Good busy? Productive busy?"

Sue said, "Confusing busy. Annoying busy."

Flash shook her head and spent the next twenty minutes covering their adventures in detail. Flash's revelations annoyed Sue, but she couldn't really say out loud that she sometimes needed to keep the two parts of her life in separate compartments. Flash concluded by saying, "You know, I never really faced any Soviets in my day, but I'm really starting to dislike the Russians whether they are intelligence officers, mafia, or mercenaries."

Sue said, "Me too."

Barbara said, "Russians. No wonder it was annoying busy. And remember, I was read into *Silicon Addiction*."

Sue hadn't known that her operation and her mother's adventure were all part of a larger program. She didn't know what to say.

Flash decided to answer. "We did some disruption, but I'm not sure that it was more than that. I think this new cyber battlefield is not one where you ever win. You just work hard not to lose. I hate to say it, but I wish we were back to hunting terrorists. That was easier and far more satisfying when you *finished* a target."

Barbara smiled. "You know, we used to say that about the Cold War."

Sue nodded. "It still makes my head hurt."

"Drink some red wine, dear," Barbara advised. "It might not help, but it certainly can't hurt."

Barbara paused as she looked over the rim of her wine glass. Finally, she said, "By the way, we have a visitor coming later in the week. It seems the local FBI want a complete debriefing on *Silicon Addiction*. There is an Army CI guy coming in from the West Coast. I think you know him. Jasper Derry?" Barbara smiled.

Flash said, "Now I didn't see that one coming."

Sue was blushing. All she could think to say was, "Me neither."

J.R. SEEGER is a western New York native who served as a U.S. Army paratrooper and as a CIA case officer for a total of 27 years of federal service. In October 2001, Mr. Seeger led a CIA paramilitary team into Afghanistan. He splits his time between western New York and Central New Mexico.